W9-BWN-622

CRITICAL PRAISE FOR
MAMEVE MEDWED'S *HOST FAMILY*

"A cuttingly funny yet heartwarming tale full of hilarious twists and practical wisdom." —*Publishers Weekly*

"A penetrating look at the different forms that the family takes. . . . It's the gentle humor, delivered with subtle grace, that makes this book an enjoyable read." —*Denver Post*

"A clever romance, full of warm and wry touches. . . . Returning to the ever-eclectic People's Republic of Cambridge, the scene of her successful debut, *Mail*, Medwed spins a similarly funny tale of romantic entanglements and divided loyalties as a woman struggles with starting over." —*Kirkus Reviews*

"Medwed understands the fears and fantasies, the disappointments and the hopes that are the landscape of family love. . . . A novel that is bound to make you chuckle." —*Newsday*

"A charming read for which Medwed's fans will most likely be waiting in line." —*Library Journal*

"Shamelessly charming, HOST FAMILY is more ambitious than Medwed's first, *Mail*. It's funnier, too." —*Boston Globe*

"Charming . . . a fun read as well as a thoughtful look at what 'family' means in this day and age." —*Readers' Edge*

"An entertaining, witty look at the wacky world of modern American relationships . . . filled with twists and turns . . . [a] bubbling story line." —*Midwest Book Review*

more . . .

"A witty, joyous novel about modern love in a similar vein to the film *American Beauty*. . . . Enjoyable from first page to last. Charming, extremely well written, character-driven in the best possible way. You'll laugh, you'll cry with sadness and possibly also feelings of joy."
—*Sullivan County Democrat*

"Cambridge belongs to Mameve Medwed. Find yourself an easy chair and settle in with the warm and witty HOST FAMILY for a complete delight." **—Arthur Golden, author of *Memoirs of a Geisha***

"An absolute delight from beginning to end. Hats off to Mameve Medwed! Her wicked wit and endearing charm grace each and every page. I don't know when I have laughed as loud and as long."
—Jill McCorkle, author of *Final Vinyl Days* and *Crash Diet*

"Medwed finds the joy and humor that exist beside our heartbreak and sorrow. . . . HOST FAMILY is a testimony to that hodgepodge of emotion that makes up the human condition. I loved this book."
—Ann Hood, author of
Somewhere Off the Coast of Maine* and *Ruby

"A funny, buoyant, good-hearted novel about modern love and the complicated, sometimes exotic accommodations people make for it."
—Suzanne Berne, author of *A Crime in the Neighborhood*

"You'll care about these people, you'll laugh—you're in for a real treat!"
—Lorna Landvik, author of
Patty Jane's House of Curl* and *The Tall Pine Polka

Also by Mameve Medwed

Mail

HOST FAMILY

MAMEVE MEDWED

WARNER BOOKS

A Time Warner Company

If you purchase this book without a cover you should be aware that this book may have been stolen property and reported as "unsold and destroyed" to the publisher. In such case neither the author nor the publisher has received any payment for this "stripped book."

This is a work of fiction. The characters and situations are products of the author's imagination. Although Star Market and Harvard are real institutions, none of the characters in the book are based on actual people, and any resemblance to Star Market or Harvard employees, living or dead, is entirely coincidental and unintentional.

Grateful acknowledgment is given to Dan Schmidt for permission to reprint the lyrics from "Tapeworm of Love" by Honest Bob and the Factory-to-Dealer Incentives. © 1997 by Dan Schmidt.

Copyright © 2000 by Mameve Medwed
All rights reserved.

Visit our Web site at www.twbookmark.com

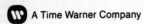 A Time Warner Company

Printed in the United States of America
Originally published in hardcover by Warner Books, Inc.
First Trade Printing: January 2001
10 9 8 7 6 5 4 3 2 1

The Library of Congress has cataloged the hardcover edition as follows:
Medwed, Mameve.
    Host family / Mameve Medwed.
      p. cm.
    ISBN 0-446-52166-3
    I. Title.
  PS3563.E275H6 2000   99-29473
  813'.54—dc21   CIP

ISBN 0-446-67661-6 (pbk.)

Cover design by Honi Werner

ATTENTION: SCHOOLS AND CORPORATIONS
WARNER books are available at quantity discounts with bulk purchase for educational, business, or sales promotional use. For information, please write to: SPECIAL SALES DEPARTMENT, WARNER BOOKS, 1271 AVENUE OF THE AMERICAS, NEW YORK, NY 10020

For Elinor Lipman

PART ONE

FRANCE NATIONALE
CHARLES DE GAULLE 2
1
A 421 FRANCE

For the third time tonight, Daisy Lewis steers her car along Church Street. The crowd lined up for the Harvard Square Movie Theater snakes into her lane. A shredded-blue-jeaned couple stops in the middle of the street, gesturing wildly. They both sport ponytails. Silver hoops thread through at least three of their ears. Daisy sighs. It's so hard to tell anything these days, to sort people, sexes, even beliefs. She feels like plowing them down, this pair who are now hugging on the yellow line like some permanently inserted traffic cone. She honks her horn; they don't move. Pedestrians seem to be reproducing at the same rate as Mildred and Stanley, the guppies Sammy had when he was five. Taking over the Square like the infestation of lice that once ran rampant through the first grade. *Her* Square, she thinks. "My life," she says.

Daisy checks the doorway of the Unitarian church for witnesses. Nobody's there except a street person mounded under a pile of what must have once been quilts of many colors but have all aged into an indeterminate gray. Age and change, the two enemies she's sleeping with. And Henry, she adds, though lately there hasn't been a whole lot of that. She pulls into the spot marked FOR CLERGY ONLY and tries to tamp down her guilt. Will God get her for taking the place of a man of the cloth? She is, after all, the half-Jewish daughter of a bacon-addicted mother and an atheist father whose last visit to a house of God was at his own christening in the one-room schoolhouse-*cum*-church in Benkelman, Nebraska. Besides, she believes in the separation of Church and State. How can you have a parking space designated For Clergy Only and not for a forty-two-year-old North Cambridge ex–food bank organizer now community relations manager *slash* ombudsman for the Star Market chain?

She looks at her watch. What's more, no clergy would want her to be late for the awards ceremony. For the public acknowledgment of her good works. Sort of good works. She hurries toward Brattle Street, hobbled by the unaccustomed high heels and her new tapered skirt. These days, since she sometimes freelances from home and since her office next to the meat freezer requires her to dress less for success than to pad herself for warmth, she is not the fashion plate she might choose to be. She will, of course, be late. Henry is coming from French class, five minutes across the Yard, five minutes more to the Loeb. She hopes he's not wearing that ridiculous beret he affects on Extension School nights. But that's not her worry, she reminds herself. What Henry wears, says, or looks like does not reflect on her. She wishes she believed that.

She passes the Yin and Yang Restaurant and breathes in the smells of soy and sesame oil. As usual, the dining room, except for a clueless tourist, is empty. Twenty-five years ago, she had eaten chop suey in one of these tattered booths during freshman week. The next day she and her roommate had ended up in the infirmary. There, their fluids were replenished by Cokes laced with sugar to get out the bubbles, their underarms packed in ice to bring down the fevers of food poisoning.

By now, Henry will have started on the white wine and food-from-many-nations, each platter crested with a paper-flagged toothpick denoting country of origin. She pictures him talking up a sultry beauty in Kente cloth or a vision of health in dirndl and clogs. He will have already leapfrogged over the group of Japanese business students, a navy-suited mass of male solidarity. He will skirt the Latin American Kennedy students, men, older than the others, sent to Cambridge by their governments. She should have walked. "Why didn't you walk?" Henry would ask with a nod at her hips. "Beautiful night. We all can use the exercise."

Daisy pulls in her stomach. It's not that she's fat. But something happened when she turned forty. Along with the cake and champagne and silly hats and the subscription—from Henry, he thought it was funny—to *Modern Maturity*, she also found herself the recipient of pounds that frosted themselves onto her hips, her knees, unnipped her once nipped-in waist, cushioned her once chiseled chin. She'd always been pretty: Miss Latin Club in seventh grade, Miss Stonehouse Road Junior High first semester in eighth. She still was, in a forty-two-year-old way.

Daisy pats her hips, the mounds that haven't seemed to dislodge despite the five free aerobics classes she'd been enticed into from a flyer tucked under her windshield wiper. "I'm not sure this is for me," she told Heidi, whose purple spandex circled a thigh the width of Daisy's wrist. Heidi lowered her eyes to Daisy's problem area. "You'll live to regret this," she warned.

Now Daisy pushes open the heavy glass doors of the Loeb Theater and thinks that there are many things she has probably lived to regret: that she has only one child, that that child is now in a dormitory room sleeping on one of the three pairs of extra-long sheets that will probably never be washed and changed, let alone washed and changed by a mother's loving hands. She remembers her great-uncle Herbert, whose parents emigrated to Cambridge for the four years he was at Harvard and re-created in their rental an exact replica of Herbert's childhood room down to the green-shaded desk lamp and the doily snowflaked across the maple bureau top. She can identify. She pictures Sammy one mile away in Pennypacker Hall. They moved him in two weeks ago. Since then, they've heard very little. She's taken to hanging out in the Square—at the Coop where at some point he has to line up to buy four syllabi's worth of books, at the sandwich shops and pizza joints where she's run into scores of his old high school chums. "Oh, Mrs. Lewis," they'll say, "I've just bumped into Sammy at the Kiosk." Or, "Hi, Mrs. Lewis, Sammy was in front of me at the ATM a minute ago." And Daisy would wander to the bank or the magazine stand, where sightings of Elvis seemed more likely occurrences than sightings of her here-on-earth and geographically proximate son. He might as well be at Stanford, where he would have been if he'd gotten in. "So count Harvard as your safety," Henry had said.

"And be tainted as a legacy?" Sammy was indignant, vowing until the last moment to seek the egalitarianism of UMass.

Daisy looks around her. The lobby of the Loeb is thronged with a United Nations worth of costumes and multicultural faces. There are saris from India and sweaters from *Vogue,* pleats from Talbots and plaids from the Highlands, ripped jeans from Camden Lock and pressed jeans from Place de la Concorde. Daisy lingers at the edge of the crowd, searching for Henry, but before she can find him, Elizabeth Malcolm, the head of the Harvard International Office, spots her and hurries over with the businesslike tat-a-tat of her sensible pumps. "Oh, Daisy," she says, shaking her hand with such energy that if Daisy had had rotator cuff problems she'd be scheduled for surgery. "I've been waiting for you. I thought we'd have the ceremony before everybody gets too tipsy hanging out at the bar."

Daisy looks toward the bar, where three young men in elbow-patched tweed and mufflers with stripes of three different universities she can't identify are talking quietly. What seems like a stingy supply of half-gallons of generic reds and whites lines a folding table covered by a paper cloth. Two trays carry plastic cups the size of shot glasses. Cocktail napkins with *Veritas*es on them are shaped to form an H and a U. It would probably take a trayful of glasses even to begin to get tipsy, Daisy decides. She wonders if UMass with its lack of endowments might have a less Puritan, less miserly approach to celebration.

"Have you seen Henry?" Daisy asks Elizabeth, who is writing *Daisy Lewis Host Family Honoree* on a *Hello, I'm . . .* sticker.

"Over there." Elizabeth nods in the direction of another folding table laden with foil lasagna pans, each boasting, as she'd predicted, a flag signifying country of casserole. "He found the French contingent immediately. He's doing so well, has made such strides with the language"—she giggles—"that I couldn't resist putting *Henri* on his name tag."

"I'm sure he's thrilled," Daisy says.

"Not that I'd really know," Elizabeth goes on, "even though I had three years at Winsor. My ear." She points to her lobe, on which is clipped a pearl the size of a ladybug. "Besides, in college, Spanish was considered more important for social work."

Daisy is about to ask whether heading up the office for international students at Harvard can be even loosely interpreted as social work, but thinks better of it. She notices a Chinese woman sitting in a corner looking both bewildered and sad.

Elizabeth notices too. "Let me rescue Wang Ling, and then we'll get this show on the road."

Elizabeth puts her hand on the Chinese woman's shoulder and nods energetically. Daisy looks back over to Henry—or, rather, Henri. The French contingent must consist only of women, since the ring-a-rosy around Henry is entire female. She is relieved to see he is not wearing the beret, though she detects an inch of blue wool peeking out from his breast pocket. Even at this distance she recognizes the smug turn of his mouth and his index finger raised to its most pontifical. She waves in his direction, but Henry, so intent on conversation, doesn't notice her. She's sure he's speaking French from the way his lips are pursed in the exact position high school teachers instruct you to use when making the French *u*. He looks like he's sucking lemons. But though his face is vastly disapproving, his hands loop through the air as if he's spinning worlds of sugar plums in front of the uplifted faces of his adoring audience. A waterfall of charm, she's all too aware, which he can turn off and on like a garden hose.

Daisy is about to make her way toward him when Elizabeth Malcolm, one hand pulling the Chinese girl, grabs her elbow and leads her over to the microphone. "Will Henry Lewis come over here," she announces in a burst of static that accelerates into a high-pitched hum.

In seconds, Henry is at Daisy's side, smiling like an ad for Colgate. She smells something suspiciously like Old Spice, though she assumes that whatever it is comes in a bottle reading MADE IN FRANCE and costs three times as much. "You're late," he whispers through the pearly whites.

"Parking," Daisy says.

"You should have walked." His hand, which he's placed at the small of her back, moves a little lower, where he does the pincer test for fat.

Up close she notices that his beret is arranged with the kind of care waiters use to fan a napkin across a serving plate on the tables of the fancier restaurants. "I should have done a lot of things," she hisses under her breath. In spite of the beret and the *Henri* name tag stuck to his lapel, it delights her to realize that his straight and healthy teeth are a blatant giveaway of made-in-America orthodontia, a comforting world of retainers and rubber bands, of tumblers of milk and bowls of vitamin-enriched cornflakes. Not a nation of muddy coffee, filthy Gauloises, red wine rubbed on the gums of infants in their bassinets.

"Students and their host families, may I have your attention, please?" announces Elizabeth Malcolm. She is enunciating carefully with pauses between words for those for whom English is not a second language but maybe a third or sixth.

The room quiets down. All multinationed faces are raised toward Daisy and Henry Lewis, who stand shoulder to shoulder, their big American smiles a testament to their even larger, more bountiful, more all-encompassing big American hearts. "Darling," Henry says.

"Honey," Daisy says.

Elizabeth Malcolm claps her hands. "We're here to honor Daisy and Henry Lewis, dedicated host family for twenty years." There is a round of polite applause. "Here, here," say the British guys over at the bar in the voices of bored MPs during those sessions of Parliament you sometimes see screened on C-SPAN.

Elizabeth Malcolm clears her throat. She pulls the microphone out of its socket. She's the spitting image of a talk-show host about to wander out into the audience. "Twenty years ago," she begins, "as students themselves, they hosted their first international student. And every year, another one. And now their son is a freshman at the college, almost the age of many of you here." Elizabeth stops, an ear cocked for a chorus of Wows! Though none are forthcoming, she is not at all deflated but proceeds with even more enthusiasm. "They are an exemplary family," she says. "A *Harvard* family," she emphasizes. "An American family." She holds the microphone aloft in a Statue-of-Liberty pause-for-a-moment-of-silence salute. "And in a world of shifting relationships," Elizabeth goes on, "alternative lifestyles, they are the rock of stability, the very model of a model family." She reaches behind her and whips forward a folder of padded crimson leatherette embossed with a Harvard seal, a replica of Daisy's and Henry's old diplomas, now tucked away in an attic cabinet. "So without further ado . . ."

Next to Daisy, Henry shifts, fidgets with his sleeve. To his credit, he looks as uncomfortable as Daisy feels. Or maybe it's just disappointment that he's not singled out as the model of a model French family. Though the award is for the two of them, joint property for joint hosts, Henry takes it. Daisy stretches up on tiptoes to read over Henry's shoulder:

> To Daisy and Henry Lewis, Host Family
> In Grateful Appreciation for
> Many Years of Welcoming
> Harvard University International Students
> With Generous Hospitality and Caring Friendship

"A few words." Elizabeth twirls the microphone up to Henry's mouth with an Oprah-like sweep of her arm. "Thank you very much," says Henry. "Quite an honor." His head bobbles over clusters of countries lined up like contiguous states until it alights on France. *"Merci bien,"* he adds with a slight Gallic-looking salute. *"Merci très bien."*

"Daisy?" Elizabeth asks.

Daisy shakes her head.

Undaunted, Elizabeth slides the microphone under Henry's chin. "You two, tell us about your first host-family experience," she gushes.

Henry turns to Daisy. "Dear," he says in his most unctuous, for-the-public-tone, "ladies first."

"Pilombaya," Daisy says. And it comes to her without any thought. As if it's been poised all these years on the springboard of her tongue, waiting only for the gun to go off. "Pilombaya," she says again.

FRANCE NATIONALE
CHARLES DE GAULLE 2

2

A 421 FRANCE

It was fall, twenty years ago. Henry was in graduate school. Daisy had a job running a food bank. Though this might not seem like suitable work for a newly minted Harvard *cum laude,* Daisy saw it as a natural progression from the soup kitchen where she and Henry had volunteered as undergraduates and where her heart had leaped at the tenderness with which he placed bowls of minestrone into scabbed and trembling hands. All the big moments of her life, she was beginning to realize, were flagged by food.

She and Henry weren't yet married, but they shared a Harvard married-student sublet on the Somerville/Cambridge line: 301E Holden Green, an address engraved in her soul. She wore a small diamond chip on her third finger, left hand. It had been Henry's mother's first (the first of three) engagement ring. "Do you mind?" Henry had asked. It wasn't even his father's, number two, whose marquis cut in Tiffany platinum prongs Lillian had elected—even litigated—to keep.

"Oh, Henry." Daisy had nearly wept from happiness. "I

don't need a ring to signify my commitment to you." But she had been thrilled, nonetheless. Number One had been Lillian's favorite, the only husband she hadn't divorced with ten typed pages of complaints expensively documented at a top New Jersey lawyer's high-end hourly rate. Number One had died, two months after their wedding, of malaria in the jungles of Africa, where he had been sent on a mission from the Department of Agriculture. The ring was almost perfect, only a black carbon dot of imperfection you couldn't even see without a jeweler's loop. But if the ring wasn't unflawed, Daisy's life certainly was. She and Henry took bubble baths in the claw-and-ball-footed tub. And every morning and night, all over the housing complex, thin and lumpy Harvard-issued mattresses creaked on their half-sprung flimsy Harvard springs.

It was a community of newlyweds and live-togethers. The youth and hormones that triggered love and sex danced in the air like the dust motes that rose from unswept floors and unmade beds. Every afternoon at four, she would come home from work and pore over recipes. Baked Ham Aloha from the back of the box of cloves. Spaghetti Provençal from the label on the olive jar. She scoured through the books her mother had given her: *Campbell's Soup One Hundred Casseroles*, where cans of cream of mushroom, cream of celery, and poisson cheddar cheese would trick gourmets into thinking they were tasting the long-simmering sauces of Escoffier. *Two Hundred Ways to Make Eggs. A Month's Worth of Low-Cost Heavenly Hamburger Dinners*. This contained Henry's favorite: sweet-and-sour meatballs, with Dole pineapple chunks, green peppers, and onions swimming in a sauce of sugar and soy pasted together with cornstarch.

Once she decided on the menu, Daisy would rush to the market across the street, where Julia Child was rumored to shop, though Daisy personally had never seen her pinching the cantaloupe. Beneath the photographs of Julia kissing Jack the Butcher, Daisy would, in her culinary ignorance, buy the ready-made cans of Dinty Moore beef stew and fast-frozen broccoli stems that Julia Child wouldn't feed to the neighborhood stray.

Often she would take pity on some of the bachelors in Henry's department and insist he bring them back for a taste of home cooking and domestic bliss. Only later did she learn— it was Henry, of course, who pointed it out—how terrible those meals were, how close in texture, flavor, ingredients, and additives they came to the Swiss steak, chicken thighs tetrazzini, mystery meat on toast then served in the Harvard student dining halls.

Years later, over take-out sushi or a platter of grilled vegetables with extra-virgin olive oil, she'd turn to Henry. "Remember those wonderful dinners back in our first apartment," she'd say with a nostalgia for creaking bedsprings, footed bathtubs, and cream of mushroom soup.

"Do I ever," he'd harrumph. "At my last reunion I don't know how many people brought them up. They were so terrible. And so bad for you!" Then he'd dip the yellowtail into the soy sauce, splattering the placemat for emphasis.

"You used to think they were wonderful."

"I used to think a lot of things were wonderful."

Like soup kitchens. Like community activism. Which, she could hardly bear to acknowledge, were starting to be replaced in his affections by upscale restaurants and high-tech gadgets touted for leisure time. What happened to his idealism? To the bleeding-heart liberalism he flaunted as a badge?

"It was that first trip to Paris that made the scales fall from my eyes." He'd chuckled. "And that terrible American blandness from my palate."

Twenty years ago the blandness of his palate was not an

issue. They were crazy in love, she with his mother's first husband's engagement ring; he with the collection of little poems she'd tuck nightly under the mildewed bed pillows, regulation issue of the fully furnished apartment. Nevertheless, they thought they should hold something jointly, an equal share in an object as a testament to their future coupledom.

They considered buying a sofa together. Their across-the-hall neighbors, Helen and Hitch, did that. By second semester they were in the process of breaking up. Each wanted the sofa. One wouldn't buy out the other's half. Daisy and Henry would sit over coffee trying not to hear Helen scream about how she chose the upholstery, and Hitch's even louder shouts over how he was responsible for the frame of kiln-dried wood. One day when Hitch was at class, Helen borrowed a saw from the super and hacked the sofa down the middle. Forlornly, the two halves straddled the street on trash day, their edges jagged like cartoon drawings of broken hearts.

Even though Daisy and Henry were convinced that anything they bought together would never be cut asunder, they were a little uncomfortable nonetheless. "What could we do that would be a shared venture?" Daisy asked Henry.

"Buy stocks? Mutual funds? Take out a joint checking account? A two-for-one special? A ticket for the lottery?" Henry suggested.

She had nodded toward the outside hall, where even as they spoke, Helen was dragging away cartons of slotted spoons and spatulas. "Something of no monetary value. Something as a symbol of our love."

"We could have a kid," Henry said.

"Well, of course we'll have scads," she'd agreed. "Two girls and two boys. But after marriage."

"And honeymoon."

So when the letter had come from the Harvard International

Office asking for volunteers to be host families, it had seemed like a sign, the very symbol they were looking for. Besides, they wouldn't have to put the students up; they'd be housed in dormitories and student apartments. Daisy and Henry would be there to supply support, friendship, advice, and the occasional delicious meal of sweet-and-sour meatballs à la Waikiki. In short, to be living examples of American family values and of American life.

"It'll be like having a kid for a year," she'd said.

"You make it sound like a lease," Henry had joked.

"Better. Parenthood without the diapers and two A.M. feedings and responsibility." Exactly what her mother always said when pining pointedly for a grandchild. "And if it works out we can have a new kid every fall. A whole family even," she'd exclaimed.

"We can choose a different country every year. Then when we're ready to make our world tour . . ." chimed Henry, who, back then, didn't think "foreign country" meant only France.

"We'll have friends in every port," she finished. That didn't sound right. She paused. "A different cuisine in every pot," she added triumphantly.

The first student had been Pilombaya. They knew this about him: He was a "mature" student. He was from Indonesia; he had been a customs inspector in Jakarta and was being sent by his government to the Kennedy School. He had many interesting hobbies and liked all sorts of recreational activities, none of which he named. This came in a note painstakingly printed out in red ink on lined paper. He would contact them on his arrival in the fall.

Dutiful pupils that they were, Daisy and Henry had pored over the atlas. In the Widener Library they checked the encyclopedia for indigenous crops, the climate, crafts, the names of political leaders of the right and left, the local cuisine. This was during a time when you couldn't get nasi goreng or pad thai at your neighborhood joint; a time when your wooden salad bowl was stamped MADE IN VERMONT, not hewn by the hand of native peoples on the island of Timor. Looking for verisimilitude, they'd even gone to a revival of *Krakatoa, East of Java* at the Brattle, coming out excited about sinuous pearl divers and sun-toasted bodies slicked with sweat.

"Maybe he'll turn up in a peasant costume, with fire in his eyes," Daisy had said.

"We've taken on a responsibility, Daisy. We can't stereotype. Besides, a customs inspector at the Jakarta airport? A person who makes sure you don't take plants out and bring plants in, let alone artifacts and dope. I wonder what he'll study. Could be the guy's even been known to take a little bribe."

"Now *you're* stereotyping. What Harvard student would take a bribe?" Daisy had been incredulous. "Perhaps customs inspector is a front for something else."

"My very point. Not crook. Not thief—undercover agent, revolutionary."

They were in a booth at Mr. Bartley's Burger Cottage. Having devoured the Sean Connery while Henry was downing the Derek Bok, Daisy had gone on and on spinning plots of intrigue and international derring-do to complement the posters of Bogie and James Cagney on the walls and the thrillers stacked next door on the Harvard bookstore shelves.

It was mid-September when Pilombaya turned up. They had just been to dinner at a classmate of Henry's whose wife had spent a year at a Swiss finishing school topped off by a course at Le Cordon Bleu.

"This is delicious," Daisy had exclaimed over the lentil-and-sausage dish from *Mastering the Art of French Cooking, Volume*

Two. "Do you drain the liquid from the can or use it in the sauce?"

"No can," said their hostess the way you might dress down a misbehaving child. "But it's very easy; you soak the lentils overnight." Daisy didn't even know what lentils looked like in their natural state, she and Henry having come from households where you had to open a tin, tear or pierce a sealed plastic bag, or defrost an ice-encased block of frozen peas to get to the food.

"Don't tell me you make your own sausages," exclaimed Henry. "You grind them up and stuff them into skins?" They had both studied her hands then, delicate and beringed, the nails painted to expose stark white half-moons.

She followed their eyes and fanned out her fingers. "French manicure," she explained with a little *comme çi comme ça* shrug. Then she served Henry another helping of thin slices of sausage cushioned on the perfectly mushless lentils. These were topped by real chopped Italian parsley, not the dried kind Daisy always used well past its blurred-from-use expiration date.

"As for making my own . . . no," she admitted. "But I discovered handmade ones at a little Portuguese hole-in-the-wall in Inman Square."

Walking home, their belts loosened, their tongues tingling from the final course of an "easy as pie to make" lemon sorbet—as if pie were easy to make—Henry had sighed. "I'm ready for bed."

"I'm tired too."

"Not sleep! Sex. The natural outcome of all that good food."

"It was a wonderful meal," Daisy admitted.

"I think we need to change our culinary ways. Not to put down your tuna noodle casserole . . ."

"I understand."

Henry had been gentle. "The times are changing. People are

into healthy food. We should start watching *The French Chef*."
He reached for her hand. "There's no reason we can't rise above
our mutual humble background of total immersion in Velveeta
cheese and Lipton's onion soups."

Daisy had put her arm through Henry's. She was looking
forward to bed, to sex. To Sunday morning, when they might
sleep in till noon. Then, after breakfast, Henry would sit at his
desk, his brow adorably wrinkled in concentration while Daisy
would stretch out on the secondhand sofa whose back folded
down into a single bed and devise plaintive pleas for donations
of canned spaghetti sauce.

Daisy rubbed her cheek against the rough tweed of Henry's
jacket. She was content. She liked this rehearsal for marriage,
this stand-in for the real thing, for the long-running successful
production to be. Everything seemed right: the crisp air of
early fall; the piles of bright leaves crunching under their feet;
the lighted bookstores, their aisles potholed with students
cross-legged on the floor flipping through *On the Road* and *The
Confidential Guide*; the coffeehouses where gleaming espresso
machines whooshed and hissed their pitchers of milk into
foamy white clouds. In Cambridge, the arrival of the students
every year was like the swallows coming to Capistrano, the
whole city energized, transformed.

"What's this?" Henry's shoulder stiffened against Daisy's
chin. They paused at the end of the little courtyard around
which the Harvard married-student apartments were ringed,
each entry with its black painted number under a low-wattage,
cheaply encased bulb. At their entry, 301, a figure was shad-
owed against the doorway surrounded by suitcases and crates.

Daisy checked her watch; it was almost midnight. "Rather
late for someone to be moving in."

"If it weren't for the suitcases, I'd be suspicious," Henry said.
Last year they'd been mugged a block from the movie theater

they'd just left; a figure had hovered in a dark doorway, then emerged to grab Daisy's wallet containing a five-dollar bill and two symphony tickets, and Henry's checkbook along with his Coop card and one free-hot-fudge-sundae certificate. The cops had been scornful when Daisy suggested that to find the perpetrators they need only turn up at Friday's performance of the *Eroica*.

"But, of course," Henry went on, "all that luggage could contain stolen goods."

As they drew closer, Daisy realized that this figure didn't seem daunting—unlike the hulking bad guy with a tire iron sticking out from his hooded black sweatshirt who had snatched her purse. This was a small, slight silhouette almost trembling in the autumn breeze and not much taller than the stacked cartons next to him.

All at once it came to her. "Pilombaya!" she cried. "Our student. He was due to arrive about now."

Pilombaya stepped toward them, beaming, bobbing, nodding, bouncing. "Host family?" he asked.

Daisy extended a hand. "I'm Daisy," she said. His hand in hers was tiny. His hair was black, sleeked back with oil. He was shorter than Daisy. The top of his head came to the middle of Henry's chest. He wore a tan suit with flared trousers and a crimson tie, which when he moved under the light Daisy realized was dotted with embroidered *Veritas*es. Over one shoulder he carried the kind of leather—though this looked like vinyl—pocketbook French and Italian men sport. Over the other shoulder hung a camera. She sniffed a faint odor of mothballs mixed with the heavier smell of oil and cologne. "Husband?" he asked, nodding at Henry.

Daisy turned to Henry. Instinct warned that this was not the time and place to discuss or explain her matrimonial state.

Henry must have had the exact same thought. "Nice tie

you've got there," he said with the neat block of a basketball
guard.

Pilombaya ran his fingers lovingly over the red silk. "Friend
from my country give me," he explained. "He visit Harvard
Coop in nineteen sixty-four."

Daisy eyed his luggage. "Isn't your room in the dormitory
ready yet?"

"I came first to host family," he said, his smile huge with be-
stowal. Abruptly the smile faded. "Too late to get key. 'Office
closed, try tomorrow,' policeman said. He help me find street
on map. I ring bell," he added, "but nobody open door. One
lady going out tell me not to go in. Not good welcome, kind I
expect in America." He shivered dramatically. "Cold here. Not
like home."

Chastised, Daisy and Henry filled their voices with welcoming warmth and gestured welcomingly. It took three trips up
their three flights of stairs to bring Pilombaya's luggage inside
the comfort of their not-quite-matrimonial bower, where it
monopolized two-thirds of their combination living room, library, guest quarters, study, and storage facility, all crushed
into a twelve-by-fourteen-foot space.

Pilombaya mopped his face with a batik handkerchief. He
folded it into a tiny square. He put it back in his pocket. Then
he began pulling the lobe of his ear with one hand and patting
his trousers with the other. He twitched, scratched, jiggled his
foot, ran his tongue over his teeth. Though he was not, in the
annals of beauty, terrible looking, Daisy did not find him at-
tractive. Not that she didn't like exotic men. But he was too
small, and the way various parts of his body were jumping reminded her of fleas.

Daisy looked at Henry, who was now gamely examining
some postcards from the stack Pilombaya had laid out on the
milk crate that served as a coffee table. Henry was almost hand-

some, with his square, solid face and receding hairline that made him appear more like an egghead than he was. His tall frame and wide shoulders fit the worn preppy clothes he favored even though he was a graduate of Hoboken High. And he was nice, she thought, approving as he feigned interest in Javanese dancing techniques.

After the postcards, Pilombaya brought out an album of photographs. Though Daisy and Henry yawned dramatically and asked each other the time, Pilombaya seemed unable to acknowledge American social signals. Most of the pictures were of Pilombaya and his car: Pilombaya standing in sunglasses, his hand on its hood; Pilombaya standing in a batik shirt, leaning rakishly against the fender; Pilombaya standing with the door open, pointing into the interior; Pilombaya sitting on a blanket with his back against a whitewall tire. The car was varnished to a patent-leather shine. Behind it, Daisy could make out a palm tree and some ferns. "Nice greenery," she said.

"Nice car," Henry said.

Pilombaya beamed. "Fully air-conditioned," he said. "I remove heater, put in cooling system." Daisy thought of her own car—her sister Rachel's hand-me-down—whose upholstery was ripped and repaired with duct tape, whose radio was stolen, whose floor was lined with candy wrappers as dense and varicolored as autumn leaves. Oh, brave new world that had such disappointments in it. "Americans have nice cars too," he allowed. He leaned over and unzipped a Garuda Airlines carry-on bag. "I show slide now. Have you Kodak Carousel?"

Daisy shifted with the burden of her capacity to disappoint. "Not yet," she said. "Kodak Carousels are the kind of thing that married people buy, married people with families."

Pilombaya looked puzzled. "No family?"

"Well," Daisy began. "Family, yes. I mean I have a family. Henry has a family. And of course"—she cleared her throat, made a phony little laugh, the prelude to a joke—"there's always the family of man!"

"This man?" Pilombaya pointed to Henry.

"Henry," Daisy pronounced with the kind of authority you use to state an incontrovertible fact.

"Mr. Henry." Pilombaya nodded.

"Actually, Mr. Lewis," Daisy said.

"Ah. You Mrs. Lewis?"

Daisy shook her head.

"But husband, yes?" he asked.

"Not yet," she said.

"Family?"

"Sort of," she admitted. "Though in the interest of full disclosure, not technically."

"Children?"

"We plan to get married first," she said.

Pilombaya's brows knit with concentration as if he were trying to decode a language not offered in the Harvard catalog.

Studying him, Daisy felt a sudden motherly—no, host-familyish—rush of sympathy for Pilombaya. She remembered a family tree of Bloomsbury she once studied for hours trying to fit together Vanessa and Clive and Duncan, Roger, Angelica, Carrington, Ralph, Lytton, even Bernard Berenson and George Bernard Shaw. "Never you mind," she addressed him with the voice one uses for a kindergarten student who's been suddenly overstimulated.

"So actually who is host family?"

"Henry and I."

"But you and Henry aren't husband and wife. You have no children. That is not definition of family I find in my English/Javanese dictionary."

She noticed the sad and defeated droop of Pilombaya's shoulders and felt terrible. "But we will. We plan on getting

married and having at least four kids. We'll be your trial host
family. Your practice host family. Your host family in the
wings."

Pilombaya's head bobbed like a puppet's on a string. "Host
family?" he implored.

"Host family," Daisy and Henry sang.

Assuaged, Pilombaya asked to spend the night. It was too
late to get the key to the dormitory. Besides, he preferred the
warmth of his host family to the impersonality of a Harvard
room or a hotel cubicle.

Daisy unfolded the sofa, trying to ignore the ridge that
humped and twisted down the middle like the spine of some
extinct dinosaur. A night on that would send you begging for
the impersonal yet real mattress of a dormitory room. She dug
out her one set of matched sheets, a present she'd inherited
from her college roommate, who had broken her engagement
and become a lesbian. With the bed down and Pilombaya's pile
of luggage, the room was so small that Daisy had to scuttle
sideways around the bed while Henry's and Pilombaya's backs
were flattened against the wall like terrorists lined up for the
firing squad.

It seemed only minutes after they had shut the door of their
bedroom when Pilombaya called out. "Host family?" he ventured, his voice plaintive as a child's.

Daisy and Henry peered out. Pilombaya sat on the edge of
the sofa, resplendent in blue pajamas and a matching bathrobe
whose lapels were rimmed with gold. His hair, Daisy noticed,
seemed sleeked with yet another layer of oil. She thought of the
danger to her roommate's rejected bridal pillowcases, their
hemstitched edges, their two-hundred-and-fifty-thread pure
cotton content, their pale pink flowers strewn across a field of
hunter green. Henry's mother, Lillian, had often laid her
jumbo-rollered curls on these same pillowcases. Under the

scent of Ivory Snow, you could still discern a faint whiff of her Joy.

Pilombaya hugged the tops of his arms. His teeth chattered. "Is cold," he said.

"Not really," Henry said. "It's only September, and a mild one at that."

"In my country . . ." he began.

"It's very warm," Henry finished. "We've studied the weather charts."

Daisy took the quilt from the master bed. Bunched under her nose, it reeked of sex. She noticed spots from pizza and a grease stain from a carton of take-out onion rings. Still, Pilombaya's combination of mothballs and exotic lotions from the East would probably vaporize their more American smells.

She added the quilt to the two blankets already on his bed. She demonstrated how the storm windows slid down on tracks in case of a chill. Pilombaya pushed the glass panels and screen back and forth, giggling. "Americans," he said with admiration. "Do you have hand-held calculator? Walkie-talkie? Stereo? Touch-Tone telephone?"

No, replied Henry, but Daisy owned a waffle iron, which made incredible French toast, which he would show Pilombaya in the morning. He would also rearrange his plans to help Pilombaya move into his dormitory room. He could commiserate with how eager Pilombaya must be to get settled in his own digs.

Pilombaya slept eighteen hours straight, through the American breakfast of French toast, through the American lunch of peanut butter with Marshmallow Fluff. At noon, Henry convened an emergency study group session and fled to the Pamplona Cafe. Daisy tried to work at her bedroom night table, feeling confined like someone under house arrest. She was cross, angry that this near perfect stranger had appropriated the very center of where she lived.

And as if in punishment for her xenophobic thoughts (if Harvard knew, would they strip off her host-family badge?), three more days passed before Daisy could fold up the living room couch and take Pilombaya to his dorm. He was missing his country, having trouble with jet lag. He wanted to spend more up close and personal time with his host family, to get to know the American way of life—their customs, their food— before he moved out on a larger, more institutional scale.

"See you later," Henry had said, retreating to his carrel at the library.

"But we're both hosts," she complained. "Our *joint* project, lest you forget."

"You can shuffle your appointments around," he pointed out. "Besides, it only takes one host for one hostee."

What were two days out of the rest of your life? Daisy figured, sounding even to herself a little too Pollyannaish. Like those posters that say if life gives you lemons, make lemonade. Besides, Mrs. Moynihan's fourth grade probably wouldn't mind postponing their Young Volunteers community service at the food bank. She called the school and was told that, anyway, half the class had been sent home with lice; they wouldn't be let back for at least five days and many doses of Kwell. In her clunker of her sister's reject car, about which Pilombaya didn't even begin to hide his disappointment, she took him to Concord, to Lexington, to the Museum of Fine Arts, to the Gardner. They walked one-half of the Freedom Trail before the soles of his made-in-Indonesia shoes gave out. At every tourist spot, Pilombaya thrust his camera into Daisy's hand. In front of a pumpkin, next to a Texaco sign, against the Golden Arches, Pilombaya smiled straight into the lens. On one outing, he asked a passerby to photograph the two of them. She'd had a meeting that day and had worn a suit rather than her usual patched jeans. She was pretty sure Pilombaya preferred her dressed up. He himself was always dapper, either in batik or a jacket and tie. She admired his high standards, sympathized with his difficulty in keeping up with a host family who had none. She thought of the British dressing for dinner in the colonies.

On day four, Henry and Daisy loaded the car, leaving the living room with its folded-back bed and its visible area rug looking like an encampment from which the enemy had just fled. At the door to his dormitory, Pilombaya turned to them. For the occasion he wore a fresh batik shirt whose sharp creases from neat folding seemed part of the design. He smelled of more recent applications of both mothballs and cologne. He held his camera in front of him like a shield. "I want picture of me with host family," he said. "Camera has timer." He set the camera on top of a gatepost, adjusted it, and squeezed between Daisy and Henry, his chin tilted up, his mouth a jack-o'-lantern's smile.

Now Daisy thinks of twenty years of hosting families. They scroll past her like a crowd being scanned with a camera's wide-angle lens. A sea of faces, many colors, but mostly shades of brown. In the early years of the program they chose students from emerging African nations, a husband and wife with six children from Afghanistan who two minutes off the plane left the children with Daisy and Henry to buy a TV. ("One hour, no more," the husband had promised with a wag of his fingers, and returned in five.) They had hosted Pakistanis, Turks who arrived right wing and went home radicalized, a Brazilian member of parliament whose shirt was open to the waist even in January, a Malaysian couple whose curried vegetables sent both Henry and Daisy to the infirmary with swollen tongues, a Uruguayan whose mother came to visit and got arrested for shoplifting a full-length mink coat, which she stuffed into a medium-size Filene's Basement bag. Daisy remembers how well she and Henry managed everything, how exemplary they were. How in spite of the cultural gaps, the international office kept getting testimonials. The parents of their students begged them to come to Bangladesh, to get to know the real Chad.

Though Daisy herself reveled in good works, from time to time Henry would complain. "Are you out to save the world, Daisy? You can't let these lost souls invade our lives."

Slowly, Henry started to revolt. "I'm sick of the third world," he protested. "I want Europe—Paris, London, Vienna, Rome. Especially Paris."

How could she reply to such a statement? Did she dare to tell Henry she took it as an omen when her high school teacher announced that, according to Henry James, the daisy is a flower that doesn't flourish in European soil? Though the same teacher had made comments about Daisy Buchanan and Daisy Mae, it was the Daisy Miller analogy she never forgot.

And the Daisy Miller analogy she never told Henry. Instead, when Daisy explained they could do more good for people of less advanced nations, that these students really needed them, Henry was forced to agree. *"But,"* he added, "I want someone to practice French on. I want a nice place to stay in Paris. I want delicious and recognizable food. I don't want to do good."

Now, Daisy turns and listens to Elizabeth Malcolm talking about all the good they are doing. She hugs the award to her chest. For a minute she is tempted to put it in front of her face. She follows Henry's eyes toward the group of French students, who naturally attract notice. From their center beams Giselle, proud to be connected to such celebrated award winners. Only last week she was assigned to them when the Senegalese man Daisy had chosen (French-speaking, she'd pointed out) had at the last minute opted for the Sorbonne. "Nice enough," Henry had reported after he'd volunteered to pick her up at the airport and deposit her at the graduate student dormitory.

Giselle is pretty in an overdressed, French kind of way, Daisy has to admit. Why do French women seem to have a special gene for folding a scarf? Her own scarf, a maybe too flowery Liberty print, which was adjusted this afternoon at a rakish angle and looped into an impressive knot, now hangs dead center around her neck like the kerchief on her childhood Brownie uniform.

"We need a photograph," Elizabeth Malcolm announces. She gestures toward her assistant; she brings over a photographer from the Harvard Information Office who is lugging a camera the size of a small child. Elizabeth squeezes between Daisy and Henry. Daisy notices she is wearing Ma Griffe. She motions to the Chinese student in a corner and crooks her finger at a majestic African in full tribal robes. Elizabeth directs them both to Daisy's right.

"*Alors,* Giselle," she hears Henry call out. The young, tousled redhead in all black except for her brilliant scarf bordered in the interlocking C's of Chanel jumps in two gazelle/Giselle-like leaps to Henry's side.

"Say cheese," commands the Harvard Information Office photographer.

"*Fromage,*" Henry says, and Daisy wants to strike him dead.

FRANCE NATIONALE
CHARLES DE GAULLE 2
3
A 421 FRANCE

Daisy and Henry walk away from the Loeb. Daisy carries the award in one hand, her too-large pocketbook in the other. Henry is toting his backpack stuffed with tapes and French grammars, which he'd stashed behind the lobby's ticket office. Daisy notices he's got the kind of backpack all college kids cart, although Henry is forty-five. When he was a freshman, everyone was lugging around the ubiquitous green bookbag with the cracked rubber lining that looked like, and even substituted for, the laundry bags some students sent home to their mother on the Greyhound bus.

Henry is silent. Daisy is thinking that perhaps their marriage started to go bad when Henry took up French, when Henry moved from yak milk and curries and Mongolian hot pots and parathas to vintage Beaujolais, pâtés, and baguettes. Maybe this is what happens to twenty-year marriages: dull familiarity or its opposite—who is this person I used to know?

"How about sushi?" Henry asks.

"Great," Daisy agrees all too quickly. Could it be a good sign that Henry picks sake and *ebi* over Cahors and cassoulet?

Daisy turns in the direction of Roka, their regular Japanese hangout. There they always request a table served by Sachiko, who brings them, along with the hot and scented towels, little bowls of pickled beets and white radishes cut like chrysanthemums. "On the house." She'll giggle behind a starburst of fingers as delicate as a geisha's fan. Sachiko knows Henry wants his Deer in Spring sake hot and Daisy, her Kirin beer ice-cold.

Henry pulls her elbow. "Wait, there's a new place over by JFK Street," he says.

Daisy stops. She doesn't like new places. She doesn't like JFK Street, which she continues to call Boylston even though its name was changed in the early seventies. She doesn't like that Henry has started to study French when the German all the undergraduate science majors took was once foreign language enough for him. She doesn't like that Sammy has gone to college and his room at home is neat for the first time since she brought him from the hospital. Every four years she gets her house painted the same gray that it was when they bought it; she wears her hair in bangs and turned under at her ears the way she's worn it since she was twelve; she still plays her Cole Porter LPs. She's proud of twenty years of wifely fidelity to the boy who carried her boxes up the stairs the first day of freshman week. And to the man who bears less of that boy in him than she would like. She studies Henry, impatient, forward looking, eager all of a sudden for new things, for change. She hates change. There's something to be said for a long-term marriage, if not, if not—and the thought is fleeting and for a second races her heart—if not always for the husband whom you're locked into the long term with.

Daisy and Henry wait for the light at Boylston. A huge chartered bus passes in front of them, its windows filled with silver-haired passengers who peer down from on high, pointing and gesturing, some even clicking cameras, as if the pedestrians are so many local-color specimens. Yet another senior citizen group making a pilgrimage to the Square. Elderhostel, AARP. She catches herself. Not so many years before she and Henry will be eligible. Since Henry turned forty-five, he gets mass mailings from the AARP to Dr. Henry Lewis, though Henry in fact never actually earned his Ph.D. These he tosses in the wastebasket without even slitting open their envelopes. "How can you take offense?" Daisy asked. "You who gave me a subscription to *Modern Maturity*."

"That was a joke," Henry had explained, indignant. "This is an insult. Even you ought to be able to tell the difference."

The *even you* was a bit of an insult itself. Daisy had bristled. But had kept her mouth shut.

The bus chugs past like a curtain opening on a screen. When Daisy looks across the street, she sees, suddenly revealed, the familiar shape of her only child.

He's in the middle of a pack of baseball-hat-on-backward, backpack-slung-over-one-arm, ripped-jeans, and denim-jacketed kids. Daisy can tell he's laughing from the way his shoulders jiggle, the way his chin tilts sideways. He has his hand on the neck of a girl whose blond ponytail swings from side to side like a cow's tail swatting a fly. She's laughing too. In fact, the whole crowd is laughing, probably, Daisy believes with the sure sense that eighteen years of motherhood has conferred on her, at one of Sammy's jokes. He is so adorable. He can be so funny. She tries to take a closer look at the girl. She's pretty, she's sure. Good enough for her son, she hopes, as if there were anyone in the world worthy of such charms. God, how she misses Sammy. Though her instinct is to yell across the street, she restrains herself. This is the Sammy whose first choice was Stanford. Though for reasons, he insisted, that were only partly geographical. This is, after all, the same Sammy who at thirteen used to cross to the opposite side of Mass Ave from Daisy and Henry just in case he might run into one of his junior-high buddies in Harvard Square. "I'm dead meat if any kids see me on a Saturday night with my *parents*," he had explained.

Daisy had said she understood, but she was secretly sad. After all, she and Henry were not the kind of parents their own parents were. Her parents looked gray and middle-aged at forty, the way real senior citizens do now, her mother in a starched apron and space shoes for her bad feet, her father in his too-narrow tie and Mister Rogers cardigan. Nor did she and Henry resemble Lillian at forty, with her helmet of hair frozen into a style popular in 1955, her glitter-dusted T-shirts, her backless mules. Middle-aged, Daisy's mother would put on white gloves, her father a tie, to go to the movies. Middle-aged, Daisy and Henry wear jeans and sneakers almost everywhere.

"It's Sammy." She nudges Henry and points.

"All grown up," says Henry.

"You think?" she asks, registering how young he looks, how vulnerable.

"All grown up," insists Henry with a surprising emphasis.

By the time the light changes, Sammy and friends have already crowded into the doorway of the frozen-yogurt store.

Henry takes her arm. Under her sleeve she feels a forceful pinch of the skin. "No, Daisy," he commands.

Does she look wistful? she wonders. Does it show?

"We are not going into the yogurt place," he continues. He twists his mouth the way he does when he's about to make a little joke. "We're going to have our sushi and eat it too." Henry pauses. "Besides, Sammy's all grown up. He's got his own life. We . . . *you* have yours and *I* have mine."

*   *   *

The restaurant is called the Sea of Japan and occupies the basement, which once contained a record store that burned down,
and, before that, a hot dog place that went belly-up during the
health-food craze.

Daisy can still smell charred linoleum, and, over that, the
sauerkraut that used to smother the German sausages. It's interesting how the smells of a place can be uncovered like so
many archaeological layers. She wonders if the people who now
live in their old Harvard student housing can ferret out the ves-
tiges of a dinner of sweet-and-sour meatballs or overcooked
London broil. Does the mattress carry in its springs the scent
of their old lust? Remembering that old lust, a sadness seeps
down that seems the exact opposite of that once rising heat of
desire. A desire she remembers not in her loins, but in her
head, the way you remember a favorite book pushed years ago
to the back of the shelf. Of course, that mattress would have
been tossed out decades before, turning into landfill on some
hazardous waste site that is Cambridge's dumping ground.

Only one other couple is sitting in the restaurant, and
Daisy's certain it's not a good sign that this couple is not Japanese. They are a robust pair whose ancestors could have been
Vikings sailing around the fjords. This is reinforced by the
awkward way they stab at their noodles with chopsticks like
crossed swords. Noodles slither down the sides of their bowls
and onto the placemats like slippery eels.

Daisy thinks of Roka and Sachiko and of a menu she knows
by heart. Here the walls are damp. The floor smells as if it had
been swabbed by a sour mop. Next to the cash register, two
waiters and a cashier looked bored. There is no sushi counter
with gleaming cases of iced fish. No sushi chef with a ban-
danna wielding his knife like a baton. "This doesn't seem exactly popular," she says to Henry.

"Because it's new," he replies. He has already followed the

nod of the cashier, who, doubling as the maître d', is pulling out a chair at a corner table. "You always like to do the same old things," he says to Daisy. It is not a compliment. "Lately I'm finding myself open to new experiences. Besides, it's quiet here. We don't know anybody. We've got a lot to talk about."

This surprises Daisy, who has begun to think they don't have anything to talk about. She assumes they'll discuss the award ceremony, when to have their new student to dinner, what local seafood to serve, what sights to show her in the greater Boston area, though from the way Henry carried on at the award ceremony, he's already been polishing his hosting skills along with his French.

In minutes, Daisy knows, they'll quickly exhaust the topic of Sammy, who is closemouthed about trooping any news from the college front. Then they'll finish their meal in the kind of pained silence she's become rather used to now that Sammy's not here to compare batting averages, dissect his teachers' abilities, let them in on who is going steady with whom. Maybe she'll ask about those new experiences Henry is finding himself so open to. Does the redheaded Giselle have something to do with them? she wonders. She studies the beret tucked into his pocket. Maybe these are experiences she doesn't want to know about.

The menus are as big as a Rand McNally atlas but not so thick. She picks chicken teriyaki on rice, a choice that, though bland, seems safe. Henry chooses the sushi deluxe.

"Are you sure?" she asks. "Do you think it's fresh?"

Henry raises his eyebrows in a weary oh-what-I-have-to-put-up-with way that implies he can't be bothered to answer such a stupid question. His chin tightens with an I-can-take-care-of-myself clench.

The waitress slaps lacquered bowls of miso soup onto the table with such force that some of the liquid spills over, making amoeba-shaped puddles. These quiver like a lower but definite form of life. The waitress does not apologize.

Daisy nods at her retreating obi-wrapped back. She lowers her voice to a whisper. "So far the service seems so—oh—un-Japanese."

"She's Korean. Can't you tell?" Henry says in the semidisgusted tone he's been using lately to correct her pronunciation of words like *au revoir, boeuf en daube,* and *politesse.*

Should she be able to tell the difference between a Japanese and Korean? Is it as hard as picking who's a Norwegian, who's a Swede? Shouldn't her years of hosting international students have fine-tuned her country-of-origin identifying skills? Still, that the waitress is Korean in a restaurant called the Sea of Japan is hardly promising.

And not only for the food, Daisy realizes, when Henry, after three noisy slurps (the Asian show of respect, he insists), sets down his empty bowl.

"I've been thinking a lot about how to approach this," he says.

"Approach what?"

"And I've decided that the best thing is to come out with it." Henry is looking at Daisy, but as soon as she returns his gaze his pupils start to dart around in their sockets like a bee searching for a petal to alight upon. The very opposite of his masterful locking of eyes at parties or with prospective clients for his computer company.

"Then, well, do," Daisy says. Her voice is reasonable, measured. Underneath the table, in her lap, her hands are gripped together so tightly her engagement ring pierces skin. She squeezes harder. Funny, but for twenty years she hasn't given one thought to this ring's tiny flaw. And yet, now she pictures the carbon dot of imperfection wiggling through the hard-as-a-diamond diamond and soundlessly, invisibly, seeping harm into her vulnerable flesh.

"It's the marriage."

"Whose?" Daisy asks.

Henry lifts the bowl to his lips, gazes out over its rim, a hollow prop that, tucked under his nose, makes a kind of silly mustache. Daisy smiles.

"It's not funny," Henry says.

"It could be," Daisy explains. "A new man for your mother. Sammy about to elope. Colonel Mustard on bended knee with Miss Scarlet in the library. Elizabeth Taylor ready, once again, to tie the knot." Frantically she casts about for other examples. She needs jokes to divert the flood, charm to deflect the bomb. Stop, she wants to cry. You're unwinding the wrong reel. *Reasonably* happily-ever-after will be more than acceptable.

"*Our* marriage. I think it's run its course."

Daisy stops breathing. She feels like one of those quarterbacks writhing on TV who've been kicked in the gut. She drops her chopsticks into her soup. She gasps. She clutches her stomach. Her voice, when she summons it, sounds tinny, like the voices coming from cheap speakers attached to your car in the parking lots of drive-in movies. "Like a horse put out to pasture? A car that flunked its one-hundred-thousand-mile checkup and needs to be traded in?" She touches her chin. "Needs to be traded in for a new model," she says.

"That's beside the point," Henry says.

"Aha! I have a point," Daisy exclaims.

Henry puts down the bowl. "The point is," he says, "this marriage's dead."

"The point is . . ." Daisy starts. She pauses. What is the point? She has no point, only a feeling of pointlessness. Of powerlessness. "Excuse me," she croaks.

She staggers on rubbery knees to the ladies' room, which,

after pulling open the door to the broom closet, then the door to the water heater, she identifies by a demure Madame Butterfly painted on a wooden arrow. This in contrast to the gents, where a samurai slashes a lethal-looking sword.

She's ready to fall on her own sword. Instead she slumps onto the none-too-clean toilet seat and buries her head in her hands. The tears pour, accelerated by the pungent smell of a plastic peach deodorizer. Her skin is clammy with shock. It's one thing to be dissatisfied, another to be the object of somebody else's dissatisfaction. A somebody else who knows you almost better than you know yourself. She takes three deep breaths, then a series of short pants she remembers from Lamaze. Courage, she tells herself, and realizes to her horror that she's given the word a French inflection.

She freezes. The faucet drips. The fluorescent light buzzes. First she's speaking French; next she'll be speaking in tongues. Get a grip, Daisy, she chants, get a grip. Maybe it's time to slide out from under Henry's all-pervasive influence. Her world doesn't have to collapse just because her marriage does. A marriage with symptoms any diagnostician might pronounce progressively terminal. Still, even if you know the end is in sight, you're never prepared for it. Especially if you're on the receiving end of the rejection.

The toilet paper roll is empty. One soggy paper towel lies crumpled in the sink. Daisy wipes her eyes on her sleeve. She starts to think of toilets. The toilet on the third floor next to Sammy's room, across the hall from Henry's study, has never worked right. The flushing mechanism is temperamental; the seat is cracked; the handle sticks. Its continuous gurgle shoots their water bill into the stratosphere. Only last week she and Henry decided to replace it. "You need a power flush," the plumber advised. "Trouble is, though, sounds like a gun going off. We installed one in our ladies' room. Come over any time during business hours and fire the cannon."

She'd gone that afternoon. She'd tried matchsticks, toilet paper, gum wrappers—all were whirled away into a vortex with no diminishment between first flush and third. True, it made a racket, but powerful technology deserved a powerful accompaniment. There was something satisfying about the loud whoosh compared to the puny and ever-constant trickle they'd settled for.

"Go for it," Henry had said. "We don't want a repeat of the linen-closet horror."

It's not the *horror* of the linen-closet episode that comes to her now—the time when Sammy, in an excess of toilet-training zeal, stuffed a whole roll of Scott tissue into the toilet, which overflowed into the downstairs linen closet where all the wedding china, linen, and crystal were stored—but rather the *triumph* of their coupledom, how together they lugged garbage bags of tablecloths and sheets to the cleaners, how Henry had washed the wineglasses and water goblets by hand, how they had sponged the shelves and scrubbed the placemats, how they had risen to heroic action like Londoners during the Blitz.

If her marriage ends, the toilet will never get replaced, she supposes. As soon as she thinks this, she is amazed. Her world as she has known it for twenty years is falling apart, and she focuses only on the most inconsequential domestic details. The loss of a power flush rather than the loss of a husband. But it makes sense. She can wrap her mind around a toilet. Marriage, husband, love, life are territories too vast to get a purchase on.

She pictures Henry, uncomplaining, emptying wineglasses of their sewage, coaching her in quantum theory, cradling her on their Holden Green bed, breathing along with her in childbirth classes. She forces herself to remove this halo she's just awarded him. She replaces it with his beret, a gesture that stirs anger into a batter of what had been pure sorrow. Someone starts pounding on the door. She can just about make out a gasped "Emergency."

The Nordic woman looks worse than Daisy feels. "All yours," Daisy says.

"I've never felt so bad," the woman groans.

"Me too," Daisy says with a sad nod of shared sisterhood. "Believe me, I can sympathize."

Maybe they're both in the same boat. A boat navigating the perilous waves of the Sea of Japan. Maybe the Sea of Japan is the destination of choice for breaking up. Maybe the Viking waved his chopsticks and vanquished the Viking-ess. Restaurants aren't always what they seem.

Nor are husbands. Unlike Henry, she would have muddled along, played it safe. For Sammy's sake. She pictures her hulking son, his scratchy beard, his size-twelve moccasins. How long can she cling to Sammy as an excuse? The way she'd explain the extra pounds by announcing she'd just had a baby when, in fact, she'd set out to buy candles for Sammy's first birthday cake? No, she'd stayed in the marriage for her own needs. Out of fear. Out of loneliness. Out of her instinctive tendency to cling to the husk when the core is gone. She slides back into the booth. Does Henry look a little sheepish?

"The point is," Henry reiterates, "this marriage is a shadow of its former self."

"I guess you're right," she says. Surprising Henry. Surprising herself.

Henry lets out a long whoosh of relief like the fired cannon of a power flush. "That's what I've always liked about you, Daisy—your reasonableness."

My doormattedness, thinks Daisy. "Is that all?" she asks.

Having been so easily let off the hook, Henry can afford a spurt of generosity. "You're funny. You're pretty. You're smart.

We had good times. A great son. It's not that we never loved each other."

Daisy notes the past tense.

"Like some people we know," he adds.

Daisy assumes he's thinking of her best friend, Jessica, who married serially for money, for looks, for a warm body in bed, for regular sex, for a Saturday night date, for somebody to put on lipstick for. Are all these such bad reasons? she wonders. Maybe having someone to share a box of popcorn at the Cineplex is enduring enough. Maybe love has a cycle that, like all living things, ends in death, and the big question is knowing when to call it quits.

"And what about our son?" She has a sudden tragic picture of Sammy: child of divorce, victim of a broken home.

"He's all grown up. Jesus! Most of his friends come from families split apart."

Daisy has to agree. When Sammy was in elementary school, he used to invite classmates home for play dates. "Your mother's house or your father's house?" these friends would inquire. And he'd decry his own lack not only of multiple dwellings but also of stepparents and half brothers, vacations that came in a variety pack, and what seemed like endless combinations of doting grandparents. Not to mention the two turkey dinners, the two desserts, the quadrupled number of presents on every holiday.

Then she remembers reading an article on how divorce is so much harder on older children, how, surprisingly, they are so much more susceptible. She thinks of telling this to Henry but suspects he will only put up an argument. She touches her hand to her forehead, then moves it to her pulse. She is taking the temperature of this news, the pulse of this news. Her pulse is steady, her temperature only slightly elevated, which might just as well result from the aftereffects of the miso soup than from the toppling of her world. She knows that divorce is high on the Richter scale of stress, one of those life changes that you need to gird all your psychic forces for. She realizes that she, who can't stand street names being altered, isn't exactly a poster child for going with the flow. Still, she's doing okay under the circumstances. It's not like the viruses that get into the computer systems, the viruses that Henry is such an expert on. These cause complete breakdowns, for which Henry's company is summoned. The breakdowns or, rather, their treatments, provide for Sammy's tuition, paid off the mortgage on their house, allow her to hold a job that doesn't supply a living wage. She is having no crash. No system-failure icon is parading across her screen. Just a small meltdown in the ladies' john. All that's left is to hope that her feelings come in manageable portions, the way you introduce a baby to new foods.

Sometimes in bed, Henry will recite the names of the computer viruses: Taiwan, Enigma, Monkey, Maltese Amoeba, Green Caterpillar, Tequila, Bubonic, Mosquito, Invader, James Bond. Beside them, the word *divorce* seems ordinary, benign. *Divorce. Divorce,* she repeats, trying to get used to it.

Not that Henry has exactly mentioned the word yet. She is pathetic, squeezing a drop of comfort from such a technicality. Behind the shield of a menu she takes a few more Lamaze pants. She knows divorce is as inevitable an end to a dead, shadow-of-its-former-self marriage as "They lived happily ever after" is to a fairy tale.

Their dishes arrive. Henry's sushi is set out on a platter the size of a TV tray table. Her plate is smaller, oval. The teriyaki looks shiny, the colors a little faded like the plastic food left too long in the windows of Asian restaurants.

"Anything else?" the waitress asks. "Watah, more beeah?" Her accent is pure South Boston. No chopped Asian syllables— Japanese or Korean—have ever passed her frosted fuchsia lips.

"No, thank you," Daisy says and turns to her dish. Her reasonableness has not yet reached her stomach, which is churning madly. She has no appetite.

Henry, on the other hand, attacks the food as if he's William the Conqueror subduing the Saxons.

Daisy rakes the rice with her chopsticks. She clears paths, builds hills, landscapes her plate.

"Must you play with your food?" Henry asks. A drop of wasabi sits on his chin like a witch's wen.

"You no longer have any right . . ."

"I suppose that's true. Of course it is," he cedes the point. He indicates her plate. She pushes it across to him.

"Just for the record," she asks, "is there someone else?"

Henry's *shinko maki* is poised an inch from his lips. He studies it as if the answer lies somewhere inside its seaweed-wrapped, vinegared-rice interior. "That is not the issue" is what he says.

"Which pretty much answers my question," Daisy says. She has a sudden picture of a red-haired Frenchwoman with a jauntily tied scarf. "Nice enough," Henry had conceded after he'd picked her up from the airport. How nice? What degree of enough? That they're *English* words she can't translate is the ultimate irony. She fingers her own scarf, which is starting to feel like a noose. "Scorned wife. What a cliché."

"One, you're not scorned. Two, clichés are only clichés because they're based on repeated human experience."

"Who are you, Roman Hruska making a plea for mediocrity?"

"You have every reason to be upset, Daisy," grants Henry, patronizing her in his most irritating, helping-profession way.

Henry has finished his tray of sushi down to the last slice of ginger, the last daub of wasabi paste. Now he is starting in on her plate. He slides the chicken off its bamboo skewer. He eats systematically as if with every mouthful he is checking something off a list.

Daisy gulps down her beer, considers ordering another, then decides not. She needs to be alert. Going through one of life's major stresses will require high functioning. To deal with ensuing miseries she will need to be at the height of her capacities. That deep down might lie a layer of relief like the trace of Lillian's Joy in their old pillowcase is a faint hope, a slight possibility. There might be comfort in being one of the many— those bitter middle-aged women left for nymphets. Women who confide their stories outside the schoolyard gates waiting for their soon-to-be psychologically damaged sons and daughters to be released from first grade. Women in the aisles of the supermarket buying a frozen stir-fry for one, who tell you about losing their house, dividing up the groceries, about having to take a job beneath the level of their abilities. "I was a Phi Bete at Wellesley and am supposed to feel lucky filing insurance claims at an hourly wage?" the mother of Orlando and Atticus complained. Women who rush to therapists to head off, at the couch, a dysfunctional family in the making, the blight of single motherhood.

But Sammy is grown, she tells herself, and she and Henry have long ago grown apart. And even though she knows young adult children will suffer from the end of their parents' marriage, Sammy is resilient. She sees him surrounded by a pack of friends on Boylston Street. She's pretty sure that in his troubles—if he's not too busy to acknowledge them—many comely shoulders will be offered up.

This comforts her until she scans the shoulders of the opposite sex available to her own tears and produces only the blood-stained, butcher-aproned ones of the guys at work.

"Done with your dinnah?" asks the waitress. A rhetorical question since she is slapping dishes together in a very un–Miss Manners stack. She winks at Henry. "Looks like you were wicked into that deluxe." Ignoring Daisy, she still manages to bump her slightly with the edge of the tray.

Daisy is about to say "I beg your pardon," then changes her mind. She'll have to get used to people fawning all over Henry, ignoring her. Her friend Jessica, the still flawless beauty who at forty-one was discovered in Bread and Circus and asked to audition for a Veuve Cliquot ad (which she refused, afraid the widow connection might jinx the ever-diminishing prospect of marital bliss), used to complain that when she left Edward, she sat by the phone while Edward—that cold drink of water who never said a word—was so in demand at dinner tables in Cambridge and the near suburbs that he was never home to answer his own ringing-off-the-hook telephone.

Henry signs the credit-card slip. In light of their changed situation, Daisy slides across a twenty-dollar bill. Henry refuses it. Nicely, she notes. And she is grateful that he doesn't point out who is the source of the four twenties and two fives that are now folded up and tucked into the zippered compartment of her purse.

"Which reminds me," Henry says now. "One thing you won't have to worry about: I'm not going to ignore my financial responsibilities."

Is financial responsibility the last to go in the peeling off of responsibilities? Daisy wonders. After sexual fidelity, trust, honor, all the stuff of marriage vows. She feels like a kept woman. She doesn't like being the kind of person someone else needs to be responsible for.

"What about the toilet?" she's compelled to ask.

"That's one expense we might forgo." He sticks his Visa into his pocket. "This was excellent," he tells the waitress. "We'll"—he pauses—"*I'll* have to come back again."

"It was terrible," Daisy says when the waitress is not quite out of earshot.

"Considering you didn't touch a bite, how could you tell?"

"Easy," Daisy says. She sweeps her arm indicating the now empty room, the sour-smelling floor, the basement windows with their lack of light, the mold crawling up one wall, the bored waitstaff. She rolls her eyes. She is stating the obvious, her posture claims.

"Well, it's no surprise your reaction wouldn't be positive."

"What's that supposed to mean?"

Henry sighs a long-suffering sigh. "Daisy, I don't want to get into a pissing contest with you."

"Which would be weighted in your favor, speaking anatomically." She takes pleasure in her own joke. She supposes she will miss Henry at least anatomically. She does miss the old days and all the rollicking sex. She loved when they lived together in sin; she adored the heightened calisthenics of their early married years when they were trying to conceive a child. In the end, though they had wanted four, and had screwed enough for fifty, it was Sammy, the result of that one instant when all the stars of her eggs and of Henry's sperm were aligned perfectly, who was their hearts' single delight.

In the last couple of years, however, neither she nor he has been particularly interested in the other's anatomy. On the fewer and fewer occasions that Henry would move onto her, that she would open her arms and legs to him, they came together with the memory of love, with old motions that were so familiar they were automatic, with past feelings whose strong imprint disguised the absence of present ones. Habit has a lot to account for in the longtime marriages that a husband and wife are habituated to.

When they climb up out of the restaurant, it's dark. It's turned colder. Daisy shivers; she tightens her scarf. Henry takes

out his beret and angles it jauntily onto his head. Daisy thinks
he appears ridiculous, this computer consultant, this expert on
computer viruses, trying to look like some cadmium-yellow,
burnt-sienna-spattered artist in Montmartre.

"The car's at the church," she says.

"At the For Clergy Only spot," Henry says almost gleefully
as if he's only too happy to chalk up yet another of her offenses
in his miles-long list of grievances.

"How did you guess?"

They are crossing Brattle Street. The health-food store on
the corner has a window display of piled-up autumn leaves.
Peeking out here and there are bottles and vials of elixirs, vitamins, lotions for the skin, scents of carrots, cucumber, fig leaf
to attract the opposite sex, boxes of Daily Detox Tea to cleanse
the system, St.-John's-wort for depression, *Ginkgo biloba* extract
for mental acuity, Chamomile Essence to promote harmony
and well-being for the whole family. Daisy looks at Henry.

Henry turns to her. "The award? Didn't you take it?"

She shows him her empty hands. "I thought you had it."

"I gave it to you."

"No, you had it last. I saw you put it down on your side of
the booth."

"Shall we go back?" Henry asks.

"*You* could," Daisy replies.

Henry shrugs. "Why bother. Considering the circumstances."

Daisy can't help but agree. She thinks of Chamomile Essence
to promote harmony and well-being for the whole family. She
pictures the words on the award: "Daisy and Henry Lewis, in
grateful appreciation for generous hospitality and caring
friendship." She wonders what the Korean waitress will do
with the award when—if—she cleans up the booth. Add it to
the lost-and-found? Try to look them up? To find their ad-

dress? Wait for Henry, the satisfied customer, to rush back for another sushi deluxe?

Of course it will be thrown into the trash along with old chopsticks, empty soy-sauce containers, used and crumpled Wash'n Dries.

Henry must think so too, because he starts to talk about host families. "In a way, it will be more realistic," he says with the enthusiasm only the self-justifying can summon. "After all, the traditional family is pretty much kaput. We'll be showing them what passes in this country as the American family norm."

"What are you talking about?"

"Host families," he says with the disgust of someone who has to explain things to the terminally obtuse. "We can each be host families. We can each pick our own students to host."

"To show them the joys of single parenthood?"

"If you want to put it that way." He stops in front of Bob Slate's stationery store. Behind the glass, postcards are fanned out from around the world: the Taj Mahal, the Colosseum, Victoria Falls, Big Ben, and, naturally, the Eiffel Tower. "On second thought," Henry says, "I'd just as soon walk."

"See you at home," she says. It comes out automatically. She pauses, tries to find a better word. There must be one to reflect the external changes that are roiling the meaning of something both so simple and so profound as the concept of home. "See you back on Avon Hill," she corrects herself.

Henry doesn't seem to notice the fine gradations in her vocabulary that are signifying her quick adjustment to the shock of the new. His eyes are still on the comforts of the old—the Eiffel Tower and an exhibition of wedding invitations, engraving one-quarter off this month. He gives a wave of dismissal. "Later," he says.

Walking to her car, Daisy contemplates host families. She

doesn't have to get someone from lower Borneo or upper Pakistan. She doesn't have to grow accustomed to native costumes or oddly spiced cuisines. She doesn't have to talk slowly, sounding out vowels with exaggerated contortions of her lips the way she did with the developmentally disabled helpers at the food bank. She doesn't have to host someone to whom she has to apologize for a surfeit of consumer goods, doesn't have to explain that her house with five bathrooms for three people was the by-product of conspicuous consumption of a Victorian nouveau riche who made a killing in copper-lined pipes.

Since this evening's ceremony, since the subject of Pilombaya has come up, she can see him in front of her eyes, smell him under her nose. She remembers how disappointed he was that they didn't have a Kodak Carousel, that they'd never even considered a Touch-Tone phone. He should see them now: microwave, dishwasher, Cuisinart, five TVs, CD players, three computers, beepers, digital diaries, call waiting, call forwarding, voice mail, e-mail, fax, something that turns on the house lights at the first step on their walk, burglar alarms, fire alarms, car alarms, heat detectors, water purifiers. She thinks back to their student-housing days. They had nothing. They had everything. The irony is that all this accumulation has only resulted in a loss. Has it set up a barrier so they couldn't find each other across this mountain of things? Or is it simply the piling up of objects to hide the cigarette burn, the chipped veneer, the pale white blemish that stains the coffee table's mahogany, the small imperfection in a diamond engagement ring?

A couple is walking in front of her. Each has a hand in the back pocket of the other's jeans. Well, if Henry can order up a young French girl with an artistically knotted scarf, she can order up a French man, a man to whom a beret is not an affectation but a right. In high school, she was, in fact, an ace in

French. In college she did so well on the placement exam that she passed out of having to take any language at all. Her high school French teacher, Monsieur Bookerman (Monsieur *Livre-homme*, they called him), said she was a natural, suggested a year at the Sorbonne. He put his hand on her breast once in the back of the bus during the French Club's trip to Quebec. He was just being French was his excuse. French Canadian, she had exclaimed since they had just crossed the border into Saint Joseph de Beuce. He had not been complimented. He had examined the offending hand, which had been sliding its way down from the alligator on her Lacoste. He had waggled his fingers. *"Français. Parisien."* She hadn't pressed charges. How could she, against a bald not-French man with sad eyes and garlicky breath who wore an enameled fleur-de-lys in his lapel?

When she reaches her car, she spies a note crunched under the windshield. Her first impulse is to leave it there since it doesn't look like one of the usual flyers for four shoes for the price of two or even a handout from her own place of work, offering two jumbo Wisks for the price of one giant Tide. She picks it up. It's a message on a piece of lined paper torn from a notebook. Across it is scrawled in red Magic Marker, *You should be ashamed of yourself,* and signed, *A concerned and outraged parishioner.*

Daisy tucks the note into her purse, opens the car door, and turns on the ignition. She wonders if she'll pass Henry on Mass Ave. Shall she stop, honk her horn, pull over, ask if he's changed his mind? Wants a ride home? Home. The word sticks in her throat. She's calling it Avon Hill, she reminds herself. She turns off the car. Gets out. Opens her purse. Puts the note back under her windshield. She heads in the direction of the Charles River, to Jessica's building, to the lobby where the concierge will call up, check that Jessica's both home and alone, then will buzz her in. She is ashamed of herself. But not for parking in a For Clergy Only parking space. For what? For being the kind of woman a kind of man like Henry would want to leave—and for reasons that seem linked to the language of French. For this terrible news about to be sprung on her son. For being half a host family after twenty years of being a whole. For hanging on to a stale marriage well past the expiration date.

FRANCE NATIONALE
CHARLES DE GAULLE 2
4
A 421 FRANCE

Jessica lives on the ninth floor of a modern high-rise behind the Charles Hotel. Edward bought the apartment in a frenzy of real estate speculation and marital optimism. After the third law firm managed to crack the antenuptial agreement, it became hers—though Jessica claims it was not superior legal-eagledom but finally wearing Edward down. She has two children by her first husband the hunk, a buyer of men's accessories at the downtown Filene's where she used to model part-time in her college days. Kiki is at Dartmouth, Karl at Berkeley, though it's Kiki with the navel ring and Doc Martens and Karl with the boat shoes and pressed madras plaid from J. Crew. "Go figure," Henry would say every other time Jessica's name came up.

Daisy has known Jessica since nursery school in Bronxville, where they pressed their handprints into each other's Play-Doh dishes. In third grade they mixed their mothers' perfumes in a pain-free version of blood sisterhood. At Harvard they found themselves three rooms apart down the same corridor. Jessica is closer than a sister, closer than Daisy's sister, Rachel, who lives in Winnetka and sells Mary Kay cosmetics from a pink-painted Cadillac.

The cute concierge is on duty—the one whose CD is being seriously considered by the higher-ups at Sony. Last year, the cuter concierge sold a story to *Ploughshares,* and it's about to be anthologized in the annual O. Henry Awards. This is one of the things Daisy loves about Cambridge: The waiter is playing Uncle Vanya at the ART; the guy selling notebooks at the Coop composes symphonies; the girl who cuts your mat at the frame shop shows her sculpture in a Fort Point Channel gallery; the young man who whacks your weeds is a linguistics post-doc. "Believe it or not, *Miz* Lewis, *Miz* Sherman is in," the cute concierge says.

The elevator is lined in brass so shiny Daisy feels trapped in the mirrors of a fun house. She can't avoid her reflection. Even the plate studded with floor buttons beams back the spark from her engagement ring. What does she see? A nice-looking forty-two-year-old woman with swollen eyes in her award-receiving dress, a lank scarf drooped around her neck. Under its twisted-to-the-front point, she can make out the *Hello I'm . . . Daisy Lewis Host Family Honoree* sticker slapped on her chest. She tears off the sticker, crumples it into an ashtray beneath the No Smoking sign. There's still a little corner of white adhesive that she can't get off. She unknots the scarf. She stuffs it into her pocket. Depending on the angle, she resembles either a candidate for liposuction or a gangster's moll who is packing a gun. Maybe that's better than looking like someone's mother. Or someone's wife. The mother of a grown son. The wife of a husband who no longer wants to be one.

"Daisy!" Jessica exclaims. She kisses each cheek, then holds Daisy at arm's length. "What's the matter? You look terrible!"

Jessica herself looks wonderful. Her glossy black hair is cut with the kind of expensive, angular simplicity that only men named Christophe or Massimo can provide. Her face is powdered Kabuki white, her lips lacquered Chinese red. She's wearing jeans and a peach silk tee. Reading glasses slide down her nose, signaling she's at work. This is confirmed by the laptop propped on the coffee table in the living room.

"What's the matter?" Jessica asks again.

All of a sudden Daisy doesn't want to say. Naming things makes them real. Then you have to deal with them. "What are you working on?" she sidesteps. "What are you in the middle of?"

Jessica inspects her with an appraising eye. She pulls Daisy over to the sofa, plumps up six fat pillows the color of butter, and pushes Daisy down into them. "It's the feuding Franklins."

Daisy shakes her head. Jessica writes celebrity biographies for *Boston Bean & Cod*, a high-class scandal sheet with shiny ads and impossible-to-make-without-a-restaurant-stove recipes. The feuding Franklins are three brothers who inherited a plumbing-supply dynasty from their father and are running it into the ground. They communicate by memo. The only time they meet is at the annual first night seder at their mother Bessie's house, where they have perfected the art of a devotion so filial they rotate who sits next to her through the bitter herbs, the charoses, the gefilte fish down to the flourless Barton's chocolate cake. Jessica has slept with two of them: Abe and Morty. Or was it Lawrence and Abe?

Jessica picks up a bunch of papers. She shoves them into a leather folder embossed with the pattern of alligator skin.

"You'd be amazed what my research has turned up. For example, Bessie the Battle-Ax Franklin, the slumlord whose passion is the eviction of orphans and widows and disabled vets, spent a week in the hospital last year. Guess what they found out?"

"I give up."

Jessica takes off her glasses. She sticks them on the nose of a marble art deco head. "The hospital did test after test. Each brother engaged his own personally selected specialist. They solicited second, third, fourth opinions. Booked the suite at Mass General last occupied by King Hussein and his retinue. With a view of the Charles." Jessica turns toward her own view of the Charles, where sculls glide under the bridges even though it's night. "Abe, Lawrence, and Morty took turns sleeping on the couch. And last year Morty even had a new wife."

"And?"

"She's suing for divorce, claims Morty should have hired a hostess rather than chosen a bride."

"Not that. Bessie."

"They discovered she had a parasite." Jessica opens her folder and starts pulling out pieces of paper. A Post-it attaches itself to a vase, another to the welted edge of the sofa's upholstery. "I have the name of it somewhere. Oh, never mind."

"A parasite from what?" Daisy asks.

"That's the best part. Gefilte fish! She caught it from rolling the raw fish into balls and tasting it to see if she put in enough salt."

Daisy smiles. She laughs. Jessica hoots, a whoop-de-whoop like the song of a rare bird. They each grab a butter-colored pillow and hold it to their ribs. Daisy laughs so hard tears stream down her cheeks. Then she starts to sob.

Jessica stops. She flings her arms around Daisy. "Honey," she croons.

Daisy smells Opium, the crushed pomegranate of Jessica's lipstick, the lemon of her shampoo, the lavender of imported soap. She remembers when Jessica smelled of Prell, Tangee, Jergens, pink Camay, Cover Girl not quite covering Clearasil.

She remembers the sugary fragrance of her own mother's Jungle Gardenia mixed with Jessica's mother's My Sin.

Daisy cries some more.

"Oh, honey. Oh, sweetie-pie," Jessica soothes. "Men," she diagnoses. "No second, third, or fourth opinion needed here."

Daisy nods.

"Henry?"

"Who else?" Daisy blows her nose on a peach Kleenex, which pops up from a silk-covered cube like a jack-in-the-box. She looks around the living room: white linen walls, white upholstered chairs, watercolors in pale pastels. She thinks of her own house, the rambling Victorian with its footed tubs, walls that need paint, floors that need washing, a kitchen stove with permanently attached pliers to turn the knob, the running toilet now doomed to run forever without its power flush. She thinks of the graceful rooms, the fireplaces, the molding, the way the light slants in and burnishes the books on the shelves. For a second it occurs to her that she could move, buy a chic, sleek apartment with nobody's balled-up socks in the corner, nobody's computer magazines falling into the shower. Then she pictures Sammy's room. It's neat for the first time in eighteen years, the bed made, the bureau and desktop cleared. There are no sneakers set out in the upstairs hall like the shoes left to be polished in the corridors of European hotels. "Why do you keep these here?" Daisy had asked after having tripped on one of them.

"The smell, Mom. I don't want to sleep with it."

Though the room is cleaned to unrecognizability, it's still a shrine. She goes in there often. It's calming, like a monastic cell where one can pray. Though she misses those boy smells—the ripe socks, the rancid shoes—there's still enough trace of Sammy to draw her in. Funny how leaving the childhood room of her child seems more difficult than giving up a whole life of adult rooms with Henry.

"So? Henry?" Jessica prompts.

Daisy hesitates. How to word it? she wonders. How to contain such a huge thing in a paltry collection of syllables? She daubs her eyes. Blows her nose. "The marriage . . ." she starts. She stops.

Jessica takes her hand. "Which is only to be expected. What is it, sweetie, a fight? A midlife crisis? There are always blips. And even more space for them in a twenty-year marriage, I assume, though I can't exactly speak from experience."

"This is no blip."

"You mean . . . ?"

Daisy nods.

"Oh, Daze."

Daisy sobs against Jessica's shoulder. She worries about the peach silk. For the award ceremony she brushed on mascara and a bronzing powder promising a blush of Saint-Tropez. Will the dry cleaner be able to erase these stains of vanity, this trail of sorrow? Jessica, unlike Daisy, is not the kind of person who would be distracted by laundry, by plumbing, in the midst of tragedy.

Jessica pats Daisy's back. She smoothes her hair. "Not that I'm surprised."

Daisy stiffens. "What do you mean?"

"I mean," Jessica explains, "from one who's known you forever and is, well, fond of Henry, I've noticed—how can I put this?—a certain lack of pizzazz."

Daisy focuses on the word *pizzazz*. It's a ridiculous word. A word a pep-squad leader might use, or a copywriter extolling Viagra or Geritol. A word one knows not by definition but by sound. Pizzazz. There was plenty of it in the early days. Even though Henry was not her first love. That distinction belonged to Richie Rego, unsuitable juvenile delinquent-in-the-making, a crushed pack of Camels tucked into his T-shirt sleeve and pizzazz up the kazoo. She thinks of her second love, Oliver Foreman, the NYU film school student to whom she lost her virginity. And for whom she also lost her appetite, having dropped fifteen pounds during a summer of love when her stomach was so clenched with pizzazz that Oliver used to drag her to restaurants secure that she would never order more than a few lettuce leaves.

Daisy feels defensive. "What long-term marriage has pizzazz?"

"You're right. Some other word. Lifeless, maybe? Empty? Not that it isn't a trauma. The end of a marriage always is." Jessica pauses. She clears her throat. In her gentlest, Mother Teresa orphanage-interviewing voice, she asks, "Is there anyone else?"

"The language of French" trips unbidden off Daisy's tongue. She has a sudden image of a petition of divorce. Her eyes scroll down its pages, which have a high cotton-rag content and are heavily watermarked. Under *alienation of affections,* she sees *the language of French.* Under *cause of inevitable breakdown of a marriage,* she sees *the language of French.* Under *third party interference,* she sees *the language of French.* Under *worm in the marriage, wrecking ball, virus,* she sees *the language of French.* "I should have known when he started to put his bread on the table instead of the plate. When he started to drink his coffee in one of those soup bowl–sized cups." Daisy sighs. "The signs were as unmistakable as lipstick on the collar, a crumpled florist's bill." *J'accuse,* she wants to say, *j'accuse* the French, though she acknowledges a certain redundancy.

And of course it's a natural segue from *j'accuse* the French to *cherchez la femme.*

"In my unlimited experience there's always a woman, or at least the hope of one," says Jessica.

A possibility—no, a certainty—Daisy isn't ready to contemplate. Instead, she thinks of the award left behind in the Sea of Japan. It may still be on the seat, she imagines, wedged against a Japanese or Japanophile hip. Or slipped to the floor splattered with soy sauce and trampled by a legion of hobnailed feet. Not that you find many Japanese or many feet in your bad-food, bad-service, downscale, downstairs, and in-the-basement restaurants. "And they just gave us an award," she cries.

"Who?" Jessica asks. "The Great Institution of Marriage Society?"

"No, Harvard."

"I understand the crimson arm on this side of the Charles is o'erreaching, but why would Harvard be interested in your marital difficulties? Afraid a loyal alum's fortune is going to be pilfered away in alimony?"

"For being a host family. An exemplary host family. You know for those international students that come to Harvard."

"Do I ever. As I recall, didn't you have to get somebody's mother out of jail?"

"That was only one instance. . . ."

"Then there was that real leech you used to complain about. What was his name? Pill something. Sounded like a disease and its remedy."

"Pilombaya," Daisy says. She is amazed how after all this time his name has come up twice in one night.

She remembers the Thanksgiving she and Henry celebrated their first year in Holden Green. Lillian was in Florida. Her parents were making the three-day drive to Winnetka to her sister's new split-level in an up-and-coming development. She and Henry had refused invitations from his adviser, her food bank canned-goods supplier, from the couple across the hall who moved in after Helen and Hitch broke up. "It'll be just the two of us," they'd crowed.

It was the three of them. Pilombaya called. He had been reading about Plymouth Rock. About the Pilgrims and the Indians. That she and Henry host an Indonesian seemed to him to be the equivalent. What time was dinner being served?

It was a dinner that never should have been served. The turkey didn't defrost. The stuffing never cooked. The filling of the pumpkin pie shifted in a glop to one side when Daisy took it out of the box.

"So much for our cozy dinner for two," whispered Henry, hacking frozen turkey into the garbage pail.

"He's been doing homework on the Pilgrims and the Indians for a week. How could we not ask him?" Daisy whispered back.

"Easy," Henry had said. "There is no reason on earth to leave yourself open like this, to be so available, willing even, for every foreigner, every stranger to take advantage of."

"He's our responsibility. . . ."

"Baloney. What about me? Where do I fit in? Besides, the dinner stinks!"

"The dinner is wonderful," Pilombaya said back in the living room. His plate was puddled in cranberry sauce thinned to the consistency of blood. "Could we make trip, Daisy, to Plymouth to see the rock?"

Just then, Jessica knocked on their door, took one look at the sorry remains of the sorry meal, Henry's tightening jaw, Pilombaya's Pilgrim-like colonization of their table, Daisy's free-wheeling misery, and fled without the turkey baster she'd come to borrow in the first place.

"Sometimes the third world is too much with us," Henry had groaned, after dropping Pilombaya home.

An insult Daisy, who folded clothes for Oxfam, who demonstrated against injustice in Guatemala, whose very profession fed needy immigrants, took personally.

"I feel invaded!" Henry had added, *"literally."* Then pulled the door behind him so hard the knob came off in his fist.

"Pilombaya wasn't that bad," Daisy tells Jessica now. "In fact, he was really rather sweet," she elaborates with the rose-colored glow only time and distance can provide. "But I feel a little guilty that on the very night of our receiving an award as host family, we are de-familying ourselves."

"Count yourself as part of the zeitgeist. The fractured family as poster child for planet Earth."

"The exception is still possible."

"You and Henry had a run longer than most."

"Which makes the ending harder. All those years—pizzazz or no—they have to count for something."

Jessica gives Daisy's knee a squeeze. "Oh, honey, of course. But one door shuts and another door opens." There's a newspaper under her computer folded on a page of ads. Jessica slides it out. She waves it at Daisy. "Take it as an opportunity. The first day of the rest of your life."

"Ugh."

"I assume that's for the cliché and not the profound concept behind it. Don't scoff at an opportunity for meeting new men."

Daisy's first thought is: Has Jessica been going through the personals? Is her beautiful, smart, sexy, rich, popular best friend that desperate? And what does that say for Daisy as the comparatively plain-Jane sidekick to Jessica's dazzler? And her second thought is she has no idea what Jessica's talking about. "What *are* you talking about?" she asks.

"Host family. If Henry can *cherchez la femme,* you can *cherchez*—oh—*le garçon.*"

"I think that's a waiter," Daisy says.

"Don't change the subject."

"But I get your drift." Daisy shakes her head. She feels weighed down with sadness. Pumped up with fear. "This is not something I want to think about. You don't replace a man in your life the way you replace a carton of soured milk."

"Well, of course not. Not right away. Still, after a decent interval, you could pick out your own French beau like a mail-order bride." Jessica sits up. "I've been checking the travel section." She strikes the side of her head. "My God! You can leave France to Henry and head for the boot of Italy."

In spite of herself, Daisy grins. For three weeks last summer Jessica spent sun-drenched days and man-saturated nights in the hill towns of Tuscany. "At least I had high school French," Daisy admits. "The only Italian words I know are pasta dishes in restaurants."

"You can always learn. Don't think that there aren't men lurking in the groves of adult education."

"I can't even begin to imagine being out there."

"Give it some time. Sap can rise in the most dormant of trees."

Is she dormant? Daisy wonders. Has she been tamped instead of tapped? Perhaps she's been closed so long she'll never be able to open up. Or like Rip Van Winkle she'll awaken to a world unrecognizable.

She thinks of Sammy's social life. He seemed to travel in a pack of teens. Even the girls he escorted to the junior and senior proms arrived flanked by other Laura Ashley–clad beauties. How could you tell whether it was Caroline, Jenny, Hannah, or Lucinda who was Sammy's designated date? Again, she pictures Sammy across Boylston Street in the middle of a group. After all, the ponytailed girl could be a ponytailed guy; earrings dangling from ears could belong to either sex.

Jessica stands up. The neck of her T-shirt is scooped to expose her delicate clavicle; her jeans taper to the instep of her polished lizard boots. No matter Henry's opinion, Jessica is proof that dowdiness is not the fault of the Land of the Free and the Home of the Brave. Should Daisy blame her midwestern relatives for her lack of style? Is the gene for plain sown above the fruited Plains?

"Time for me to go home," Daisy says, using a word that seems suddenly in the process of being redefined like one of those obsolete terms linguists at the Académie Française hold Jesuitical debates about. She wonders if Henry's wondering where she is. Is he worried she's in such despair she's driven herself into the Charles? Or headed to Logan Airport for parts unknown without even a change of underwear? She reaches for her purse. Maybe he hasn't even noticed that she's gone.

"Let's go out and get a drink first. Doctor's orders. A change of scenery and something to dull the pain," decrees Jessica.

The Rialto bar is just across the courtyard. In the elevator down to the lobby, Daisy concentrates on Jessica's reflection in an attempt to ignore her own. She's not surprised that Jessica was surrounded by men in the hills of Tuscany. In their junior year of college they spent a summer traveling through Europe on a two-month Eurailpass. To save money, they slept on trains. One night they were jolted awake at a deserted railroad station at two A.M. It was going to take an hour to fix the track, announced a conductor in a rapid Italian that was translated for them by a Neapolitan who had for three years driven a taxi in New York. When Daisy and Jessica realized they were stopped in Pisa, they were determined to see the Leaning Tower. By the time Daisy had buckled her sandals, Jessica was striding twenty feet ahead. All of a sudden, a line of Italian males materialized seemingly out of nowhere. They formed a single file behind Jessica like ants trailing after a picnicker. *"Bella. Bella,"* they cried, raising their hands in gestures easy enough to recognize.

Daisy figures the Rialto bar is an appropriate name for two people who have been talking of Italian and their memories of Italy. Though there was no romance in Venice. It was a week so rainy that *impermeàbiles*—cheap plastic raincoats as thin as cellophane—were hawked on the crest of every bridge. She and Jessica had terrible colds, not helped by the damp walls and the smelly canal under the window of their *pensióne*. The *signóra* mothered them with bowls of *pasta e fagioli* and pronounced them too pale and weak for an evening walk to the Rialto.

More than two decades later, confronting another Rialto, Daisy still feels pale and weak. She looks around the bar. She has a first impression of men in pinstripes, women in gray tropical-weight wool. There's not a sweatshirt among them, not a backpack either, though one woman dangles a red ostrich-skin version from one shoulder. This is studded with silver zippers, rings, and chains. Daisy is not surprised to see MADE IN ITALY embossed across its flap. No wonder there aren't any students at such a restaurant.

At which Jessica is, of course, a regular. She kisses the maître d', asks after the bartender's girlfriend, who broke an elbow at the gym. A busboy whips out a photograph of his newborn son. A waitperson stops to praise Jessica's articles on the Franklin brothers, who reserve a regular table on alternate Thursday nights, a corner booth tufted in velvet with a view onto a courtyard. After the Franklins, the waitperson informs them, Julia Child gets next dibs, then visiting rock stars, *Fortune* 500 CEOs, and Nobel laureates.

Daisy crushes the scarf in her pocket and tries to look interesting and thin. "It's all in your mind," her mother used to tell her during her fits of adolescent angst. "Think beautiful and you will be; think special and you will be."

Now Daisy tries to think herself at least special enough to be a regular. When she'd suggested the Rialto for a birthday or anniversary, Henry would counter with a craving for moo goo gai pan or Ethiopian doro wat. A surprising choice for a Euro-centric who pooh-poohs the third world. Better value was his excuse. On those nights when he calls to complain he's going to eat a corned beef sandwich at his desk, maybe he's at Espalier or Maison Robert consuming delicacies *en croûte*. Why pour a fine Beaujolais down the throat of a wife who's happy with a Tsing Tao? A wife who's soon to be an ex. For whom it would be a shame to stretch the food budget to a cheaper two when one alone can dine so well and so expensively. Daisy pauses. Maybe it's not *one* dining. She has a sudden blinding vision of Henry spooning foie gras between the glistening, pillowy lips of somebody young and beautiful and French.

Daisy's eyes move from the bar to the tables next to the window. She's relieved to see academic types in scratchy tweeds, even a few earnest women in their jewel-colored Marimekko tents. Which you can't find in the Square anymore. "So loud, so big, so unflattering," Jessica used to pronounce. "So Cambridge." But Daisy had loved being so Cambridge. Henry had liked the dresses too. They fit their Dansk bowls, their bent-birch Swedish furniture, the rippling glass vases that were replicas of the ones still in the collection at the Museum of Modern Art. Those were happy years. Their Scandinavian years, as Daisy now thinks of them. They had hosted a Finn named Riitta Liisa, whose radiant complexion convinced Henry to send away for a build-your-own-sauna kit.

In time, though, Daisy's elbows broke clear through the Marimekko sleeves. The hemline frayed into a fringe. Once-vibrant reds and purples blanched. And Henry moved from the love of all things Danish to his obsession with French.

Jessica grabs Daisy's hand and pulls her to the bar. "Two

Campari and sodas," Jessica commands. She turns to Daisy, "All this talk of Italy, seems the natural choice."

Daisy and Jessica climb onto barstools a two-cell-phoned, two-beepered pair has just left. The seats are still warm, almost hot. A man stands behind them. Daisy feels puffs of breath on her neck. She smells a cologne she thinks she recognizes from inserts in beauty parlor magazines. "Size six, Dolce and Gabbana," the man says to Jessica.

Jessica squeaks the barstool around to face him. "Bug off," she orders in the tone of one hit on by a constant chain of Lotharios.

"Though you'd be a four in Calvins. Same in DKNY. Eight in Moschino; they tend to run small."

"I'm not impressed," Jessica says. "Get lost."

Her words bounce off him. The man who won't get lost is hardly someone you'd impress anybody with. He's in his thirties, dark, tanned not beneath the Caribbean sun but under the ultraviolet lamp of a salon. He wears a necklace of gold linked chains with an ID bracelet to match. A shirt opened Harry Belafonte–style is tucked into jeans with such crooked seams they were probably stitched by exploited child laborers from the underdeveloped underbelly of the continent. Around the waist, his flesh rolls like a doughnut circling its hole.

He turns to Daisy. His eyes slide from her torso to her ankles and then back again. It's not the ogle of a wolf but the appraisal of a tailor. "Size ten in Levi's 501; nine/ten, the Gap; eight, relaxed fit." He smiles, teeth as white and glossy as a denture ad. "Though in that dress it's kind of hard to tell."

Daisy supposes she should be grateful he hasn't cast her into the high double digits of what is euphemistically called woman plus. "It's been years since I've bought jeans," she confesses. "I tend to wear the castoffs of my *husband*."

"*Niente converzatione,*" Jessica whispers. "Don't encourage him." Followed by "*Estranged* husband, Daisy." She can't help herself.

"Jessica," Daisy exclaims.

"So you're Jessica," the man crows with the deductive glee of a Sherlock Holmes. "And you are Daisy. The flower."

As opposed to what, Daisy wonders, the daisy wheel in old IBM Selectrics?

"Love me. Love me not," he goes on. "Nice name. Nice and simple. Barry," he says. "Barry Sweiker." He holds out a hand to Jessica. Who ignores it. Then to Daisy. Who, as an apology for Jessica's rudeness, feels obliged to clasp it in her own.

His hand is damp. Nerves? Or just moisture accumulating on the glass?

"So Daisy, Jessica, can I get you girls a refill?" he asks, then announces, "The same again, plus another Seven and Seven on the rocks."

"No thank you," Jessica says.

Daisy raises her eyebrows at Jessica. She looks past her. In one of the corner banquettes, she can almost picture Henry. With an old French wine and a young French woman. He holds the glass to the light, swirls the ruby liquid, sniffs, samples a few drops on the tip of his tongue. There will be champagne flutes on the table for later, with the crème brûlée. Henry leans toward a downy cheek, nuzzles an inch of sylph-like neck . . .

The scene switches to the Sea of Japan. Chopsticks poke some wilted seaweed. Sauce congeals, then thickens to mud. "Yes, please," Daisy says. "I'd love another."

Barry Sweiker brings their drinks to a table just being vacated by a plump couple in matching navy gabardine. He nods in their direction. "Size fourteen, Wranglers; sixteen, Lees. Wouldn't recommend any designer brand. Your Guess?, your Polo, the European"—pronounced Europeen—"manufacturers, your Sergio Valente, wouldn't be cut wide enough," he says.

Broad in the beam would be the term Daisy's father would use. In the Nebraska of her father's childhood, all women were broad in the beam, wide-shouldered, with hands toughened by working in the fields, scrubbing overalls against rippled washboards, putting up a season's worth of preserves. Their bodies were efficient machines, not works of art you cordon off with a gold tasseled rope. Daisy studies this couple, more dude ranch than farm. What is she, a chameleon who takes on the colors of whatever person stands next to her? She's been in this bar ten minutes, has met this totally inappropriate guy sporting an ID bracelet and holding that most uncool and dated of drinks, a Seven and Seven, and already she is measuring people by the width of their waist and the length of their inseam.

Barry Sweiker grabs another chair for Jessica. Who, before she can even refuse to sit, is halted by a ringing inside her pocketbook. "I know. I know. Don't say a word," she warns Daisy as she unfolds a cell phone the size of a credit card. "You're kidding!" she exclaims into the receiver. "I'll be there in half an hour." She tucks the phone back inside her bag. "We'll have to go, Daisy," she says. "Further developments. Seems Morty's wife is suing him for divorce and naming Bessie as alienator of affections. There are rumors of assault. Or at the very least, poisoning." She stops. Puts her hand on Daisy's shoulder. "I'm taking you with me."

Again Daisy looks over to the corner banquette. Though three businessmen in gray suits and red ties are studying menus there, they're only short-term parkers on what she's come to see as the site of Henry's dalliance. Shared upholstery means shared guilt, she decides, and glares at them. Maybe Henry didn't go home. Maybe he's out somewhere ordering kir royales for two to celebrate dumping her. "I've decided to stay," she protests.

"I refuse to abandon you."

"I'll be okay," says Daisy. "I insist."

"She'll be fine," Barry Sweiker pipes up. "Yours truly's a gentleman."

"Daze . . ." Jessica's chin tilts toward Barry Sweiker, toward their empty glasses. "As your best friend . . ."

"Go," Daisy orders.

As soon as Jessica leaves, Barry Sweiker drains his drink with an ungentlemanly gulp, then rolls the ice cubes around, using his finger as a swizzle stick. "So, Size-nine/ten, the Gap, your best friend Jessica says you and your husband have split."

"Not exactly."

He holds up a hand traffic cop–style. On his fourth finger he wears a class ring with a big red stone. "Far be it for me to trespass on territory marked No Trespassing."

"I appreciate your tact," Daisy says.

"Something you have to have in my business," he allows. He pauses dramatically.

Daisy knows that this is her cue to ask *what is your business*. Educated person that she is, she might hazard an educated guess. "I assume you've got something to do with jeans."

He stares at her astonished, as if she's Descartes just inventing *Cogito, ergo sum*. "You're one smart cookie," he exclaims.

A Harvard graduate, could she be anything less? After all, her diploma has to be good for something. She casts a discreet eye on his school ring. A high school ring, she figures. From across the table she can make out an eight, perhaps a five. If she's calculated right, she marched to "Pomp and Circumstance" in the crepe-papered high school gym ten years ahead of him.

Barry Sweiker pulls out a case of denim-colored plastic.

From inside he extracts a card; he hands it to her. CATERPILLAR
JEANSWEAR, it reads, A DIVISION OF MOTH MANUFACTURING.
BARRY SWEIKER, MARKETING. At the bottom, offices are listed
in L.A., Miami, Boston, New York.

"Caterpillar jeans," Daisy says. "I'm sorry, but . . ."

"I'm not surprised you haven't heard of us. We haven't hit
the big time yet," he explains. He emphasizes the word *yet* as
if it will be only a matter of days before Caterpillar will be
right up there with Ralph and Calvin and Giorgio.

"I'm sure you will," Daisy says, though she is far from sure.
"It is a funny name for jeans," she adds, especially if, like her,
you associate caterpillar with combines, tractors, fork-lift
trucks.

"Not if you think of it." Barry Sweiker grins.

"How so?"

"Hazard a guess."

"I'm not a good guesser."

"You're just being modest. I like that in a woman." He puts
down his drink. "Caterpillar jeans"—he waits a beat—"turn
you from a worm into a butterfly."

"I get it. Though I'm not sure how many people care to
think of themselves as a worm in the first place."

Barry is shocked. "We'd never come out and actually say it,"
he says. "It's the silent message. Subliminal."

"I see."

"Besides, butterfly as a brand name was already trade-
marked."

"Not that I've heard of Butterfly jeans, either."

Barry Sweiker pounds his fist against the table. Their glasses
jump. "My point exactly," he says, triumphant. "Butterfly
jeans went into Chapter Eleven."

He orders another round of drinks. Daisy is surprised that
she's agreed both to more booze and to staying at this table

across from an infant Caterpillar jeans salesman in conspicuous jewelry, who prides himself on prescribing relaxed fit for flabby thighs or pencil legs slightly flared to accommodate boots. Henry's announcement, along with the Campari and sodas, seems to have numbed her into senselessness, robbed her of all sense.

Or maybe not. Perhaps, like practice tests for SATS, like warm-up exercises, a chance to hone your dating skills with somebody you'd never want to date will build much-needed confidence.

Their drinks are delivered by an anorexic barmaid whose left ear is pierced with a border of dark metal hoops that look like the overstitch on a gimp wallet Daisy made once in summer camp. Barry studies her retreating back, an art lesson of perspective with a diminishing thin black line. "She'd be perfect in our size-four Caterpillar Capri," he says.

Daisy takes another sip. She is starting to develop a taste for Campari and soda. Keep eating asparagus, she used to tell an unconvinced Sammy, and one day you'll find you're an asparagus freak. This advice hasn't applied to her marriage. Old wives don't always translate into the comfort of old shoes, the pleasures of leather when it is broken in. Those years of marriage piled up like sandbags don't always protect against the hurricane.

Barry Sweiker is stirring his drink with a stubby finger. This one's garnished not only by a slice of orange but also a maraschino cherry bobbing on the top. She must be looking at it longingly because he lifts it up by its stem. "You want?" he asks.

"If you don't."

He shakes off some drops of liquid onto a cocktail napkin, then reaches over and pops the cherry into her mouth. She feels like a bird being fed a worm or, rather, under the circumstances, a caterpillar. She's perking up. Getting ready to emerge from her chrysalis. Is this the effect of alcohol on an empty stomach? The fact that a man, any man, is paying her enough attention to figure out her size in jeans? To give her the cherry from his drink?

"Frankly, I never touch 'em." Barry dries his hands. "Red Dye Number Two."

"Once in a while you have to live dangerously."

"I hear you. I feel the same way about a T-bone. About surf and turf. Sometimes you have to take a little risk." He pauses. "So, you want to talk about the estranged husband?"

"No."

"That's okay," he says. "I'm fine with that."

"He's not nice," Daisy says, and hears the word come out "nishe."

"I'm sure he isn't. How can he be, separated from a girl like you?" He waves over another round of drinks, which arrive with an alacrity the Sea of Japan could take a lesson from. He reaches for her hand. "Me, I've never found the right girl."

"That's too bad."

"Hey, I'm not complaining. Don't get me wrong. I've got hope. I've got opportunity. I meet plenty of beauties in my line of work." He strokes her fingers in a zigzag of O's and X's as if he's playing both sides of tic-tac-toe.

"I'd better go home," she tells him.

"So early?" he asks.

She looks at her watch. It is after ten. "So late," she says.

"And I haven't even found out what you do," he says, progressing to a bunch of rhythmic squeezes that feel like the tightening band on a blood-pressure machine.

She pulls her hand away. She digs in her pocketbook and finds her card. It's a Star Market card, shiny as a Visa, the gold

of an American Express. Under the Star Market logo is printed
DAISY LEWIS, OMBUDSMAN.

"Well, what do you know." Barry Sweiker lets out a slightly
asthmatic whistle of admiration. "Pretty fancy."

"Not really," Daisy says.

"You're just being modest."

"There's a lot to be modest about."

"Don't put yourself down." He studies the card. "So what's
this ombudsman, anyway?"

"Community relations."

"I see. But why not ombuds*woman?*"

"You have a point."

He leans forward, his eyes intent. "Tell me. Do you need a
college degree for that?"

"It certainly helps," she lies. "Though the job is the natural
offshoot of my early training. When I first graduated, I organized a food bank."

"You mean for poor people?"

She nods. "Soup kitchens. Shelters. Day care. The elderly.
Wherever there was a need."

"I'm impressed," he says. "I have to confess that I myself
can't pass one of those Salvation Army folks without opening
up my wallet right on the spot."

"But once the food bank became established," she goes on,
"I felt I'd accomplished my goals. I took some time off. Then I
decided I wanted to do something more . . ."

"More creative," he interjects.

"Exactly." She *has* been known to get pretty creative answering complaints about the ten-item infiltration in the five-
item checkout line. Why bother to explain that she fell into
this so-called career when the food bank's biggest donor offered
the part-time work and flexible hours mothers crave because
"you're a cute kid with a nice smile and a Harvard degree."

"I consider my *own* job pretty creative," Barry Sweiker says now.

"Of course, along with intellectual challenge, I'm committed to something that still makes a contribution to the community," Daisy confides. Listening to herself is like having an out-of-body experience. Who is this person talking? Who is this person this person's talking to?

"I can buy that," he says.

She stands up. He stands up. "Can I see you home?" he asks.

"My car's nearby."

"We could mosey on over to my room at the Sheraton. It's got cable. A minibar."

So here it is. This is what she's got to look forward to. Propositions by jeans salesmen in bars—which, however ridiculous, still hold for her a pathetic element of flattery. For a moment she thinks, Why not? She's always played it safe. Married young. Was faithful. Raised a kid. Took on the conventional roles of mother, of wife, accumulated the kind of job history that marks a woman who chose to put family first. To do good works. And look what it's got her? Why not take a risk?

"We could rent a video." Barry Sweiker grins.

Daisy studies him. He's not exactly the metaphor for the first day of the rest of her life. The risk has to be worth the taking. "I don't think so," Daisy says.

He sighs. "I didn't expect you would. In my line of business you learn to tell the nice girls from the sluts."

Not the compliment he intends if you figure nice guys finish last and nice girls get abandoned first.

"I've got your card," he says. "You've got mine. Don't forget when you're in the market for jeans . . ."

"Think Caterpillar," she intones. "From worm to butterfly."

"From your lips to God's ears."

"Thanks for the drink. The drinks."

"No problem. Take care," he calls after her.

Out in the courtyard, an elderly man and woman with twin clouds of white hair and matching canes hobble past. Their free arms clutch. "A little bedtime toddy would be lovely, dear," the woman tells the man. Two backpacked students skip in front of them. The boy's hand caresses the girl's neck. "Want to catch the late movie at the Kendall?" she asks. He hooks her close. "Let's go back to your place," he moans against her collarbone.

Daisy nears a bench where a couple sit so entwined you can't tell where his denim starts and hers ends. They are kissing with loud smacks. They laugh. They grunt. They rock together, legs snaked around legs like the caduceus on doctors' prescription pads. "Sugar," sighs one. "Oh, baby. Oh, baby," croons the other.

Daisy turns to them. Fury balloons inside her. Her cheeks burn. Her eyes smart. Her voice when she hears it seems to spurt from the mouth of a foreigner. "Stop that!" she yells. "Stop right now. This is a public place. You should be ashamed of yourselves."

FRANCE NATIONALE
CHARLES DE GAULLE 2
5
A 421 FRANCE

Ashamed of herself, Daisy walks along Church Street to her car. At the corner of Palmer, a group of young people crowds the sidewalk in front of the Border Cafe. Daisy is picking her way carefully, watching for uneven bricks and, poking up from them, the twisted roots of trees. In her unaccustomed pumps, overwhelmed by Henry's bombshell, by three Campari and sodas, by the fears of a future in which "dating" unfolds to reveal an infinite chain of Barry Sweikers, she is teetering. All she needs now is to break her writing wrist, her walking ankle. Or worse, a nose, a jaw to compromise even further the face she turns to meet the world. She thinks back once more to the pyramid of stress, in which divorce and empty nest lie right under the pinnacle of death. Not that Henry's actually said the D-word, but she's pretty sure it's hovering up there on the Ouija board that is her life.

A few kids are sitting on the curb. They're holding the beepers the restaurant issues in place of the more conventional reservation list. These vibrate to announce who's next in line for cheap chicken fajitas, burritos, enchiladas of a *verde* nature's never seen, and pitchers of beer. Daisy searches the pack for Sammy, to whom such a place would be a natural habitat. This is his favorite restaurant, he once admitted, he who has dined with his parents in France at tables displaying menus studded with a galaxy of Michelin stars. He who has had his teething gums rubbed with the finest vintages. "The mango margaritas are amazing!" he'd protested.

"You mean they don't demand your ID?" she had asked with the shock of one whose college drawer stashed the false licenses a roommate's boyfriend had financed his tuition by manufacturing. "You are only eighteen," she had exclaimed. And looking like twelve, she noted, her motherly eye transforming a bumpy, dull-razor-scraped cheek into the silken, Ivory-soaped complexion of the newborn.

And because she is scanning the crowd for Sammy, Daisy misses the stump of a chopped-off rotted elm. She catches her heel on it. She pitches forward. But before she falls, four hands grab her and set her upright like a toy soldier caught in the act of toppling. "Thank you so much," she says. "I feel so silly."

"Is dangerous. Trees all over Cambridge cut down from Dutch elm disease. Sticking up for people to trip on." One rescuer tisks.

"Is a tort waiting to happen," chirps the other one. "Should be law school moot court case."

"In Japan, we say nail that sticks up gets hammered down."

Daisy looks at them. They're two Asian men with black leather jackets and sleek slides of gleaming black hair parted on opposing sides. Daisy thinks of bookends, of mirror images. Alike but with a difference. One hesitates. Then studies her. "I know you," he says.

"You do?"

"Daisy Lewis!" he exclaims as if he has just confirmed the identity of an amnesiac.

"Host-family award," explains the other young man. "We were at the party." With the choreography of synchronized swimmers, they each unzip a jacket to reveal the same *Hi, I'm . . .* stickers that Daisy's dress still bears a remnant of. One reads Hiroshi Tanaka, the other Masamoto Teramoto. They both are printed *Osaka, Japan, and Harvard Law School LL.M.* Hiroshi Tanaka's eyes scrutinize her shoulder purse, then search her coat as if for contraband. "Where is it?" he asks.

"Where is what?"

"Your award. Testimonial with Harvard seal in fine presentation case?"

What does she say? That it's drowned in the Sea of Japan? Or, more likely, tossed into the Dumpster in back of the restaurant? One thing she's sure of, that Henry hasn't rushed back to claim it for his trophy cabinet. "My husband's got it," she says.

"And where is husband?" Masamoto Teramoto asks.

"Business," she says. An answer any Japanese would understand.

Which is a correct assumption, since they both nod understandingly. "Very nice. Your husband takes time from busy business to be host family."

"It *is* nice," Daisy agrees.

"Congratulations on such big honor," says Hiroshi Tanaka.

"Is honor for us to save award winner of best host family from falling in the street," adds Masamoto Teramoto. "To help someone who wins prize for helping foreigners."

"Who represents best values in America," says Hiroshi Tanaka.

"Who shows that Americans are not the selfish individuals the media portrays," says Masamoto Teramoto.

"Who gives big university like Harvard intimate scale," says Hiroshi Tanaka.

Daisy's head bobs from Hiroshi to Masamoto like a spectator at a tennis match. They go on one-upping each other in heaping such praise that Daisy quickly realizes that, as its object, she is pretty much irrelevant. The minute Hiroshi Tanaka stops to catch his breath, she interjects a thanks.

They both bow to her, their hair flapping over their brows like flags whipped forward by a sudden wind. Masamoto Teramoto points to the offending tree stump, which is sticking up with all the stubbornness of a court case in the making. Wreathed around it are empty beer cans and ripped containers that once held fast food. He nudges an empty Big Mac carton with an impeccably polished toe. He giggles, placing his hand in front of his mouth. "Americans may be good hosts," he adds, "but they have dirty streets."

"And dirty streets," adds Hiroshi Tanaka, "to use an American—*native* American—phrase, is happy hunting ground for disease." He strikes his brow in a gesture so exaggerated that Daisy wouldn't be surprised to see a cartoon lightbulb explode over his head. "I have idea. Come drink margarita with us."

"We love margaritas. Better than sake. Great American invention," Masamoto Teramoto puts in.

Daisy doesn't bother to explain that margaritas are Mexican. "I've had too much to drink already," she confides.

"We could go to Computer Cafe and play video games," suggests Hiroshi Tanaka.

She supposes she should be flattered. First Barry Sweiker, then this duet of students not much older than her son. Is her sudden singleness sticking up so much it needs to be hammered down? She shakes her head. Hiroshi Tanaka reaches for her hand. His arm grazes her breast. An accident? she wonders. Or a deliberate act that could be inviting a sexual harassment case? She remembers reading about the courtship rules for Antioch students. *Do I have permission to touch your shoulder?* a suitor was cautioned to ask. How she had laughed from her secure position outside the battlefield of sexual politics. Now the laugh's on her, catapulted into the war zone minus nineties social skills. With the kind of stereotyping the Harvard International Office would make rules against, she pictures Japanese men wooing hostesses in bars while at home their wives prepare their husbands' baths. Or these same Japanese husbands, fathers, sons, on sex tours to the flesh pots of Thailand and Indonesia. She bows her head. *"Sayonara,"* Daisy says.

She makes her way to her car. Pizza cartons, diet Coke cans, Starbucks cups, advertising flyers litter the sidewalks. She's no doubt a contributor, she thinks, abandoning her award like the leftover wrapper of somebody's lunch.

When she reaches her car, she sees there are a few more messages pinned under the windshield wiper. *What kind of worm*, asks one in magenta Magic Marker, *would usurp this parking place? Asshole,* states another, scribbled in pencil on a receipt from Newbury Comics. *God will get you for this,* promises a third.

If she'd gone off with Barry Sweiker and been called a slut, would it be any worse? At least there'd be a man to appreciate a body in or out of its jeans, never mind that both man and body fall far from the ideal. Would she be called a cradle robber if she'd agreed to a video game with the Japanese Tweedledum and Tweedledee? In spite of cultural differences, she'd still be flanked by two men with good manners and high test scores. When Daisy looks at her car, she expects to see the tires slashed, a hieroglyph of key scratches across the metallic paint. But there is nothing. And when she gets inside, the car starts right up. Business as usual in Harvard Square, she hums. Then stops. Not quite. She thinks of Henry, of marriage, of these first forty-two years of the rest of her life. Has God already gotten her for this? she wonders. But then she's not sure that God can get you for simply taking His parking space.

To compensate for the drinks she's consumed, Daisy drives up Mass Ave ten miles under the speed limit. She grips the steering wheel in both hands at precisely ten and two. She looks in all directions. She turns on the radio. Somebody is interviewing a woman called Sunshine Hawk and her partner Sedona Eagle. They are Smudgers, spiritualists who drive bad vibrations from people's houses. For two hundred dollars an hour, they will burn sage to shoo away baneful influences from the home. "I honor all cultures. I honor all traditions," Sedona Eagle announces in a voice that clearly sounds as if it deserves to win a host-family award. She totes a whole crosscultural bag of tricks: High John the Conqueror incense, African beads, Indian bells, a tape of Japanese drummers. There are many ways, she says, to bring light to a benighted house.

When Daisy pulls up in front of her own house, she's surprised to see it looks the same. No peeling paint to signify a state of benightedness, no dark and gloomy aura to symbolize a baneful influence. Upstairs in his study, Henry's computers whir and hum, lights blink on and off, a screen-saving parade of happy faces and burbling fish float across their monitors in undisturbed rows. What hint would there ever be that the Devil's Dance or Maltese Amoeba were attacking Henry's files at the very instant these contented fish go swimming by?

Daisy raises her eyes to the roof of the house. Even with the streetlight on, it's hard to make out the one foot square of new wood on the fascia. Last year they'd had an infestation of squirrels in the walls. All day squirrels chased each other in the ceiling over her bed, behind the refrigerator, at the top of the living room's bay. Daisy could hear the scrape of their toes, dropped acorns rolling down the slope of an eave, the broom-

like sweep of their tails. It had taken the wildlife control officer three weeks of setting traps, studying the nooks and cran-
nies of their roof, following a trail of little nicks to find the
hole—no larger than the bathtub drain—where they had
squeezed through, nested in a pile of Sammy's baby clothes,
and reared enough offspring to make a polygamist proud. "It's
probably only temporary," the wildlife control officer had
warned as he tarred and patched and hammered a solid-looking
Band-Aid of new wood. "Once they get in, the darned critters
nearly always find a way to get back."

Now Daisy fits her key into the lock with a not entirely sure
hand. The door creaks open on its meant-to-be-oiled hinges.
The house is unusually quiet. The grandfather clock on the
landing ticks. The refrigerator grunts and groans, spitting ice
cubes into its automatic ice cube tray. But no Billie Holiday
sings out from the CD player. No sales pitches for Veg-O-
Matics or cubic zirconias burst from the TV. Maybe at such a
moment she'd welcome the dance of the squirrels overhead.

The house is black. Henry hasn't even left the hall light on
for her. Perhaps it's the prospect of a divorce lawyer's billable
hours that has Henry monitoring more than usual the expen-
diture of every kilowatt. At least he hasn't turned off the answering machine, whose red signal shines with a steady,
unblinkable stare. A Post-it sticks to the phone. *Jessica called,*
it reads. *Have gone to bed in the guest room. In the a.m., we'll talk.*

Daisy walks through the first floor, turning on all the lights.
She even pulls the chain in the pantry, flicks the switch in the
guest john under the stairs. She turns on the lamp made from
shells her grandmother collected on the beaches of Florida the
first and only time she left Nebraska. She presses the button on
the desk lamp that angles out over the hump of torn leather
and sprung springs that the family has colluded on designating
Henry's chair. She sinks down into Henry's chair. It smells of

him. The seat is scooped out to accommodate his bottom. There are dents in the back where his shoulders hit. She can trace the shape of fingers where he rests his hands. For twenty years she's been laminated onto Henry the way thin sheets of wood are glued together to make a butcher's block.

She looks at the Post-it: *Have gone to bed in the guest room.* She's been set adrift. No rudder. No anchor. But she hasn't panicked yet. She didn't go off with Barry Sweiker despite the enticements of his minibar. She's found her way home without maiming either herself or an innocent pedestrian. She gets up. She goes to the phone. It's after eleven, but she knows that even if Jessica's finished the Franklin brothers' update, there's still *Nightline.* Jessica's allegiance to Ted Koppel forms a constant in a whirl of more fleeting, less satisfactory relationships.

"Just checking up on you," Jessica says. In the background Daisy can hear the TV and the closer clink of ice cubes.

"More Campari?" she asks.

"Strictly Poland Spring," says Jessica. She takes a loud sip. Daisy pictures the cut-glass tumbler. She knows the heft of its expensive leaded weight. "Tedsie's talking to some Middle East sheik with the cutest headband. Trained at Harvard. They're discussing chemical warfare." She pauses. "So how are you?"

"Just dandy."

"Why am I not convinced?"

"Because you've known me practically from the womb."

"And held your hand through all the agonies and the ecstasies." She sighs. "And can see how, hating change, you have settled for less than you deserve. Dare I say that Henry's bombshell might be a change for the best?"

"No," Daisy nearly yells. She waits a beat. "Did you finish the Franklins?"

"I'll say. I'm not sure their booth will be quite so regular when this comes out." Jessica lowers her voice. "Honey, I hated to leave you. Was everything all right?"

"Just fine. We exchanged business cards."

"Your Star Market Advantage card? The one that gives you the discount on the fruit of the week?"

"Very funny. He invited me to his room. To check out the minibar. To watch a video."

"I suppose you have to start somewhere."

"This is not funny. This is very serious."

"Oh, Daisy, don't I know that. I, the queen of divorce."

Daisy feels herself begin to cry. She tests the waters with a few sniffles. She squeezes out a tentative tear, which turns into a flow. She remembers a cartoon in a book of *New Yorker* drawings. A woman lifts her knife to cut an onion. In the end she is sobbing up a storm.

Daisy sobs up a storm. "We were so happy in Harvard student housing. In that terrible apartment on the Somerville/Cambridge line."

"People are always happy in their first wretched apartments. The bigger and better the apartment, the greater the misery."

"That's a conclusion from a scientific study? An official Gallup Poll?"

"A private Jessica Sherman poll. People grow up. They grow apart. They get interested in other things."

"Like French! Like Mademoiselle from Armentières, parley voo? Like, like the Desmoiselles d'Avignon?"

"That's art history."

"I know that!" Daisy wipes her nose on her sleeve.

"Where's Henry? Or dare I ask?"

"The guest room."

Jessica chuckles.

Daisy manages half a smile. She looks across the hall through the arched doors to the living room, which is flamed with her profligate's light. On the mantel rests a photograph of Sammy in his high school graduation robes flanked by his beaming parents. Next to this is a color print of Daisy, Henry, and Sammy riding a Ferris wheel when Sammy was five. They are all grinning, though Daisy's grin, unlike theirs, was simply a mask for her fear. The way she feels now, Daisy could be back on that Ferris wheel. Her stomach plunges, her throat knots, her voice pitches higher, close to a scream. "What about Sammy?" she shouts. "A child of divorce. The product of a broken home."

"Not yet," Jessica assures. "And besides, he's not a child. Now he'll have something in common with every other young person he knows." She pauses. Her words become softer, kinder. "Sweetie, maybe it's time for you to get some sleep."

As if she could, Daisy thinks, when one of life's top ten bestseller lists of stress will keep her tossing and turning throughout the night. But she *is* tired, she has to admit.

"And just think," Jessica adds, "for once you'll have that stingy-sized rickety antique bed all to yourself!"

Daisy starts to turn off the lights, then stops. Why not leave them on? She no longer has to be subject to somebody else's input on how to lead her life. Especially when that life loses its component of jointly held domesticity. Besides, it's fall, the days are shorter, the sun is weak. She needs all the light she can get. In the papers you're exhorted to procure an hour of sun every day for vitamin D. In the stores they're selling light boxes; doctors prescribe sitting under them the way they prescribe a course of antibiotics or physical therapy. Daisy thinks about vitamin D. When Sammy was two he swallowed a whole box of candy-colored chewable vitamins. She'd spooned ipecac down his throat. Immediately he'd thrown up a rainbow-hued stream, a concoction so fascinating it had stopped his tears.

The vitamins were shaped like letters of the alphabet. The D was the blue-green of a robin's egg. She'd written an irate letter to the manufacturer. Poison disguised as candy, she'd complained, a sugarcoated exterior, the equivalent of the polished apple given Snow White. The vitamins were taken off the market, "thanks to the vigilance of people like you," the president of the company had oozed his gratitude. And had sent along two cartons of adhesive tape.

Now the robin's-egg blue D forms in front of her eyes. Then she sees three other D's, all in black: darkness, depression, and divorce. If she can combat darkness by artificial means, how will she manage the depression that seems inextricably linked to divorce? She walks up the stairs, flicking on the ugly chandelier that the previous owners left, the two-bulbed sconce that illuminates where the landing twists. From the top step she looks down on a house ablaze.

Daisy tiptoes to the bathroom, trying to ignore the closed door at the end of the hall. What is wrong with this picture? she wonders when she reaches for her toothbrush. She peers closer around the washbasin and realizes that Henry's blue extra-soft Sensodyne is no longer leaning against her red extrafirm Oral-B. She pulls open the medicine cabinet. His half is empty. Only a tumbleweed of dental floss and some Mercurochrome stains mark shelves once stuffed with nose drops, aftershave, Tylenol PM, mouthwash, razor blades, mustache wax. Through the mirror she can see the hook on the door from which her bathrobe dangles in unaccustomed unaccompaniment. She is not surprised to find his shampoo and conditioner missing from the lineup along the bathtub ledge. In the few hours she has been with Jessica and warming up her social skills with Barry Sweiker, Henry Lewis has been systematically removing himself from the matrimonial house, the matrimonial bathroom, the matrimonial bed. She's amazed that someone whose slobbiness she's berated for twenty years has been so organized. Maybe it takes a lifetime stress event to whip you into shape. Or perhaps—this comes as a sudden flash from the battle-of-the-sexes front—he's been mapping this strategy for longer than she dares to contemplate.

Which is further evidenced by a bedroom closet empty of his clothes, a bureau top swept clean of his brushes, small change, ticket stubs.

Daisy plops into the exact center of the bed and spreads her arms and legs out to its edges like the man in the da Vinci drawing. Jessica is right about this bed, though for years she and Henry have been defensive about it. "It keeps us close," Henry used to say. "Great for bundling up on cold winter nights." That in hotels and motels they paid extra for king-sized oases was a sin they refused to confess, all the while delighting in pillows the size of logs and a blanket you could spread a whole extended family across. Theirs is an antique four-poster with a slightly smaller than standard mattress on wooden slats, a legacy from Henry's great-uncle, who died in it after ninety-five years of contented bachelorhood. The mattress she and Henry bought, testing out a warehouse full of double welting and hand-tied springs. Now, though, despite their informed consumerism, there's a ditch in it excavated by husband and wife derrieres in wedded juxtaposition night after night.

Floating over the bed is a canopy, an intricate pattern of white net strung by a group of women on an island off the Carolina coast. Imagine creating such a thing, the time it takes, the care. She assumes you start in a corner, proceeding in small increments—a piling on of tasks until the final result is achieved. Probably, like most things, it's hard at first, becoming easier as you move along. Daisy studies the canopy, trying to find a pattern of rougher knots, then more graceful ones to prove her hypothesis. But all she can see is a layer of dust, a huge gray pelt of it that she has never noticed before but which has been gathering ominously, atom by atom, over more than a thousand and one nights of Daisy and Henry's sleeping forms. She's never washed it, supposing—what?—that it was such an open weave, dirt would not settle but just drift away. How will she wash it? Wisk? Tide? Bold Plus new and improved? Woolite for all things delicate? It comforts her to think that in the morning, among more earth-shattering events, she'll have ordinary domestic tasks to face.

Daisy snuggles under her quilt. She waits for insomnia to strike. The half-empty closet is, after all, a symbol that her life is emptying. The absence of wing tips and Reeboks under the bed is an absence not to make the heart grow fonder but to make it race. She rolls over to Henry's side of the bed. On his pillow she smells the scent of his hair. Underneath her rises the scent of his flesh. Maybe—she looks at the canopy—her life won't be swept away but simply swept clean. She falls asleep. If not exactly the sleep of the just, the sleep of the self-justified.

FRANCE NATIONALE
CHARLES DE GAULLE 2
6
A 421 FRANCE

Something jolts her awake. It's three-thirty in the morning. The windows are rectangles of pitch black slate. But there's a line of light shining from the hall through the bottom of the door. Then she remembers. She'd turned on every bulb to protest the guttering of her marriage, or maybe just the miserliness of a husband who switches off every switch marked On, who monitors the length of long-distance calls, who'll go two miles out of his way to save a twenty-cent toll. But what woke her up?

She hears it again. A half–wild animal, half–wild human retching sound from the direction of the bathroom. It echoes along the corridor emptied of Henry's stuff, which, she now realizes, muffled noise better than the insulation they'd had blown into the walls after the old asbestos filling was declared hazardous.

She creaks out of bed, limbs heavy with sleep and the complications that preceded it. She wraps a blanket around her shoulders. She heads for the hall. She smells it even before she's cracked the door an inch from its jamb. Throw-up. A smell any mother can recognize and, on occasion, any wife.

She crawls back into her bedroom, shuts the door, climbs back into bed. She's relieved that since abjuring wifely duties she has no duty to clean it up. She's also a little pleased. How untouched could Henry be by the dissolution of a family if he rushed home and proceeded to be systematically dissolute? He's stinking drunk, she exults. He has some sorrows he needs to drown. She presses the quilt to her nose. Not that Henry is a drunk. But there've been times. And that's discounting college, where on Saturday nights every stall contained a heaving head.

Only two years ago, they had been in Austin for the third wedding of one of Henry's oldest friends. The hotel was posh, gilt putti and crystal chandeliers everywhere, racks that baked the towels, a bed swathed in mosquito netting, though she couldn't imagine a mosquito buzzing a trail to the twenty-seventh floor, and a rose marble bathtub the size of a small continent. The day before the wedding, there had been a bachelor party at a ribs shack and a girls' night out at a lakeside grill. By eleven, Daisy had sunk into bed leaden with Texas barbecue. By three A.M. Henry was throwing up a matched set of barbecue all over the rose marble and the heated towel racks. "Ish not the beer," Henry had insisted, "but the Slivovitz." He placed all the blame on the second cousin from Dubrovnik.

"You could have refused," Daisy had said. "Saying no wouldn't exactly cause an international incident."

"And be labeled a spoilsport? Not to mention a lack of grace toward someone from abroad."

By five, Henry had collapsed on a corner of the pale rug. At six, Daisy started scrubbing out the bathroom with the spot-ridding obsession of a Lady Macbeth.

Later, after the wedding, they headed back to their room to check out. "My aching head," Henry cried.

"*My* scraped-bare knuckles."

Just leaving their door was the maid, with her arsenal of buckets and mops and sponges and brooms. In one hand she held a can of Lysol raised like a tear-gas canister police use to quell rioters. She pointed it in the direction of Daisy's stomach. "Sick?" she asked.

Simply a husband soused on Slivovitz, Daisy was about to answer when the maid cradled the Lysol in her arms and started rocking it.

"Pregnant?" she diagnosed.

"Morning sickness," Henry declared and handed her two twenties and one ten.

Back in bed, Daisy finds it now impossible to sleep. Like a perverse variation of Proust's madeleine, the throw-up has released a stream of memories. She thinks back to Sammy's eleventh birthday party. They'd stuffed ten children in the rear of the station wagon and taken them to a *Star Trek* movie, where they'd plied them with popcorn, Raisinets, and strings of red licorice. As they headed home on the Central Artery during rush hour, it had started to snow. "I feel sick," groaned John Haddad. He threw up on Andy Sheffer, who in turn threw up on Eric Jacobson; on and on it went like a Caucasian chalk circle of vomiting.

Henry stuck his head out the window. "All we can do is keep going," he gagged. "Classic chain reaction. Geez, Berton Roueché should write this up in his *Annals of Medicine.*" Snowflakes dusted his hair as he drove a carful of screaming, writhing, vomiting eleven-year-olds wearing ruined down parkas to the line of waiting parents pulled up at the front of their house.

And though they'd had the station wagon professionally

cleaned, even fumigated, the neighborhood kids went on strike against her car-pool days. "I can still smell Andy Sheffer's throw-up," insisted one and then another.

Daisy thinks about family stories, the folklore created by long-term relationships. "If you tell that one more time . . ." Henry used to warn. "Everyone in the whole world and his brother has heard that," Sammy would complain. But they were the groans of someone listening over and over to a corny and familiar joke. "Not that again," they'd say. Please that again, they'd think. It's the stories that knit a family together, Daisy supposes, an at times secret language recognized only by a linked group. "Remember when . . ." they'd remind each other.

We've got a history, she'd console herself after puzzling over why the joy had escaped from her marriage like the air from a punctured tire. Did the emptiness surface only in the widening gap between her do-good and his live-well desires? Between her running in place and his forging ahead? Now the course of her history, of her family, will be changed. External forces have been brought to bear. Age, hormones, French, the plain old vulnerability of the human organism. We're all susceptible to love and its mutations: lust, flattery, a Campari and soda to ease your loneliness. It's been a strange night, starting with a prize, ending with a loss. Daisy wonders if she should check the bathroom again, show a little wifely concern despite the bound-for-extinction adjective.

But before she can deconstruct the semantics of checking on Henry, she hears a violent thud followed by a long, low moan.

She jumps out of bed, wrenches open the bathroom door, to find Henry crumpled in a heap, arms wrapped around his stomach. His face is white; he's drenched in sweat. "I'm dying," he wails.

Looking at him, Daisy thinks he might be. "I'll call an ambulance," she gasps.

"No." Henry gives the bottom of her nightgown a weak tug. "Just drive me to Emergency."

Maybe he's not dying, she thinks. After all, would he still be cheap in the very throes of death? "Can you make it down the stairs?" she asks.

"With your help," he says, his face pathetic with gratitude.

He leans against her. His body next to hers is hot as fire. She can feel him trembling. She's scared. He is, after all, still her husband, the father of her child, the onetime love of her life. "I'm dying," he repeats.

"No you're not," she insists. "Don't you dare."

She gets him into his shoes and coat. Not so difficult, since his arms and legs are as limp as a Raggedy Ann's. She throws her own coat over her nightgown and slips on a pair of Sammy's rubber boots. What a duo they make, she in a high-necked flower-sprigged faded flannel nightgown more often seen in the corridors of women's dormitories than in a marital if single-occupancy double bed; Henry in soaking, soiled, wrung-through-the-mill pajamas, the perfect candidate for the industrial-strength detergents with which, at work, she surrounds herself. Henry's head swivels around on his neck. "How come every light's on in the house?" he pants accusingly.

Which relieves her. If there's miserliness still pumping through those veins, can life be far behind?

He lies sprawled across the backseat like a sack of groceries, protesting every bump in the road as if it's a personal, deliberate assault. "Easy, easy," he says, "I'm in agony."

In the emergency room, Henry is whisked off on a gurney while Daisy fills out insurance forms. It's quiet in the ER; more noise comes from the TVs angled out from the ceiling on their metal buttresses than from the accident-prone. "Your husband did *what?*" exclaims a talk-show host.

The attending physician, who does not possess the movie-star looks of actors playing doctors on the big or little screen, has bruised eyes and sunken sallow cheeks. He stares at the rickrack on her nightgown. "Can you tell me what your husband had to eat, Mrs. Lewis?" he asks. "Breakfast? Lunch?"

Am I my husband's keeper? Daisy wonders. His calorie counter? His nutritionist? "I'm not sure. I don't remember breakfast. Lunch he gets at work."

Does she detect surprise, disapproval? The family that eats together . . . might just as well be marching across his prescription pad. Is the end of their marriage plastered across her face, a symptom easy enough for a doctor to diagnose? "This morning I had to leave for my office at the crack of dawn," she lies.

"Dinner?"

"That we shared," she acknowledges.

"Consisting of . . . ?"

"Oh, my God. Sushi," she exclaims. "It must be a parasite!" she adds, thinking of Bessie Franklin.

"He ate only sushi? At dinnertime?"

She nods. She remembers reading about one kind of sushi—blowfish—that is highly dangerous. There are chefs specially trained in cutting out its poisonous sac. Fugu chefs, a Japanese student they once hosted, had instructed them.

But Daisy doubts there are blowfish specialists in Harvard Square restaurants. And she can hear Henry in his green-curtained cubicle, cataloging his symptoms with a vigor that hardly calls for the coroner.

"Did you eat the same thing?" the doctor persists.

"No."

"I see."

"In fact I ordered the teriyaki," she nearly apologizes. She pauses, re-creates the unpalatable plate on the table of the Sea of Japan, hears again the unpalatable conversation that accompanied it. "But Henry ate mine. I lost my appetite."

"Lucky for you," the attending physician says. He makes some notes on a clipboard. There are ink stains on his fingertips, Daisy notices. Hardly sanitary.

"We'll admit him," he says. "He's feeling pretty sick," he adds. It's a pointed remark. *You ordered the teriyaki, you should have eaten it* hovers in the air unstated but, to Daisy's ears, as loud and clear as a broadcast from the ceiling-hugging ever-jabbering television set.

There are more forms to be filled out, a bed to be found, a computer search, an extensive medical workup. It'll take a while, she's told by the emergency room nurse. Daisy wonders if she should ask to see Henry. Is that what good wives do? What about half-good wives? Or even rotten ones? What is the protocol here? She can imagine the moans from behind the green curtain escalating into shouts when Henry lays eyes on her. His wife. His poisoner. *Mea culpa,* she wants to confess, but *culpa* for what?

The morning television shows are now marching across their multiple screens. *Good Morning America, Morning News, Morning Business Report, Early Edition, New England This Morning, A.M. Coffee Hour.* Under her coat, Daisy still has her nightgown on. She'll go home, shower, dress, notify Henry's office, her own. And, of course, she'll have to tell Sammy his father's in the hospital. For a second she hopes it won't affect his first batch of exams coming up. She catches herself. It's time to adjust her priorities.

At home, adjusting her priorities, she showers. She washes her hair. She puts on clean jeans and a black ribbed turtleneck. She lines her eyes. She glosses her lips. She adds earrings from

Mexico and a bracelet from Afghanistan. Former foreign students' hostess gifts. She looks pretty good for a forty-two-year-old mother of a college freshman, an ex–food bank organizer, a supermarket sounding board, a discarded wife. Let Henry admire what he's about to miss.

A bunch of messages blink from the answering machine. Jessica checking in, the cleaning woman whose bursitus is acting up, the Electrolux man regretting her hose is too old to be fixed, Sammy to announce he's dropped his laundry off, the voice of Brigitte Bardot with a "massage of congratulations pour Henri and Day-zee on their 'ost familee award," and her boss, Bernie Houlihan.

Daisy calls Bernie Houlihan. "You got a package here, kiddo, the size of a twenty-four-boxed carton of your giant economy Tide."

"What is it?"

"Beats me. It takes up so much of the office I'm calling you from the counter where Mary Lou stamps the checks."

"I'm on my way," Daisy says. She thinks of the "office," the closet behind the meat counter, her igloo, always freezing from the refrigerated vaults next to it and smelling of the fat being trimmed from the lamb. It's big enough for a bridge table, a telephone, two rickety chairs. Bernie's contributed his jar of M&M's and a girlie calendar. "Are you one of those feminists?" Bernie had asked, hammering a big-haired, big-boobed Miss January to the wall. "Will this get your dander up?"

"Only my sympathy," Daisy had replied, feeling sorry for models grinning in such frigid surroundings with only a G-string between them and their goosebump-vulnerable flesh.

To mark her territory, Daisy's tacked a photo of Sammy on the bulletin board next to the one of Bernie with "the wife," the long-suffering Doris, and their five towheaded grand-daughters. On the bridge table, a peanut-butter jar holds her

Magic Markers and a pair of scissors made for left hands, although she has always favored her right.

She dials Sammy's number. He's at class, reports his roommate, who sounds cruelly awakened from a very deep sleep. "I'd take a message, Miz Lewis, if there was a pencil or a slip of paper within three feet of this desk."

Then what is on this desk? Daisy wonders. "I'll get him later. It's not important," she adds automatically.

At Star Market, Billy and Jimmy—two men who, though called by children's names, are well near retirement—stand behind the meat counter hacking at chicken breasts with the kind of cleavers that are valued as stage props in murder mysteries. "How's it going, Daisy?" asks Billy. "Hey hey," sings Jimmy in syncopation with the cleaver chops.

Bernie's leaning in the doorway, tossing back handfuls of M&M's after separating the blue ones from the chaff. These go into the pocket of his blood-stained butcher's apron. Though Bernie is "management," he's not above helping out when there's a run on ground round. Past his shoulder she can see the carton nearly the size of the bridge-table top that's holding it. Whatever can it be? Daisy's heart soars. Then sinks when she zooms in on the logo of a butterfly and the words CATERPILLAR JEANSWEAR stamped above VIA MESSENGER.

Bernie helps her hoist it onto a grocery cart where, too big to fit into the basket, it wobbles on the rim. "That's some mother," he says. "A secret admirer?" he asks.

"What kind of secret admirer would send such a package to someone's place of work?" she says.

"So it's business."

"Hardly pleasure." She wheels her load out to the parking lot. She jams it into the back of the station wagon, then drives to the rear of the market, where the produce trucks have already made their morning deliveries. There's nobody around, she's relieved to see. She gets out of the car, pulls the package onto the ground, and slices through the sealing tape with the Swiss army knife Henry gave her when he got a newer one.

There's a card on top. *For Daisy, a perfect ten.* This is signed *Your friend Barry Sweiker,* followed by a *P.S. Thanks for last night.* Daisy sticks the card in her pocketbook and pulls off the tissue paper, which is the exact color of Gulden's mustard, extra-hot.

Inside is a stack of enough denim garments to outfit two months' worth of activities at summer camp. Daisy unfolds a shirt, three pairs of pants, one with a drawstring, two short shorts, one white with fringe, which laces up from the crotch to the waist, a vest, a wraparound skirt, a jacket with rhinestone buttons and silver studs, one set of farmer's overalls. She rubs the short shorts between her index finger and her thumb. The fabric feels flimsy; it appears to iridesce. But the fact that they are short shorts more suitable to twenty-year-old limbs than forty-something's chubby thighs holds in it the essence of a compliment.

Over by the chain-link fence, several feet from where the trucks pull up, sits a trailer. There people leave their green garbage bags full of clothes for Goodwill. Usually a man sprawls just at the entrance, writing receipts that donors use to justify charitable deductions on tax returns. He's absent now, probably on a coffee break. For a second Daisy considers making a charitable contribution herself, a goodwill Goodwill gesture for a size-ten lover of short shorts. Certainly the jacket with the rhinestone trim would gladden a cowgirl's heart. But then she thinks of the card in her purse, its signature, from "Your friend." What kind of friend would turn a friend's gift away? Daisy packs up the box, sticks it back in her car, starts the ignition, and heads toward the hospital.

*   *   *

At the desk, the receptionist punches some keys on the computer. "Mr. Lewis is stable." She smiles. Daisy smiles back. She's relieved that Henry is stable, surprising herself. A woman scorned, she should want him to suffer. Instead, she reacts like a wife. She feels like a wife. Maybe yesterday's shock was only a bolt of mid-autumn night's madness. Maybe recovering his health, he'll recover his senses. Daisy and Henry—Mr. and Mrs. Lewis—will be just as they always were. She stops. Is this what she wants? she asks herself.

She decides to find her way to the cafeteria. She's had little sleep; she's spent half the night in the emergency room, has been home, to Star Market, back to the hospital with not a drop of caffeine to fortify her. She's feeling a little peckish, as her Nebraska relatives would say. Not to mention the need to counter the effects of the Campari and sodas and the implication of the poisonous meal she didn't touch. She has a sudden desire for bacon and eggs, French toast slathered with butter and drenched in maple syrup, coffee with real cream so thick it will barely pour. Would the hair-netted, rubber-gloved ladies behind the counter offer such fare in a hospital cafeteria? Especially in Cambridge, this city of the terminally aware? She has a sad vision of bowls of granola, low-fat yogurt, stewed prunes. Of twenty different kinds of herbal tea. What will they give Henry? A scoop of Jell-O? A cup of consommé? She's read that the Japanese eat a breakfast of seaweed and pickled yams. What do they serve in the cafeteria of French hospitals? They probably don't have cafeterias, only cafés—where the Breakfast of Champions is a *petit déjeuner des champignons*.

She asks directions from a harried woman in surgical garb. "Follow the blue arrow," she instructs. Daisy follows a blue arrow along winding corridors that are crisscrossed with other colored arrows. She tries to sniff out the scent of sizzling sausages, of bubbling oatmeal. But she smells only the antiseptic used to scrub the linoleum. On two sides march lines of closed doors marked by black-lettered signs. These announce obscure-sounding medical specialties she prefers not to know about.

When she reaches the end of the corridor, she is face-to-face with double doors; CANNON AMPHITHEATER is written over them. She freezes. That the arrows terminate at a cul-de-sac is not what stops her. It's a sign propped on the kind of chrome tripod you see in the lobbies of hotels announcing Stevie Stern's bar mitzvah in the Rococo Room, Em and Bal Peters's silver anniversary on the mezzanine, registration for B & L Asset Management in the Paul Revere Chamber, refreshments to follow in the JFK Hospitality Suite. Here the movable letters of a movie marquee spell GRAND ROUNDS, then: HOST FAMILIES: A COMPARISON BETWEEN PARASITES AND THEIR HOSTS IN FISH FROM THE GULF OF MEXICO AND THE SEA OF JAPAN. TRUMAN WOLFF, M.D., PH.D., 7:00 A.M.

For a long time, Daisy stands in front of the Cannon Amphitheater thinking of signs. HOST FAMILIES: A COMPARISON BETWEEN PARASITES AND THEIR HOSTS IN FISH FROM THE GULF OF MEXICO AND THE SEA OF JAPAN, she reads again. It's a literal sign for someone at the literal end of the line. She's followed the blue equivalent of the yellow brick road and has landed at her own fully personalized Oz. She pushes the metal plates screwed into the doors.

Which swing open on a lecture hall whose seats are littered with balled-up foam cups, shredded napkins, paper saucers stained with the crumbs of breakfast that some lucky souls got to eat. A jacket is tossed over a slide projector. A lab coat lies bunched on the floor. In one corner there's a table set up with a coffee urn; three lopsided jelly doughnuts dot a tray that must once have held several dozens' worth. Assessing this evidence of recent occupation, Daisy assumes the room's just been vacated. The only person besides herself is a tall, thin man on the stage, stuffing papers into an NPR tote.

He looks up. He's got a nice face with fine features topped by an unruly mop of dark hair peppered with gray. He seems exhausted, a mirror image of her own exhaustion, she imagines, taking comfort in this company of shared bags under eyes and heads heavy with weariness nodding slightly on the wobbly stems of their necks. "Any questions?" he asks.

"I'm afraid I missed the lecture," she says. She walks down the center aisle to the stage.

"No matter. You didn't miss much." He pulls the cord of the movie screen behind him. This retracts into its roll with a sharp snap.

Daisy jumps.

"Sorry. These things are like window shades. You put the wrong tension on them, they flip out of control."

"Like life," she says.

He laughs. "Like life."

"The lecture sounds—sounded—really interesting," Daisy says.

"It's a fascinating topic. Do you know that worms have the genetic structure of human beings?"

"My goodness," Daisy exclaims. Are worms more genetically advanced than butterflies? Which, if true, would make a surprising irony. But she refrains from asking the kind of dumb question that would reveal her as an English major whose science requirement was filled by plants for poets and bones for drones.

"Parasites are a marvel," he goes on. "And their subtle differences . . . you could write a book. Of course I have written a book. No, it's my delivery. I'm stiff as a board. Wooden as a cigar-store Indian."

Daisy checks out his arms and legs, which look supple, graceful even. He has beautiful hands with long, attenuated fingers, the kind of hands that would span octaves effortlessly. Artist's hands. Lover's hands. She pinches herself. What is wrong with her?

He smiles, a mouth full of white, charmingly irregular teeth, eyes that crinkle in the corners so that they look like children's drawings of little suns. He's wearing a lopsided bow tie patterned with red ladybugs. Movie-star cheekbones without the movie-star glamour that makes a person feel so inferior. "I should sign up for one of those Dale Carnegie courses. A parasitologist misses a lot of opportunity to practice his social skills. Too much time in the lab doesn't help you to win friends and influence people," he says.

"I don't think you have to worry." She wiggles out of her coat.

"Truman Wolff," he says. He extends his hand.

She takes it. It feels as beautiful as it looks, soft and angular in all the appropriate spots. And his equally beautiful left hand, she notices, lacks a wedding ring.

"Daisy Lewis."

"Daisy Lewis. Daisy Lewis," he repeats. "Are you staff?"

"I'm afraid not."

"Which makes sense, since I certainly would have remembered you." He pauses. "Are you just wandering by? Or do you have a particular interest in parasites?"

"Yes. Yes to both questions. I got lost on the way to the cafeteria. But my husband was just admitted. He'd eaten bad sushi for dinner. He might have a parasite."

Truman Wolff is all business. "Usually parasites take longer to show up. Of course there are always special cases." He gives her a penetrating look. Is it the eye of a clinician hunting for a diagnosis? Or the eye of a man evaluating the opposite sex? No matter, these eyes are the green of the sea, the forest, a certain brand of piccalilli consumers agitate to keep stocked on the shelf. He knits his brow. "Did you eat this sushi too?" he asks.

"No. In fact, I'd lost my appetite. I didn't even touch my own teriyaki plate."

"All to the good. What were his symptoms?"

Daisy thinks of the retching noises behind the bathroom door, how she had dismissed them as the end-of-a-relationship drunkenness. "Throwing up," she says. "I mean vomiting."

"Anything else? Numbness? Muscle weakness?"

"I'm not sure."

Truman Wolff rubs his chin, which is adorable, with its slightly skewed cleft. "It could be ciguatera poisoning. Certain toxins in predatory fish present immediately. You didn't notice any flushing during the night?"

"I wouldn't."

"It is hard to tell in the dark," he acknowledges.

Daisy nods. What should she say? Is this her life from now on? Spilling the beans of marital breakdown and separate rooms to any member of the male persuasion who bothers to ask?

Who is also a doctor, she reminds herself. A healer. A person who took the Hippocratic oath. A professional to whom confidentiality is as sacred as it is to a priest. A man who's probably heard as many intimate confessions as a priest. She takes a deep breath. "I mean, we didn't sleep together. We don't sleep together. We're estranged," she explains, grabbing on to Jessica's word. She feels a blush rise to her scalp. She pulls at her turtleneck. "We're in the process of breaking up."

Truman Wolff straightens his bow tie, which flops back into instant crookedness. "How about joining me in the cafeteria? I've got a hankering for bacon and eggs. For sausages."

*   *   *

In the corner of the cafeteria, Daisy tears into her bacon and eggs like a different person from the wan, delicately stomached, exemplary host-family half at the Sea of Japan. She can't remember ever having breakfast with a man other than Henry or Sammy or a visiting relative. Not since college, anyway, when the kids on her corridor might crave blueberry pancakes in the middle of exams. What a difference a few hours make. A sick husband, a shower and clean clothes, a gift of jeans from a new admirer, a path not taken, the path misread and—presto!—Truman Wolff.

Since they were both heading toward breakfast, it would have been rude to refuse, silly, even, to insist on separate tables. But at the same time she thinks this, she panics. She's a cue ball set off by Henry and ricocheting crazily from man to man. Who's next? The Boston Strangler? She's never been so out of control. Not surprising, for a woman who's clung to a safe marriage, raised a successful, socially responsible child, taken nonthreatening jobs some of her classmates might have viewed as a waste of a Harvard degree. "You always settle for less," Henry had told her.

Over the years, when she and Henry were considering both large and small leaps into the unknown—to get a pet, adopt a child, try skydiving—she had always balked. "It could be great," Henry would point out.

"It could be terrible."

Now she looks at Truman Wolff. Disasters come in threes, cautions the old wives' tale. But she herself is living proof that it's not always easy to predict what—or who?—the disaster will be. Or where to start counting from. She's heard warnings to the recently bereaved not to make sudden life-changing decisions. It won't be hard to be careful, she tells herself, she who has perfected being careful her whole life. Even if the end of a marriage tends to shake things up.

But if she's shaken up, Truman Wolff seems completely content. He savors his unhealthy-choice breakfast. He slices his sausage with the skill of a chef. Daisy imagines him sectioning tissue samples onto slides for a microscope. Around them the cafeteria bustles. Trays clatter. People talk. Newspaper pages crackle. A parade of white-coated figures marches back and forth; the only difference between the servers and the servees are the hair nets the servers wear. Scattered about are men and women in street clothes, family members of patients. These seem tired, worried. They are not digging into hearty breakfasts but are sipping coffee from thick white mugs. They have a dazed dimension to the eyes, and their clothes look as if they've slept in them. Daisy feels a prick of guilt. She has not given enough thought to the husband whose body is racked with pain, infested with probable parasites while she is nibbling on toast and sopping up eggs.

Truman Wolff holds up a slice of bacon. He swivels it. *"Dermatobia hominus,"* he declares.

"Pardon?"

"The human bottfly."

"The bacon?" Daisy asks. She studies the glistening strips on her plate. She pictures hospital admission forms, curtained cubicles. She shudders; she can't stop herself.

Truman Wolff plows ahead, not noticing. "The method of entrapment. These Club Med types turn up at the ER with a price to pay for their fun in the sun. Maggots need oxygen. They have breathing tubes that pierce your flesh. If you stick bacon over your skin, the little buggers will poke their breathing tubes straight through. Thus, Dr. Watson, when you pull off the bacon, you can catch the worm. *Quod erat demonstrandum.* It takes about twenty-four hours."

Daisy imagines bacon taped to people's ribs, to their shoulders, to their thighs. She supposes you'd have to wear old clothes you don't care about. Subtly, she pushes her own bacon to the edge of her plate.

Though not subtly enough, since Truman Wolff points to her breakfast, which is now partitioned like children's chinaware. "Sorry," he says, "you won't be surprised to hear I've been accused of possessing a one-track mind."

"I never . . ." Daisy begins.

"Let's change the subject." He devours his bacon as if he's swallowing evidence. "So," Truman Wolff asks, "what do you think of the Red Sox?"

Daisy laughs.

"Politics? The weather?"

She shakes her head.

"Now that we've exhausted the important topics," Truman Wolff states, "what came between you and your husband?"

"You *are* direct."

"I warned you, no social skills." He pauses. His voice is gentle. "We can go back to the Red Sox if you want."

Daisy feels her eyes start to fill. She pulls a wad of Kleenex from her pocketbook. Out flies Barry Sweiker's card and lands with the precision of a paper airplane at the intersection of Truman Wolff's crossed knife and fork. Daisy watches him trying unsuccessfully to avert his gaze from *P.S. Thanks for last night.*

"That's not the reason," she says.

"I never thought . . ."

She reaches over. She grabs the card. She squeezes it into a ball. She tucks it under the rim of her plate. "It sounds fishy, but it's completely innocent."

"I wouldn't even begin to judge. . . ."

Daisy studies the metal napkin dispenser, which is flanked by French's mustard and Heinz ketchup. The dispenser is empty. Both jars are down to the dregs. "French," she reads. Déjà vu all over again, she thinks. "French," she says.

"French?" he asks.

"The reason my husband and I are breaking up."

His eyes open so wide they look like two green Life Savers. His fork is suspended in the air, a slice of sausage speared on its tine. "You've got to be kidding."

"Unfortunately, no."

"I don't mean to intrude on something so personal. Hell, I do mean to intrude." He studies his fork a foot from his mouth as if it's something flying through the air unattached to any body part. "Would you care to elaborate?"

Would she ever. It comes out in a rush, the dam-burst of emotion that Daisy supposes is what psychologists mean when they say letting it all hang out is good for you. She tells this complete stranger the story of her marriage, the story of her life. Her voice barrels across the years with the speed of an actor she once heard cover all of Shakespeare's plays on a ten-minute tape. When she comes to the part about host families, Truman nods so vigorously his mug takes two telekinetic steps.

"Something I know a bit about myself," he confesses.

"Your lecture, 'Host Families, the Sea of Japan,'" Daisy says, "which drew me to you in the first place. I mean, which prompted me to open the doors to that lecture hall."

"And I'm very glad you did."

"Me too," Daisy concedes, not quite able to meet his remarkable eye. "Though, of course, you were speaking of parasites."

"There's a real correlation with human families. The assumption of a parasitic mode of life," Truman recites with such loving attention to each word he could be quoting poetry, "is a habitudinal reaction to the intensity of the struggle for existence."

"That's brilliant." Daisy is awed. She knows she has heard something profound. If she had a pencil she would write it on a napkin the way, in movies, would-be Picassos dash off their masterpiece. But the napkin dispenser is empty. The intensity of the struggle for existence, she says to herself, trying to memorize the sentence the way she had to memorize "Casey at the Bat" in grammar school. She struggles for the apt analogy, but her brain cells feel as scrambled as these eggs she's wolfing down. The second she has this thought, the word *wolfing* flashes in her head as big and bright as a neon sign atop a Las Vegas casino. Wolfing! The symbols are everywhere.

Truman Wolff seems to have read her mind. "We have a lot in common. Host families. French."

"We have French in common?" she asks.

He nods. "Your turn first." He grins.

She tells him about Henry's metamorphosis from Henry to Henri. The segue from French lass to French class. His affectation of a beret. Her suspicions about Giselle. "Though in all fairness, I can't completely blame French," she explains. "The marriage just started to go bad, from the inside, a slow progression. Like a tapeworm," she says, pleased with herself.

"An apt analogy," Truman approves. "It is not in the interest of a parasite that *great* harm should result to the host from its presence."

"That's right. We just went along not really noticing until outside forces—French—finished the marriage off." She pauses. "Francophilia," she says. "Sounds like a disease. Like hemophilia."

"The symptoms of which I'm an expert on. Francophilia, that is."

Daisy shifts her plate to one side. Puts her elbows on the table and props up her chin. Truman Wolff's eyes move to her hands. Is he focusing on the glint of her mother-in-law's first husband's engagement ring? She sticks her hands in her lap.

Like Barry Sweiker, she knows the power of the subliminal. "So, your turn," she says.

"My ex-wife—we've been divorced a year—is named Michelle."

"My husband, Henry, has been known to call himself Henri. In front of a camera, he says fromage. The place where I work he refers to as L'Étoile."

He shakes his head. "Michelle's from Billerica, Mass. But I can't help but think that, like a person's DNA, there's some genetic code inherent in a name which is programmed for inevitability."

Daisy agrees. Though if a name is a self-fulfilling prophecy, then what about Daisy with its love-me, love-me-not component, a petal-plucking odyssey to a romantic fate? And what about Wolff? But then she reminds herself that his name is Truman and is comforted. "Go on," she encourages.

"She left me for the under pastry chef at Maison Robert," he says. He sighs. "The symptoms were there from the beginning. French lessons. Two weeks each summer at Cordon Bleu. A collection of Editions Gallimard lined up on the bookshelves. The damn CD player always blasting Edith Piaf. She said I lacked joie de vivre. Like I was some kind of Tin Man from *The Wizard of Oz*—all I needed was a little French to give me a heart."

"I don't know you very well," Daisy admits, "but it seems to me even on such small acquaintance that you have a very big heart."

He smiles. Some toast is caught between his teeth. This touches her. "I even thought about studying French myself," he confesses, "hoping a romance language would bring—well—romance."

"I wouldn't touch French with a ten-foot pole," she advises. "I studied it in high school. It's highly overrated. Good for ordering a croissant." She thinks of Jessica. "Italian's by far the better choice."

"You may be right. La dolce vita." He shreds his napkin.

They give a collective, ruminating sigh.

"Not that it's all been bad," Daisy feels obliged to point out. "Twenty years leaves room for plenty of peaks among the valleys. Henry and I do have a wonderful son."

"And I—Michelle and I—have a daughter we dote upon."

"Isn't it amazing how something good can come of something bad?"

"It's one of the more humbling, more awe-inspiring facts of nature. Do you know, for example, that a pearl is a reaction that forms around a parasite?"

The cafeteria is emptying. A hair-netted woman clangs their plates together and stacks them on a cart. She has a surly look on her face. She has places to go, things to do, she seems to growl, if only they would hurry up.

Daisy checks her watch. "My God! I'd better go see Henry," she exclaims.

Truman pushes back his chair. He grabs his NPR tote. "Anytime you need a consultation," he offers.

FRANCE NATIONALE
CHARLES DE GAULLE 2
7
A 421 FRANCE

On the way to the elevator, Daisy passes a bank of phones. She grabs one in the middle of the row. At her left a woman sobs. "How can you do this?" she cries. "How can you be so cruel when he's really sick?"

"The guy's a doctor, for chrissakes!" the man on her right shouts.

She dials Sammy.

"I'm just heading out to class," he says.

She explains about Henry, that he's in the hospital, that it's something he ate.

"Is it serious?" he asks.

"Enough to be hospitalized. Though the doctors insist it's not life-threatening."

"Do you need me right away?"

"No. He's stable. Getting better."

"I'll stop by," he says, "between French and biology."

She hangs up. The woman still sobs. The man still yells.

Daisy shakes her head. That's exactly where I am, she thinks. She presses the elevator button. Between French and biology.

When she swings open the door to Henry's room, she's glad to see that he's in a double, even though no one occupies the second bed. In spite of Henry's guilt-driven reassurances, her prospective financial status is not conducive to the surcharges a single would entail. She's ashamed, dwelling on money matters when the focus should be on only the medical.

"There, there, darlin'," singsongs a nurse in a voice that isn't too many months removed from County Cork. She holds a compress to her patient's brow. Bags heavy with fluid flank a pole like coconuts about to drop. These drip into a tube taped to Henry's wrist, where veins pop out like knots in a rope.

Seeing him hooked up like this, Daisy feels terrible.

"I feel terrible," Henry groans.

"Of course you do, dear," soothes the nurse, whose jolly red cheeks, twinkly blue eyes, colossal breasts, and wide, competent hands illustrate the archetypal mother in a fairy tale. Daisy pictures Henry's mother, Lillian, who, between her tango lessons, mah-jongg club, husband hunting, and pedicures, hardly had the wherewithal to find some baking soda for his chicken pox. She feels sorry for him. She thinks of *The Wizard of Oz*, of Truman Wolff's Tin Man analogy. Has Henry turned to French to make up for a lack of mothering?

"But every minute you're a wee bit more on the road to recovery," says the nurse, whose name, Daisy reads from the badge, is Siobhan O'Sullivan. She squeezes out the compress, cradles Henry's head, and feeds him water through a straw. He sips weakly with all the strength of a Mimi wasting away from TB in the garret of *La Bohème*. If Daisy turns sideways, Siobhan O'Sullivan's breast hides the glass so it looks as if she's nursing him.

It's a tableau straight out of Michelangelo's *Pietà*. The only

French equivalent Daisy can find is that icon of Gallic pride, Marianne, once bearing the face of Brigitte Bardot, who outgrew the honor. Why? For the motherly wrinkles of middle age, her maternal commitment to animal rights. Daisy is appalled by the glamour-mongering French, who have now cast Marianne with the features of a young Catherine Deneuve.

Daisy moves closer to Henry's bed. She studies his features. Henry is still pale, his face still slicked by a feverish layer of sweat. But some color pricks his cheeks; his eyes are no longer the glassy marbles you see on dead fish. Perhaps his desire to end their marriage is a disease-driven anomaly he's not responsible for. This sustains her for two seconds until she acknowledges that no chicken-or-egg argument could confuse the actual clear sequence of events.

Siobhan O'Sullivan settles the water back on the night table and turns to her. "Well, see here, darlin' "—she strokes his arm—"this pretty lass just come in must be your wife."

In an instant, the color is leached from his cheeks. His eyes go flat.

"Daisy Lewis," she introduces herself. "Have they identified the parasite?"

"Parasite?"

"From the sushi, Henry, my"—she hesitates—"husband," she spurts, "ate for dinner last night."

"The things some people contaminate their bodies with." Siobhan O'Sullivan shakes her head.

Daisy understands where she's coming from, a country where cabbage is cooked to the consistency of limp wet wool, where a Dublin friend once put the Brussels sprouts on to simmer while they went to a production of *Man and Superman*. "The veggies should be about ready," she'd said three hours later, after they'd left the Abbey Theater and were waiting for a bus.

"I wouldn't let raw fish within ten kilometers of my dinner plate," Siobhan O'Sullivan continues. "No, it's salmonella poisoning."

Daisy has a momentary stab of disappointment. A parasite would be more interesting, an object to study, to dissect, a foundation for her and Truman Wolff to build a conversation on. A parasite would provide a reason to bring Truman Wolff in to consult, to introduce a fourth party to what she suspects is an unfairly weighted triumvirate. "Salmonella," she repeats with a distaste that marks it as a lower link on the chain of poisoning.

"The teriyaki. The chicken was undercooked. We've run some tests. There's a couple from Norway who ate the same thing, poor dears, and are now filling up two beds at Mass General."

"*I* ordered the sushi," Henry manages to point out with an amazing vehemence given his weakened state.

"Are you saying all this is my fault?"

"*I* ordered the sushi," Henry repeats. "The thing speaks for itself. *Les faits parlent d'eux-mêmes.*"

"Now, now." Siobhan O'Sullivan tut-tuts. "I'm going to get out of here and let you lovebirds have some privacy."

"Don't go," Daisy exclaims, like a kindergartner on the first day of school. She is astonished to see that she has actually grabbed a handful of the nurse's white nylon skirt. Reluctantly, she releases the clot of cloth. This springs back to its original unwrinkled sheen—the advantages of man-made fibers, Daisy notes. "I mean I have some questions," she adds.

Siobhan O'Sullivan folds her arms across the shelf of her chest, which has room for a few more appendages plus a suffering patient's febrile head. Daisy wishes she could soothe her own addled brain against that inviting maternal breast. "Which are . . . ?" the nurse encourages.

"This salmonella. Is it dangerous?"

"Very. Why just last week, two people died. Fifty were hospitalized. Over four hundred got sick." She ticks these numbers off as if she's reciting items on an inventory. "A church supper in Maryland. Tainted ham." She chuckles. "The septic system got a workout the city fathers never counted on."

"People died?" Daisy asks. This is not the solution to her problems that Daisy wants to encourage. She feels a sharp sting of fear.

Which is mirrored in Henry's ashen face and breathless gasps. "Am I in danger?"

"Not when I'm watching over you," Siobhan O'Sullivan boasts.

"Is there an antidote?" Daisy asks.

"None. Only palliative care. But this one's on the mend. Passed the crisis with flying colors, he did. Who knows but quick as a wink he'll be back home with his wife and his son."

"That's a relief," Henry says.

"Is it?" Daisy asks.

"That I'm on the mend, I mean," Henry has the need to clarify.

But before she can ponder this and produce a retort, the door swings open. With two giant steps and the whoosh of nippy Cambridge air, in strides the six-foot-one hunk of adorableness that is her son.

Daisy has the sudden desire to fling her arms around him, to proclaim to Henry, to the nurse, *Look, this is mine.* "Sammy!" she hoots and swoops toward him like some giant bird with wings outstretched.

"Mom," he says. His voice carries a warning that causes her to fold her elbows to her ribs. PDAs—public displays of affection—it cautions, are not suitable for young men over the age of ten. She thinks of the couple on the bench. Until, of course, he falls in love. Still, he angles his cheek toward her. She kisses it, surprised as always at the bristle of a beard on the once downy baby skin. She feels reduced to one in a series of maiden aunts whose dry pecks at family gatherings were an indignity he'd politely tolerate.

"What a fine strapping lad," Siobhan O'Sullivan announces. She heads for the door. "I'll leave you with your family for now, Mr. Lewis, but don't overtire yourself. Don't forget, you still are very weak."

Henry gives a corroborative moan. Sammy rushes to his side. Against Henry's ghostly skin, white bed linens, a hospital johnny of washed-out beige, walls the shade of jaundiced flesh, Sammy's a riot of color—green parka, blue hat, yellow scarf, the cuffs of red socks under faded jeans. Not to mention his robust good health, ruddy cheeks, a mop of curly brown hair with golden lights, eyes the shade of an August sky, and, when he removes his scarf, pink blotches on his neck. Pink blotches on his neck! Daisy looks again. Love bites? she wonders, then dismisses the thought. More likely chafing from a too-tight collar, too-scratchy scarf, maybe a minor allergy.

"So what happened, Dad?" Sammy asks.

"Your mother poisoned me."

"Henry!" Daisy cries.

Sammy laughs. "Then she didn't do a very good job."

"Not good enough, since they tell me I'll survive."

"Your father has salmonella poisoning," Daisy explains, "from dinner last night at a new and terrible restaurant he chose."

"The poisoning came from the teriyaki your mother ordered," Henry points out. "Which she didn't touch," he adds.

"And why was that, I wonder?" Daisy feels obliged to ask.

Henry ignores her. He rolls on his side toward Sammy and undulates his IV tube, a gesture Daisy finds more than a trifle flamboyant. "I myself had the sushi. It was delicious. Without flaw," he goes on as if he's a diamond merchant on Forty-seventh Street. "I only had the teriyaki to help your mother out."

"They say a good deed never goes unpunished," Daisy replies.

"Well, you've certainly seen to it."

"Are you saying that I deliberately poisoned you? That I could tell by looking at the chicken that it was bad?" She pauses, indignant. "You can't always tell from the outside that there's something rotten at the core," she insinuates. "But I certainly knew right off the bat that the restaurant was no good."

"So you're prescient, along with all your other gifts."

"Hardly. Or I would have tumbled to"—she hesitates—"certain clues immediately. Still, how much ESP does it take? A damp-basement, nearly empty restaurant with untrained, inattentive staff—"

"Just starting out and looking for support, a little tolerance."

"Why did you go there, anyway?" asks Sammy.

"To celebrate receiving our host-family award," instructs Henry. "Ironically," he adds.

"Oh, so that's why," says Daisy. "Speaking ironically, of course, since the award was left behind with the tip. A tip instead of a suit for damages!"

Henry ignores her.

"What was the name of the restaurant?" asks Sammy conversationally in his long-perfected oh-you-guys peacemaking tone.

"The Sea of Japan," Daisy replies. "Cross it off your list."

"*Au contraire,*" says Henry. "I give it my imprimatur."

An answer Daisy finds to be pretty much the vocal equivalent of his affectation of a beret. Still, she is incredulous. "Even though it poisoned you? Even though at this very minute the two other patrons dumb enough to set foot in that den of bacteria are now barfing up their teriyaki in the corridors of Mass General?"

"You certainly know how to stack the deck. Why not give a new restaurant opening in Harvard Square a bit of rope. The benefit of the doubt. In all things—and you should know this, Daisy—it takes some time to work the kinks out."

"Sometimes the kinks won't work out. The tapeworm settles in for the long haul." Daisy thinks of her marriage. She supposes twenty years might qualify as "some time." "Sometimes you just have to throw in the towel."

"Is this the *restaurant* you're talking about?" Henry asks in a way Daisy finds needlessly sly. He turns to Sammy. "It was fine."

"Fine enough, I repeat, that you left your host-family award there. Like a dog marking its spot. A wild animal leaving its spoor—"

"It was *your* host-family award too, let me point out. I, for one, will go back."

"For the flawless sushi, I presume. Not the award."

Henry sighs the sigh of a man whose crisis of health has not yet passed. "I'm afraid this conversation is tiring me. Do I need mention that Nurse O'Sullivan just minutes ago brought your attention to my weakened state?"

Sorry, Daisy considers saying, but it lodges in her throat with a satisfactory stubbornness.

"Anything I can get you, Dad?" Sammy gives Henry the kind of pat you'd give a pet. "I could go to the cafeteria."

"What I need you couldn't find in any cafeteria."

"What do you need?" Daisy snorts.

Henry ignores her. "Let's switch to a neutral subject," he says. "Sammy, how's French?"

Since when is French a neutral subject? Daisy wonders. Since Henry started studying it? Since he moved from the conjugation of *Madame* to the conjugation of *Mademoiselle?*

"Okay," Sammy says.

"Just okay?" asks Henry.

For how long has Henry been so out of touch with his son that he doesn't realize "Okay" qualifies as a superlative? The northern lights, R.E.M., courtside seats for the Celtics, a winning lottery ticket—these would all be deemed by Sammy to be "okay."

"We're reading Alexandre Dumas. It's a bit of okay."

"Ah, *Les Trois Mousquetaires, Le Comte de Monte Cristo,* Dumas *père,* Dumas *fils,*" intones Henry. "Have you been working in the language lab? How's your accent? We could practice a little conversation." Con-ver-sash-see-own, he pronounces it.

"Sure, Dad."

"Right," Daisy says. "What's French for salmonella poisoning?"

"Very funny, Daisy," says Henry, who does not look amused. He turns to Sammy. "Don't you just love the language?"

"It's okay," he says, in which, this time, Daisy's ears detect a diminution of enthusiasm.

"How about biology?" Daisy asks. "What are you dissecting?"

"What are you conjugating?" asks Henry.

"Who's your lab partner?"

"Have you mastered the subjunctive yet?"

"How does that chart go: species, genus, family, class, phylum . . . ?" muses Daisy, summoning up a morsel from her plants for poets past.

"I thought we were talking about French," counters Henry.

Daisy realizes she and Henry must sound like competing interviewers trying to get the attention of some dignitary on *Meet the Press*. What about the tax credit? Any names for the White House pet?

"Come on, you guys." Sammy holds up his hands in a cease fire. "We're studying the flu of nineteen eighteen and the ebola virus."

"Too bad your mother couldn't get her hands on a sample to sprinkle on my California roll."

"Which we'd have no need for if we continued giving the Sea of Japan what you insist is its well-deserved chance."

Sammy groans. "Enough, you two. Seriously, Dad, will you be coming home soon?"

"No doubt any second. With medicine these days open heart surgery is practically done on an outpatient basis. I could be on my deathbed—probably am—and they'd still kick me out of here. Those bean counters," he complains, as if he isn't one. "But as for coming home . . . I take it your mother hasn't told you yet."

"Henry," Daisy warns.

"Told me what?" Sammy asks.

"Your mother and I—" Henry begins.

"Not now," Daisy interrupts.

"Are splitting up?" Sammy finishes.

Daisy is furious. How could Henry break the news like that? As casually as if he's announcing the dry cleaner lost his navy pants. Together they should have planned exactly how to drop the atom bomb that is the dissolution of their marriage; they should have consulted therapists, parenting books. They should have role-played the presentation as if everything were at stake. Everything is at stake, she knows. Sammy's happiness, his whole world. She thinks of nervous breakdowns, post-traumatic stress syndromes, alcohol, drugs, delinquency. She thinks of the red fire of anger and the black hole of depression. She thinks of his sex life—does he have one?—of his sexual orientation—is it flexible?—of his midterm grades. She studies him.

If Sammy has had his security blanket pulled out from under him, he is giving no sign. "Quite frankly," he confesses, "I'm not surprised."

"You're not?" asks Daisy.

"See," says Henry.

"I figured you might split up once I left home."

"You did?" asks Daisy. "You might have let me in on this."

"Oh, Mom. I recognize the symptoms. So many of my friends have been through this. Lack of communication is your number one problem."

"Baloney."

"You're just in denial, Mom. Perfectly natural."

"Sammy! Spare me—"

"Mom, most of the kids I know have families that divide and multiply like—well—like the amoebas we study in biology. It's pretty common. Plus we've been analyzing family structure in Intro to Psych."

"A little knowledge . . ." grumbles Henry.

"Don't worry. I had a good childhood," Sammy says.

Daisy studies him. She recognizes the twitch at the corner of his mouth that appears when he's trying to put a brave face on things.

He chews a fingernail. He pulls at his ear. "Well, guys, gotta go. A lab," Sammy explains with such an extra-cheerful how-are-we-feeling-today breeziness he could be Nurse O'Sullivan.

"French?" Henry asks.

"Biology?" Daisy asks.

"Whatever. Take care, you two." And in a tone Daisy finds just slightly patronizing, adds, "We'll talk."

At the door, he stops. "Mom, I left some laundry. . . ."

As soon as she hears his footsteps recede down the hall, she turns to Henry.

"Henry," she starts.

"Don't start," Henry warns.

"I take it all systems are go as planned. This little crimp in the line, this salmonella poisoning, isn't going to force you to come home to recuperate?"

"I've made other arrangements. In all fairness, Daisy, I could hardly justify burdening you with my precarious health." He points to the clock opposite his bed. "Speaking of which, I need my rest," he says. He rolls over, thrusting the solid wall of his back to her.

When Daisy gets off the elevator, she squeezes through a crowd waiting to get in. Not until she reaches her car does she realize she has brushed shoulders with the red-curled, silk-scarfed, French "other arrangement" bearing the name of Giselle.

At home, Daisy dumps her coat on the hall bench and walks to the kitchen. Clues to Sammy's recent presence are everywhere. A bowl sits on the table. In it three Cheerios float in a puddle of milk. The newspaper lies opened to the sports pages. A nearly empty carton of orange juice and a bagel with a bite out of it stand on the counter. The portable telephone hangs off the edge of the garbage pail. A paper towel roll is unfurled like a carpet across the linoleum tiles. Crumbs dust the toaster, whose base is dolloped with strawberry jam.

Daisy cleans up without her usual resentment. "I'm not the servant here," was once her constant refrain. "Pick up after yourself. I refuse to lift a plate." And when she was really mad: "I pity your wife!"

Now she is only too glad to do it. Rinsing out his bowl and sponging away his crumbs makes her feel nurturing even though he's not physically in the sphere of her concern. It's the old tree-falls-in-the-forest conundrum. If he's not here to see her clean up his mess, will he still know she's taking care of him? Especially now since his united-we-stand parents are about to divide, if not necessarily fall. She scrubs at a particularly tenacious blob of jelly. From under the sink she pulls out a canister of Lysol and spritzes the countertop with the ferocity of the team of fumigators who once came to annihilate a nest of wasps. Bee Busters they were called and wore the helmeted white suits of astronauts. She gives an extra-violent spurt to the side of the refrigerator. It feels good. For a second she understands the male attraction to weaponry, its power, the almost sexual release. Funny, she thinks, that at the very minute she is machine-gunning bacteria in her kitchen, Sammy is probably cultivating viruses in his lab. And Henry? What's he cultivating? she wonders. Is he making space in his hospital bed for Giselle?

Daisy walks into the laundry room. Sammy's laundry bag lies in front of the dryer, spilling its darks and lights like the treasures bursting from Santa's sack. She sighs. All his whites are gray; his darks are grayed. Though she's instructed him how to do laundry, heat up a chicken pot pie, change the sheets once a week, vacuum the dust kitties under the bed, she has no illusions that he will pay any attention to her manual of domesticity. It's what Jessica says: You tell your kids not to have sex without any expectation they will listen to you. You make the token proclamation still knowing it's tokenism.

She separates the whites from darks. Makes two piles. From both piles the smell of Sammy rises up. She wants to bury her head in them. She wants to cry. This child that she and Henry came together to create, this combination of her smile, his teeth, her hair, his feet. Now she and Henry have drifted away from each other; there's a gap between them like the space between this pile of denim, this mound of underwear.

She picks up a shirt whose sleeve is twisted inside out. She gives it a shake. Something small and silky falls to the floor. She bends over it. Scoops it up. It's a pair of bikini underpants. Of the softest silk. Of the palest pink. A ruffle of lace trims the impossibly small waist. She examines it. Slightly soiled. Slightly frayed. She pictures Sammy. The face of a child. The beard of a man. The pink marks on his neck. She stops. Her baby is having sex. Is her baby having sex? She's horrified in the way she supposes all mothers of sons are horrified to acknowledge that their child's affections have turned away from the maternal breast. But if her baby is having sex, it dawns on her, then maybe in this ocean of family breakdown, he has found an island of pleasure to keep him afloat.

Daisy puts the laundry into the washer, adds the underpants, pours in colorfast Wisk, and, as an afterthought, sets the machine to Delicate. She's feeling delicate, fragile, vulnerable. Angry and confused. And sad. She remembers how as a newlywed she would match Henry's socks on the long table in the middle of the Laundromat; these are my husband's socks, she'd think, my *husband's*, she'd marvel.

She pictures the box of Caterpillar jeans in the back of her car. Perhaps the owner of the underpants would like the white denim cutoffs, admire the work that went into the dungaree jacket with its rhinestone trim. Still, given the size of that triangle of silk, its owner would swim in both of them.

The washing machine shakes, rattles, and rolls. Some days it sounds like a herd of elephants; others, a dance-hall floor. She and Henry have talked about replacing the machine, which they bought when they moved into their house. They'd studied *Consumer Reports*, read through the list of brands: Kenmore, Maytag, Westinghouse, GE. They're all good American names

solidly backed by five-year warrantees, she'd insisted. Badly
produced American products with a planned obsolescence in
five years, Henry had argued.

"Are you wanting a foreign make?" asked Daisy, meaning
French. Le Cornue ovens, Moulinex mixers, Verdette refrigerators.

"They're often superior," replied Henry, meaning French.

Now Daisy feels a sudden loyalty to this dependable household product they were so rudely hoping to replace. For years
it's provided good service. Kept her whole family clean. Its
chugs and thumps are comforting. So what, a few vibrations,
the tremors of age. Should it be discarded in the prime of its
useful maturity for something new? Turned in like an old wife
for a younger one? She puts her hand on its lid, which is warm
and slightly damp. She strokes the sticky enamel. She can
identify.

Under her fingers the pink silk bikini is being agitated.
She's agitated herself. Back when she and Henry first met, the
lace-trimmed elastic would have easily spanned her own wasp
waist. Nevertheless, she comforts herself, the size-ten jeans
Barry Sweiker's professional eye diagnosed are not exactly a
symbol of the "before" in a before-and-after ad. She remembers a bookstore display of a gargantuan pair of Levi's hanging
over an eight-foot stack of the novel *The Giant's House*. These
were not made to order, explained the clerk, but part of the
regular Big Guy merchandise. Maybe, as ombudsman, she
should request a pair to promote the Hearty Helpings line of
frozen food she has introduced in response to community activism.

Does serving as ombudsman win points for creativity and
social good? Is it an occupation you might want to flaunt at the
twenty-fifth reunion of your Harvard class? If it's a fine filler
job for a wife whose husband and child are her primary con-

cerns, how about as a career for a woman whose husband and child have headed off for opposite shores? But before she can ponder these questions, the washer kicks into rinse at the same time the telephone rings.

"Daisy?" Henry asks.

"Who else would it be?" At first she's irritated. At second thought she's flattered. In Henry's view, it is possible that another voice could be answering this phone, a phone for which he pays the monthly maintenance.

"In all their infinite wisdom, the powers that be have decided to kick me out tomorrow. I've got my briefcase, but there's a bag full of papers I've left behind. In the study between the desk and the easy chair. A Sharper Image bag. I'd be really grateful if you'd drop it off at the hospital."

"Why not," Daisy states, admiring her own magnanimity.

"Thanks." He pauses. Daisy hears the rustle of sheets. "I thought it went okay with Sammy. Didn't you?"

She's not about to let *him* off the hook. "There's always the rebound effect. People can have delayed reactions to trauma. To shock."

"You sound like a textbook page. As if you're quoting chapter and verse out of Sammy's Intro to Psychology."

"Which they'd hardly teach at Harvard if there wasn't documented proof."

Henry seems to consider this. Or at least he doesn't put up an argument. "He's a good kid" is what he finally says.

"There's no disputing that."

"Well, we did *something* right."

Daisy doesn't want to think about what they did right, since that would inevitably lead to what they did wrong. Once she starts she'll cycle into Heavy Duty, bypassing Delicate. "Lighten up, Daisy," Henry has told her on more than one occasion, "you take everything so seriously."

"Sammy has a girlfriend," she announces.

"How do you know?"

"Pink silk bikinis in his laundry bag."

His delight crackles over the phone lines. She can hear him slap the night table with what she presumes is his non-IV'ed fist. "Well, I'll be!" Then he turns somber. "Safe sex?"

"I hope. It's not that he hasn't been indoctrinated."

"We—*Sammy and I.* We'll have to have a talk."

"Where can I reach you if I need you? I mean if Sammy falls apart. If the house falls apart?" *If I fall apart,* she amends silently. "If Sammy needs a father's advice as well as a mother's love?"

There's a long silence. Followed by so much throat clearing it sounds as though he's had a relapse. Then: "I might as well tell you. I'm moving in with Giselle."

"Giselle!" exclaims Daisy. She slams her hand against the telephone book with the kind of karate chop she's seen sumo wrestlers use to divide the Manhattan directory. She's furious, indignant. But not surprised. "Giselle's a baby. Our student. She hasn't been here long enough for us to have her to dinner yet!" she yells.

"Sometimes things happen fast."

"I'll bet they do." She looks at the phone book. She opens it at random. SAVE ENERGY announces an ad for water heaters. She sighs. "So where can I reach you?"

He rattles off a number so fast it's clear he's committed it to heart. Has committed his heart. What could be a surer sign? It's an 868 number. Cambridge. She writes it down.

"And the address?" she asks.

She senses him hesitating. Hears the sip of water through a straw, the ping of the glass placed back on the night table. "Is that really necessary?" He sighs.

"To forward your mail."

"Why don't you call me. I'll come and pick it up."

"What if there's a power failure? The telephone lines could go down."

"Unlikely."

"Anything could happen," she persists.

"Daisy . . ." he says, conciliatory.

"There could be an emergency." She's aware of her own voice getting desperate, taking on a crazy edge. Like spots in front of her eyes, the titles of disaster movies line up: *Titanic*, *Earthquake*, *Meteor*, *Volcano*, *Twister*, *Crash*, *Outbreak*, *Typhoon*. In quick succession march the plagues visited on the Egyptians: blood, frogs, lice, wild beasts, cattle disease, boils, hail, locusts, darkness, the slaying of the firstborn son.

The slaying of the firstborn son!

Henry croaks out an address.

"Can you repeat it?" Daisy asks, pencil poised over the Star Market swiped-from-her-"office" memo pad.

"301E Holden Green," he rasps, certain of his doom. "02138," he adds, sealing it.

"You're kidding!"

"I'm afraid not."

"But that's *married* student housing!"

"*We* weren't married when we lived there. Giselle's sublet it. From a French couple who were called back to Paris suddenly when the government changed."

That in the middle of such a revelation, Henry still manages to pronounce Paris "Paree" infuriates her. "But that's *our* apartment! We were so happy there!"

"You wouldn't recognize it," he placates. "They've got rid of the footed tub. Put in a shower, carpeting." He's on a roll now, self-serving, gaining steam. "They even have a regular schedule to fumigate!"

"Asshole!" Daisy yells. "Worm!" she screams and slams down the phone.

It takes her through the rinse and spin cycles and forty-five minutes of drying time before she can collect herself enough to go find his papers. In the study, she sorts through them, looking for what? A sign of a sharper image in a Sharper Image shopping bag? Underpants marked *peau de soie,* a lace brassiere tatted by nuns in Alençon, a handkerchief blotted with a brand of lipstick sold only in the Galeries Lafayette? She sticks her nose in the bag. No scent of Rive Gauche or Je Reviens. She shuffles the papers. No *billets doux* penned on Cartier ivory stock. Only bills. Not for flowers or chocolates, she checks. Notes on software in Henry's sloppy hand, business letters, an inventory. She picks up a page that is headlined "Recent Virus Report." French Kiss leads the list. She pulls her hand away.

She sinks into the easy chair. Henry will be French-kissing Giselle in the same rooms that had contained Daisy's own premarital bliss. And given Harvard's miserliness—despite the shower and roach-free kitchen shelves—probably in the very same bed. Just like the white nylon of the nurse's uniform, those springs have a memory no matter how many times the mattress has been aired. How many coats of China white did it take to cover the bathroom's mural of hearts and arrows they'd painted on Valentine's Day? How many extractor fans does it take to extract old cooking smells? For someone who idolizes French, Henry has no respect for the past. What kind of man would introduce a new bird to an old love nest? Still, if those who ignore the past are condemned to repeat it, then Giselle's tenure isn't exactly supported by a long-term lease.

For almost half an hour, Daisy sits in the chair, sad and furious. It's all Harvard's fault, she's convinced. It was at Harvard where she first met Henry. It was a Harvard apartment from which her marriage was launched. It was the Harvard host-family program that introduced Henry to Giselle. Even now, Harvard is housing her son in a dormitory, her husband in 301E Holden Green. What is Harvard? Some virus invading her family, breaking down the structure she has so carefully built up? And of course, if Harvard taints all things, Truman Wolff, medical school parasitologist, is spoiled goods, thus leaving free of contamination only the Barry Sweikers of this world. She groans.

She looks at the desk drawers, which are so stuffed they're impossible to shut. Spilling out are the family photographs she's always planned to file and sort. She picks up two snaps of Sammy as a baby. In the full flush of motherhood, she was convinced she could identify Sammy at the quarter-year mark, and at eight and two-thirds months. Now she's not so sure. Why didn't she at least pencil in the dates?

On Jessica's pristine shelves, blue leather albums line up like a full *Britannica*. Jessica's whole life, husbands, kids, work, is contained in those pages, dated, labeled, preserved archivally. Instantaneously, she can produce Kiki at Dartmouth and Karl at Disney World. This is exactly the distraction Daisy needs. Organizing the Kodak moments will be step number one in taking charge of her life.

She wrestles open a drawer. Even more photographs fall to the floor. Henry. Sammy. Her mother. Her last dog. Her first prom. Each black-and-white, each color shot tugs at her heart. She stuffs them back in. She shuts the drawer. A corner of blue sky pokes out. She yanks at it. It's the photograph of her and Henry with Pilombaya. They're arranged in front of some Harvard-looking red brick. Holden Green maybe, or a building at the Kennedy School. She and Henry look so young, so happy. Though off-center, out of focus, not fully formed. Perhaps because of the light, their edges are blurred, causing them to appear transitional.

Between them stands Pilombaya. In contrast, he has the sharp outlines of a cartoon character. He's scowling into the sun. Solid. Definite. Rooted to the spot.

FRANCE NATIONALE
CHARLES DE GAULLE 2

8

A 421 FRANCE

Daisy folds Sammy's laundry, which is now as warm and sweet smelling as newly risen bread. It's heartening how something so grungy can be transformed by hot water and soap. She remembers the bouts of lice in grammar school, the repeated shampoos with Kwell, her conscientious boiling of the comb, the obsessive way she picked the nits. She thinks of Henry's poisoning, his sullied fluids replenished by the IV, his body nurtured by the ministrations of Nurse O'Sullivan. At least some nasty things have an antidote.

She stacks Sammy's clothes into the laundry basket. She places the bikini underpants on top. She smoothes and adjusts. They look like a pink satin bow you'd find crowning a wedding gift. This gives her pause. How quick is the progression from mixing his and her underwear to exchanging vows? As mother of an only son, when does she have to start panicking? She packs the basket in the back of the car next to the box of jeans. Between them she jams in Henry's bag of papers. Driving to the hospital, she feels like she's operating a delivery van.

She pulls alongside a No Stopping Anytime sign. For one second it crosses her mind that she might pay Henry a visit, show uxorious interest—ex-uxorious interest—in the state of his health. She dismisses this thought. He could be so much recovered she'd be drained of all sympathy. She could run into Giselle. Or, worse, she might lose her temper and attack a sick man for fouling a love nest of twenty years ago. What's the point? she acknowledges, impressed by her maturity. She leaves her hazard lights flashing. Danger ahead!—the signs are everywhere.

Inside the lobby, she hands the package to the receptionist. "You can take it up yourself," the woman instructs, barely lifting a kohl-rimmed eye from a heaving-bosom-covered paperback.

"But I'm double-parked," Daisy pleads. She dangles her car keys as evidence.

"There are meter maids all over the place," the receptionist warns with ill-concealed glee. "I'll see if I can find an *orderly* to deliver this." Her eyes shift back to her book; its embossed, lightning-bolt letters spell out *Dolores: Abandoned in Her Prime.*

In a rush to rescue her Volvo from ticketers whose zeal, Cambridge residents suspect, is fueled by a bonus for every car tagged, Daisy runs by a clump of lab-coated doctors holding clipboards and speaking in hushed tones. "Daisy Lewis?" a voice inquires.

She stops. It's Truman Wolff. He detaches himself from his colleagues. Though she knows statistically the chances of running into him at the hospital where he works are high, she's still surprised. Weeks can pass without a glimpse of her next-door neighbor. She can go for days in her office never seeing the produce man, whose own cubicle is two aisles away between Cheez Whiz and Reddi Whip. Here he is. What does a twenty-five-dollar ticket matter anyway?

"So how's the patient?" Truman Wolff asks. His name is embroidered on the little pocket over his heart.

"It's salmonella," Daisy explains. "He got it from my teriyaki. He says I poisoned him."

Truman Wolff laughs. "I'm sure you would do no such thing." He pauses. "So you've come to take him home? Fortunately, recovery from salmonella is quicker than from a parasite."

"He gets discharged tomorrow."

"That's good news." He raises an eyebrow. "Isn't it?"

"He's not coming home." As she says this, Daisy hears her voice start to break.

Truman must too, since his forehead knits with doctorly concern. To be treated with such I-feel-your-pain kindness, Daisy imagines, must cure many ills. "Daisy . . ." he begins.

"I'm fine," Daisy insists, feeling not at all fine. What is wrong with her? Who is she? A wife in shock? Dolores, abandoned in her prime?

"Excuse me for being precipitous," Truman Wolff says, "but do you have plans for dinner tonight?"

Back in her unticketed car, she speeds to Quincy Street. She parks at a loading zone in front of Pennypacker Hall. Her hand on the ignition, she hesitates. She remembers the angry scribbles excoriating her for appropriating a For Clergy Only parking spot. Well, she's not the only person taking what doesn't belong to him. Besides, she's unloading a load. If her litany of sins were simply traffic related, she'd be declared a saint. She hoists the laundry basket on top of the carton of jeans and stumbles across the sidewalk. She has either to crane her neck to peer over the pink silk underpants or screw her eyes through one of the basket's lattice openings. Both ways are cumbersome. What pains she takes to insure her son's snowy shirts.

Not to mention the pristine state of what his girlfriend wears next to the most intimate part of her anatomy. If she is a girl-friend, Daisy qualifies, the way only a mother's instincts make such an observation possible.

"Can I help you, ma'am?" asks a six-foot-three giant whose arms match the span of an eagle's and whose manners would do any Emily Post–quoting mother proud.

He sails her bundles up the three flights of stairs to Sammy's room as if he's carrying feathers. Panting behind him, she gasps her undying gratitude.

"Sammy's a friend," he confesses with a good-bye salute. "He's an okay kid."

Which makes her chest fill fair to bursting.

The door creaks open with a tap of her fingers even though there are signs up and down the corridor warning of thieves. She knows her child's room immediately, the way a mother blindfolded can sniff out her own infant from a crowd dusted with the same baby talc. The way a mother *ought* to be able to identify the age of her child in any photograph. It's the smell of sneakers, the tattered posters, the view of total devastation she recognizes. The halls are quiet. From the floor below, Bob Dylan twangs "Don't Think Twice, It's All Right." She could search this room, sift through these books and CDs and socks and half-eaten candy bars like an archaeologist examining shards. She could check the suggestively wrinkled sheets for clues to Sammy's sex life like an anthropologist documenting the customs of a tribe. But she is a moral woman, she tells her-self. And besides, Sammy could right now be heading back from class. She finds a Post-it on his desk. A pen on the seat of a chair. She sticks the Post-it on the top of the box of Caterpil-lar jeans. *Maybe these would suit a friend,* she writes, *hugs and kisses from your Mom.*

*   *   *

Truman Wolff rings the doorbell on the dot of seven. Daisy buckles her trousers. She loops a chain of silver beads around her neck. It takes her three tries before she can fasten the clasp. Her hands aren't working right. Neither is her brain. Why did she accept this invitation? Separated from Henry a matter of hours, she has already nibbled bacon across a breakfast table from a man not her husband and is now primping for a dinner date. Is she a slut? Or merely a relic from an earlier time? After all, these days, happily married career women share meals with male colleagues, have drinks with male friends. She herself has broken the bread of a submarine sandwich, a giant Whopper, a tuna melt, with Bernie or Jimmy. There's no difference.

But there is a difference. Otherwise why would she be so agitated? She's mistaken the hand cream for the moisturizer. She's smeared lipstick outside the lines even though she can paint the shape of her mouth in the dark. She would have been ready ahead of time if she hadn't felt compelled to try on half the clothes in her closet. There are advantages to Henry's leaving. Since Henry's cleaned out his side of the closet, she has discovered apparel she didn't know she had. She is disgusted to hear her heart pounding with teenage anxiety over her "date." But it's not a date, she consoles herself, just two people having dinner together as friends, two people brought together by a medical interest in parasites. She could as easily be eating with a colleague, a former professor, a community activist, with Jessica. Besides, what's the alternative? Staying home alone in a half-emptied house to agonize?

An hour before, skirts and sweaters scattered on the floor like sprawled bodies outlined in a crime scene, she'd called Jessica, agonized. "What shall I wear?" she whined.

"It depends on where you're going."

"But I don't know where I'm going. Where *we're* going."

"Then black."

Now the bell rings a second time. Daisy brushes lint off her black sweater. "Coming," she calls.

"I was afraid you'd forgotten." Truman Wolff grins. "Or got a better offer." He is wearing a bow tie with yellow butterflies. He carries a bag that reads HARVARD MEDICAL SCHOOL COOP.

"Just a few last-minute wardrobe adjustments."

"And well worth it too," he approves. He cranes his neck to the hall behind her. He rustles his bag. "Not that I don't mind standing here staring at you . . ."

Daisy feels her just-blushed cheeks blush. "Sorry," she apologizes. This is all new to her. New and terrifying. Calm down, she instructs herself, you're too smart to jump blindly from one man to the next. As a woman of a certain age, of a certain experience, she is entitled to the reasonable hope that Truman Wolff will be a friend.

Daisy shows him into the living room. He looks around. He scrutinizes a Piranesi print of the Colosseum. He flips through a book of Rosamond Purcell's photographs. He straightens a pair of pottery candlesticks. He slides his fingers along the sofa's cut-velvet covering. "Nice place," he says. "Makes me realize what I've missed now that I'm back in the kind of digs I used to live in while studying for my doctorate."

Daisy nods in empathy. She knows what it's like being thrust into the past. She feels her own life boomerang. Back to dinners for one. Back to no child in the house. Back to wardrobe worries. Back to Holden Green. Back to Pilombaya. She steels herself. She examines Truman's beautiful hand—the hand of a healer, of the diagnostician who identifies the parasite and prescribes its antidote. His healer's hand is now rubbing the nap of a square of upholstery, turning it from dark to light, from light to dark. Is Truman Wolff about to tell her he's across the hall from Henry and Giselle, in the former quarters of the ever-feuding, sofa-splitting Helen and Hitch? "Are you in student housing?" she manages to ask.

"Might as well be," he says. "Since I've got a med school appointment, I'd probably qualify for some of those nice places held for Harvard faculty. But no, I rent an apartment on Oxford Street. It would do fine if I were ever there long enough to fix it up."

"Because you're in your lab?"

"That, and traveling."

Traveling. Daisy's heart lifts. She loves traveling. She's socked away a nest egg made from bits of her jobs and a small inheritance. For the first time since college, she's got no strings. Her work hours are flexible. Hell, she could fax back ameliorating letters to disgruntled customers from an island off the coast of Mauritania. She could go around the world visiting the twenty years of foreign students she was host family for. And if, pleading middle age and a delicate stomach, she decided to forgo the pleasures of Bangladesh, there are cheap tickets these days to England. And to France.

The thought of France must color her face in such a way to provoke Truman Wolff to add, "Traveling for business, that is." He holds up the package. "Speaking of which, I brought you a present."

"For me?" Daisy feels the delight of a child.

"Though I'd better forewarn you. No chocolates. No flowers. No *Sonnets from the Portuguese*."

"What a relief."

"It comes from the conference of Parasitologists held in Miami last week. Going there on the plane, I sat next to a Platter."

"A platter?"

"Exactly."

"Of food? Someone left food next to your seat?"

He shakes his head. "Not that kind of platter."

Daisy feels incredibly dumb. As if there's a field of science of which she alone is ignorant. Maybe platter is a new noun form of the tectonic plates that seismologists are always talking about.

"A Platter. Of the Platters. The music group."

Daisy laughs.

"He slept the whole time. I was sorely disappointed. I had questions about harmony, group dynamics, how to keep your tap shoes shined. I was calculating the odds over whether he'd pick *Entertainment Weekly* or *The Economist* from the stewardesses' pile. Not to mention how eager I was for a few bars of 'The Great Pretender.' I'd better warn you right now I've got peculiar musical tastes. I've been collecting records particular to my line of work."

Daisy remembers reading a newspaper feature on the songs of dolphins. "The humming of parasites?" she asks.

"Not exactly," he says. "There's 'Cockroach' by Albert King, a great blues song. 'Lice' by Solid Frog. Cards in Spokes did 'Tapeworm.' So did Pig Face. There's an old sixties song by Brute Force called 'Tapeworm of Love.' Plus 'The Caterpillar' by Ray Camps. And 'Caterpillar Crawl' by Dick Dale."

"'The Caterpillar.' 'Caterpillar Crawl.' I could have guessed," says Daisy.

"Am I missing something?"

Daisy shakes her head.

He thrusts out his package. "Which is all by way of introduction. So, here."

Daisy opens the bag and pulls out a sweatshirt. It's red with a bug on the front. TRIBOLIUM CONFUSUM, TRIATOMA INFESTANS, INTERMEDIATE HOST reads the caption. Daisy thinks of her Latin. *Confusum* is not confusing to define; intermediate host she understands. *Infestans* she can guess. She studies the bug, which looks deceptively domestic. Like a housefly or a cock-roach. Both she's known personally. On the back of the shirt, it reads HAVE A PARTY. HOST A PARASITE. At the bottom is printed CONFERENCE OF PARASITOLOGISTS, INTERNATIONAL SYMPOSIUM ON STRATEGIES IN VIRUS-HOST RELATIONSHIPS, EDEN ROC HOTEL, MIAMI, FLA.

"It's called the assassin bug," Truman explains. "Found in the cracks of mud houses."

"Oh," Daisy says, "then I gather it's not part of the insect population of Cambridge, Mass.?"

"Unlikely." Truman smiles. "In the interests of science, I feel obliged to inform you it's also called the kissing bug."

"That's a rather odd juxtaposition," Daisy says, "speaking se-mantically." She pulls the sweatshirt over her head. It falls to her knees. "I love it!" she cries.

"They only had extra large."

"Which makes it extra comfortable."

"It suits you. Beautiful," he says.

She beams. She twirls. Then she has a sudden thought. Is it a compliment to say you look beautiful tented in a sweatshirt that sticks a parasite on your chest? A parasite that bears the opposing names of *assassin* and *kissing* connoting murder and love? She stops herself. Why look a gift horse—a gift *bug*—in its *Triatoma infestans'* mouth? "My manners again. Would you like to take off your coat? Have a drink?"

"Better not." He surveys the room. He sweeps his arm dra-matically. "Everything's so cozy, so warm, it would be too easy for me to settle right in."

Daisy's confused. On the one hand she's created a welcoming environment. On the other, she's heard the warnings about no-see-ums in tropical paradises, those insects you can't recognize until they sting. At least her crumpling walls are of plaster and not of mud. And it's only dinner, she reminds herself.

"So what'll it be? Fancy or non?"

"Non. Anyplace I can wear my bug."

"Sushi bar or Mr. Bartley's Burger Cottage?"

"What is this, twenty questions? I'll give you one guess."

They find a table in the corner at Mr. Bartley's Burger Cottage. Daisy's chair is so close to the back wall it's impossible to angle her legs to avoid some contact with the length of Truman Wolff's imposing tibia.

Truman Wolff looks up at the poster of the young Elvis. Next to it, Humphrey Bogart teeters a cigarette at the side of his mouth. Truman Wolff laughs. "Let's enjoy the human contact and not worry about our interlocking appendages. You know," he says, as casually as if he's discussing the shaker of Parmesan cheese he's now chugging around the salt and peppers, "there's a parasite, the loa loa worm, that can enter the body, for example in the foot, then travel up the leg. . . ."

"Oh, dear," Daisy says.

"And if you're careful, you can catch it the exact moment it migrates across the eye."

Daisy shudders. She tries to imagine a worm wriggling across Truman's sea green eye. She concentrates on a silky eyelash the color of freshly tilled Nebraska earth.

"It's quite elegant really, the way it works. I'm rather fond of it."

"I'll take your word for it. I mean I hope that I can take your word, that I'll never have the actual experience myself."

"Unless you venture into the jungles. Or dine anymore at— whatever was the name of that restaurant?"

"The Sea of Japan."

"No wonder. One of the most polluted bodies of water on both hemispheres."

The waitress approaches their table. She gives Truman an

appraising, approving smile. She turns to Daisy. "Nice sweat-shirt," the waitress says, "though I pity whoever comes across that bug. A citation, for sure. You can count on it." She's a motherly woman with wide hips and upper arms that jiggle as she writes down the order for their root beer floats. Daisy glances around her. The other waitstaff could be this waitress's sisters and brothers. Real-looking people with bunions and bad backs and mortgages, as opposed to the starved actors-in-training who work at the Rialto restaurant.

Unlike the Rialto bar, she's comfortable here. And almost comfortable with Truman Wolff now that she's adjusted to their knees, which knock together with the rhythm of a pendulum. She orders the Alan Dershowitz. Truman, after some sallying back and forth between the Evander Holyfield and the Howard Stern, settles on the Seiji Ozawa.

"Make mine rare," Daisy instructs.

"If you don't mind a suggestion," Truman Wolff begins, "from a professional . . ."

Daisy is about to protest. She always gets her steaks pink, her tuna seared. When she grills hamburgers at home, the outsides are black, the insides just one pass beyond raw. "I can practically see the pulse," Sammy would cry. Then she thinks of Henry's ordeal after the Sea of Japan. His bathroom retching, which she had attributed to mere drunkenness. His IV dangling over his pale and suffering arm. The weakly beating pulse of his wrist, bruised where the tube went in. "Burn it to a crisp" is what she commands.

"Good girl," Truman Wolff cheers.

"Though Bartley's is such an institution, I can't imagine anyone ever got sick from their hamburgers or their onion rings. No place would have lasted so long without a reputation for purity," Daisy points out. "We had a neighbor who worked at Lamont Library and ate lunch at Bartley's every single day.

Same time, same table, same meal. He was partial to the Henry Kissinger. Even after Watergate."

Truman laughs.

Daisy brushes some crumbs from a previous diner's lunch off the tabletop. Now that she's become aware of the dangers out there, she'll pay more attention to cleanliness. She's always felt somewhat casual toward dirt. One of the things, ironically, that Henry liked about her. "Daisy doesn't sweat a little grime," Henry had boasted to a friend who was apologizing for a bathroom blitzed by his teenage sons. "In that respect, she's practically French." Though Daisy had felt complimented, she'd shuddered at the remembrance of smelly unisex bathrooms in French cafés with a drain in the floor and two disgusting wells where you placed your feet. Daisy pictures the toilet-paper slipcover that Jessica constructs before she deigns to sit. In France, half the time you don't even have the privilege of a toilet seat. Jessica's kitchen counters gleam. The spigots and knobs and cabinet pulls look like displays in the window of a fancy remodeling store. In contrast, not even a household pet would want to chew his Alpo on such a welcome mat to infestation as Daisy's kitchen linoleum.

Truman must be thinking along the same lines. But of course, infestations are probably always occupying his thoughts. "In the small New Hampshire town where I grew up, we had two Chinese restaurants, Sing's and Ming's," he confides. "Somehow a rumor got started that Sing's served rat meat. The health inspectors investigated and found no rodents of any sort. But it was too late. The dining rooms were empty. Two of the three waiters were forced to go back to their small villages in Taiwan. Sing's took out ads. Offered free meals. No customers."

"That's so sad," Daisy exclaims. "Once you get a bad reputation, it's impossible to live it down."

"Not always. The local branch of the AMA decided to hold its annual banquet there. All the doctors and their wives—the doctors and their *husbands,* these are modern times—got duded up and had themselves quite a feast. Business improved. Then it really took off when a customer confessed he'd been hired by Ming's to say, as it were, he smelled a rat. Ming's went into bankruptcy. Now the only chop suey joint in town, Sing's is so swamped the quality's declined. Sing's misses Ming's. These things happen when the balance is upset. When you tinker with what has been a very successful symbiotic relationship."

Daisy can't help but agree. You introduce a new element—France, Giselle, even a parasite or bacteria that makes you sick—and everything gets shaken up. Though not always in a bad way, Daisy figures, if you count someone like Truman Wolff as a new element. She studies the poster of Elvis. There's certainly a whole lot of shaking going on. She feels she's turned topsy-turvy inside a snow dome. She clings to the anchor of Truman's knees, which prop up her own.

Their food arrives. "Delicious," Truman Wolff approves.

"Yummy," Daisy agrees.

"Still, I must confess, I cut down on beef since all those stories about mad cow disease."

"It's *British* beef, not American," Daisy points out.

"Which is a solace. Though, of course, you and I would have expected mad cow disease to originate in France." Truman Wolff picks up an onion ring from a platter of them they've ordered to share. "A platter," he'd instructed the waitress, "lowercase."

Now he dangles the onion ring in front of Daisy's lips like a mother bird delivering its baby a worm. Daisy opens her mouth. She feels cared for, fussed over. It's almost a religious experience. Spiritual. As in ceremonies she's seen in Catholic and Episcopalian churches when somebody receives the host.

And she's transported—*transubstantiated*—when Truman Wolff accompanies this gesture with the incantatory words: "Tell me about your son."

She is off and running. The saga of Samuel Daniel Lewis from the moment she brought him home from the hospital to the moment she deposited him and his three milk cartons of CDs in his dormitory room.

To Truman Wolff's credit, his eyes never wander. He holds her gaze through this fascinating account—toilet training, Little League, the darnedest things this particular kid did say—even when the lettuce on his Seiji Ozawa starts falling out.

"And your daughter?" she asks at last.

"Phoebe," Truman intones as if that word alone has said it all. She's a dancer, beautiful, the wormless apple of her father's eye. Like Sammy, a college freshman studying chemistry.

"Pre-med?"

"That. Or theater. Her mother's quite the actress."

Daisy leans back in her chair so her head is flattened against the wall, where Elvis must be tapping his blue suede shoes in the vicinity of her center part. She looks around the room. Couples chat. Students fork French fries with one hand and with the other scribble in composition books. An off-duty cop flirts with an on-duty waitress. A professor and undergraduate discuss Kafka over coffee mugs. A plate of brownies sits between them. The student's head nods up and down as if bobbing on a string. The professor's hands trace circles in the air. Daisy hears the words "Gregor Samsa." She looks down at her sweatshirt; its bug could be, she supposes, Gregor Samsa's metamorphosis.

She turns toward the counter. By the cash register, a crowd waits for take-out orders. Two young people in down jackets pick up their brown bags. They start to leave. Each moves in an opposite direction, opening like a theater curtain to reveal the unmistakable back of Samuel Daniel Lewis. The very same

Samuel Daniel Lewis whose virtues Daisy has just been extolling to Truman Wolff. Daisy is about to cry out, to leap from her chair. Here he is in living breathing color, she will crow, the illustration to go along with her text. She is stopped by the sight of Sammy's arm slung over the shoulder of a rhinestone-studded jacket bearing the impossible-to-misdecipher label of Caterpillar Jeanswear. A golden ponytail pokes through a baseball cap, bisects the rhinestones, and sweeps Sammy's arm, which sports a shirt recently washed and folded by the loving hands of guess who.

"What's the matter, Daisy?" Truman Wolff asks with professional concern. "You've gone suddenly pale."

"It's Sammy." Daisy stammers. "Over there."

Truman Wolff turns in the direction of the cash register. At the same moment, the golden-ponytailed, Barry Sweiker–denimed young woman lifts an angelic profile to the chalkboard of daily specials.

"It's Phoebe!" Truman Wolff exclaims.

Immediately, Daisy and Truman Wolff reach for their menus and fold them out like screens to hide behind.

"You didn't tell me she was at Harvard," Daisy whispers.

"You didn't ask," Truman whispers back. "I try not to brag," he adds.

Is that a criticism? Daisy wonders. Has she been playing the my-son-at-Harvard record so much that it offends the ear? Or is it simply Truman Wolff's natural—and endearing—modesty? Before she can ponder this, along with the exact nature of her son's and Truman's daughter's relationship, at least one question is answered when Sammy leans over and gives Phoebe a long, hard movie-star kiss.

Daisy has a fleeting thought of Sammy's dislike of public displays of affection. "Oh, Ma, stop." He'd cringe. So much—*everything,* she realizes—depends on the circumstance.

Now Sammy takes his order of onion rings with their signature stains of delectable grease, and the two large cardboard containers of Coke. These are put into a handled shopping bag. Phoebe fishes her wallet out of the jeans jacket. She pays the cashier, dumps her change in the jar marked FOR TIPS. Why isn't Sammy treating? Daisy understands the rules of dating have changed. Should she offer to float Truman's Seiji Ozawa, her own Alan Dershowitz? Now that she's out in the world, she'd better learn its millennium etiquette. Who pays when and for what? What set of rules applies? She makes a note to ask Sammy, who, hip to hip with Phoebe, is hotfooting it through the door.

"Well," sighs Truman.

"Well," echoes Daisy.

They are like two stunned victims in the wake of a tornado. Turned upside down by forces beyond their control. Turned helpless onto their backs like Gregor Samsa. They struggle to get their bearings.

"It's not necessarily bad," Truman says at last.

"Not necessarily," Daisy concurs. She thinks—wisely—that now is not the time to tell him about the pink bikini underpants.

"Could even be an advantage," adds Truman, warming to his subject. "It's pretty logical once you think about it. Mutual attraction passing through the genes to the second generation."

Daisy supposes she should consider the scientific implications of Truman's statement, about whether there is a genetic marker for desire. When you dissect a worm, for instance, can you predict the worm it will be attracted to? But she's stuck on the words: mutual attraction.

Later, after coffee, a shared banana split, and conversation skirting the Sammy/Phoebe axis, Truman Wolff takes her home.

In front of Daisy's door, he turns to her. His face is shy. His bow tie is starting to come undone. She can smell mustard, onions, sauerkraut on his breath. "I had a really nice time."

"Me too."

"Can we do this again?"

"We'll see," she says. She pats her kissing bug. She nods. "Why not. I guess so. Yes."

Truman Wolff puts his hands on her shoulders. He leans over. He brushes his lips against the tip of her ear.

PART TWO

FRANCE NATIONALE
CHARLES DE GAULLE 2

9

A 421 FRANCE

The alarm rings at eight. Truman Wolff reaches over Daisy to her night table and presses the snooze button. He snuggles against her, then falls back asleep. Though Henry left her bed two years ago, Daisy still isn't used to having the alarm clock on her side. She rolls onto her back. She looks up at the ceiling. The plaster is cracked. A water stain bears the outline of a map of the continental United States. There are some black splotches that look like mold. In places, the paint is as crosshatched and peeling as a bad case of eczema.

She never noticed such things from the four-postered canopy she and Henry used to share. Reality was shrouded, like the netting overhead that, despite its holes, collected a marriage's worth of dust. When Truman Wolff moved in, he brought, as dowry, his bachelor's queen-size bed. The four-poster went in the basement, its sagging-in-the-middle mattress and sprung box spring put out for the trash. She was sure some student scavengers would grab it. Nobody did. It sat at the curb rejected even by the garbage composter until she called the city and arranged for the truck that collected old refrigerators to pick it up.

She and Truman made more changes. She shifted to the opposite side of the bed from where she'd slept for twenty years. She took over Henry's study. Truman turned the guest room into a home office, jettisoning more mattresses in favor of a futon that could accommodate a family of five. Truman's coffee grinder, his cappuccino machine, his canister of dark French roast, his nutmeg grater, his stainless-steel pitchers for steaming milk claimed space on the counter where once the toaster oven stood. His books filled the shelves empty of Henry's. His undershirts and boxer shorts stuffed the highboy's bottom three drawers, which had once contained a tangle of Henry's socks. His great-grandfather's battered leather chair now stood in the front hall, the receptacle for lost scarves and mismatched gloves.

Some changes, though, Daisy's too scared to make. Every so often—in the kitchen, at the foot of the bed, on the misted bathroom tiles—Truman gets down on one adorably dimpled knee. "Daisy, marry me," he pleads. "Daisy, Daisy, give me your answer, do," he sings.

Daisy's throat constricts. "Let's leave well enough alone," she'll say. "Don't upset the apple cart. Don't tempt the gods." A stream of clichés comes tripping off her tongue as if they've been queued up forever, waiting there. "Let's take a lesson from Ming's and Sing's," she reminds him. "We're great together like this. You're always telling me what happens in nature when the balance is skewed."

Daisy is anxious. She doesn't want to repeat her mistakes with Henry. The cocoon of marriage wrapped around her little family once meant so much to her that she hardly noticed, *refused* to notice, its unraveling from joy through mild discontent into unhappiness.

And now, because of what happened at the Sea of Japan, she's having a completely different reaction: Marriage is dangerous, too full of risks. Marriage, she's come to understand, offers up a false sense of security that makes the ultimate, inevitable betrayal excruciating. Right now in her Cambridge house life is as blissful with Truman as it was with Henry back in their student days. There's a lesson here she needs to learn: Things change. Mutate. What's good doesn't stay that way.

The radio blasts on again. Another sex scandal in Washington. The French are astonished by the sexual unsophistication of the American people, the Paris correspondent reports. Look at Mitterrand, he illustrates, a wife, a mistress, two sets of children, all at the funeral, all very civilized. The correspondent has an American voice, a radio-announcer-school-graduate's voice, but his indignant syllables betray the symptoms of incipient Francophilia. He sounds like Henry. She can picture the reporter's beret, the jaunty tie labeled Yves Saint Laurent. Though his American Puritanism might be too ingrained for the Gauloises, she can imagine a copy of *Le Monde* folded into his blazer's inside pocket. The French, he elaborates in a bored *comme il faut* voice, are amazed that Americans have any interest in the sexual peccadilloes of a politician. Is she mistaken or does he say pecca*dildo*? *Pecker*dillo? Is she simply a sex-mad American? Or has she just heard a closet sex-mad American make a Freudian slip?

Truman Wolff hears it too. He guffaws. He reaches over her and shuts off the radio. He slips the tape into the tape deck. It's a version of "Tapeworm of Love" sent to Truman's lab by an MIT band with the unlikely MIT-ish name of Honest Bob and the Factory-to-Dealer Incentives. Since he liberated it from the office last week, he's been playing it before they go to sleep and when they wake up. "Some aphrodisiac," she had laughed.

"Not if you really study it."

Now she listens to the lines that repetition has made her almost memorize: "I've got a tapeworm of love/I feed it daily but it isn't enough/I like the thing that it's a tapeworm of/It's a tapeworm of love. You might think I am crazy/But I like my parasite/I can feel it wiggle in me/Every time you hold me tight/They warned me about the steak tartare/They said I could get a disease/But I don't mind being ill so much/If I can have symptoms like these. . . . It's a welcome guest in/My intestine/I don't mind the things it makes me do/Each proglottid/That I've got is/Feeding on the love I feel for you. . . ." Together Daisy and Truman sing the refrain with voices that have caused them both to be cast into the back row of their separate junior high choruses and encouraged mostly to move their lips. Now Truman slides his hand to her breast. "Darling, Daisy," he whispers, and rolls on top of her.

After Truman leaves for work, Daisy pours herself a second cup of coffee. She pulls down the Marcella Hazan bought to replace *Mastering the Art of French Cooking,* volumes one and two, which Henry took as part of their post-divorce division of spoils. Sammy and Phoebe are coming for dinner tonight. At seven-thirty. After Truman's Italian class lets out.

She must admit that when Truman first told her he'd signed up for Introductory Italian, she was more than a little worried. "That's where all the trouble started in the first place," she cried, "when Henry took up French. What if history repeats itself?"

"History never exactly repeats itself. There are variations on a theme. Even a parasite continually adapts to changed circumstances."

She shook her head.

"Besides," he added as if the very words were self-explanatory, "it's *Italian,* not French."

Now Daisy leafs through Marcella Hazan's Tuscan specialties. There are almost as many steps here as there are in Julia Child's boeuf en daube. And some of the ingredients, the truffled oils, the buffalo mozzarella, the squid ink, the zucchini flowers, are not quite what you can grab from Star Market's shelves.

She puts the book away. She'll settle on her dependable lasagna. Easy-to-assemble comfort food for Sammy and Phoebe, who at Eliot House can't get lasagna like mother used to make. Either mother, Daisy corrects herself, remembering how Truman had once let slip that Phoebe's mother used to create her own pasta from scratch, drying it on a cat's cradle of string looped from kitchen cabinet handles to drawer pulls. "Before, of course," he added, "she went completely French."

"There are more ways to a man's heart," Truman had placated when she flung her box of generic-brand dried penne to the floor and started to stomp on it.

She thinks of Phoebe and Sammy living together since freshman year. Sort of living together. Both Phoebe and Sammy have been nominally assigned to suites with three other same-sex roommates on separate floors. Each suite consists of a common room and two bunk-bedded cubicles. In both his and hers, the beds have been dismantled and divided by heavily postered and graffiti-ed plywood walls; these multiply the opportunities for trysting while minimizing already minimal space. "Interesting," Truman mulled, lingering at the doorway to Phoebe's "room." Clearly there was accommodation for only one vertical human being. It was a leap of imagination to cast two horizontal bodies on the sliver of bed. "Watch out for splinters if you stretch," Truman warned.

On Daisy's own forays to Eliot House to deliver clean laundry, a batch of chocolate chip cookies, and the electric broom on sale at Dickson Brothers Hardware that she doubted would ever be taken from its box, she was constantly reminded how love could overcome geometry and geography. "You mean you and your lover's kids are lovers too?" one or another of Daisy's friends would ask in astonishment.

"Well, it *is* unusual," she'd reply, crossing her fingers, "but it seems to work." After the initial shock, she'll sometimes qualify. In truth, she's afraid the equation is a little too neat, the double pairs too symmetrical for nature, red in tooth and claw.

Now she puzzles over the kaleidoscope of relationships. Except for Phoebe and Sammy, who have been a cornerstone of stability in their ivied brick dorm, most of Harvard's undergrads have shifted, come together, separated like so many bits of tumbling colored glass. An unlucky-in-love Charlotte or Matthew will take to his or her bed, then a few days later rise to wash his or her hair. Somebody promising is waiting at the statue of John Harvard in the Yard. New plywood walls have gone up, new comforters thrown on beds to wrap new limbs. CDs vanish; others replace them with the constancy of dying and regenerating cells. Posters of up-to-the-minute media gurus cover the old staple-gunned holes of fading ex-favorites who have been ripped from the walls.

Yet Phoebe and Sammy seem so completely, so cutely, in love. The minute she thinks this, she starts to worry about broken hearts and broken promises. "Try not to fall in love with the girlfriends and boyfriends of your children," Jessica has told her. "When they break up, you're devastated too. It's like losing a child."

"But what if they don't break up?" Daisy had countered.

"They always break up," confirmed Jessica. "One or the other will find someone else."

Daisy had been about to refute Jessica's claim. Still, she couldn't come up with any examples to support her argument. It wasn't that there weren't any examples, she soothed herself, only that she couldn't retrieve them. A natural memory loss attributable to the declining hormones of middle age. Lately she's had trouble producing just the right glowing adjective to exalt a special on chicken legs in her community newsletter. *À la recherche de Frank Perdue,* she scribbled on her notepad, then crossed it out. Elitist. French. Two words practically interchangeable. Then her mind went blank. Maybe brain cells weren't dying off, but instead were so crowded together that it was standing room only inside her head; new information had to fight its way down the aisles.

Is Jessica right? she wonders now. Maybe it's only *young* love that's fragile, vulnerable to outside influences, easy to crack with a sudden smile, a new person in class, a different grin in the carrel next to you or across the table in the dining hall. Certainly age and experience have toughened her and Truman, made them resistant to new and exotic/erotic strains. Or maybe such new strains have trouble taking hold in the less juicy middle-aged.

Would marrying Truman be a way of buying extra insurance for additional coverage? A promissory note promising security? One thing Daisy knows: A wedding ring won't vanquish woes or other loves like a cross held in front of Dracula.

"Plus ça change, plus c'est la même," Henry would say.

Two years ago, Henry married Giselle. Daisy had picked Sammy up at the airport after a week of wedding festivities in the south of France. He handed her a bag from the tax-free store at Charles de Gaulle that contained Arpege. "They were out of Joy," he'd said.

"Tell me everything," she had implored. *Nothing good* had been her hope.

"Mom," he'd sighed. He was wearing a T-shirt that read SORBONNE, but she noted with relief his Red Sox cap. "You're not supposed to ask such questions. You who've read all those Ann Landers kinds of books on how to behave with the children of divorce."

"I know," she'd said. "But tell me anyway."

He told her anyway. Henry and Giselle had been married at the *mairie* in the village of Giselle's parents' country house.

"Picturesque?" Daisy had asked.

"Very," Sammy apologized. "There was a reception at the local restaurant called Les Pommes d'Amour."

"Love apples," Daisy translated. "That's what we call the extra flesh around the hips."

"That's love *handles*," Sammy corrected. "According to Jessica, that's why she left husband number two."

"Yes, well, Jessica always was unduly influenced by looks. The food?"

"Not bad."

"Giselle's dress?"

"Okay."

"Giselle's parents?"

"Nice enough."

"Grandma?"

"Typical Lillian."

She ventured another try. "The weather?"

Sammy shook his head. "Sunny. We ate outside." If he could have made it rain, his expression said, he would have out of loyalty.

Now Daisy thinks back to her own wedding. On the designated day, Hurricane Gladys attacked. Both sets of parents were stranded at airports waiting for connecting planes that were canceled. "We'll toast you with champagne at half past four," Daisy's father had called from the airport bar. Perhaps it was a bad connection, but her father's voice sounded as if he had already started celebrating. In the background she could hear her mother's sobs. "Your mother is distraught," said Daisy's father, pronouncing it "dishtraught" and exuding jollity.

Lillian had blamed Henry for bad planning. "You're a scientist," she accused. "Couldn't you have predicted the weather?"

"I'm in computers, Mom. Not meteorology."

The caterers were late. Trees and telephone poles were downed in the storm, they pleaded. Which may have accounted for the fact that the salmon was off.

After the reception, the guests threw rice as Daisy and Henry ran to their car. The rice got wet, plumped up, turned sticky, and glued itself to their hair and shoulders. Though Daisy's going-away suit stayed pale cream even drenched, Henry's charcoal gray sharkskin looked like the drop-off station for a mutant form of dandruff. "Tsk, tsk," clucked one of the wedding guests as Henry brushed at his lapels. "People should throw rose petals. Rice will choke the birds."

Daisy had shuddered. She was superstitious about birds. Ever since one had flown through an attic window, battered itself against the walls trying to get out, and had fallen dead onto the Christopher Robin quilt of her childhood trundle. Years later, a college friend from India had told her that a bird inside the house was a bad omen.

"Did they throw rice?" she asked Sammy.

"Rose petals," he replied.

Now Daisy thinks of the auspicious circumstances of Henry's wedding to Giselle compared to her own. Another reason to refuse Truman's proposals. You can't control the paths of storms, the flight paths of birds, the path a black cat might cross as you are setting off for your honeymoon. How could she tell if the stars were aligned the moment Truman dropped to his knee?

Through Sammy, she had sent the newlyweds her best wishes, though not without a pang. More pangs came when, ten months later, Giselle gave birth to Jean and Jeanne, red-headed twins.

They live in Lexington now, easier for family life Henry has said, plus it's closer to L'École Bilingue where Jean and Jeanne have been enrolled from the moment their first baby teeth poked through their pink baby gums.

Sammy and Phoebe visit them often. Over time and through watchful waiting—not direct cross-examination—Daisy has elicited these facts: The curtains and upholstery are Pierre Deux. The dishes, bought at the Pottery Barn. Tins of foie gras from Strasbourg circle generic-brand canned peas from Star. Giselle's mother sends sachets of dried lavender and little *bouquets garnis* in their cheesecloth sacks. The house is a mess, baby paraphernalia strewn everywhere on the reproduction Aubussons. Henry hasn't got around to unpacking his books. The twins are spoiled rotten. Jeanne has constant sieges of impetigo. Jean can't sit still. They whisper about learning disabilities or an attention deficit. Giselle's nails are ragged. Her tights have holes in them. They rarely go out. On the weekends they watch Jerry Lewis videos.

For a second, these bulletins from the enemy camp make Daisy glad. And then she hates herself.

Daisy pours another cup of coffee and opens to the Metro section of the *Globe*. A man has been arrested for spraypainting spiders on somebody's car. An MIT student tried to ex out the Smoots on the Harvard Bridge. The Kennedy School has given a semester's appointment to a bigwig from Indonesia.

She turns to Ann Landers, who is advising Unhappily Married in Peoria to get counseling.

The phone rings. It's probably Truman reminding her he'll pick up the focaccia on his way home from Italian class.

"It's Elizabeth Malcolm," the voice announces. "I expect you know why I'm calling."

"I can guess," Daisy says.

"You've had a two-year hiatus. But the time's up. You *are* our award winners. So now I'm calling to see if you'll be a host family again."

Daisy pauses. "Our circumstances have changed," she begins.

"I know all about Henry and—well . . ." For a second Daisy wonders if Elizabeth Malcolm and the Harvard International Office might feel responsible for the end of her marriage, feel guilty about introducing the bacteria that spread the disease. Maybe this is a common problem. Maybe other host families have been broken up by the student they were host family to. Perhaps there are laws in place about sexual congress between hosts and hostees.

These thoughts are underscored by the way Elizabeth Malcolm spits out "Giselle" as if she is plowing right through a barricade. "I've just placed a French student with them. Someone from the Ed School. It'll be good for the twins. With the language, I mean."

"We don't have the same needs here," Daisy protests. "Besides"—she picks her words carefully—"I don't think I'm exactly the exemplary host family you're looking for. I'm living with someone, but we're not officially hitched. I'm living in *sin,*" she adds for emphasis.

"Which is exactly what I want!"

"Sin?"

"Of course not. The word is irrelevant. What constitutes a

family has changed. Especially in this country, though I dare-say abroad as well. There's no longer a conventional model. I think our students are very much aware of this and would be extremely receptive to being included in an alternative arrangement."

Daisy focuses on "alternative arrangement." She goes on to alternative lifestyle. She supposes that's what her midwestern relatives might consider her arrangement with Truman to be. She thinks of communes, of mattresses on the floor and home-made candles stuck into jelly jars, of sticks of incense burning on a tabletop. She thinks of the various configurations of cou-pledom: same-sex, no-sex, May-December, December-May, mixed-race, mixed-religion, commuter marriages, jailhouse marriages, marriages of convenience, marriages of inconve-nience, separate houses, separate tables, separate bedrooms. In comparison, she and Truman are sadly conventional. She feels sorry for Elizabeth Malcolm: She can produce neither a *Leave It to Beaver* American family nor an off-the-wall alternative one.

And because she feels sorry for Elizabeth, she says yes.

"I knew I could count on you," Elizabeth croons. "We have somebody from Azerbaijan. Doing an LL.M. at the law school. He's come from a situation of incredible and constantly shift-ing strife." She stresses the word "strife."

What is the message here, Daisy wonders, that someone in the middle of ethnic conflict would have no trouble sorting out the colliding platelets of her family life?

"His name is Fuck Hard," Elizabeth goes on.

Daisy gulps. "I beg your pardon?"

"I know. I know. Always the American dirty mind."

"Which is kind of inevitable," Daisy ventures, "given—"

"It's spelled F-a-k-h-a-r-d," Elizabeth interrupts. "He'll be a fascinating student."

"Of that I'm sure. But I'll have to pass. The name alone."

Elizabeth sighs. Although Daisy is spared the a-rose-by-any-other-name, one-culture's-swear-is-another-culture's-badge-of-honor speech, she hears it still in Elizabeth's exhaled, disappointed breath. "Well, then, do you have a particular preference for country of origin?"

Daisy considers. She knows she's let Elizabeth down. All the ends-of-the-earth places that have been flashing from the six o'clock news assault her: the war-torn Middle East, disease-ridden Africa, typhooned and flooded Bangladesh, the politically stressed and economically depressed former Soviet republics, terrorized Algeria, rioting Indonesia, impoverished Haiti, ethnically fractured Bosnia. Who could be more grateful for the warmth of an American hearth, the bounty of an American table? She and Truman have such privilege to offer the underprivileged, a window onto the developed world for those exiles from the undeveloped one. God knows, Truman might even meet up with some new and exotic parasite. She weighs this. Then says, "Italy."

"If that's what you want," Elizabeth Malcolm grunts, disapproval oozing from her every syllable. "I'll get to work on it."

Daisy is about to hang up when she has a sudden vision of Sophia Loren. The vision is so real she can see one of those movies with Marcello Mastroianni projected on her refrigerator door. Sophia Loren's breasts heave; her lips open; Daisy can just make out the glistening red tip of her tongue. "This time," she says, "we'll request a young man."

Sammy, Phoebe, Truman arrive all at once at the front door. Truman carries the focaccia. Sammy totes his laundry bag. Phoebe extends a wilted, straggly bouquet. "These were the last ones at the supermarket," she apologizes.

"A little water and they'll perk right up," Daisy says. "Did you get them at the Evergood?"

Phoebe nods.

"Remember, Sammy?" Daisy asks.

"Mom . . ." Sammy warns.

"My lips are sealed," Daisy promises. It was the seventh-grade dance. By the time Sammy had got around to asking his number one and two choices, they had already accepted the more prompt invitations of other admirers. At the eleventh hour, a classmate looking for better offers and finding none agreed to go with him. She wouldn't ordinarily have accepted so late an invitation, she had explained, except for her mother's financial sacrifice to transform a duckling into a swan. While his friends bore beribboned florists' boxes nestling corsages of tea roses, Sammy had stopped at the Evergood for the last wilted bouquet of orphaned flowers. These he had fastened with rubber bands, tin foil, a few garden chives as greenery. When he tried to attach this creation onto his date's shoulder, he stabbed her with a safety pin. Blood spotted the pink taffeta. "Cheapskate!" she had exclaimed and refused even one dance with him. Later she sent the cleaning bill.

"I think Sammy told me this story once," Phoebe admits.

"Never on my life," Sammy protests.

"You probably had too much to drink," Phoebe suggests.

Sammy looks at Daisy. "Not I," he says. "It was junior high!"

"My very point. You should have seen *my* junior high."

Truman knits his brows. "What *about* your junior high, Phoebe?" he asks.

"You know," Daisy says. "I went to junior high myself. I wouldn't live through that again for anything."

"Me neither," agrees Truman, "though I was essentially out of it."

"Why does this not surprise me, Dad?" Phoebe asks. She turns to Daisy. "I think she should have appreciated Sammy's originality," Phoebe adds. And Daisy is touched by her loyalty.

In the kitchen, Daisy puts the flowers in a vase. She pours in water. The flowers don't perk up but droop dispiritedly over the rim like a yellowing fringe. Daisy sets them in the center of the table anyway. She's the kind of mother who frames her child's fingerpainted squibbles, who places his kindergarten twisted lumps of clay next to her Staffordshire.

Phoebe sits between Sammy and Truman. She and Sammy lean into each other the way lovers do. He brushes a strand of hair away from her eye. She straightens his collar. Daisy's heart bursts. If Sammy made a wilted corsage for Phoebe, Daisy is sure that Phoebe would wear it with absolute pride. Will this be a lasting love? she wonders.

The lasagna is only slightly overcooked, the cheese burned only in the little circles where it started to bubble. She cuts the lasagna in large squares for Sammy and Phoebe—after all she did go not just to junior high but to college once—smaller ones for her and Truman. She tosses the salad, slices the focaccia. Truman pours the wine. "How's school?" he asks.

"The usual," Sammy says.

Daisy, of course, wants to ask what does the usual mean. But she holds back. She is, after all, the mother of a young adult, even though he looks no older than the thirteen-year-old of the wilted bouquet and the Clearasil-ed chin. Even though he's a cohabiter. Even though she and Henry were addressing wedding invitations at about his age.

"We could ask you the same, Dad," Phoebe says.

"That's right," Daisy jumps in. "How did Italian class go today?"

Truman leans back and sips the wine. He tears off a piece of bread. He studies it. He turns it over and over like a naturalist with a fascinating specimen. "It must be a right brain–left brain kind of thing, but I'm terrible at languages."

Daisy smiles. She can't imagine Henry ever admitting he was terrible at anything.

"Me too," Sammy says. "In fact I've given up French."

In spite of herself, Daisy is startled. It's not as if he's confessing he's given up hamburgers, or rock and roll. It's not as if he needs a permission slip from Mom to be excused from PE. French is only a language. And in the context of her family, a rather loaded one. Certainly a mastery of English is more than enough.

Sammy must see the surprise on her face, because he says, "I know. I know. Dad is really pissed. I think he takes it personally. Like an insult to Giselle. Like my communication with Jean and Jeanne—'your *frère et soeur*' Dad calls them— will be limited. Like they're really going to talk only French at home. Give me a break. How French can they be, born here at Brigham and Women's?"

"Actually," Truman points out, "they probably have dual citizenship since their mother is a native of France."

"Whatever." Sammy shrugs. "I've already fulfilled the language requirement and there's other stuff I want to take. Why study something when you're bad at it?"

"The very question I ask myself," Truman declares.

"Daisy, this lasagna is really excellent." Phoebe scoops up another gargantuan slice. Daisy loves that Phoebe is a hearty eater, that she's not one of those parsley-sprig-and-boutique-water kind of college girls. That as a child of divorce, as a child of an absent mother who ran off to Colorado with a

French chef even, she has not succumbed to the dime-a-dozen eating disorders she might be psychologically profiled for. Of course, it helps to have your Scarlett O'Hara waist sashed by a full magnetic field.

"What a treat," Phoebe goes on. "The lasagna they serve at school would be the perfect subject for Dad to investigate."

"Yes, a study of the parasites in the Harvard dining halls. That would certainly set the scientific community on end," Sammy joins in.

"Not to mention hordes of parents storming the dean's office to rescue their kids from dysentery," Phoebe adds.

"And collecting evidence for a class-action lawsuit," chuckles Sammy.

"Actually, you've raised an interesting topic." Truman strokes his chin. "Dining halls and cafeterias, with their steam tables, their salad bars—"

"Dad, lighten up," Phoebe cries.

"Provide just the right sort of open environment for—"

"Dad!"

"Pathogens of the—"

"Truman, they're just joking," Daisy feels the need to instruct.

The phone rings. Sammy digs through platters and pans until he finds the cordless under a fish-shaped pot holder whose dorsal fin has been singed into a threadbare blackened crest. "Lewis slash Wolff residence," he announces.

He listens. He roots for crumbs in the lasagna pan. He licks his fingers. He frowns in concentration. "Livio?" he says. "I'm sorry," he adds in his best English-as-a second-language voice, "but there's no Tancredi here."

"I'm afraid there is." Truman jumps up from the table and grabs the phone. His expression is rueful. He clears his throat. *"Buona notte,"* he says. He pauses. *"Ciao,"* he embellishes.

Daisy, Sammy, and Phoebe watch him with an air of expectancy. Could Elizabeth Malcolm at the international office have found an Italian student for them so quickly in the interval between cocktails and dessert?

The pause stretches to infinity. Truman turns his back to them. He hunches over the phone like a spy spinning a plot of nuclear sabotage. *"Si,"* he says. More silence. Then, *"Si,"* he whispers again.

Time passes. Truman seems to writhe as if he is contorted with pain. *"Che bella giornata"* he finally manages to get out, each word wrenched from him with the agony of an extracted wisdom tooth.

What is going on? Daisy wonders. What is this code?

"Si! Si! Si!" erupts at last like the grand finale of a fireworks display after a bunch of duds. *"Buona notte. Buona notte. Ciao. Ciao."* He puts down the phone. He tucks it back under the fish pot holder as if that's its power source. He turns toward the three quizzical faces raised up to him.

His own face is red. Through both exertion and embarrassment, Daisy assesses. He sinks back into his chair. "That was Livia," he declares as if the words are self-explanatory.

"Who seemed to be calling for someone named Tancredi. Who was garbling a language that didn't seem to be anybody's native tongue," Sammy persists.

Truman laughs. "Boy, wasn't it ever," he exclaims.

"And Tancredi?" Phoebe prompts.

"Tancredi is"—he stops—"yours truly," he admits with a whistle of breath that could be relief.

Some obscure parasitical reference here? Some inside joke? "I still don't get it," Daisy says.

Surprising Truman, who looks as if he's given the lecture and all the students should feel both instructed and satisfied.

But he is a patient man. "It's Italian class," he explains.

"We're all supposed to choose a partner and talk nightly, in Italian, on the telephone."

"And you chose this Livio? A man I gather rather low down on the chain of fluency?"

"Actually it's Livia," he says, emphasizing the *a*. "She's a solid-state physicist and equally inept. We need to be paired with people at the same level of ability," he elaborates.

And there's no dumb student who's a male? Daisy wants to ask. Instead she nods. Truman and Livia are the last two to be chosen for the team, the bottom two in the slowest reading group. She reminds herself of the shining scientific star she's hitched her own star to. A man who walks the corridors of Harvard Medical School like a god and the halls of Harvard night school as a near illiterate. "About the Tancredi?" she asks.

"Livia is Lurleen Liverman-Goldberg. She has one of those hyphenated last names that feminist mothers insist upon."

Daisy is familiar with that generation of children bearing the hyphenated names their feminist mothers insisted on. She can do the arithmetic. She calculates that Livia must be considerably younger than herself, the product of a non-bra-burning, Tupperware-distributing mom. But she knows enough not to say anything. She understands that just because Henry went a particular route, lightning doesn't strike in the same place twice. The man in her bed is the man at her table. If she's careful, there's no reason things won't stay that way.

Truman goes on, "So they call her Livia Monte D'Oro. Wolff is easy—Lupo—but just like there's no Italian equivalent of Lurleen, there's no Italian equivalent of Truman. I chose Tancredi. I saw the opera once."

"I like it," Daisy says. "Tancredi, Tancredi," she sounds out. It trips off her tongue as if it's always been sitting there.

Truman reaches for her hand. "I knew you would," he says.

*   *   *

After Phoebe and Sammy take their foil-wrapped packages of leftovers and freshly folded laundry and head back to the dorm, Truman and Daisy decide to leave the dishes and go to bed. Maybe it's the influence of Italian, the fact that Truman has a language partner called Livia who could just as well be Livio for all he cares, maybe it's the name Tancredi, maybe it's because the kids (who will always be kids as well as young adults) are out of the house, maybe a combination of all four, but Daisy is sure they have never made love more operatically. She feels the swell of the orchestra, the aria, the chorus of voices raised. Truman's hands beat amazing rhythms on her breasts, on her thighs. Together they rise in crescendo, make an adagio descent. "Darling Daisy," Truman sighs, "please marry me."

This is the second time he's asked this month, but Daisy is not about to point this out. For a minute she's tempted, caught off balance by a good dinner, by great sex. She catches herself. Who, after all, but Daisy Lewis has a better command of the fact that marriage is not a vaccination against the strains of Giselles or Livias or any other unwelcome varieties? "Let's stay like this," she whispers into an ear as pink and delicate as one of nature's perfect shells.

"We can't always stay like this," Truman murmurs with the *andante doloroso* of an opera's lament.

Something wakes Daisy in the middle of the night. Squirrels in the walls? A siren screeching outside in the street? She goes into the bathroom. She pours herself a glass of water. She smears cold cream under her eyes and at the base of her neck. She sits on the toilet. She picks up a *Harvard Gazette* rolled in the basket filled with magazines and joke books for short-term and long-term bathroom tenancy. KENNEDY SCHOOL ENGAGES INDONESIAN HIGHER-UP proclaims the headline. DIGNITARY TO

OFFER SEMESTER'S SEMINAR is written below in slightly smaller type. Daisy studies the photograph of a gray-haired distinguished man wearing a bespoke suit. Her eyes move to the caption underneath. *Pilombaya,* Daisy reads.

FRANCE NATIONALE
CHARLES DE GAULLE 2
10
A 421 FRANCE

The invitation comes in the mail. It's addressed to Mr. and Mrs. Henry Lewis by a calligraphic hand and on stiff wedding stock bearing the Harvard seal. A reception for Pilombaya, former Harvard student, now minister of finance, a member of his country's cabinet. On the bottom is scrawled in ink the color of royalty, the thickness of blue blood, *Please bring the whole Lewis family. Very truly yours, P.*

Daisy studies the confident script, firm strokes slanting to the right and curling upward, the large emphatic *P.* From the bathroom, she fishes out the *Harvard Gazette* from under a pile of medical journals and the *New York Review of Books.* It's hard to square the photograph of this titan of his government's cabinet, his strong masculine handwriting, with the mothball-smelling, body-parts-jiggling, handheld calculator-craving Pilombaya of all those years ago. The VIP shown here is probably chauffeured to work every day in a silver Rolls-Royce fitted with every gadget in the universe: TV, phone, microwave, refrigerator, surround sound, a heating system to warm your toes and cool your brow.

Daisy looks into the mirror that hangs over the hall table. She studies her own brow. How will Pilombaya fit the face of a twenty-two-year-old Daisy crazy in love with Henry and living in sin in Harvard married-student housing with the forty-four-year-old Daisy maturely in love with Truman Wolff and living in sin in the Cambridge Victorian that witnessed the death of her marriage and the seeds of Henry's new one? The hall is dark. The fan-shaped window over the door emits a gray light as furled and dense as cigarette smoke. In such a light, Daisy can see the face of her youth. And over it, like the artist painting on top of an earlier portrait, lies the less dewy face of Daisy in her middle years.

She pushes away three unmatched gloves and sinks into Truman's great-grandfather's chair. Its springs creak. Its angle is oddly pitched. It has the cracked leather of old skin. When she rubs her hand along the arm, pieces flake off. She can identify. What the hell is *the whole Lewis family?* Immediate? Extended? Intergenerational? She, Henry, and Sammy? Truman and Phoebe? Giselle, Jean, and Jeanne? The unnamed Italian man she and Truman are host family to? The unnamed French woman assigned to Henry and Giselle? The conventional RSVP can't begin to circumscribe such shifting and expanding combinations.

Daisy picks up the invitation. She goes to the telephone. She dials the number listed for replies. "I'm calling to accept the invitation for the reception for Pilombaya," she says to the all-business no-nonsense voice—female—that answers the phone.

"Name?"

"Lewis."

"Number?"

"You mean telephone?"

"No, number in party."

"Well, that's the problem," Daisy confides.

The woman on the end of the telephone is clearly not interested in the problem. "Which is in the nature of what?" she snorts.

"In the nature of," Daisy sputters, "how many of us there are."

"And?"

"And . . . it's complicated. It could be as few as two, as many as . . ." Daisy decides to eliminate Jean and Jeanne on the strictly nonjudgmental basis of age. She does a quick calculation. "As many as six."

The woman coughs. She rustles a few papers. In the background, phones ring, faxes whir. Daisy can hear the scrape of chair legs, the banging of drawers. Clearly this woman has more important things to do, these sounds proclaim. As does her voice when she says, "General Pilombaya has left instructions to include the whole lot of you." The way she talks, she might as well be saying, You bunch of bums, whom, if it were up to me, I would never invite. "So shall I put down six?"

"Yes, but . . ."

"But?"

"But I can't speak for all of them. Some of them are at a different address."

"I see," she says. "Well if you can give me that address, I'll stick another invitation in the mail for them."

"Mr. and Mrs. Henry Lewis," Daisy begins.

"Whom, if I'm not mistaken, we already have on our list of guests."

"This is another Mr. and Mrs. Henry Lewis." Daisy's glad it's not an uncommon name. There are probably dozens of Mr. and Mrs. Henry Lewises in the greater Boston area. She's released from the kind of explanation she'd have to make if there were, say, two sets of Mr. and Mrs. Mortimer Quizenberry. Or two sets of Mr. and Mrs. Truman Wolff. Still, she feels a stab of feminist anger. Why couldn't Giselle have hyphenated her name to distinguish her from Daisy, who, both generationally and as wife number one, has first dibs on the name in its unadulterated form? What's more, Henry Guerard-Lewis would be just the ticket for a die-hard Francophile.

"Mr. and Mrs. Henry Lewis's address is?"

Daisy rattles it off. She hangs up the phone. She congratulates herself for being so fair. Twenty years before, she and Henry shared Pilombaya. Twenty years later, they should share him still. As soon as she thinks of Pilombaya, she hears the words "General Pilombaya," which only now does she begin to register.

She looks again at Pilombaya's photograph. No medals band his chest. No epaulets drape his shoulders. His suit is plain. He wears no hat. No Indonesian equivalent of an eagle pins his tie. No Indonesian equivalent of the Croix de Guerre thrusts from his lapel. Is he in mufti for Harvard, while in his own country he dons the uniform of a dictator?

This sets up a new series of worries. Is he a good guy or a bad guy? She thinks of the political upheavals at Harvard in the seventies. The constant chant, the constant challenge of what side were you on. Is having hosted a general, who was not a general then, still a blight of political incorrectness retroactively?

She drives to Star Market, where she thinks she'd better put in a few hours at work. Since she and Truman have been living together, she's adopted the habit of answering complaints and composing her newsletter at home, then faxing them in. She writes in bed on a clipboard and with the Magic Markers she keeps in her night-table drawer. She props her head against the pillows, wraps herself in the sheets. These are usually rumpled and tangy with the smell of late-night and early-morning sex. She gets her best inspiration, she tells Truman, on first awakening. She has read somewhere that this transition time between unconsciousness and consciousness is the hour of peak creativity. She feels guilty about appropriating this for herself since she's fairly sure peak creativity applies not to those Magic-Markering marketing newsletters but to novelists toiling in the realm of great literature. Which, she has to admit, in Truman's besotted eyes, means her. He delights in her every syllable. He pronounces her a genius of the turned phrase. The architect of the apt adjective. "You're the Dorothy Parker of fruit!" he's said to her. "Star's star ombudsman!"

She feels like a fraud. To justify his vision of her, she should be writing the perfect rondel, the pithiest haiku. In her book, to be the Dorothy Parker of fruit isn't quite the compliment he insists it is. Her job doesn't *really* contribute to others the way the food bank did, or enrich society with the power of art. Continents away from Truman's cutting-edge science, community relations is more the edgy cutting down of words to promote the largest number of mostly unnecessary consumer goods. To placate the dissatisfied, to soothe them enough to get them to come back into the store and empty their pocketbooks.

To be a lover does one need to be blinded by love? In bed, Truman itemizes her virtues the way he once ticked off the pestilences that fell on the Egyptians: beauty, brilliance, grace, creativity, sexiness, exemplary motherhood. Some nights he adds her cooking, her driving skills, the way she can touch her nose with the tip of her tongue, pound a nail straight into its stud. You're gilding the lily, she tells him.

"The daisy," he corrects.

She, on the other hand, sees Truman through the eye of the more perceptive sex. That Truman is—so far—pretty terrific is a conclusion based on her superior female observational skills.

But if I'm so terrific, she almost hears him ask, why won't you marry me?

She parks her car, nipping a stranded shopping cart. This careens into a woman carrying two bags of kitty litter and a six-pack mix of Dr. Pepper and Orange Crush. The woman drops a bag of kitty litter, which tears against the shopping cart. The kitty litter starts to seep out like the sand funneled through an hourglass measurer. Daisy gets out of the car and runs over to the woman. "I'm so sorry," she exclaims. She picks up the bag. She tips it rightside up. Kitty litter pours onto her jacket. "Let me go inside and get you another one."

Three purple Velcro rollers crest the woman's hair. She's wearing a purple nylon jacket with lipstick to match. She has a defeated-looking face, eyes turned down at the corners, a capillaried nose. Daisy pictures her at home with her cats; sliced bologna fills her refrigerator; in the freezer sit frozen chicken fricassee dinners caked with ice.

"Don't bother," the woman says. She points to the purple Velcro rollers. "No time. Got me a date." She hoists the kitty litter over her shoulder and stomps off, leaving a Hansel and Gretel trail. When she reaches her car, a BMW, she turns back. "Have a good day," she says, flashing the kind of smile you see on a member of a cult.

So far Daisy has not been having a good day. This is confirmed when she winds through the meat lockers to her office to find Billy, Jimmy, and Bernie sitting at her bridge-table desk shuffling decks of cards. "Well, look what the cat dragged in," says Bernie, not the most felicitous phrase for one whose jacket is littered with kitty litter.

"Long time no see," says Jimmy, eyes fixed on his hand.

"Where you been?" asks Billy. "What's that stuff all over you? You look just terrible."

Clearly Billy is not from the Truman Wolff school of compliments. "Thanks," Daisy says.

Billy waves a jack of clubs. "Don't mention it."

Daisy surveys her office, which looks as if it's been captured by an invading army. Bernie's bowl of M&M's stands smack in the middle of her table. Her jarful of sharpened pencils is thinned out, the points blunt or broken, the erasers chewed off. From the wall, new half-naked ladies part their come-hither lips. One is tacked over Sammy. Another curtains Bernie's long-suffering Doris and three-quarters of their grandkids. The room smells of cigarettes dangling from two of their three mouths, of rancid fat, of fresh-cut meat, of cold coffee left around too long in cracked and mottled mugs. Fury starts in the pit of Daisy's stomach and rises to her mouth. "You've taken over my office!" she shouts.

"Not that you're ever here," Billy points out.

"Especially now that you're *faxing,*" adds Jimmy.

"Faxing!" repeats Bernie. And they laugh with the laughs of men who have Dorises at home and Cindis and Mitzis on their walls at work.

But then Bernie must have second thoughts, because he turns to Daisy. "You want we should clean this up for you, kid?" he asks.

Daisy remembers when she was pregnant with Sammy; she and Henry were visiting graduate student friends at Berkeley who unrolled two futons for them, one thick, one thin. As a concession to her pregnancy, she claimed the thicker one. When she came back from the bathroom in the middle of the night, Henry had shifted onto her mattress. No matter how she kicked and shook him, he wouldn't stir. She tossed and turned like the princess on the pea, the concrete-slab floors pushing into her ribs. In the morning, Henry had protested total innocence. "I'm a heavy sleeper," he'd said. "I just rolled onto your mattress by accident."

Nothing is an accident, Daisy knows. Truman tells her that science and nature are all part of a grand plan. Sammy tells her that according to his psychology text, everything has a meaning, everything is ordained.

But even if everything is ordained, you still have to fight for what is yours. Parents boss; husbands control; children demand. Your territory is always being encroached upon. No matter how hard you protect your own space, somebody on the outside is always trying to tear down your wall, penetrate your fort. She thinks of Truman on bended knee.

Now Daisy surveys her office. Sometimes, however, the fort isn't worth protecting at all costs. At any cost. The table is rickety; one leg is bound with tape. The walls are stained. It's hard to block out the sounds of cleavers hitting butcher block, of freezer doors banging, of clattering shopping carts. A cubbyhole behind the meat lockers is not exactly a corner office overlooking Central Park. You need to pick your fights, both Henry and Truman, in different decades, in different contexts, have advised.

"So Daisy," Bernie asks, from behind his fan of cards, "you want us to get out of here?"

"No, stay. I can work just as well—even better—from home," she says.

"Especially with your fax," Jimmy says.

"Though I'm sure you miss having us boys around," Billy adds.

Bernie puts his cards facedown on the table. "Don't peek at them," he warns Billy and Jimmy. "Follow me," he orders Daisy.

Daisy follows him. He goes to a counter where lamb chops lie on unfurled Saran Wrap in neat rows. Daisy thinks of those waxed-paper rolls dotted with little round candies that were so popular in elementary school. She used to peel them off, sometimes in symmetrical stripes, sometimes at random, depending on her mood.

Bernie peels off three fat lamb chops. Wraps them carefully, ties them up with butcher's string, though this seems an unnecessary flourish given the tight swaddles of Saran. He hands them to her. "By way of apology," he says. "For you, your hubby, and the kid."

Daisy is about to correct him on the hubby part, then stops herself. After all, certain words are only technical. Does Doris call Bernie hubby? Is Doris to Bernie the little wife? Words of honor, of respect no matter how many cheesy-looking pinups you have lying around the place. If Doris visits Bernie at work, Daisy's never seen her. Maybe Doris never lets Bernie into the kitchen except to stock it with leftover meat. But she's only accepting lamb chops, not writing a thesis on family relationships, she reminds herself. "Thank you, Bernie," she manages.

She drives to Harvard Square. She has to pick up the cleaning, drop Truman's watch off to be repaired. Her red Magic Marker's dried up, the green is getting thin. Now that she's working more from home, she'll have to lay in more office supplies. She needs paper clips, Scotch tape, folders for the files she plans to organize. Post-its on which she can scribble reminders to organize her files. She pulls into the For Clergy Only parking space without a second thought. It's amazing how the constant repetition of a crime numbs guilt. She wears the blinders of a recidivist.

She tucks the lamb chops under the seat, out of the sun. It's cold enough that an hour in the car won't breed any bad bugs. She wonders if lamb can grow salmonella the way chicken does. Or does each brand of meat or poultry give birth to its own genetically unique bacteria, like mad cow disease in British beef?

She makes a note to ask Truman. She smiles. She's lucky to have Truman to ask such questions of.

In the stationery store she finds Post-its the color of Granny Smiths and of Dubble Bubble bubble gum. She adds a purple Magic Marker and a shocking pink. The folders come in royal blue, orange, and yellow. She buys four of each. She thinks of the color of meat, of chicken, of milky pounded veal. Ground beef, speckled sausages. Drab like the walls that surround the butcher's enclave, like the standard-issue gray metal furniture, like the tan paper that wraps the chicken breasts. She supposes Sammy, with the knowledge of a semester's worth of Intro to Psych, might say she's overcompensating. Buying apple green Post-its to leave your past behind. Cohabiting with Truman Wolff as a compensatory reaction to having cohabited with Henry Lewis.

She walks down Mass Ave. In one hand, she swings shopping bags. In the other, she carries a shirt professionally cleaned of its lasagna stains. She lifts its hanger a little so the plastic doesn't sweep along the pavement bricks. She is just past Holyoke Center, which contains the Harvard International Office, when she decides to stop. They have a good bathroom. Clean, nicely lit, plenty of towels, extra toilet-paper rolls. The stall doors lock. There is a hook for your purse, a shelf for your shopping bags. The soap dispenser dispenses soap. The floor is frequently mopped. Finding a bathroom in Harvard Square is not so easy as you'd think. In the windows of bars and cafés are posted signs that announce rest rooms for patrons only. Sandwich shops, coffeehouses, bookstores don't supply such amenities. The ladies' and gents' on the mezzanine of the Coop have been under reconstruction for a month. There are no public toilets. Articles have been written about this fact. There have been editorials in the newspapers, telephone calls to her fellow ombudsmen, letters to the editors, parents protesting in defense of their kids' small bladders, senior citizens protesting in defense of their aging ones. Whole paragraphs have been bold-faced in travel books warning foreign visitors.

"I read an interview with Queen Elizabeth," Jessica once told Daisy, "where she was asked for advice. 'My greatest piece of advice,' the Queen replied, 'is when you spy a convenient bathroom, use it.'"

Certain advice Daisy is not averse to accepting. Especially when it comes out of the mouth of HRH the Queen. She turns into Holyoke Center. She slips inside the elevator. Two students, white-faced and coughing, get off at the Harvard Health Services. A man with a Ché Guevara mustache and three brief-cases gets on. Daisy rides up to the floor where the international office is located. Because of her years of hosting, she claims squatters' rights to their facilities.

As she swings the door into the ladies', Elizabeth Malcolm is swinging out. "Oh, Daisy," she says. Her voice is casual, as if it's the most ordinary of occurrences to see Daisy Lewis's hand on the knob to her office ladies' room. "We've just assigned your student to you. Andrea Mosca from Livorno, due to arrive sometime next week."

"Andrea!" Daisy exclaims. "I asked for a man."

"I know you did, Daisy. And so did I, on your behalf. Alas, the system's not perfect. Sometimes it slips up. Sometimes we have to make a rush judgment. We can't always fill both re-quests: first-choice country, first-choice sex."

"But . . ." Daisy counters. Look what happened with Giselle, she wants to say. Then she stops. She never would be living with Truman Wolff if what happened with Giselle hadn't hap-pened with Giselle. History won't repeat itself. She's a grown-up. What prejudices can she lodge against a sweet young girl she hasn't even met?

No doubt Elizabeth is thinking the same thing, because her

words are the clipped, on-the-record syllables smoothed by overuse. "We've sent Andrea your name and address. I'm sure it will be a successful placement. I know you will do your best."

Doing her best, Daisy decides to leave the subject of sex and move onto geography. At least she's got an Italian. Andrea will be the daughter she always wanted. She'll be an Italian partner worthy of Truman. A coach who will help him improve. Daisy is sure it's only Livia's low-level language skills that are drawing him down. Out of graciousness, Truman would always lower the volume on his brilliance for the sake of a fellow student in line for a dunce's cap. Andrea will be a sister to Phoebe as well as Sammy, a second daughter to Truman. Thus she could cement a relationship, rather than open fissures in it. In a family trying to blend, she will fill in the gaps.

Daisy swings the ladies' room door back and forth. It squeaks a little. The hinges need oiling. She supposes, in her capacity as a regular, she might mention this to the maintenance staff. Daisy wonders about the number of bathrooms proportionate to the population in downtown Livorno. She hasn't been doing her usual homework in preparation for her host-family duties. After Giselle, the bloom is off the rose. But maybe Pilombaya's return as cabinet minister, Andrea's arrival from Italy, might force the incipient bud. Daisy holds the door open. She hangs her dry cleaning on the nearest hook. "I assume you've also given Andrea our telephone number," she tells Elizabeth. "That you've told her to get in touch."

Elizabeth looks huffy. "After all these years, Daisy, I'm surprised you even need to ask."

Outdoors, she heads toward Brattle Street. A flea market is set up on the filled-in section that comprises the T station, the kiosk where you can buy the *Jerusalem Times* and the *Toledo Blade,* the pit where kids from Cambridge Rindge and Latin skateboard, where punks show off their tongue studs, where suburban teens come to score drugs. Where one crackpot yells "Jesus Saves"; the other "Down with the President."

She riffles through the bins. She surveys tables with crystals on them. Tables piled high with rough wool sweaters from Ecuador. Boxes with baskets from China, silver earrings made in the Yucatán. One vendor in a Harvard football shirt is selling what seems like a Harvard education's worth of texts: *Introduction to Economics, Language in Action, U.S. History, The Art of India, Chemistry, First Year French.* The books look pristine, as if their owner never cracked their covers. Daisy studies the football shirt. Its muddied exterior smacks of the gridiron, of the goal posts, of the thirty-yard line. Very different from the facsimiles that Japanese tourists buy by the dozens in the Coop's specially designated Harvard insignia room.

At the next table three milk cartons abut each other. A sign attached to one of them is scribbled *Ephemera.* Inside lie dusty engravings taken from old books, the rotogravure sections of newspapers, city maps of nineteenth-century Cambridge. She once bought a map here that shows her own house drawn like a child's rendition—pointed roof, two window eyes, one door mouth, a curl of smoke from a chimney—standing in the middle of acres of green land. Now houses, apartments, condos have filled in all of this.

She picks up an etching of Mount Vesuvius, which is erupting dramatically. Trees and rocks, whole villages are madly plummeting. The sky is ominous. Sparks fly like little bugs. Daisy thinks Truman might like this given the Italian theme, the force-of-nature theme. It's a masculine etching, suitable for a man's library, a man's study, a man's half of a bedroom graciously shared. It will make a nice balance to her collection of etched ballgowns from *Godey's Ladies' Book.* "How much?" she asks the man behind the table. He has gray bangs cut straight across in a Dutch boy cut, a Fu Manchu mustache, a Sir Walter Raleigh goatee, a Winston Churchill unlit cigar stuck between his teeth.

He smiles a Groucho smile. "For you, sweetheart, I make a good price."

"And that is?"

"Such gorgeous eyes."

"The price?"

"Let's see a smile, sweetheart, on that pretty face."

Daisy smiles. She can't help herself.

"That's better. For a beautiful girl, a special bargain."

Daisy is not sure what delights her more, the beautiful or the girl. "Which is . . . ?"

"Twenty dollars."

"Will you take ten?"

"An old man's got to make a living." He does some Groucho things with his eyebrows. "Darling, for you a compromise. Fifteen."

"It's a deal," says Daisy. She reaches into her purse.

"Why don't you look around while I wrap this up," the man suggests.

Daisy moves down to the third bin. This is filled with documents: Boy Scout records, diplomas from the turn of the century and earlier, somebody's army discharge papers, old marriage certificates. There's an award for best all-around camper from Camp Pocahontas on Sebago Lake, Maine. A blue-ribboned citation from the Cambridge City Council for a composer whose song was chosen to be played by Guy Lombardo and his Royal Canadians. A Kiwanis badge. A mayor's commendation. A cardboard-backed report of a no-hitter game in Little League. The papers are torn, stained, crumpled with age. Even the framed ones are yellowing, foxed, the glass discolored or cracked, the nails poking out from splintered wood.

She picks up something in a ripped and filthy red leatherette case. She opens it. She stares. She gasps.

Perhaps she has even yelled, for the man turns to her. His cigar wobbles. Concern crinkles his brow. "Sweetheart," he asks, "are you all right? Are you okay?"

Speechless, she manages to nod. She studies the document, which looks like it's bearing the remains of many meals. Like it's been trampled on by many feet. Left out in the rain. Left out in the sun. But she can still read the words HOST FAMILY AWARD. The words HENRY AND DAISY LEWIS.

"How much?" she demands.

The man reaches across and takes it from her. He holds it at its corner the way the parents of Sammy's friends touched their kids' befouled jackets after Sammy's eleventh-birthday bash. "It looks like it's got a lot of age," he hedges.

Daisy knows exactly how much age it has. She knows that the browning edges denote not antiquity but soy and teriyaki sauce. She keeps her mouth shut. She could claim it. Say it's mine. Say I'm not going to pay money for what rightfully belongs to me. Why does she want it anyway? She remembers clearly the awful circumstances surrounding it. How it was left at the Sea of Japan, a restaurant that went out of business a month after its opening. It's an award she wasn't sure she wanted when it was awarded to her. And yet for some God-knows-what reason, some reason years of analysis might not even begin to probe, she wants it now. "How much?" she asks again.

The man sighs. He is already starting to fold it in newspaper, to place it next to the wrapped Mount Vesuvius. "Two bucks," he states. "Plus tax."

FRANCE NATIONALE
CHARLES DE GAULLE 2
11
A 421 FRANCE

Daisy turns the key in the lock and steps into the hall. She glances in the mirror. She tosses her head. Her hair flies out, then springs back. She admires her new haircut, swagged architecturally over one eye. "The perfect frame for your face, Daisy," Vito de Bruno, né Victor Bronicek, crooned. "It's about time you changed from that retro look." Two neighbors have already stopped her on the street. "Looking good," high-fived a fifteen-year-old. "So becoming, dear," a grandmother clucked.

Daisy's feeling fine. It's not even noon on Friday and she's already managed to change her hairstyle and find a dazzling black dress on sale at Clothware. Tonight is the party for Pilombaya. Yesterday's worries of the twenty something–year gap between hosting Pilombaya and feting him, Pilombaya's exalted and iffy status, inevitable tensions between Henry's family and hers, Sammy's divided loyalties, how she looked, what she wore have disappeared. For reasons that she accepts as superficial—a new dress, a new do—she's almost looking forward to the reception at the Kennedy School.

From the den she hears the sound of the TV. A certain perkiness signifies morning cartoons. This puzzles her. It's been years since there's been a child in footed pajamas sucking his thumb in front of Road Runner and Mr. Magoo. "Anybody home?" she yells.

"Me," Truman calls. "In here."

Daisy walks into the den, where Truman is sprawled on the easy chair. He balances a bowl of popcorn on his knees. He sips coffee from a Save-the-Square mug. Daisy stands in front of him. She preens. She flips her bangs.

Truman doesn't look up. "Have a seat," he invites. He points the mug toward the TV. "This is brilliant," he announces.

Daisy follows his gaze. On the screen, a nasty cartoon bug dives into a green sea. Identical bugs hike through a forest in which trees are hung with white sacs of eggs. Angel bugs with wings and halos fly through the air. Corpses of bugs litter the ground. "Olive Oil is the enemy," a bug-in-the-throes declares.

"What is this?" Daisy asks. "Dr. Seuss?"

"*From Head Lice to Dead Lice,*" Truman says with the kind of reverence you might use toward a groundbreaking PBS documentary.

"Which is something I should be familiar with?"

"Not at all. It's brand-new." Truman chuckles, causing popcorn to bounce over the rim of the bowl.

Now the scene switches to a yuppie kitchen with granite counters and glass-fronted cabinets. A little girl leans over the sink. A man dressed as a woman pours olive oil into her hair, then with a special comb starts picking nits.

"Why is that man dressed as a woman?" Daisy asks.

"For comic effect. Isn't it obvious?"

"I see," says Daisy, who doesn't exactly see. The little girl winces. Bugs beat the dust. Children trade hats and start scratching their scalps. The school nurse, played by the same man now sporting a frilled cap and white pantyhose, reiterates in a falsetto a five-step program for eliminating lice. "No laughing matter," this man *slash* woman warns.

The music soars; more corpses drop. When THE END flashes across the screen, Truman claps, then presses rewind on the remote. "I think I'll play this again," he says.

Daisy shakes her head. What is going on? She remembers reading about Howard Hughes who in his later years, eccentric if not mad, holed up in a hotel room growing his fingernails into claws, watching *Ice Station Zebra* from beginning to end to beginning in a continuous spiraling reel.

Truman hits the Play button. *From Head Lice to Dead Lice* starts to repeat itself.

"What is going on?" Daisy asks.

Truman looks up. "Great hair," he says. "I've been invited to give a talk to the Cambridge elementary schools this afternoon," he confides. "There's an epidemic of head lice. After, I'm being interviewed for *Nit Notes*."

"*Nit Notes*? Is it the *New York Times* of parasitology?"

"Very funny, Daisy." Truman awards her a token "Ha." "But this is entirely serious."

Daisy looks at the screen. The bugs are again crashing to the ground. "I wonder why they show them in cartoons," she muses, "rather than actual photographs."

"That would scare the mothers," Truman explains. "Like a monstrous thing attacking their child. Sometimes Daisy, reality, for mothers if not for scientists, is too hard to bear. That's why this film is so brilliant. The Mary Poppins spoonful of sugar makes the medicine go down." He considers. "Still, lice have a certain beauty once you're trained to recognize it. There's an artist from western Massachusetts who photographs only parasites. They're a revelation, really. Haunting. Brilliantly lit. They're regularly exhibited. To rave reviews. We'll have to go take a look at them."

Daisy is pleased. Truman has not categorized her as one of those delicate mothers but somebody with the capacity to find beauty in ugliness. Now Truman fast-forwards to the little girls trying on hats. His focus is laser-like. His absorption rivals the 100 percent absorbent sponges in Star Market's houseware aisles. She adores his complete immersion in whatever interests him: Italian, cartoon lice, lasagna, Bartley's burgers, community relations, and the Dorothy Parker of it—Daisy herself.

The phone rings. Though it's on the table next to Truman, he doesn't seem to notice it. Daisy goes out into the hall. She picks up the extension.

"Is this the residence of Daisy Lewis and Truman Wolff?" asks a voice. It's a deep voice, tremulous with the vibrato of Rossano Brazzi about to intone "Some Enchanted Evening" in the late-night showings of *South Pacific* that have always set her swooning. With regret, she assumes this call is not for her but rather another assignment generated by Truman's Italian class. Truman's Italian must be improving. Perhaps his professor assigned Livia to somebody else and awarded Truman this maestro of enunciation whose very tones conjure up olive groves and cypress trees, linen jackets worn like capes from the shoulders, and Chianti bottles wrapped in straw.

"This is Daisy Lewis speaking," Daisy says.

"For me, a pleasure," the voice answers. "And Truman Wolff?" it asks.

"He's here," Daisy says. From the other room, the school nurse warbles. "Though at the moment he's somewhat tied up."

The voice laughs. "Not—as you say—literally, I hope."

"No," Daisy says and laughs herself.

"Let me make an introduction," the voice announces. "Andrea Mosca. From Livorno. The Harvard International Office gave me your telephone number to call you when I arrived in America. You and Dr. Wolff are my host family."

Perhaps all the men dressed as women in *From Head Lice to Dead Lice* are confusing her powers of gender recognition, but Daisy could swear that the voice of Andrea Mosca is distinctly masculine. Of course, to her untrained ear, Japanese sounds feminine; German, a grandfatherly guttural; French oozes sex, the sex of both sexes. She needs to consult her in-house expert. "Hold on a minute, please," she says. Then, remembering her host-family manners, adds "Welcome to Cambridge." She walks across the hall, uncoiling the phone cord. "Truman, it's our Italian student. I need your help."

Truman pushes the Mute button; the characters go silent, their lips opening and closing like underwater fish. Then he presses Pause, and the frame freezes; the child bends her head over the sink. The female impersonator/mother holds aloft his/her jar of olive oil. Truman grabs the telephone next to him. "*Buon giorno,*" he says.

Daisy holds her own phone to her ear. "Truman Wolff?" the voice asks.

"*Si.*"

"Andrea Mosca."

"*Benvenuto.*"

"*Grazie.*"

At the rate they're going, Daisy's sure they'll never get to the bottom of this. Given Truman's stop-and-start language skills, she can no longer wait for him to solve the mystery. "Are you male or female?" she interrupts.

"Daisy!" Truman sounds shocked, as if she's challenged the

bella figura that is so intrinsic to the way Italians present themselves.

Andrea Mosca laughs. A belly laugh that starts with a rumble and gathers volcanic mass. Already, Daisy likes him/her enormously.

"Male," Andrea Mosca states. "Americans and English often make that mistake. The *Andrea*, I guess. Just think of *Andrea Doria*."

"Of course," Truman concedes.

Daisy thinks of the *Andrea Doria*. Wasn't that a ship that went down like the *Titanic*? But then aren't boats feminine? Sailors are always talking of her hull, her stern, always naming their boats the "Little Missus" or the "Roberta Marie."

"Andrea Doria was a great Italian explorer," Truman informs Daisy.

"I know that," Daisy lies. While all the boys in grammar school were reading explorer books—Lewis and Clark, Magellan, Christopher Columbus, Captain Cook, Fridtjof Nansen, Vasco da Gama—she was devouring Clara Barton and Florence Nightingale. A bred-in-the-bone trait that no amount of feminist enlightenment can sway. When Sammy was young, she and Henry gave him equal opportunity to pick Tonka trucks or Barbie dolls. When he chose the trucks, they were both relieved.

"There's Andrea Bocelli," Andrea Mosca adds now. "We call him the thin Pavarotti."

For a moment Daisy wonders if to have the rich voice of an Andrea Mosca you need the waistline of a Pavarotti.

"Yes," Truman says. "Andrea Bocelli. I think I've heard of him."

"We can't wait to see you," Daisy breaks in, taking up her host-family duties. She's amazed at her powers of adjustment. Only days ago she prepared herself for a female, accepting with reasonable good grace whatever Elizabeth Malcolm had assigned. And now she's been rewarded. Andrea Mosca turns out to be the male she wanted in the first place.

"And I am eager to meet my American family," Andrea allows.

Daisy remembers Pilombaya's note at the bottom of the Kennedy School invitation: *Bring the whole Lewis family*, it read. She explains about the cocktail party, about Pilombaya, their student from two decades ago. "With my former husband," she adds. "We're divorced. We have a son together, Sammy. Truman, Dr. Wolff, is—"

"I understand," Andrea cuts in. Of course he does, Daisy assures herself. Europeans are worldly. She wouldn't have to explain to an Italian or a Frenchman what she might more carefully have to parse for somebody like Pilombaya from a nation in its earlier stages of development. Still, considering what she's read about Italian families, Daisy supposes that he comes from a world of additions rather than subtractions, a world where ex-wives and former husbands aren't jettisoned, but where mistresses and lovers swell the already swollen ranks.

She tells him the time and the place. In seconds he has located the Kennedy School on his map. "There'll be name tags," she explains, "so we'll have no trouble identifying you."

They all say *ciao* and hang up their respective phones. Daisy can hear Truman reanimate his lice.

She's making coffee in the kitchen when Truman comes in to her. He's holding the tape in one hand. With the other he cups her breast.

"What's this?" Daisy asks. "Lice as foreplay?"

"Guess so. There is the word 'licentious,' after all." He pulls up her hair. He nibbles the nape of her neck. "I've got an hour before my talk."

Lying in bed in the middle of the day, Daisy feels licentious.

Deliciously lascivious. Her hair is clumped and knotted, damp with the calisthenics and heat of making love. The sheets are twisted, the blankets and quilts tossed to the floor. Lipstick smears the pillow case, whose edge bears a swathe of her mascara, warm brown, which in the eyes of the flea market seller might endow her linens with the positive properties of age. There are positive things about age, she admits. Decay, of course, but maturity, a ripening. Middle age ain't bad; middle-aged sex can be wonderful. She's pleased her desire for Truman surmounts worries about her hairdo and an already made bed, the kind of worries that managed to cool a great deal of her and Henry's ardor in their later and troubled marriage years.

Is this the difference between marrying the man you love, Daisy wonders, and living with him?

Truman's leg wraps around hers. His cheek is against her breast. "I love you, Daisy," he says.

"I love you too."

"In which case—"

"Oh, Truman. Everything is perfect just the way it is."

For his lecture to the Cambridge schools, Truman wears a spiffy suit and his ladybug bow tie. Since he's not sure how long his interview with *Nit Notes* will last, Daisy arranges to meet him at the Kennedy School. She leaves a message for Sammy and Phoebe on their answering machine. Before she can get to the beep, she's forced to listen to rap music with lyrics unintelligible except for the jackhammer pounding of the word *love*; this is followed by Sammy and Phoebe's attempt at harmony—"We can't come to the phone right now but please"—proving that they have inherited both her and Truman's musical skills. She's tempted to remind them to dress up, that Pilombaya is not one to understand ripped jeans and faded T-shirts bearing the drugged-out faces of long-departed rock stars. "See you there," she says, instead. "And incidentally, our new student, the one we're host family for, is going to attend. Andrea Mosca. Look out for *him*."

The party is held in one of the reception rooms with windows overlooking the Charles and its bordering park directly below. Daisy can see the JFK fountain ringed by strollers. Toddlers in bright sweaters and jackets dash and tumble like a continual spill of colored marbles. Runners, skateboarders, dogs, Rollerbladers, elderly couples out for a predinner constitutional move at varying speeds along the river's paths. The light is sharp. The leaves are starting to turn. Autumn has always been her favorite time of year. The beginning of school, new students to host, the sense that anything is possible. Crisp McIntosh apples fill barrels in the aisles of grocery stores; Indian corn decorates neighbors' front doors. Across the river in Boston, the beacon on top of the Prudential Tower flashes clear skies ahead, a promise of perfect days strung together like pearls. From this distance the world seems sharp-edged, translatable. Like a puzzle, the pieces fit together, but you can still make out the lines that separate them. Closer up, in her own world, for instance, you see the clumps, tangles, knots. How do you get perspective on anything when you are smack dab in the middle of it? How do you find a handle for the long haul in such a shifting universe?

A table is laid with name tags arranged alphabetically in a checkerboard design. She finds the *L*'s; she's the first of the Lewis clan to arrive. Their name tags are all there—Henry, Sammy, Giselle. Under her, Henry's, and Sammy's names shines a gold star, next to which is written *General Pilombaya's Original Host Family.* A nice touch, Daisy thinks, although Sammy wasn't even born when Pilombaya and his luggage turned up on their doorstep in Holden Green. And she and Henry weren't even married then.

She's glad to see a tag for Andrea Mosca. Though she'd called earlier to have him added to the list, she hadn't been sure that the secretary had actually copied down Daisy's carefully spelled syllables. "He's a man," she'd clarified.

"Our names tags aren't gender specific," the secretary snorted. Implying that it must have been a long time since Daisy Lewis had made her way down Harvard's enlightened corridors.

Now, Daisy surveys the room, which already holds a crowd. There's a cluster at the refreshment table, and a cluster over by the side window where she can make out between elbows and hips a receiving line. She pastes her name tag on the shoulder of her chic black dress and makes her way toward this person from her past.

Who, if he weren't wearing his own name tag and a glittery tribal-looking cap, she would hardly recognize. Unlike most people, age has improved him, not to mention the burnishing that those in high places acquire. His hair is gray; there's lots of it brushed back under the cap and gleaming with the patina of rich silver. He's filled out—wide cheek bones, broad shoulders, an assertive jaw, penetrating eyes. His suit, slate-colored and silky, looks European: French, Saville Row, possibly Italian. And though he's not taller, he seems bigger somehow, a man of stature. Which only goes to show you. How do you know how somebody will turn out? Twenty years ago and crazy in love with Henry, would she have predicted a pompous Francophile?

But before she can make projections about Truman, Pilombaya steps through the throng of admirers. "Daisy Lewis!" he exclaims. "I'd recognize you anywhere."

She holds out her hand.

He clasps it between both of his. He kisses her on each cheek. "I have perfect recall of your sofa bed." He laughs.

"With that lump down the middle where you unfolded it. You must have been so uncomfortable."

"I was so cold."

"I remember," she says. Should she apologize? For Cambridge weather and ridged mattresses and dinners cobbled together with cream of mushroom soup and canned pineapple chunks? Yet how else can you appreciate four-star hotels and the riches of a Kennedy School? The deprivations of youth are important. Has Sammy had too little of the cold to appreciate the warmth?

"Those were happy days," Pilombaya says, still squeezing her hand. He's wearing a heavy gold ring, which cuts into her palm. She's not surprised when she looks at it to see it's the biggest, goldest, most deluxe Harvard ring you can buy at the Coop. She winces. If he keeps holding her hand like this, she'll have *Veritas* engraved on her flesh. She remembers his necktie of little *veritas*es. Tactfully she slips her hand away.

He reaches into his pocket. He pulls out some photographs. "Picture of my car," he says.

Daisy studies three poses of a black Mercedes the size of a small house. Flags fly from the hood; reflected palm trees line its glossy surfaces. In one corner she can just make out a small uniformed leg. "Very nice," she says.

"Is nice," he agrees. "Ess class. Global positioning system. Lumbar massager. Four-corner air-sprung suspension with variable damping. Sixteen-way power seats. Ten-fan ventilation. Eight airbags. Cell phone to recognize seven languages."

"And a partridge in a pear tree," Daisy finishes.

Pilombaya frowns. He's puzzled. Is there a gadget he forgot to request? He grabs the photos back. He presses them against his heart. "Concord. Lexington," he continues, "With you and

Henry I had my first Big Mac." He giggles, then looks around. "Henry?"

"He'll be here," Daisy says. She's aware of a line forming behind her. She recognizes a couple of deans and the holder of a controversial chair. There's a law professor in the middle of a tenure fight and somebody who just won a MacArthur genius grant. "Why don't I go look for him?"

"Yes. Yes." Pilombaya beams. "And bring over the whole family. This is my Harvard family," he boasts to a woman next to him who sports on her lapel a small card typed STAFF. She doesn't respond. She holds some sort of walkie-talkie; her eyes scan the room like the eyes of secret servicemen protecting presidents.

Daisy searches for Henry. She passes the refreshment table, garlanded with extravagant bouquets of flowers. She notes platters of interesting things on bamboo skewers, bowls of shredded coconut, bean sprouts, nuggets of tofu, shrimp crackers, an array of sauces—soy, peanut, chili—pineapples halved, the insides cubed and pierced with toothpicks topped with miniature flags, rice spilling out of banana leaves like fruit from a cornucopia. "Daisy!" a voice calls out.

Daisy turns around to face Jessica, who is wearing a black leather skirt and a triple rope of pearls. "What are you doing here?" Daisy exclaims.

"I might ask the same of you." Jessica's eyes move to Daisy's name tag and widen with surprise. "You've got to be kidding!"

"About what?" Does Jessica think Daisy's good for only jeans salesmen in bars, not dignitaries in Harvard halls?

"You were General Pilombaya's host family?"

"Over twenty years ago."

"You and Henry?"

Daisy nods.

"But why didn't I know about this?"

"I'm sure you did. I think you even met him once. He stayed with us in Holden Green. We had trouble getting rid of him."

"The guy you gave the quilt from your own bed?"

"The very same."

Jessica presses her fingers to her temples. "I must have blocked him out. Mostly I remember a lopsided turkey and a room in utter disarray." She shakes her head. "But look at him now. I should have become a host family myself."

"Every Harvard student, every alum, had equal opportunity."

"But then I would have chosen some Italian, grown fat, and now be hanging laundry out a window in Sicily while he's with his mistress on the Isle of Capri."

Daisy studies Jessica's stranglehold of pearls. The skirt over shimmery metallic pantyhose, the open-toed, sling-backed stiletto-heeled shoes. "I see you as the mistress, not the wife."

"I suppose you mean to flatter me." Jessica tilts her head toward the receiving line. "But this person bears no resemblance to the one you used to describe."

"People change."

"Imagine hearing this come from you, the queen of the status quo."

"No longer." Daisy smoothes her hair.

"A new cut. It suits you," approves Jessica.

"People can change," Daisy repeats.

"Sometimes for the better." Jessica tugs at the hem of her skirt. "I'm here to write General Pilombaya up for *Boston Bean & Cod.* Why don't you introduce me. Tell him I'm your very best friend in all the world."

Daisy is delighted that the tables have turned, that she's able to do something for Jessica. Working with Jimmy, Bernie, and Billy, separating from Henry, living with Truman Wolff, she's not exactly a treasure trove of eligible men. It amazes her that it's she, not Jessica, who wandered into the arms of Truman Wolff simply by following a snaky blue line on a hospital corridor. Jessica's the beauty, but Daisy's got the man. Jessica may be the mistress, but Daisy, if she wished, could be the wife. Her goodwill spills over. She wants everyone to march off into the sunset hand in hand with a sublimely perfect match.

Though she has her doubts about Pilombaya no matter how distinguished he's become. Once he was nearly impossible to get rid of. And here he is again. Henry might say a bad penny keeps turning up, a computer virus can reinfect its PC; Truman no doubt would make some allusion to parasites. Yet Jessica's eager to take him on. There's no disputing tastes, Daisy sighs, tallying Jessica's husbands interwoven with a few layers of badly behaved lovers and men married to first-priority wives.

She is just about to steer Jessica to the receiving line when she spots, over by the name-tag table, Henry and Giselle, Phoebe and Sammy (in neatly pressed khakis and matching oxford shirts), and Truman all in a row. They look as if a tour guide brought them here and, before depositing them, warned them to "stick together; don't wander off."

"Well, there's Tolstoy's one happy family." Jessica points. "You'd better go sort them out. I'm perfectly capable of telling Pilombaya myself that you and I have a history."

Daisy is waylaid by an elderly man who is a student at the Harvard Institute of Lifelong Learning and who has just come back from a tour of Indonesia sponsored by the Institute. Because of the Harvard connection, the group had been entertained at the presidential palace in Jakarta. General Pilombaya had shaken each of their hands; he had presented each of them with a commemorative pen. "Actually, a cheap ballpoint," the man confides, "which was a disappointment considering the riches of the area." The tour members are all here, he explains, gesturing to a few white heads over near the windows, others at the buffet. Several wear hats similar to Pilombaya's. One large woman looks upholstered in batik. "Have you visited?" he asks.

"I'm afraid not," Daisy says, and he looks so sorry she adds, "but I hope to as soon as possible."

The man rummages in the pocket of a blue seersucker jacket, the kind reunioners from low-numbered and vastly depleted Harvard classes wear to fly the banner of their year. "Let me show you some photographs, young lady," the man insists.

By the time Daisy has admired Javanese puppets and a tour-group ristaffel in which most of the tourists' heads are cut off, only Truman is left in the spot where she had spotted him.

"How was *Nit Notes?*" asks Daisy, slipping her hand into his.

Truman laughs. "The lecture was great. A better response than on grand rounds. No eating in the audience. No rustling potato chip bags and pull tabs snapping from soda cans. I was interviewed by a ten-year-old who did as good a job as anyone on *Nature* or *Scientific American*." Truman leans over. He kisses Daisy. He scratches behind his ear.

Daisy follows him to the buffet table, where Sammy and Phoebe, Henry and Giselle stand on opposite ends.

"Hi, Daisy," Henry says.

Giselle puts out her hand. Daisy takes it. She studies Giselle. Giselle looks exhausted; her hair needs washing; her sweater at the elbow is unraveling. On her feet are flat ballet slippers; she's slashed a line of lipstick across her mouth; she hasn't even bothered with a scarf. Life with year-old twins and with Henry would deplete anybody's fashion sense. "Who's with the kids?" Daisy asks.

"The au pair," Henry says. "She's *fantastique.*"

"She's impossible," Giselle corrects.

"She's very involved with their French."

"She's more involved with French-kissing any, as you say, Tom, Dick, and Henry."

Is the *Henry* for *Harry* a deliberate substitution, Daisy wonders, or just a slip? She looks at Henry, who hasn't seemed to have noticed it.

"She's terribly French," Henry boasts.

"Which is the problem," Giselle laments, "that she's so terribly French."

"Have you introduced yourself to Pilombaya yet?" Daisy asks.

"Giselle insisted we hit the refreshments first," Henry says. He shudders. "She seems to think we can make a dinner out of this." He frowns at his plate, which holds two skewered chicken satays in a watery puddle of peanut sauce and one cashew nut.

"It's either this or Stouffer's French bread pizza, maybe Franco-American macaroni and cheese," pronounces Giselle. Her eyes turn mischievous. "What you Americans call fusion cuisine."

Daisy looks over at the receiving line and sees a gap; the crowd around Pilombaya is thinning out. He is talking excitedly to Jessica, his hands chopping the air. He bounces up and down on the balls of his feet. His hat doesn't move. Daisy wonders if it is attached, like the occasional skullcap she sees on a student in the Square, with a bobby pin. She gathers Henry and Giselle, Sammy and Phoebe, wrests Truman away from the seersucker-jacketed man showing off his ballpoint pen, and herds them to the guest of honor.

Who jumps in delight. "So this is the whole host family," he chants. He nods at Jessica. "And best friend."

Daisy introduces each of them to Pilombaya, who solemnly shakes each hand in turn, looks into each eye with a penetrating gaze. Daisy would not be surprised if he produced a commemorative ballpoint for each of them. "Ahhh, Henry, Daisy's husband," he says.

"Ex-husband," Daisy explains.

"Former husband," Henry amends.

"Our son, Sammy," Henry says. He pauses. "My wife, Giselle."

Pilombaya seizes Truman's elbow. "Daisy's husband," he deduces.

"Not exactly." Daisy sighs. She pushes forward. "And Phoebe . . ."

"Daisy's daughter," Pilombaya declares.

"Truman's daughter, *my* daughter," Truman states.

Pilombaya looks perplexed. He wrinkles his brow, he tugs at his ear. Daisy can practically see the lightbulb go off as he says, "Then Giselle is Truman's former wife?"

"Close enough," Jessica breaks in. "What really matters is they're *all* your host family."

"And you, Daisy's best friend, have the mind of a diplomat."

"Nice hat," Truman says, seeking neutral ground.

"Yes, native to my country. Would you like to try it on?"

Before Truman can answer, Pilombaya has grabbed the woman with the name tag marked STAFF and told her to fetch the camera. He organizes them into two rows. In the back row, Truman wears the hat for two photos, then Phoebe, then Sammy, then Henry. The film runs out by the time the hat reaches Daisy, Giselle, and Jessica, who are lined up in the front. One row of native dress is enough, Daisy says, to give an Indonesian flavor to the whole group of them. After all, you need only a few strings of saffron to color a whole bowl of rice. She hands the hat back to its owner, who replaces it jauntily on his silver locks.

As they start to dislodge from their photo-session formation, a young man approaches them. He's tall, with a dazzling smile and a head of ebony curls. His jacket hangs from his shoulders like a cape. The top three buttons of his shirt are open, exposing more silky curls. His chest is broad, his waist narrow, on his feet are boots shined to the color of a vintage Barolo. "Daisy Lewis?" he asks. He gives the kind of wink Marcello Mastroianni might grant Sophia Loren. "Truman Wolff?" he inquires. His words throb operatically.

"God!" Jessica exclaims.

A god, Daisy thinks.

"Wow!" Phoebe cries.

"Andrea Mosca," introduces this god, this movie star, this baritone. And with the crash of cymbals, the roll of drums, chimes, "My host family, I presume!"

FRANCE NATIONALE
CHARLES DE GAULLE 2
12
A 421 FRANCE

Truman, Phoebe, and Sammy are lined up in Daisy's kitchen, towels around their shoulders, their heads slathered with olive oil. Andrea Mosca watches from the table. His blue jeans are ironed into knife-blade creases. His white shirt rivals a Clorox ad. A silky, lice-free tendril falls against his forehead with the kind of casual chic that is no accident. Daisy pictures small dark Frenchmen, their stingy mustaches and not-good teeth. Compared to them, Andrea is *David* by Michelangelo. And as soon as she makes this analogy, she can't help wondering what works of art lie fig-leafed under that designer denim and 250-thread-count glazed cotton plucked from Egyptian fields and exported to the Via Veneto.

She switches her focus to Phoebe. Why does she seem to be wearing lipstick and eyeshadow to be de-loused? Usually she's the perfect Harvard Square granola type who'll show up at a candlelit restaurant, at the first night performance of Pirandello at the Loeb, at the opening of Degas at the Museum of Fine Arts, in farmer's overalls and laced-up work boots with nothing on her face but oil of kiwi moisturizer from the Body Shop. She has the kind of natural looks Daisy's mother-in-law—*ex*-mother-in-law—would rail against. "A little color on the cheeks," Lillian would suggest. "Foundation, lip-liner. What nature gave us girls can always use embellishment."

Daisy feels a sudden twinge for Phoebe's male equivalents: those L.L. Bean–clad boys whose one jacket and tie is a father's hand-me-down. How can a mere mortal compete with a monument's marble curls a louse would never get to first base on? She blots the back of Truman's neck. Still, the exhaust coughed from the gnarl of traffic around the Piazza della Signoria could oxidize any statue's most art-appreciated body parts. Nothing escapes outside influences, Michelangelo, after all, is the name of one of Henry's computer viruses. She bends forward. She smiles. Truman's head smells like the pesto in red-sauce restaurants.

"You really don't have to witness this humiliation, Andrea," Phoebe groans.

Andrea laughs. "If I hadn't been late, I'd be one of you."

Daisy is relieved he's not the fourth head in the row in front of her. Nit-picking involves an intimacy she'd be uncomfortable with in someone she's just met. Even though she is his host. Even though he is a hunk. You need to get to know a person, to develop closeness over time, to be able to start mucking about in his hair. In contrast, Sammy is the issue of her body; Truman's body spends its nights conjoined with hers. She's connected to Phoebe through both of them. She thinks of the worms in sushi. To complete their life cycle, Truman has explained, they travel from host to host, first swallowed by a crustacean, then by a fish, then by a marine mammal, and finally by the seafood lover who is bowled over in gut-wrenching agony when he interrupts the cycle. Is Andrea the interrupter?

Or the lucky outsider, the witness to this in-house feeding-frenzy chain.

"It's all Dad's fault," Phoebe says.

"It's sort of after the fact to start assigning blame," Sammy points out.

"I agree," says Daisy.

"*Mea culpa. Mea culpa.* No good deed goes unpunished," Truman admits. "Here I'm contributing to my community, addressing an auditorium full of kids, their teachers, their parents . . ."

"And you come home with a party favor," Daisy finishes. The kids were so taken with Truman, with his jokes, his blackboard drawings, the prettified lice puppets supplied by the K–3 faculty, they jumped all over him. It pleases Daisy that Truman is not the kind of cold scientist who would spurn a child's embrace. Who would repel a tousled-haired moppet for reasons merely sanitary. She thinks of celebrities holding AIDS babies. Of good Samaritans helping out in leper colonies. A nit is a small price to pay for one's humanity.

Although, of course, it's not just *a* nit. And they're not confined to Truman's humanitarian head. She tears the stainless-steel nit-picker from its package. She examines it. Catching the light, it sets off a sunburst of rays like a child's drawing of a magic wand. She trusts that form follows function. The Banisher, it's called.

"Daisy"—Truman's voice rises in alarm—"stop waving that thing around like a medieval instrument of torture."

"It probably was a medieval instrument of torture," Sammy considers. "I bet its design hasn't changed since the Middle Ages. There are, no doubt, castles in Transylvania with dungeons full of nit combs."

"Yeah, right," Phoebe says. She turns toward Andrea. "Have you ever seen such a thing?"

"I've not had the need." Implying we of the *bella figura* repel parasites.

"There are probably nit combs unearthed in archaeological digs," Sammy goes on, "studded with rare jewels and lying in the cases of museums misidentified as hair ornaments."

"You'd think they'd invent a computer chip that would zap all the little buggers." Phoebe sighs. "Or a special laser beam." She is examining an oil-slicked lank of hair with the kind of tenderness one has for treasures one is soon to be separated from.

"Believe it or not, there are some afflictions impervious to modern technology," her father instructs. "Often the old-fashioned, old wives' solutions stand the test of time. The best way to get rid of certain worms, for instance, is to wind them around an available branch of a tree. Nothing beats a needle for a splinter. Tweezers and match for a tick." He rubs some oil from his chin. "Speaking of ticks . . ."

"Dad," Phoebe says. She looks over at the kitchen table, where Andrea sits drinking one of Truman's cappuccinos. It's completely authentic, he'd announced, worming—*tapeworming*, Daisy amends—his way into Truman's heart. It's amazing how once you start using parasitic analogies you see them everywhere.

"Is this the best approach for introducing Andrea to our family?" Phoebe asks.

Andrea chuckles. His cup rattles. The cloud of steamed milk deflates. "It's, as you Americans say, a trial by fire. Or rather trial by olive oil."

"But not yours, not *your* olive oil," Phoebe is careful to point out. She nods in the direction of the extra-virgin oil in its pottery flacon, the *olio* circled by a wreath of green leaves and gold inspection stickers decoupaged around its base. One of a bounty of hostess/host family gifts, along with a bottle of grappa, a panforte, a tin of biscotti, and a small etching of Dante's house.

The olive oil now coating their hair shafts is not only not extra but not even virgin. Just an ersatz brand in a giant economy plastic vat, the rotgut made-in–New Jersey twin of zinfandel in a jug. She found it at the market next to CVS, where she had debated the properties of three different combs. That she fell for the Banisher only underscored what she had known all along, had in fact built her second career on: the power of the right word to assuage a complaint, to clinch a deal. She bought two of them.

Daisy remembers the chemicals that, out of ignorance, she had squeezed onto Sammy's hair when he was in grammar school. She feels guilty about this. Guilty every time a food group or toiletry has moved from the in list to the out. What disasters have been caused by her complicity in a toxic shampoo? Maybe Sammy's dropping French is simply the by-product of some mother-induced attack on the foreign-language portion of his brain. It's impossible to keep up with the changing rules of what is good for you. The glass of red wine helps your heart but hurts your breast. The apple a day is sprayed with Alar. Fat is bad. Some fat is good. Bodies need fish oil and olive oil. All oil is the enemy.

"Only olive oil," said Truman, presenting his head for her ministrations. She'd been touched by the gesture. Surely it was a leap of faith that he would offer up to her this wrapping for his excellent brain. That the infestation and its deliverance would be put in her hands. "Olive oil," he'd repeated. "If I learned anything watching *From Head Lice to Dead Lice,* it's that."

She'd been careful, then, not to remind him about the lesson he hadn't learned: the warning about trying on other people's hats. A scene from the video that he'd viewed in its entirety more than twice.

"Ouch!" Phoebe yells as Daisy starts to comb. What was a glorious ponytail is now an endless blond obstacle course. In the years of fifty whacks across the wrist, lice-infested grammar-school children would have their heads shaved. Maybe those kids in crew cuts grinning at you from yearbook photographs, their ears huge in relation to their cropped crowns, represented strictly a reaction and adaptation to parasites.

The phone rings. "Let the machine pick up," Truman orders, but Daisy has already grabbed it with her non-nit-picking hand. Like Pavlov's dog, she can't ignore a ringing phone, a ringing bell.

"It's not a good time," she says to Jessica.

"You're not going to believe this," Jessica steamrolls on.

"Just let me guess."

"You're not going to believe what I'm doing right now."

"I may surprise you."

"I'll give you a hint. It's nothing to do with sex."

"Which never crossed my mind," Daisy admits. "I bet it's related to a one-syllable, four-letter word that begins with *l* and ends with *e*."

"So you've got it too!" crows Jessica with a misery-loves-company lilt.

"Not me." Daisy feels suddenly proud. She's been passed over like the firstborn son the pestilence missed. "But Sammy and Phoebe and Truman are here at the sink even as we speak." She tucks the phone under her chin and rakes a strand of Phoebe's hair.

"Ouch," Phoebe yells.

"Are you okay, Phoebe?" Andrea jumps up in alarm.

"Easy, Mom," Sammy commands. "Phoebe's scalp is sensitive."

"How did *you* escape?" asks Jessica.

"The hat." Daisy tries not to sound smug.

"So it *was* Pilombaya's hat," Jessica deduces. "We thought about that."

"But Truman's lice," Daisy has the need to confess. Blaming Pilombaya would be a breach not only of diplomacy but also of morality. The poor country–rich country kind of thing. The tendency to dump the whole shebang on the underdog. But this time the city slicker's guilty, not the country mouse.

Jessica seems to perk up. "Then it's Truman's fault, not Pilombaya's. He was so worried that he might have passed it on to you, he made me call."

"The point is not who's to blame but what to do about it," quotes Daisy from every mother's parenting book.

"You're right, of course." Daisy hears Jessica step away from the phone. "Don't worry, Pilombaya," she consoles. "Daisy says Truman's responsible."

Daisy startles. The comb jerks. Phoebe cries out again. "Poor Phoebe," Andrea soothes.

"Careful, Mom," Sammy warns.

"So Pilombaya's there. In your apartment? In your living room?" asks Daisy.

"Actually the bathroom. We're about to attack the little buggers, but I thought I'd better check with Truman, the. in-house—in your house—expert on parasites. We bought some shampoo at the drugstore, but there are warnings posted all over the bottle. I'm a bit concerned."

"But how did you get it? You and I didn't try on the hat."

"I know. I must have picked it up from close proximity."

How close? What proximity? Daisy wonders. Can a louse jump from one head to the next like movie supercops who leap from skyscraper roofs to penthouse balconies? Or do scalps need to touch?

"I'm worried about my hair," Jessica confides.

"Better to worry about your health."

"*That's* beyond salvation. It's my crowning glory I'm focused on."

How like Jessica to fret over her hair and not the flesh, skin, cells, subcutaneous layers the hair springs from. "Truman recommends only olive oil," says Daisy. She details the steps toward a cure that she has watched in *From Head Lice to Dead Lice* while Truman nods his approval, adding one or two footnotes of his own.

"I've got only extra-virgin," Jessica says.

"The cheapest brand's the best."

"But maybe not so good for the hair." Her voice brightens. "You know, I've had special olive-oil treatments at Diego's for fifty bucks a shot. He uses the purest, most expensive brand from the most famous olive groves in Italy."

"Beauty is not the result you're looking for here," Daisy warns, eyeing the red wax–sealed cork on Andrea's *olio*. "I recommend a nit comb called the Banisher." She hisses the syllables with the venom of the Wicked Witch of the West. "Sammy says it looks like a medieval form of torture."

Jessica sounds unimpressed. "Thank Truman for his advice," she says. She giggles. "We'll give you a progress report."

As soon as Daisy hangs up the phone, it rings again.

"You won't believe this," Henry cries.

"Lice," Daisy says.

"You too?"

"Not on your life."

"Giselle bought some shampoo made out of carcinogens. I'm practically sanding my scalp with chemicals."

"Truman recommends olive oil."

Daisy gets back to her work. She has a vision of kitchen tables, that symbol of family in literature, in television sitcoms, in the social programs of government brochures. All over Cambridge, she sees Norman Rockwell gatherings. The mother extends her platter of roasted chicken. The pigtailed daughter, the freckle-faced son hold their knives and forks aloft; the father has just put his newspaper aside. The dog or cat looks up from its own bowl of kibble or tuna chews.

The scene shifts to the same family gathered around the kitchen sink. The mother hoists a carafe of oil to her shoulder like those Bible pictures of Ruth bringing water from the well. The son, the daughter, the father bend their heads. All over Cambridge, Pilombaya's celebrants, Truman's audience, are repeating this ritual at sinks in every zip code from 02138 to 02140. Daisy's heart swells with this connection to her fellowman. General Pilombaya, the Indonesian VIP, has lice. Dr. Truman Wolff, the famed parasitologist, has lice. Henry Lewis, computer-virus expert, has lice. Sammy and Phoebe, high-SAT, Ivy League overachievers, have lice. Schoolchildren from Brattle Street mansions and Cambridgeport three-deckers have lice. Daisy understands Truman's insistence on parasites' place in the universe, the benefits of symbiotic relationships. Talk about a common denominator.

Andrea gets up from his chair. He walks to the sink. He touches Daisy's shoulder. "Can I help?" he asks.

His eyes are the blue of the Adriatic, his skin the pale terracotta of Florentine clay. What would have happened, Daisy wonders, if she and Henry had been assigned a first exchange student like Andrea? A butterfly rather than the early Pilombaya in his caterpillar larval stage? Would they have even married, let alone win a host-family award? Would they have set down roots in Cambridge either together or apart?

She remembers the photograph of Pilombaya inserting himself between the two of them. Though they're all grinning, only Pilombaya looks happy. Henry and her smiles seem fake, the tips of their mouths clothespinned to turn up. Their eyes are strained. Over Pilombaya's shoulders, their arms stretch toward each other, but their fingers don't touch. She remembers Pilombaya commandeering their sofa in the living room; how they stumbled over him on the way in, on the way out. He took from them their space, their time, their quilt, their earnest do-goodedness. She studies a cluster of white bubbles caught between the tines of the Banisher. Is this where the first infestation began, the first microscopic segment that grew into a tapeworm twenty years old twenty years long?

"Daisy?" Andrea's hand is still on her shoulder. He gives a gentle nudge. "If I'm going to be a member of your family, you let me, please, participate?"

"I can see how you might want to share this unifying experience," Sammy says.

"Andrea!" Phoebe exclaims. "We don't want *you* to get lice."

What about dear old mom? Daisy could ask.

"We don't want *any*body else to get lice," Truman says.

Daisy yearns to plant a kiss on the pesto-smelling, oil-slicked back of his neck.

"I have to admit I am feeling a little left out," Andrea confesses.

Daisy hands him the backup Banisher, which he releases from its shrink-wrapped Houdini's trap as if he's been doing it forever.

Daisy thinks of the eeny-meeny-miney-mo she used to play in the schoolyard at recess. She thinks of the three-card monte set out on the streets of New York, ready to be wheeled to yet another block the second a patrolman comes into view. She thinks of shell games once played with scooped-out coconut husks, now plastic cups. The marble lies under which box? The rabbit hides in which hat? She feels like the moderator of *The Dating Game.* On one side sits the bachelor. On the other grin the three bachelorettes. "Pick who you want," she says. Though, given the definition of *Homo Italianus,* she's as sure of the outcome as those sharks in Times Square whose three-card monte games are fixed.

With none of the token indecision an American might assume as a concession to the constitutionally guaranteed equality of three lice-ridden citizens, with none of the care an American might take to avoid the appearance of playing favorites, with none of the effort an American might expend against making a choice on the basis of gender, Andrea awards Phoebe his Banisher.

Daisy and Truman are on their way to an exhibit of photographs of parasites. The photographer is Constantina Katsoulis, who started out working for *National Geographic* and now shows exclusively on the white walls of fourth-floor Newbury Street galleries. Her photographs of tapeworms and bloodsuckers and leeches and lice sell for two thousand dollars. There is a waiting list for some of them. A German publisher is issuing a coffee table book.

"If you want such a book on your coffee table, nudging the cheese, the nuts, the bowls of crudités, the onion dip," Daisy points out.

"It's art," Truman replies. "As hauntingly beautiful as anything by Rembrandt or Michelangelo."

Daisy has her doubts, especially about the Michelangelo. Besides, she can't imagine a nit having any appeal, even matted in linen and framed in gold leaf. She remembers Truman's insistence that the parents of infested children be spared actual photographs. Only cartoon bugs with Donald Duck eyes and Mickey Mouse ears were acceptable.

How ironic that she and Truman are dressed up to go to look at nits when what they want is to get rid of them. Right now, the house has been fumigated. The sheets washed and tumbled in the dryer extra long on extra hot. The clothes carted to the cleaner. Every blessed comb and brush bubbling away in saucepans and kettles and Dutch ovens on all four burners like a chamber music quartet. If they'd bought stock in olive oil, they'd be millionaires.

Along the Longfellow Bridge, the traffic stops and starts. Even joggers of the Sunday painter variety pass their car with an enviable speed. Truman shifts into Neutral. He turns to her. "You know, Daisy, marriage would be a piece of cake after what we've been through. All this upheaval. Lice. The kids. Families divided, reconnected—maybe in the case of Phoebe and Sammy connected more than we might have intended. Still, we're a real family, not just a host one. We've even banished—for the time being—the Banisher."

Daisy puts her hand on Truman's mouth. "Shhh," she warns, "from your lips . . ."

He kisses each of her fingers, then starts over again. "Don't you think as a couple we can withstand anything?"

"Of course," she says.

"Even marriage," he insists.

Can we? she wonders. Can anyone?

Constantina Katsoulis is wrapped and knotted in assorted lengths of black silk like one of those keening Greek chorus mothers you might see in a modern version of Euripides. Her arms are thin and spidery; her small head bobs on an elongated stem of a neck; her eyes are as black as her dress and bulge slightly. Her body looks segmented; its parts seem to move independently of each other. Daisy is reminded of the earthworms childhood bullies used to slice, how the two sections would set out in opposite directions, how the neighborhood kids would form a circle around them and monitor their progress like judges at an Olympic meet. "Children who torture animals, helpless insects," her mother used to warn, "turn into serial killers." Which had convinced Daisy, swatting a fly, slapping a mosquito, that she was heading for a life of crime. A childhood fear that had not served to mitigate her grown-up Banisher-flourishing vengeance against lice.

Now, as she looks around the gallery, she wonders what kind of childhood experiences lead someone to pick as her life's work the photographing of parasites. She has to agree with Truman that there is something beautiful about them: their arrangement, their shadows, their light. A tapeworm's segments resemble folded lengths of diaphanous Fortuny silk. Sex organs curlicue like calligraphy on Japanese scrolls. A caterpillar, cocooned in wasp larvae, lolls on a green leaf. A flea with gossamer wings and the kind of golden luminescence Daisy has seen in Russian icons flies against a black velvet scrim, a necklace of fungi circling its throat. A deer tick sports bristly spines and comical ears; a lamprey eel is the blue-green of the sea. The tiny coiled worms in sushi—shrimp-colored with the pearlized finish of frosted pink nail polish—are set out like a display of earrings at Tiffany. Some parasites take the shape of flowers; others, white grapes.

Daisy accepts a plastic glass of retsina from a circulating waiter. She nibbles a celery stick stuffed with hummus. On the buffet table rest slabs of feta cheese and fat Greek olives. The napkins are patterned with bugs printed against Ionic columns. Around a centerpiece of funereal-smelling lilies marches a ring of inky rubber spiders, the kind that splatter the windows of toy stores every Halloween. Truman has already been taken aside by a white-haired woman bent over by a half a dozen scarab necklaces. "It's tee-nee-uh-phobia," she hears him explain into a scarab-clipped ear. "Fear of tapeworms. I'm a tee-nee-uh-philiac myself."

Daisy groans. What is it about men, their tunnel vision, their nit-picking, their obsession with cars and computers, with French and Italian, with maggots and mites? "Boys have a one-track mind," her mother used to warn, hardly meaning parasites.

Now Daisy's eyes wander past her own personal taeniophil-iac. Thirty people, dressed mostly in shades of black, fill two exhibition rooms. Daisy is surprised at how many variations of black there are. She is also surprised that this is the color of choice for so many Bostonians; but perhaps the influence of galleries reconverted from warehouses in TriBeCa and SoHo is spreading north. Daisy herself is dressed in a suit the sea green of a lamprey eel.

"What a delicious dress," a man her age points out. Cheese spills from his mouth, which must, she thinks, be affecting his choice of adjectives. He himself is wearing a black V-neck and black jeans. "I find color to be quite daring."

"Thank you," says Daisy, who has never been called daring before.

"Incredible work, don't you think?"

"I do," Daisy says.

"Constantina has grown in remarkable ways. Her camera's eye can squeeze the essence of beauty from anything."

"They are remarkable," Daisy agrees.

"And the message is so profound. That our world is a parasitic one, that we feast off each other; that our bodies are hosts to nature, to nature gone awry, to nature raw in tooth and claw . . ."

"I think it's red. Red in tooth and claw."

"Irrelevant nit-picking," he scolds, "when the meaning is perfectly clear." He goes on. "We are hosts, we are symbiotes; nature has a balance that we can't accept but which we must accept." His hands are swirling through the air like locusts.

Chunks of cheese lodge between his yellowish teeth like mortar between bricks. "Forgive me. I get carried away."

Daisy smiles a smile she hopes is polite but not encouraging. He's encouraged. "I'm Vincent."

As in van Gogh? She nods.

"And who are you?" he asks.

"Daisy Lewis," she says.

"Ah, yes," he says. He pauses. "The painter?"

She shakes her head.

"The poet, then?"

"Not that, either," she says.

"The columnist for the *Globe*?"

"I'm afraid no."

"Well, I know you're somebody."

"That's a relief," states Daisy.

Whose irony is lost on him. "I've got it! One of Constantina's photographer friends?"

"Sorry," she says. "Community relations for Star Market. Ombudsman."

"That's interesting," he says in a tone implying nothing could be less.

"Former food bank organizer," she stresses, twisting the knife.

"Good for you," he says. "Well, it's been nice making your acquaintance." He searches the room. "Excuse me, but the crowd's thinned around Constantina, and I haven't yet proffered my congratulatory kiss."

Daisy watches him make his way toward Constantina, who is talking to Truman. Constantina's hand rests on Truman's arm. Her face is very close to his, closer than the distance in those studies sociologists say Americans are comfortable with. She examines the photographs of parasites matted in black and off-white, framed in stainless steel and carved wood: parasites moving in on their hosts, attaching themselves. She thinks of Giselle moving in on Henry. Of being a host herself. Of Pilombaya's return. She thinks of Constantina standing so close to Truman. Of Jessica so close to Pilombaya she's caught his lice. She thinks of Truman's talk of marriage on the bridge. Of bridges between old lives and new. Is she being stupid? Stubborn? Out of habit? Out of fear? Why can't she and Truman continue as they are? Why is she so resistant to moving forward? So content to stay in place? She shivers. She downs the rest of her glass. Will the day come when she will have refused Truman too many times?

Constantina takes hold of Truman's other arm. She leans her head against his cheek. She kisses him.

FRANCE NATIONALE
CHARLES DE GAULLE 2
13
A 421 FRANCE

At four in the afternoon, Daisy carries the paper into the living room. Though normally she'd be at the kitchen table with the *Globe* and coffee by eight A.M., she's spent all morning scrubbing counters to expunge the smell of olive oil. As a result, her whole schedule's skewed. Now is her first chance to put up her feet. She turns on the lamp. She stretches out on the sofa. She opens the page to Ann Landers. Under the window the radiator hisses. In the hall the clock beats out the seconds. Comforting sounds, she notes, soothingly familiar. Between ticks, however, she begins to hear something else: a faint fluttering. A soft peeping. She sits up. A squirrel? A mouse? Lice escaped and crawling around her living room? Maybe Cambridge's run-of-the-mill vermin have grown so fat and happy on their Mediterranean diet they've evolved into begging for their supper and seeking new territory. The noise seems to come from the fireplace. And sure enough, as soon as she looks there, she can just make out a small gray bird swooping dizzily near the hearth. A bird. A bird in her house! A bad omen, a student from India once warned.

She dials the Audubon Society, where she's forced to wait through three loops of recorded cheeps and trills until the not surprisingly birdlike chirp of Chip Merkel offers his help.

Daisy explains.

"It's probably a chimney swift," Chip Merkel volunteers. "Unusual at this time of year. Though not unheard of." He instructs her how to get rid of it.

She carries a towel over to the bird, which, exhausted from frantic circling, practically swoons into the terry-cloth nest. Daisy studies this small blur of gray feathers. Its beak opens to her. Its eyes beseech her. It manages a few weak peeps. A mother bird's child? she wonders. Another bird's mate? Gently she carries it to the window and releases it.

She settles back on the sofa. Her legs feel rubbery; her head, wobbly. She's not going to dwell on bad omens, she decides. There are enough real problems in life without making them up. She turns once more to Ann Landers.

"Dear Ann Landers," writes Worm in the Apple. "Last year my husband and I celebrated twenty years of marriage. We renewed our vows with a full-dress church wedding flanked by our children. When he kissed me, I was delirious with happiness. He left me the next day. Five months later I met someone else completely different. This is it, I thought. Now he's gone too. My question is: How do I ever get love out of my system?"

"Like the worm in the apple," Ann Landers replies, "a fine relationship can develop rot. But once romantic love enters our system, it's hard to shake. Concentrate on the love you have for your children. And try to protect yourself by forging your own identity free of outside influences."

Daisy stuffs the newspaper in the fireplace. She lights a match to it.

*   *   *

That night, she twists and turns in bed. She coils and uncoils her legs. She wriggles. She shifts. Truman sleeps beside her. The blankets, her half as well, are wrapped around him. He's cocooned, shrouded. Like a bug in a rug. Like an Indian baby in its papoose. Like Constantina Katsoulis's photograph of a caterpillar encased in wasp larvae. With every toss Truman tightens the blankets around himself, leaving her more and more exposed. At this moment her two bare shoulders and one and a quarter bare leg lie open to the chill November air.

Not that she's cold. On the contrary, she has baked herself into a sweat. Rivulets slide between her breasts. Her underarms are slippery; there's a thick condensation on her upper lip. Daisy would like to blame this on hormones, the they-don't-make-them-like-they-used-to insulated walls of a nineteenth-century house. But it's marriage that's causing steam to rise from the tips of her toes to the ends of the liceless locks on her head.

Dammit, why can't everything stay the way it is now? To hate change seems entirely sensible. From experience, she knows how the bad stuff can progress like the slow onset of a disease you hardly realize you have, how the ax can get lowered when you least expect it. She's raised her child in an intact marriage, launched him from a disintegrating one. Why would she ever want to risk repeating her failure with Henry?

Especially when you consider the possibility—the *probability*—of that worm in the perfect McIntosh, in Truman, her *someone else completely different*. However devoted Truman is to her, there are always Livias and Constantinas, always new parasites: young women in white lab coats whom Truman is showing the ropes. Doctors and nurses and physical therapists swarming the hospital. Divorced mothers of Phoebe's friends. Community outreach chairwomen signing Truman up to speak to them. Dental hygienists and bookstore clerks and meter maids and gourmet cooks. How long can Truman stay immune? How can Daisy protect herself? By not risking commitment to this seemingly perfect specimen? Is he too good for her—an ombudsman, a failed wife? Will she screw it up?

She never worried about such things with Henry. Why? The ignorance, the arrogance, of youth. The sense that not much was at stake. Perhaps playing it safe numbed her into oblivion. Did Giselle poison the well? Or is Giselle the just desserts for Daisy's own refusal to see? If so, then maybe she's changed enough that paying attention pays her dues. Caution is the homework that heads off the failing grade.

Not that exchanging vows would make Truman invulnerable to the endless parade of the female sex. But when the inevitable occurs, the lack of a wedding ring is one less obstacle to a fast escape.

And yet marriage shouldn't have to terrify her. Particularly marriage to this mostly sweet man with the not-so-sweet profession who is lying under snatched covers in her very own bed. In *their* bed, she corrects, which they bought jointly, taking turns reading off her MasterCard number, then his American Express, to the operator who answered 1-800-MATTRES ("you leave off the last 's' for savings") after the second ring. "Divide it down the middle," Daisy'd instructed, "tax, shipping, everything."

The operator giggled. "This is a first," she allowed, "in the three years I've been doing this."

"*Divisez en deux,*" Henry would command, dining with another couple at Chez Georges et Gabrielle.

"*Oui, monsieur,*" the invariably Irish-from-Southie or Latino-from–Jamaica Plain waiter would reply while whisking away their credit cards.

Daisy wonders if Truman's Italian would be up to such a

challenge in Pulcinella, their neighborhood trattoria where Giovanni brings two bowls of ribollita even when it's not on the menu and Luigi sets down a plate of grapes after the tiramisu. Lately Truman's been missing classes. The lab's short-handed; there are grant proposals he has to write. "Are you losing interest?" Daisy asked.

"Not in the least. Though my tin ear's a bit of a handicap."

"You don't have to continue, Truman. The best thing about adult ed. No credit. No finals. No worry about whether you graduate."

"I know that, Daisy. But once I start something, I'm the kind of person who likes to finish it."

"Stubborn."

"Yes, stubborn." Truman stopped. "Though at my age, not all learning takes place inside a class."

"I understand that. But it isn't always convenient to trek to the markets in the North End to build your vocabulary with the person who's aging your Parmesan."

"I do have other resources."

"Like?" She held her breath.

"Like Andrea. One of the reasons we chose him, need I remind you. I can practice the language on him. Luckily, our paths have crossed once or twice."

Daisy was so relieved it was Andrea that it didn't occur to her to wonder why Andrea's company wasn't being parceled out in equal allotments between the two of them. If she can lay claim to half a mattress, she can lay claim to half a student. Even though the *whole* student seems to be favoring Truman. A guy thing, she supposes, typical of the unliberated Italian male. She remembers the trail of signori following Jessica to the Leaning Tower like paparazzi on the scent of a celebrity. The by-products of Gloria Steinem, of Betty Friedan, appear not to have trickled down to the boot of Italy. In the old tradition, Andrea, buddy to men and swain to women, hangs out with Truman, not with her. Whatever Andrea and Truman have in common, she doubts it's being parsed in a common mother tongue.

Still, it does not bother Daisy that Truman Wolff will be unconversant in any language other than his own. The few times Tancredi and Livia "talk" ("Hey, Tanko, the phone," Sammy calls out), Truman reads the paper or stirs cereal between the haltingly painful syllables that five weeks into the course have not pushed forward to eloquence. In such struggles, Daisy is pleased not to recognize the Italian-subtitled symptoms of Henry's Francophilia.

So what if Truman's awkward, a bit stiff? So what if he tends to see everything in terms of parasites? He's a more appropriate companion for Daisy than some colossal dazzler.

Now Daisy leans toward her more appropriate companion. She runs a hand over his shank. She touches his forehead. His brow is cool. Untroubled. In his sleep there's a hint of a smile. He must be having good dreams.

While hers are nightmares. In matters of the heart, however, sometimes you have to take a leap of faith. That Lillian wed three husbands—and that the only one she loved didn't live long enough to test that love—didn't stop Henry from marrying Daisy. And her parents' own silent, accommodating marriage didn't keep Daisy from pledging her troth. Even a couple of tumultuous divorces haven't detoured Jessica's quest for a groom.

Daisy curls herself around Truman. She tucks her knees into his, her nose into his neck. They fit so well together, like puzzle pieces, stacked spoons, nested Russian dolls. She loops her hand over Truman's chest. It is not in the interest of a parasite, Truman has told her, that great harm should result to the host from its presence. Truman covers her hand with his own. "Darling," he sighs in his sleep. *"Triatoma infestans,"* he moans.

The phone rings.

Daisy and Truman sit bolt upright.

It's nearly two. Right away Daisy pictures ambulances, crashed cars, jaywalkers smashed between delivery trucks, upturned yellow parking cones splattered with blood.

Or fire. A cigarette left to smolder in the dorm. A toaster with a frayed cord; a halogen bulb from a lamp too close to the baseball-themed curtains a roommate's mother stitched. She sees the bird in her house; its black eyes imploring her.

Daisy reaches across Truman's back.

"Mom," Sammy sobs. "Oh, Mom."

Her stomach somersaults; her voice stays level. "Are you okay?"

"No."

"What happened?"

"Everything."

"Are you hurt?"

"Totally."

Daisy squeezes the receiver. She wouldn't be surprised if it flattened; she's got the force of one of those machines that crush cars. Truman crunches her arm till he's practically touching bone. "Phoebe?" he whispers, his mouth in her ear.

How can you not play favorites in the face of biology? "And Phoebe?" she asks.

"Horrible."

"Horrible?"

Truman groans. "Daisy, what is it?" Truman demands.

"Where are you?" Daisy gasps. "Where are you?" she repeats.

"In my room." His voice breaks. Daisy's terror mounts.

Where only minutes before she was burning, she's now ice;

her teeth chatter; one eyelid's developing a tic; she's shaking so much it's only Truman's clenching fingers keeping her from falling off the bed. "Phoebe? What's wrong with Phoebe?" Truman cries.

"I'm trying to find out."

"Andrea," wails Sammy. The word sounds wrenched out of him.

Oh, no, Daisy thinks. Andrea too! They, the *in loco parentis,* will have to phone his family in Italy. Find the vocabulary to break this terrible news. Studying a language does not prepare you for this. You learn to order in restaurants, distinguish the ladies' room from the gents', get directions to the Colosseum, ask where to exchange your travelers' checks. The words for disasters aren't in anyone's first-year vocabulary-building text.

But what disaster? "Sammy!" she yells. "What exactly is going on?"

"Andrea! Phoebe's sleeping with him!"

Her first reaction is enormous relief. Her baby's got all ten fingers; her baby's got all ten toes.

Then annoyance pricks: After all, she's been awakened and terrified at two in the morning for something less than life-threatening. Followed by surprise that Sammy, lately so taciturn, has chosen to confide in her.

Soon enough, though, such relatively mild responses boil into rage. Which so consumes her she feels about to implode like those buildings dynamited on the eleven o'clock news. Somebody's been mean to her kid. Somebody's betrayed her child. In an instant, all the layers of civilized discourse are stripped from her. At the stroke of Sammy's cry, the evolutionary gap between animal and man is closed. She's a lioness whose cub is in peril. What do you do with anger so strong? Particularly anger bound by mother love?

Dump it on somebody else. She pulls her arm away from

Truman's clasp. She turns toward him. "It's all Phoebe's fault," she hisses through bared teeth. And Truman's fault for having fathered her.

"What are you talking about?" Truman asks. "What is Sammy telling you?" He slams his hand on the mattress; the mattress buckles. "Is my daughter all right?"

"Your daughter is just fine." Daisy snorts.

Truman is full of questions now, but Daisy has no time for them. She turns her attention back to the telephone. "It's awful, Mom," Sammy is saying. "All her stuff is still in the room. Her posters, her books, her clothes, her *Sonnets from the Portuguese.* I can't stand to look at them." He sobs again.

And if Daisy weren't trying to be the grown-up here, she'd sob right alongside him. She remembers when her obstetrician placed the stethoscope on her mountain of a belly and she had listened to his little heart thump in perfect syncopation with her own.

"Why? Why? Everything was so great until that"—Daisy can hear him blow his nose with an enormous honking blast. He clears his throat. "Until that Italian came along!"

"Sweetheart . . ."

"Host family!" Sammy spits out. "We never should have started it."

"Honey."

"Mom, I want to come home."

"Let me throw on some clothes. I'll pick you up."

"But what about—well, you know—Truman? I don't think I could deal with seeing him."

"Of course not. Don't worry about Truman. I'll take care of him."

Daisy hangs up the phone and looks at Truman, the enabling father of a Jezebel.

A fact of which Truman seems ignorant. "What do you mean, you'll take care of me?" he asks almost conversationally.

Daisy jumps from the bed. She pulls on jeans and a sweat-shirt over her nightgown. She slides her feet into two moc-casins, which, though mismatched, are still a left and a right. She is about to grab Truman's leather jacket from the back of the chair, but thinks better of it. She scoops up her own down vest from the hook on the closet door. "Phoebe dumped Sammy," she says.

"That's terrible," Truman says.

"For Andrea."

"Poor Sammy." He sighs.

"Your daughter has broken my son's heart."

"For which I feel awful." He pauses. "Though I have to con-fess I'm not entirely surprised."

Daisy turns on him. "What?" she yells with enough force to wake a dozen more chimney swifts nesting in the chimney stack.

"You don't have to yell, Daisy," he says.

"Oh, yes I do," Daisy yells. "What do you mean by not being entirely surprised?"

"Well, I've told you I've been seeing a bit of Andrea."

"So?"

"And Andrea's been seeing a bit of Phoebe."

"And what exactly do you mean by bit? An earlobe? A toe?"

"Daisy . . ."

"A breast, let's say. A fistful of creamy thigh?"

"Daisy." Truman reaches for her.

She pulls away. "So while Andrea's been seeing a *bit* of Phoebe, you've been seeing a *bit* of both of them?"

"It's not like that. Andrea and I meet for an espresso from time to time at the Cafe Paradisio. To practice my Italian. Plus he's interested in the politics of epidemiology. He's taking a seminar on how history is determined by disease." He brightens. "For example—"

"It's amazing, Truman, that in the middle of a crisis you still manage to twist the subject to parasites!"

"Well . . ." Truman sputters.

"Well, maybe Andrea needs to study how his own actions determine somebody else's happiness. How, to use your favorite analogy, his Italian gene for flirting might cause a pestilence." She takes a breath. Is Sammy genetically programmed to replay a version of his mother's betrayal? Does a history of being dumped run in a family, like color-blindness or alcoholism? Now Sammy's got his own snake in the grass. Even worse, his misery comes at the first exhilarating blush of young love. Not like her, when the bacteria for souring a marriage had already started collecting on its surfaces. She stops. Horrified. Truman's frames of reference are now bracketing her. "Where does Phoebe fit into this?" she asks.

Truman plucks at the blanket. "Sometimes, Phoebe comes along."

"And you've neglected to tell me this?"

"At first I didn't realize there was anything. At first I thought it was a normal host family–induced friendship."

"With only half a family? Where was Sammy? Where was I?"

"Sammy had classes. You were busy. It didn't occur to me . . ." He gives her a lopsided smile. "You realize, of course, that the father is the last to know."

"In this case, I'd say it's the mother." She shakes her head. "Go on," she instructs.

"And by the time I tumbled to the fact that there was something between them . . . Well, it's Phoebe's life, Phoebe's choice. Her private business."

"Which I don't have a right to know about?"

"Actually, Daisy, I don't think you do. I don't think knowing about Phoebe's love life is constitutionally guaranteed even under the terms of our relationship."

"Even when it involves my own child?"

"I feel awful about Sammy. I'm nuts about him. I think he's a fine young man. I'd like nothing better for my daughter than your son. But it's not our decision to make."

"But you and I . . ." Daisy might as well be speaking Italian herself she's at such a loss for words. "You and I live together. Goddammit, we're intimate in every meaning of the word. You *say* you want to marry me."

"*That's* not changed."

"And yet things are going on that directly affect my child, *infect* our relationship, and you don't confide in me?"

"Our relationship has nothing to do with this."

"Our relationship has everything to do with this. You don't think how your daughter treats my son is not going to have any kind of fallout as far as you and I are concerned?"

"Let me get this straight. You assume Phoebe and Sammy were going to march down the aisle? That, as a couple, they were fused into permanence?"

"Maybe . . ."

"That's ridiculous, Daisy. Adolescent love carries as much meaning as the mating of parasites." He considers. "Actually parasitic sex is complicated. Some multiply by binary fission; blood flukes have hermaphroditic reproductive organs—"

"Truman! This is not a lecture hall."

Truman looks sheepish. "Sorry. But you can draw parallels between teenage pairing and parasites. As far as the issue of fidelity, I assume convenience and proximity are deciding factors. But you couldn't say any are monogamous."

"You may be an expert on parasites, Truman, but—"

"But what? I was a college kid once. Even I, science nerd and lab dork, was more than aware of the if-it's-Tuesday-it-must-be-Annabel syndrome that pervaded everyone."

"Except me. After all, I met Henry freshman year."

"Bingo! I rest my case."

"Well, perhaps that's not the best example, I have to admit."

"I'll say." Truman waits a beat. "What has happened between Phoebe and Sammy—which is no surprise, given the laws of nature—should hardly affect you and me."

"Oh, Truman. Lots of things shouldn't in this oh-so-perfect world. But they do and they change things."

"Not for me."

"You're just being stubborn."

"I warned you." Truman grins.

"Don't try to be charming to me. Right now I am impervious to your charms."

"I rather gather that." He pauses. "But whatever's going on between Sammy and Phoebe is separate from what's between you and me."

"Truman, we can't put up barriers, some magnetic field between them and us. They're our kids, for God's sake." Daisy thinks back to Sammy as a toddler. The laws of the jungle had nothing on the laws of the playground. She remembers how the friendships between perfectly nice mothers were tainted by whose son was mean to whose daughter. The mother of the bully was shunned, the mother of the sand thrower barely tolerated. Daisy imagines a pyramid of love with the love of a child poised at the pinnacle. This is a force of nature superseding all other loves. You can only have your heart's desire providing everything's all right with your kid. Concentrate on the love you have for your children was Ann Landers's advice.

Truman's face is turned toward Daisy. His lips form a circle of astonishment. His eyebrows arch into question marks. "So what are you saying exactly, Daisy?" he asks.

"I'm not completely sure. Only that I have to go pick up Sammy, who's in despair. And he'll be more in despair if you're here when I come back with him."

"It sounds like you're choosing sides."

"There are no sides when it's a matter of your own child."

"I'd like to think that if the situation were reversed, if it were Sammy leaving Phoebe, I would not be so—well—precipitous."

"I guess it's the scientist versus the—" Daisy stops. "Scientist versus the mother. Truman, you can't predict how you'll act until you're in the middle of it. All I know is that Sammy's waiting for me."

"Are you asking me to leave?"

"It will upset him to find you here."

"To abandon my life with you in this house? My love?"

Daisy tries not to flinch at the word "love." Hasn't he just revealed his worldview that love doesn't last, that men and women leap from one to another like lice traveling from scalp to scalp? "For the time being," she says, "until I . . . until Sammy sorts things out." She hardens her heart. "It was Sammy's house first," she feels compelled to add.

"I must say that this is something I never would have expected of you, Daisy. This is a real surprise." He shakes his head. "I thought I knew you."

"How could you, Truman, when I hardly know myself?"

Truman pulls on a pair of pants. He flings his leather jacket over his pajama top. Daisy grabs her car keys. At the bedroom door she turns back to him. His pajamas are misbuttoned. His hair sticks out in cowlicks like a child's. His bare feet against the dark floorboards look delicate and vulnerable.

"Have you a place to stay?" Daisy asks.

"There's a cot at the back of the lab. It's got a hot plate. And

under the counter a half-gallon of gin. For kicked-out husbands, infuriated wives."

"Poor Truman," Daisy nearly weeps, "but you are not my
husband. I am not your wife."

"Don't I know that, Daisy? Haven't you made that perfectly
clear every second since we met?"

It takes Daisy less than five minutes to drive through Cambridge's empty streets to Sammy's dormitory, where Sammy is
waiting flopped on the sidewalk in front of the gate. If she
hadn't memorized the line of his cheek, the slope of his shoulder, the shape of a knee, she might have figured him as one of
Cambridge's homeless settled in for the night. He's dirty, tattered, hunched. His eyes are red; his nose drips. He smells of
unlaundered clothes, unshowered flesh. She folds her arms
around him. She puts her cheek against his matted, stringy
hair, lice's perfect breeding ground.

"Oh, Mom," he howls, "aren't women terrible?"

Since she is one of them, she can't quite agree. "Not all.
Maybe some." *Some* meaning the terrible Phoebe, the terrible
Giselle. Certainly Andrea, owner of a female name in every
country but his own, has a lot to answer for.

Sammy gets into the car. From the curb she picks up his
backpack, which is not heavy enough to contain a single book.
This observation races her heart with the kind of reaction typical of a middle-class Cambridge mother worried that one of
life's upheavals might cause her Ivy League progeny to fall behind. Hold on, she tells herself. What matters the state of a
transcript when the state of a son's health is at stake?

A group of students is staggering arm in arm up Quincy
Street. "Ten thousand men of Harvard want victory today!"
they sing. Daisy examines the one-ten-thousandth man of Harvard slumped in the seat next to her. The only victory he wants

is his girl in his arms, not in those of an Italian gigolo. When you win somebody's heart, why is the custody so often temporary?

She pictures Truman on the cot at the back of his lab hefting the half-gallon of gin. She thinks of his body, whose every bend and curve she's fit herself to. She thinks of his hair, whose every strand she's sectioned and explored. Through Truman's touch, she came to life. Through Truman's eyes, she discovered beauty in photographs of bloodsuckers. Through Truman's entreaties, she saw herself transformed into material for a wife. What has she done? Taken sides when there was no need to? Telescoped her heart into room for one when there was space for a multitude? She starts the car. She reaches over Sammy. She pulls down his seat belt. She fastens it.

"Will he be gone when I get home?"

"*He*'s got a name."

"Phoebe's dad."

"Truman," she says. Oh, Truman, she thinks.

"He probably knew about Andrea all along."

We're both innocent bystanders, she wants to protest. How happy she and Truman, Sammy and Phoebe were. Two plus two equaled the four of them. Everything fit. The perfect family in its well-ordered Chinese box.

But as soon as you start thinking perfect, disaster strikes.

"It was so perfect," Sammy cries.

Sammy sleeps for three days straight. He sits up in bed only to take two measly sips of the bowls of chicken soup Daisy trots up to him. She mixes him eggnogs laced with vanilla, the way she used to when he had his tonsils out. She scoops Rocky Road and Cherry Garcia, which, when he refuses, she eats. He must be losing weight; her waistband is getting tight. She lugs the TV and VCR into his room. From Hollywood Express she rents

Marx Brothers tapes. These he plays with the sound off, his swollen eyes glued shut.

He gets up to go to the bathroom, but no soap touches his suffering flesh, no shampoo his tangled hair. Looking at him, Daisy tries not to think of missed classes, papers due, pop quizzes, falling behind.

She's falling behind. She has to plan meetings for neighbors concerned about the Dumpsters in the back of the market and trucks making deliveries in the front. She has letters to answer from shoppers whose tenderloin was tough, whose strawberries were squished. She has to schedule the one day a week when a percentage of the profits from produce will go to local schools. She needs to stake a claim to her office at least occasionally. How can she demand squatters' rights when she's not there to squat?

Yet how can she leave her son? She's obliged to watch over him when he wants to be alone, to feed him when he doesn't want to eat, to lend the support he rejects. She's read the papers; in today's *Globe* a student jumped off the observatory at MIT after breaking up with his one true love. She knows about the relation between broken hearts and suicide. And knowing this, that she still worries about missed classes makes her hate herself.

"Talk to me, Sammy," she'll beg, sitting at the corner of his bed where his position—on his back, arms across his chest, legs splayed, toes and chin pointed at the ceiling of the pasted-on glow-in-the-dark stars—seems not to have changed from days previous.

"Nothing to say. Please leave me alone."

Morning and noon, Henry calls. "Any improvement?" he asks.

"About the same."

"He must really be falling behind in class."

"Henry, only you would worry about that when your son is in such terrible pain."

On the way home from work every night, Henry stops by. The first time, he surveyed the house with an appraiser's gaze. "You've made some changes," he accused.

"Well, so have you."

"Where's Truman?"

"Staying at his lab. We thought it best."

"We? Sammy and you. Truman and you?"

"All of us."

"I suppose it is. Best. Under the circumstances."

Now Daisy and Henry flank Sammy's silent bed and look at each other with mournful eyes. She remembers how they used to take turns distracting Sammy when he had the chicken pox. How Henry would stand on his head and sing "Yellow Submarine." How she would make clucking noises and jump like a frog.

Some nights Henry will linger too long. Giselle will telephone. Dinner has been sitting on the table getting cold, she'll complain. Jean and Jeanne need a father's attention too.

"I'm not sure why she cares." Henry sighs, putting on his coat. "Since it's usually takeout or some frozen mass you boil in a pouch."

"Which is not surprising with the demands of twins." Coming to Giselle's defense, Daisy surprises herself.

"Perhaps it's a French thing, but Giselle is having a bit of trouble trying to cope."

Daisy nods. Giselle's not the only one having trouble trying to cope. Daisy doubts it's a French thing. More a woman thing. After all this time, is she discovering in Giselle a bond for sisterhood?

Henry looks around at the changed-yet-not-so-changed

house. "I've got to hand it to you, Daisy, it's peaceful here. Welcoming."

By day four, when Daisy is thinking Prozac, thinking shrinks, thinking intravenous feeding, Sammy gets out of bed. He showers. He shaves. He washes his hair. For breakfast he eats a carton of Rocky Road standing at the kitchen sink. He slings an arm over her shoulder. He pats her head. "Thanks, Mom, for all the TLC," he says. "It's time I got a life."

FRANCE NATIONALE
CHARLES DE GAULLE 2
14
A 421 FRANCE

Sammy's been back at school for two weeks. When Daisy calls to invite him home for comfort food and a mother's comforting, he pleads too much work. This pleases her. How are you doing? she'll ask. Sad but coping, he'll say, making the best of things.

Daisy herself is neither coping nor making the best of things. Sadness sticks to her with the tentacles of a nit. Unlike Sammy, she hasn't managed to get back to work. What is wrong with her? How could she have ejected Truman from her house, her life? Why can't she apply the lesson of a husband of twenty years to a lover of two? For Sammy's sake, she stayed with Henry. For Sammy's sake, she kicked Truman out. She's seized the sort of high moral ground you can only plummet from.

Daisy surveys her bedroom. A string of books the length of a body lines Truman's side of the bed. Juice glasses stamp rings on bureau tops. The kind of chaos that's forgivable when you're distracted by a driven-to-distraction son. The kind of chaos you can indulge in when you have no proximate lover to indulge. In every corner flashes a sign of Truman's recent proximity: a tie over a doorknob, a biography bookmarked with a paper clip, the bedding he was always pulling off her, which she hasn't changed since he left, a memo in his illegible doctor's script. "Do you miss him?" Jessica asks on one of her Lady Bountiful visits.

"That's beside the point," Daisy insists. "Does Sammy miss Phoebe? Is the pope Catholic? Can a Kennedy ever lose in Massachusetts?"

What she hasn't told Jessica is she's started several letters to him:

My loyalties are divided. Sammy's the only male in my life whose connection to me doesn't feel tenuous. . . .

I realize a person can't live without love even when the circumstances aren't ideal. . . .

Actually the circumstances were close to ideal; and look what I've done. . . .

I can't believe how stupid I was. . . .

I panicked. . . .

Forgive me. . . .

But when she reads them over, she hates herself. She tears up the cream-colored pages. She puts them out for the trash. What a hypocrite she is. She doesn't deserve someone like Truman. How can she ask Truman to come back the instant Sammy's out of the house? You can't relapse into and out of love as if you're in remission from a disease.

Perhaps he's written her? She runs to the mail at the first clang of the brass flap. She finds only bills, Truman's journals, Victoria's Secret catalogs.

She's on her own. She's delivered the child back to college. She's banished the man. She's now sleeping in the high-necked flannel relics barred from the pages of those Victoria's Secret catalogs. She'll learn to be self-sufficient. To look on this as a time for growth, for building her character. If she can clean up this bedroom, maybe she can find the old T-shirt that states A WOMAN WITHOUT A MAN IS LIKE A FISH WITHOUT A BICYCLE.

Which is not true. Anxiety thins her resolve to a watered-down soup. A woman needs a man. Daisy needs Truman.

She calls his lab. "He just stepped out," says the person who answers the phone. Daisy hears water running and the tinkling of glass. Test tubes and pipettes, she imagines, even though they sound like goblets clanked together in a toast. "But he was expecting your call."

"He was?"

"Wait a minute. He left a message."

"He left me a message?"

Papers rustle. A pencil clatters to the floor. "Who ordered coffee with whole cream?" somebody shouts out. "Oh, here it is," the man says. "His handwriting might as well be the Rosetta stone, but I can just about decipher it. Let's see. 'When Constantina Katsoulis calls,'" he reads, "'remind her lunch at the Casablanca, noon on the dot.'"

Daisy falls onto the bed. Her heart sinks with her. If in the womb Sammy's and her hearts beat as one, out in the world they shatter into identical jagged scars. It's her fault. *Noon on the dot.* Truman certainly didn't waste any time . . . She stops. Of course it's easier to blame the Livias and Constantinas than herself. Like blaming her extra pounds on Sammy's birth. Doesn't she know Truman well enough by now to understand that other women aren't necessarily the problem here?

"Whoops, hold on, he's just come back," the man announces.

"No! No, that's okay. Tell him I got the message. . . ."

"Constantina?" cuts in Truman before Daisy can hang up.

"It's Daisy," she says, her name an apology.

"Daisy?"

Does he sound pleased? Matter-of-fact? All the background noises—water, glass, coffee passed around—make it impossible to read the nuances.

"My sources tell me that Sammy's moved back to school," Truman opens conversationally.

"Who are your sources?"

"Phoebe."

"Phoebe?" Daisy asks, astonished.

"The very one. I gather she and Sammy are in touch."

"Oh," Daisy says. She feels a stab of caution and a pang of hope. Sammy and Phoebe are in touch? Sammy and Phoebe are back together? Maybe Andrea was a small blip on the long, smooth scan of Phoebe's heart. Maybe going off with the Italian made her appreciate what she'd left at home. Why doesn't Daisy know this? Why is the mother who nursed the wounded heart the last to be notified when the wound has healed? "So," she begins, "so Sammy and Phoebe's relationship is on the mend?"

"Not at all," says Truman with the kind of compassionate directness that Daisy supposes doctors use to inform patients they've done everything humanly possible. "I hate to tell you this, Daisy. But the truth is always best. Phoebe is clearly involved with Andrea." He hesitates. "Of course Phoebe and Sammy will always be friends," he adds as an afterthought.

It's the *of course* that gets her; the *always* a close second in the annoyance race. She remembers the ends of high school romances; how you never wanted to lay eyes again on the one who done you wrong. How the glimpse of a certain chino-clad leg walking down the corridor would send you scurrying behind the metal shield of your locker door. Back then, break-up meant clean cut.

Truman, though, might say new skin grows over an old

wound, scar tissue knits together a gash. And Daisy herself knows that no matter how you try, there are connections that can't be completely severed. That a shared past can fill in a present's widest cavity.

In her day, the opposite sex stayed opposite. In Sammy's, male and female friends are indistinguishable. During Daisy's popularity-obsessed adolescence, her mother would pick up the telephone and whisper, "Daisy, it's a boy!" *Imagine,* her whole face would say, animated with delight. Daisy and Henry, on the other hand, were used to a stream of Janes and Marys and Sarahs and Abigails chatting about homework or Saturday's interscholastic football game. Is she simply projecting when she thinks that past pain would banish future friendship between Truman's daughter and her son? Is she still too angry over the unhappiness Truman's girl caused her boy?

"So, are you okay?" Truman asks.

"Fine. And you?"

"Keeping busy. I'm working on a parasite that's wiping out rainbow trout in Colorado and Montana." His voice rises, warms to its subject. "Great stuff. It's a worm that causes whirling disease. The fish spin in circles until they die."

She's spinning in circles herself, Daisy realizes. Unlike Truman, who will always have his parasites to center him, who will always have a safety rope of parasites to keep him from whirling off the edge. Her own confusion feels like a death. Could she ever, did she ever, fill the place in his affections held for a worm? "That's good," she says, "to keep busy."

"I don't know if we'll ever be able to eradicate this one. The best we can do is learn to control it. Figure out how to live with it."

Like lots of things, she thinks. Like love.

"Is there anything specific you wanted to ask me?" Truman inquires. "A particular reason you called?" His voice sounds hopeful. Daisy catches herself. No doubt it's her own pathetic hope attributing hopefulness, pitching the precise undertone she wishes to hear.

"Not really," Daisy answers. "Actually, no."

"Then I'd better get back to work."

"Me too," Daisy says. And manages to hold off her sobs until the hang-up click.

Daisy puts on an extra sweater and two pairs of socks. It's been ages since she's visited her office, especially for eight hours. She's looking forward to it, the nip in the air from the meat lockers, the conviviality of her "colleagues" Jimmy, Billy, and Bernie. Real work as opposed to nurturing. She wants to leave her hearth and hit the road to mental health.

"So Truman's in the doghouse," Henry had said when she'd explained the steps she'd taken on Sammy's behalf. Not just the doghouse, she'd thought, but the enemy camp. Like the cosa nostra, entrance to the inner sanctum of her heart is permitted only by blood ties. "You've done the right thing," confirmed Henry, whose conviction immediately sowed the seeds of doubt.

In the front hall, she fishes out a pair of gloves from the pile on Truman's great-grandfather's chair. She grabs an only slightly moth-holed scarf. Just as she reaches for the doorknob, the mail slides through the slot and thuds to the floor. The mail comes earlier these days. There's a new postal carrier who tries to cover his route before eleven so he can spend his afternoons rehearsing stand-up comedy.

She opens the door.

He tips his postal carrier's cap stamped with an eagle logo on its blue fake-fur brim. "Did you hear the one about the tapeworm, Mrs. Lewis?"

She shakes her head.

"It's a little raunchy."

"I can take it."

He sets down his mail bag. "A guy goes to the doc with a tapeworm. The doc says he can cure it in three days. Morning and night you stick a hard-boiled egg followed by a cookie up the you-know-what. On the third day, you shove in only the hard-boiled egg. When the tapeworm comes out asking where's my cookie, you hammer it."

Daisy laughs. "That's good," she says.

"Good enough for my routine?"

"Absolutely," she says.

"Promise you won't tell Dr. Wolff. I want to test it on him personally."

"Scout's honor." Daisy gives a three-fingered scout's salute. "No danger there," she promises.

Now she shuffles through the mail: no note from Truman. Not that someone with such total absorption in a spinning fish would bother with a measly postcard to his one true love. Only his *Journal of Parasitology*, *American Journal of Tropical Medicine and Hygiene*, *Parasitology Today*, and a dentist's bill. Though she supposes she should arrange to have his letters forwarded, she's secretly glad to be receiving this daily paper trail of him. So much for clean cuts.

Between the *Bed and Bath* and the *House and Home* catalogs, an envelope slides out. *Ms. Daisy Lewis* is scrawled in an unfamiliar hand across the front. Daisy slits open the flap. She pulls out a thick sheet of stone-colored stationery bordered with Della Robbia angels beaming beatifically. *Dear Daisy,* the letter opens, in Mediterranean aquamarine ink. *I am not certain how to begin this. I am also very worried that I do not have the vocabulary with which to express easily my thoughts. Nevertheless, I have the need to apologize to you and to explain myself. I am so honored to have been welcomed into your house and at a time when you were dealing with the problem of the lice. That made me feel as though I was not a formal guest but more a member of your family. I like very much you and Truman and Sammy and Phoebe and how you make it for me to feel at home.*

Then what you must have thought about what happened between Phoebe and me. You must have concluded that I was ungrateful and rude and that my payment for your generosity was to take the affections of Phoebe away from Sammy.

I had no intention for this to happen. I have a girlfriend, Paola, back home in Italy. But Phoebe and I, against our best wishes, against what we wanted, against the friendship emphasis in the host-family relationship, fell in love.

Phoebe says she thinks you will understand because this happened to you and Truman when you were still married to Sammy's father. Phoebe also explained to me that it will be harder on the parents. She is confident to coming to a better understanding between me and Sammy and her than she is about making everything all right between all the parents. This is understandable to me because in Italy the older generation often carry on feuds long after the children have made peace— and I am not just talking about the Mafia stereotype from American movies but a situation in my own family where my mother never forgave my brother's girlfriend's family when she married someone else although my brother has married someone else too.

I am making no excuses though I am sure you understand the excuse of love. But I am sorry that my arrival into your family has caused trouble for everybody, and hope you will understand and that you will continue to be my host family. I am greatly wishing to hear from you. With warmest affection and most sincere apologies, Andrea Mosca.

Daisy reads the letter twice, then checks the state of her heart. She remembers making candy in compulsory home ec and how, boiling syrup, you tested it by dropping a spoonful into ice water, watching carefully for what the teacher called "the soft ball" stage. She's missed the soft ball stage; her heart

feels solid. Her heart has crystallized. The line Andrea probably thought would melt her—*this happened to you and Truman
when you were still married to Sammy's father*—has had the opposite effect. She got a D in home ec. You could play hopscotch
with her candies; split atoms, break glass with them. A mother
with a hurt son? An abandoned wife? A woman who's exiled a
loving mate? Andrea, *and* Truman, should have a better idea of
what they're up against.

She tucks the letter into her pocketbook.

Her office seems a haven when she finally steps foot in it. "Out,
boys!" she yells to Jimmy, Billy, and Bernie with such violence
they gather their cards and are sent scurrying. "PMS," Bernie
confides. "Doris just clipped out an article."

Her mail has been left for her in a large carton that once
crated cans of plum tomatoes. POMODORO ITALIAN STYLE WITH
BASIL AND OREGANO is advertised on all four sides. She starts at
the top and works her way down. There are complaints about
lamb "with funny little white things in it," complaints about
coupons whose redemption dates are smudged. One disgruntled consumer has included a detective's log detailing day and
hour when the deli man weighed the container along with the
potato salad. Robert N. Levin, Esq., writes that there should be
more garbage cans for refuse. "A concerned neighbor" laments
that there are too many garbage cans and the dogs are getting
into them. Ms. Patti Smith protests that the trucks are making
their deliveries too early. Merna Pilot, M.S.W., grouses that the
deliveries are going on too late. There are several notes about
rudeness from the butcher, the produce man, the person who
initials the cashing of checks. There are a few notes about good
treatment from the butcher, the produce man, the person who
initials the cashing of checks.

These she separates into rubber-banded piles and sticks with

Post-its marked *Urgent, More Urgent, Most Urgent*. She'll take them home and answer them on one of Henry's computers, which are still scattered around her house, discards abandoned the minute a new model came out.

She's having dinner with Henry tonight. "Not a good idea," she'd said when he'd first invited her.

"We'll make it Roka," he offered.

"I can't be bought."

"It's better than cooking for one."

"What about Giselle?"

"What about her?"

"Wouldn't she mind?"

"She's so involved with the twins I doubt she'd notice. Besides, we need to talk about Sammy. How best to rally our support."

"In that case."

"I'll reserve our usual booth." He'd paused. "I wonder if Sachiko's still there?" he mused. "I haven't been to Roka since we split up. Giselle hates Japanese."

Daisy spends the rest of the morning arranging for pedestrian benches to be placed near the entrance to the market. She solicits estimates for marigolds and variegated ivy to ring the parking lot. She narrows down a selection of dates for the food bank fund drive. She makes an appointment with Cambridge and Somerville Recycling. She talks to the noise control officer at city hall. She talks to the traffic control officer at city hall annex.

All in all, she's put in a good few hours. She has the same sense of satisfaction she used to get in the early years of host-family volunteering, a boomerang of generosity long lost in the time gap between Pilombaya and the award celebrating the do-good instincts that created their relationship. She stuffs her papers into a Star Market handled shopping bag, which costs ordinary customers a quarter but is one of her perks. She goes outside to the meat lockers, where Jimmy and Billy are hefting whole sides of beef and Bernie is supervising. Daisy smiles sweetly. "Sorry for losing my temper. *Mi casa es su casa.*"

"Huh?"

"My office is yours until closing time."

Jimmy and Billy can only grunt under the strain of their load, but Bernie accepts her apology with grace. "Terrible thing, that PMS," he says.

Daisy walks out through the condiments aisle. She stops at the mustard shelf, where there is a veritable United Nations' worth of offerings. How do you choose among Dusseldorf, Dijon, Coleman's English mustard, Moutard de Meaux? she wonders. Beside these stand horseradish mustard from the Lower East Side and green powdered wasabi from Japan. She studies the jars. What does it mean that such items are starting to be available at a cornflakes-and-Cheez-Doodles kind of store? What sort of we-are-the-world conclusion should one draw?

All at once a shopping cart hits her from the side. "Ouch!" she yells. Her hand flies to her assaulted hip. She looks up to see Pilombaya wielding the offending vehicle and consulting a list.

"Daisy!" Pilombaya exclaims. He is holding a jar of Patak's Original Garlic Pickle, medium hot, which he drops into his cart, its landing cushioned by two bags of triple-washed mesclun mix.

"Pilombaya!" Daisy cries. "Or should I say General Pilombaya?"

"Pilombaya is very acceptable." He grins. He tries to push his cart to the side but succeeds only in ramming her more. "I hurt you very much?"

"Not at all," Daisy lies. "What are you doing here?" she

asks. Do generals who occupy, however temporarily, an exalted Harvard chair push shopping carts past jars of ketchup and piccalilli, check expiration dates and fat content, sniff the pineapple, squeeze the Charmin, in this melting pot of an America grocery chain? "What *are* you doing here?" she repeats.

Immediately the answer to Daisy's question comes stiletto-heeling down the aisle. "Lombie," Jessica announces, "I found the cutest little carrots, the tiniest, sweetest peas in their pod."

Daisy isn't sure what surprises her more: that Jessica, the order-in, home-delivery expert with a library of take-out menus from every greater Boston restaurant, (1) is in a supermarket, (2) that she's there with Pilombaya, or (3) that she called him "Lombie," if Daisy can trust her ears.

"Daisy!" Jessica shouts the instant she realizes the hip just impaled on Pilombaya's moving violation of a shopping cart graces the anatomy of her best friend since nursery school. "What are you doing here?"

"I work here, remember?"

"I knew that."

"I could ask *you* the same thing."

Jessica clutches the bag of baby carrots to her chest like a miser guarding his sack of gold. Above the stiletto heels cling crimson velvet pants topped by a hot pink satin jacket and a white aviator's scarf. Diamond studs glitter from her ears. Bracelets clatter Auntie Mame–like around her wrists. Daisy's eyes travel to Pilombaya, whose lapels look hand-stitched, whose black wing tips reflect the jars on Star Market's shelves. You've come a long way, Lombie, she wants to chant. She remembers his creased-from-packing mothball-smelling clothes from all those years ago; the shiny suits, the multicolored batiks. Now the two of them are walking fashion statements in the middle of the condiments aisle. Making the rest of the customers, including Daisy, look like patrons of fast-food joints in mid-America strip malls.

Jessica tosses the cutest little carrots and the tiniest, sweetest peas in their pod into Pilombaya's shopping cart. "Pilombaya and I are cooking dinner together," she announces defiantly. She gives Daisy her don't-you-say-one-word-more stare.

Pilombaya giggles. "Jessica and I, we are doing very much together now that we are neighbors."

"You're neighbors?" Daisy asks.

"Pilombaya's subletting an apartment in the building from a B-school professor who's been sent to D.C.," Jessica explains.

"Though I am not very often there." Pilombaya giggles again.

"Your heavy teaching load?"

"Not that. I am spending much time in Jessica's house."

"Jessica!" Daisy exclaims.

"Daisy . . ." Jessica warns.

Daisy thinks of Jessica's sleek white apartment, the kitchen counters that have never seen an onion sliced, a garlic clove minced; the king-sized bed's white satin headboard to prop a liberally oiled head, its chinchilla throw to toast bones bred in the tropics shivering with culture shock. Every cutting-edge gadget to delight the technophile. Is this America colonizing—exploiting—the third world? Jessica seducing with comfort, luxury, an alphabet's worth of modern conveniences? Or is it the other way around? Pilombaya taking root in Jessica's vast and rich terrain?

"Last weekend Henry and Giselle have us for dinner. Very nice time," Pilombaya discloses.

Daisy's eyebrows shoot up.

"Take-out Chinese," Jessica explains.

"They invite me," Pilombaya elaborates. "I ask to bring a friend."

"They must have been surprised when it turned out to be *my* best friend."

Daisy's sarcasm is lost on Pilombaya. "My best friend too," he says. "In America," he qualifies. "Except for host family," he adds.

"Speaking of which," Daisy begins, "I've been meaning to invite you too."

"I am very glad to come. I remember your good cooking in Holden Green. Hamburgers with pineapple in them. Special sauces. And my first and only Thanksgiving. The turkey had a—how do you call it?—a stuffing very original to America. Pepper and . . ."

"Pepperidge Farm," Daisy supplies.

Jessica laughs.

Pilombaya turns to her. "You know this recipe?"

"I've heard of it."

"Then we try it." Pilombaya strikes the side of his cart. He smites his brow. "I have a wonderful idea. We make Thanksgiving for you. We have big Thanksgiving celebration at Jessica's house!" He addresses Jessica. "If that's fine with you."

To her credit, Jessica doesn't flinch. "What a good idea, Lombie," she gushes, pinning a star on his forehead for best suggestion in the suggestion box.

"Jessica is very sad that Kiki and Karl spend Thanksgiving with their father in Palm Beach, Florida, so now we can have host family here."

Daisy sees herself and Sammy at opposite ends of their own dining table being good sports over a festive tablecloth and a capon-sized turkey, the runt of the litter of twenty-pound Butterballs. "We accept, Sammy and I," she says.

"And Truman?" Pilombaya asks.

"Truman doesn't live with me anymore."

Pilombaya turns to Jessica.

"I didn't tell you," she says to him. "I didn't tell anyone," she says to Daisy.

Which pleases Daisy, that confidences are kept between designated best friends even when other candidates for that friendship are stepping out into the aisle and up to the condiments.

Pilombaya is not to be daunted. "But we still invite him. And Henry. And Giselle. And all the children. The big extended family that I am learning so much about here in America."

Some things don't change, Daisy notes. You can update the clothes, improve the language, smooth the edges, sharpen the palate, send this boy to charm school, give this boy a book of diplomatic etiquette—and it's all just a gloss over the same essential doggedness.

"I insist on it," commands Pilombaya in a voice that reminds you he's a general.

"We'll figure everything out," Jessica says. "Don't worry, Daisy. Leave it to me."

"Sammy and I will be happy to come," Daisy says. She checks her watch. "Though now I've got to go." She pauses. "Dinner date," she confesses, she can't help herself.

Jessica looks so expectant, so pleased, Daisy doesn't want to douse her spirits by adding "with Henry." Instead, she says, "Check the special on veal loin today. Tell the butcher you're friends of mine. I'd give a pass to the artichokes. Not so fresh—there've been complaints." She waves her hand. "Bye, Jessica. Bye"—she hesitates. Why not? "Bye, Lombie," she sings.

She gets in her car. She leaves the parking lot. She thinks about Thanksgiving dinner. About Jessica and Pilombaya. About attractions between people and how you never can tell. She's driving on automatic pilot. When she pays attention she realizes she's heading along Mount Auburn Street near the hospital where Truman works. That the car has a mind of its own is something she's come to accept. Once, with no intention whatsoever, she ended up in front of Holden Green, a passive captive at the steering wheel of a vehicle revisiting its past life. Many's the time she's traced her carpooling route to Sammy's kindergarten, surprised to find herself pulled up to the gym years after he'd gone on to middle school. She thinks of ducks imprinted to tag along after a dog, or newborn kittens who'll attach themselves to a piece of cloth. Her car's heading toward Truman even though she's turned her heart away.

She steers slowly in front of the hospital. She watches for people entering and leaving the sliding doors. A hard-core group of smokers puffs away on a park bench. She considers the benches she's ordered to ring the Star Market parking lot. They'll probably be filled with smokers, initiating a flurry of new complaints to the community relations manager *slash* ombudsman.

A young man and woman, beepers jutting from their hips like holsters, walk arm in arm. An elderly lady bent over a cane is helped into a car by a man who must be her son. Three nurses sip coffee from Starbucks cups. This is a ridiculous pursuit, she scolds herself. Though the locals claim that eventually everybody shows up in Cambridge—and there are postcards from the Dalai Lama, Muhammad Ali, the robbers of the Brinks armored truck, movie stars, poets, Kennedys, celloists, Nobel laureates all stuck behind glass in Brattle Street eateries—Daisy knows this not to be true. People who live two blocks away she never bumps into from one year to the next.

Still, she turns into the driveway and circles the building where Truman has his lab. Where Truman now has his bed. She might as well be a teenager staking out a boyfriend's house. Does she have a stalker's psychology? Remember Sammy, she warns herself. Remember how Phoebe dumped Sammy, how Truman took Phoebe's side. Remember where your loyalties lie.

She pulls into a waiting area. She waits. A maintenance man comes out. He lights a cigarette. A bicycle messenger wheels his bike through the doors. When a car honks behind her, she presses the gas pedal and gives up her space.

She drives home on Oxford Street feeling like a fool. There are children sitting on the grass outside the Peabody Museum. They are arranged in the orderly circles of a school trip. Tourists, guide books in hand, exit from the glass flowers. Joggers run past, ears muffed in Walkmans; a Rollerblader or two weaves in and out of four-thirty traffic.

At the Agassiz School, the light switches to red. Daisy brakes. The orange hand blinks on. The Walk sign flashes its illuminated green pedestrian. She wipes her fogged windshield. In front of her, two people pass. She squints. It's Truman Wolff with a woman she's never seen before wearing a jacket the color of purple hyacinths. They each hug a bag of groceries. And they are in such animated conversation, chins bobbing, shoulders hunched with laughter, that they never once turn their heads toward Daisy's battered Volvo station wagon.

FRANCE NATIONALE
CHARLES DE GAULLE 2
15
A 421 FRANCE

Daisy is on her way to Roka to meet Henry. Henry has offered to pick her up. "I'd rather walk," she said. "I need the exercise."

"For health reasons, I assume. Since your girlish figure hasn't changed from when I used to carry your books up the stairs at Lowell House."

While this compliment bears no relation to reality, Daisy is nevertheless pleased. It has not escaped her at the reception for Pilombaya that Giselle's body hadn't snapped right back into its original contours since she'd had the twins.

"What crap, Henry," she feels obliged to point out. "You who were only too willing to pinch my hips to test what you persisted in calling avoirdupois."

"Believe me, I've always been one of your greatest fans. You must be mixing me up with someone else."

Now, as Daisy walks down Oxford Street and passes the light at the Agassiz School, she's finding it hard not to think of someone else and the someone else she saw him with. Especially since she's at the very light where earlier Truman crossed her windshield inches in front of her. The whole area might as well be roped off with police tape, it feels so much like the scene of the crime.

But what is the crime? Hers? If she hadn't been so rash, she and Truman might be trudging home from the supermarket with veal shanks for an osso buco or enough Arborio rice to put together a risotto for two. His? How can you not be reminded of funeral baked meats, so fast did the man who moved in his cappuccino machine find someone else to share his wok. She thinks of Phoebe, like father like daughter, that acorn who didn't fall very far from its oak.

A man careens around her, teetering two large pizza boxes. "Sorry," he says when she makes room for him.

Daisy nods. She smells pepperoni, mozzarella, oregano. It's hard not to feel sorry for herself. Jessica and Pilombaya are steaming baby carrots and peas in their pod. Truman and the woman in the hyacinth jacket are lugging groceries only hours after Truman's lunch with Constantina Katsoulis on the dot of noon. Are they heading to the woman's kitchen with the ingredients for a feast? No doubt Phoebe and Andrea are in one of the North End markets buying porcini mushrooms and anchovy fillets. The whole world's cooking together, eating together.

Except for Sammy, lined up in the school cafeteria, soup ladled out by ladies in hair nets and surgical gloves. A solitary Sammy sitting at a table for one spooning an institution's institutional food.

And Sammy's mother off to have dinner with her ex. Not an ideal pairing, if you consider the last time they had dinner—Japanese—Henry asked for a divorce and woke later in the night with acute food poisoning. Daisy's not so naive to suspect that one thing led to the other. If, after all, you believed in just desserts, Phoebe and Andrea and Henry and, yes, Truman would all be hunched over toilet bowls.

Now Daisy pushes through the door into Roka. The maître d' bows. He says something that sounds like "a raw shy masai," then translates, "Welcome." "A raw shy masai," echoes the woman in charge of take-out orders. The busboy bows, balancing a full tray of empty miso soup bowls. All the seats at the sushi bar are filled. Two sushi chefs, their foreheads bandanna-ed and wielding knives, bow when Daisy looks toward them. "A raw shy masai," they call out. A bunch of Japanese students have pushed tables together along a far wall; their backpacks pile into a mini Mount Fuji at one end. Scattered around the room are many Japanese families with toddlers whose black bangs are cut into bowl haircuts and who are hammering chopsticks against their high-chair trays. A few pale Western faces with light unglossy Western hair are dotted here and there, one belonging to Henry, who's secured their usual booth from many years ago. As soon as he sees Daisy, he jumps up and waves.

Daisy makes her way toward him.

"Daisy!" Henry exclaims. He leans to kiss her.

Which she deflects by scooting into the banquette across from him.

"Not even for old times' sake?" Henry asks.

"We're divorced."

"You're telling me!" Henry shakes his head. "What's that oriental curse? Be careful what you wish for?"

"Something like that."

"Is it Japanese?" Henry asks.

"I thought *you* were the expert on all things oriental." Daisy picks up the wine list. "Didn't you lecture me on the difference between Koreans and those born in the land of the rising sun?"

"Daisy . . ."

"Chinese, I'd say. It sounds like the kind of thing you find in a fortune cookie."

"You're looking nice." Henry peers over the top of his menu. Perched on his nose are half-glasses for reading, something she hasn't seen before.

"You too," she says, though she's not really telling the truth. Henry's collar is frayed; the shirt unpressed. Lint sticks to his jacket; its top button dangles by a thread. He has an uncared-for look. Though how can she blame Giselle? He should, like she should, be the only one taking care of himself.

"Sachiko's still here," Henry notes.

As soon as he says this, Sachiko glides toward them. She's carrying a tray of heated towels and little bowls of pickled beets, radishes, seaweed, soy beans, on the house. "Is nice to see you, Mr. and Mrs. Lewis," she sings, arranging the bowls on the table with the precision you might find in a Japanese rock garden where every hour somebody rakes the gravel and reconfigures the stones.

Daisy wipes her hands on the hot towels, which are scented with lemons. Not Mr. and Mrs. Lewis anymore, she ought to correct. She looks around at all the family groups, at the doting parents, their giggling kids. At the table of undergrads from Harvard and MIT. Near them she sees a young husband take the hand of his young wife. Daisy holds her tongue.

"It's been very long time I see you here," Sachiko goes on. "You are away? You are on sabbatical?"

"Something like that," Daisy cedes.

"Not exactly," Henry says. "But we're back. We're here to stay."

They both pick the sushi deluxe. Daisy wants to swap the sea urchin; Henry, the eel. Henry orders Deer in Spring sake hot. Daisy, Kirin beer ice-cold. Henry slides his chopsticks out of the wrapping, then accordion-pleats the paper to make a lit-tle stand. "Shall I do this for you?" he asks.

"If you want."

He makes an identical stand for Daisy facing his. Their chopsticks pitch toward one another like a child's drawing of a roof.

"About Sammy," Henry begins.

Daisy reaches into her pocketbook. She fishes out Andrea's letter. The Della Robbia angels are splattered by a leaky pen. One corner has been punctured by her fingernail file. In an-other corner the Mediterranean aquamarine ink has started to run like an estuary from the sea. She passes the letter to Henry.

Henry pushes his half-moon glasses toward the bridge of his nose. He smoothes the letter out against the tabletop. He picks it up. He reads it. Then reads it again. He folds his glasses and sticks them in his pocket. He looks at Daisy, eyes moving from side to side as if he's also reading her.

"What do you think?" Daisy asks.

"What do *you* think?" Henry says.

"I asked first," Daisy says.

Henry pulls his glasses back out. He studies the letter again with the kind of intensity you might bring to a subpoena the constable's tacked to your door. " 'Phoebe says she thinks you will understand because this happened to you and Truman when you were still married to Sammy's father,' " he reads. "Well, our son has no trouble spilling the beans of his parents' private business to one of his friends."

"Phoebe is—*was*—more than a friend."

"Do you?" Henry asks.

"Do I what?"

"Do you understand"—he pauses—"having been through it yourself?"

"Yes and no," Daisy says. "That is, I understand in the abstract. But when it comes to Sammy, open-mindedness seems impossible."

"And yet it's a thoughtful letter. It's hard to dislike the guy. These things do happen. I feel a little sorry for him. In a foreign country, away from home. Some girl snares him and he gets in hot water with his family, his *host* family. . . ."

"Or he snares some girl. It's amazing how men stick together, how they can be so obtuse."

"That's ridiculous, Daisy. Just because I understand this Andrea's situation"—Henry looks up—"how come he's got a girl's name anyway?" he asks in the voice of one who probably thinks Andrea's seduction of Phoebe stems from the gender confusion he'd been baptized with.

"In Italian, it's masculine," instructs Daisy, "as in Andrea Doria."

"The explorer. You're right." He shakes his head. "At any rate," he goes on, "just because I can empathize with some poor besotted soul doesn't take anything away from Sammy's pain."

"His *wrenching* pain."

"Acknowledged. The kid's suffering. I took him to Bartley's the other night and he refused a second helping of onion rings. Remember how he used to polish off three orders, and then have a John Kenneth Galbraith, an Al Pacino, and an apple pan dowdy with one scoop of chocolate, one of pistachio?"

Daisy nods. Her refrigerator was like a bucket with a hole; she couldn't keep it filled. Before she could unload groceries, the orange juice would be drunk, the box of crackers emptied, cherry tomatoes plucked from their trellised green crate, celery chomped to the end of the stalk. Followed by "Isn't there anything to eat? I'm *starving*." At times, when she bought something she knew Henry, in particular, would like (when she still liked Henry), she'd hide it. "What is that awful smell?" Henry would cry. And Daisy would find a moldy Havarti or a shriveled apricot she'd stashed under the bed, then forgot about. "Is Sammy losing weight?" Daisy asks in alarm.

"Maybe a bit," Henry says. Daisy must show the shock of a mother setting eyes on her all-bones, no-flesh son imprisoned at Andersonville, because Henry adds, "At least he was, but I think he's stabilized."

Sachiko brings Henry's sake, which she pours into two tiny celadon cups. "Shouldn't we make a toast?" Henry asks.

"To the end of Sammy's troubles," Daisy says.

"To the end of troubles," Henry says. "To the end of ours."

Daisy drinks to the end of her troubles, which are the last thing on earth she'd ever confide in Henry. She feels weighted down with the sort of catalog of disasters Ulysses faced trying to make his way home from his Odyssey. In comparison and aside from Sammy, what could possibly be worrying Henry— an unpressed shirt? A button loose? She pours herself another thimbleful of sake. "What troubles do you have to complain about?" she asks.

Their sushi deluxe arrives on red lacquered trays. The roe glistens, the seaweed shines; the shrimp is pearly pink, the salmon, as intensely coral as a reef. Henry's tray bears the sea urchin, Daisy's the eel. The sushi radiates out from a center medallion of wasabi and ginger. "Like the petals of a flower," Daisy says.

"Like a daisy," Henry says. "They probably know."

"Doubtful," Daisy says. "Mr. and Mrs. Lewis is as far as they get, and even that's a mistake."

Henry holds his *ebi* in midair, clasped between his chopsticks like a toy acrobat Sammy once owned. You'd press the sticks together and the little clown would somersault; you'd pull them apart and the clown would dance. "You can't say our marriage was a mistake, Daisy."

"Since we're no longer married, I think you might make a case for it."

Henry pops the sushi into his mouth. Some rice sprinkles the lapel of his jacket; soy sauce has dripped onto his shirt. In the past Daisy might have pointed this out; she might have called for soda water to daub at the spot, for an extra napkin to brush off the rice. Now she ignores such food fallout, since these are wifely gestures and she is not a wife. And never will be, she reminds herself.

"I've been thinking . . ." Henry begins.

Daisy waits.

"About Pilombaya. Giselle and I had him and Jessica to dinner." He frowns. "If you can call it a dinner when it's take-out Chinese." He sighs. "He's become so polished. So sleek."

"Not surprising since he's pretty high up in his country's government."

"Which is amazing when you consider that when we first knew him he was a customs inspector at the Jakarta airport." He bats some rice around with a chopstick. "But what I was thinking about was how much fun we had twenty years ago when he was sleeping on that awful pull-out couch in our living room."

"We didn't have fun," Daisy states like one of those revisionist historians academics are always indignant about. "He was a nuisance, a pest. We couldn't get rid of him."

"I know that. But when you look back, through the haze of years, through all our experiences since then, you start to feel nostalgic."

"*You,* maybe. Not me. I prefer him in his present metamorphosis."

"And *I* prefer him in his past." Henry prods his sushi so that the petals of the flower curve into segments like the legs of a bug. "Lately, there's a lot I prefer in the past."

Daisy studies Henry's face. His expression is hangdog. His mouth turns down like the mouth on the mask of tragedy. His eyes moisten. The effects of the wasabi, she assumes, the one smidgen that can clear your sinuses and send tears riveting down your cheeks. "We were talking about troubles," Daisy prompts.

"There's a new computer virus," Henry says, "French Leave. It's really wreaking havoc with the systems."

Daisy contemplates the lists of computer viruses Henry used to recite in bed the way somebody else might recite "To His Coy Mistress" with a lover's breath. Taiwan, Enigma, Monkey, Maltese Amoeba, Green Caterpillar, Tequila, James Bond, Chinese Blood, Mosquito, Bubonic, Michelangelo, Invader, Vienna, Tokyo, Haifa. Despite their names they could sound almost comforting. Now, for the first time, she notices how many connote both foreign countries and parasites. Once, it seemed exotic to share her life with someone who knew such things.

She thinks about sharing her life with Truman, who has his own exotic specialty. She thinks about meeting him because Henry was sick. She looks at Henry's jacket. She remembers brushing rice off Henry's wedding suit. Of drenching Truman's hair in olive oil, of combing out his nits. The gestures of intimacy. Does love ever go completely away? Does past love leave a present aftertaste?

"This French Leave is making data disappear. Once it infects the system, it's impossible to get it out. No other virus has stumped me quite so much."

"But you're the expert. I have complete faith."

"At least somebody does." Henry groans. "Oh, hell, Daze, things are terrible!"

"By terrible you mean this virus? This French Leave?"

"I mean Giselle. She's so, so . . ." Henry sputters, searching

for the right word. Bits of his dinner are shooting out at Daisy,
but she doesn't flinch.

"So?" Daisy encourages.

"Giselle's so *French*," he says.

Daisy sits still. She lets this sink in. Henry's fists are balled;
his jaw is clenched. "I thought French used to be the highest
accolade."

"I've been a fool. Giselle is stubborn, rude, arrogant,
slovenly, overanalytical, not physically warm, with a horrible
sense of humor." He is tallying her faults with more gusto than
he uses eating his sushi deluxe, with more venom than he em-
ploys attacking viruses. Daisy is starting to sense a backlash
here. She is starting to feel sorry for Giselle.

"All qualities integral to the French national character,"
Henry goes on. He strikes the table for emphasis. The chopsticks totter off their buttresses.

"But Henry," Daisy proceeds cautiously, "aren't you stereotyping? Just what the host-family office warned us against?"

Henry refuses to be drawn into issues of political correctness.
He shows no interest in parsing the language of diplomacy.
Daisy knows he's always had this in him, this capacity to gen-
eralize, to stick neat labels on messy things. She remembers
how, after a brief, hypocritical term of social consciousness, he
used to complain about the third world, chide her for wanting
to do good for students from underdeveloped countries. To him
anything worthwhile sprang from Europe like Athena sprang
from the head of Zeus. And the jewel in Europe's crown was
unconditionally France.

"Why do you think they have stereotypes anyway?" he asks.
"They begin with the truth."

Daisy is all too happy to exchange feeling sorry for him to
feeling mad. She has to confess that for a moment—due to a
cross-pollination of Henry's vulnerability with Truman's un-

availability—emotions long dormant were starting to rouse themselves. Now she rushes to latch on to his narrow-mindedness, a characteristic of no nationality but of Henry himself. She beats back everything she likes about him with everything she doesn't like about him. It's not an equal match.

"Frankly, Daisy, our first host-family gig was the genesis of everything bad."

"Even though you've just been preaching how much you prefer Pilombaya in the past to Pilombaya today? How nostalgia has set in?"

"I see it as the beginning of the end."

Daisy is incredulous. "You trace the end of our marriage to Pilombaya?"

"In a way. He was the start. Once we opened the door to him, everyone else followed until I met Giselle."

"*We* met Giselle. She was also my student, let me point out."

"And present at the party where we got the host-family award. From Pilombaya to Giselle, it's just a matter of connecting the dots. A straight trajectory."

Daisy's pretty sure there are holes in his reasoning, but she's had too much Kirin beer on top of too much life to begin to deconstruct the text. "What about the twins?" she asks.

"I'm not going to leave the twins. I do have some standards. Sammy, after all, was grown when we split. You know"—he leans over to confide—"Giselle not only has the worst characteristics of the French, she's adopted the worst American ones too."

Daisy sits up. She stiffens her spine. She feels defensive about her country. She needs to strengthen her borders against attack. In Henry's eyes, does she share with Giselle these bad traits of the land of her birth?

"Everything's fast food," Henry complains, "or something defrosted from the freezer. She wears these damn running shoes all the time, jeans and an old shirt; her hair's tied back with a rubber band. When I ask her so much as to sew on a button, she says 'Do it yourself.' "

"Which I wish I'd had the sense to reply back when I was lugging your suits to the cleaners and darning your socks."

"You had domestic qualities, Daisy. You even had a sense of style."

"Even?"

"You know what I mean. You always look so well turned out. In that understated Cambridge way."

Which, Daisy imagines, is the opposite of what Henry defines as that overstated American slovenliness. Perhaps to Henry, Cambridge is the exception to the rule. After all, what other American city is so often labeled *the People's Republic of*?

"And you were—are—a passable cook," Henry continues. "Some nights I dream about your lasagna."

Daisy pictures her lasagna, the recipe she got from the back of the box the noodles came in, the all too often burned layer sticking to the bottom of the pan, the tomato sauce, the Star Market brand she'd pick up in sixteen-ounce cans on the way home from work. Daisy knows the power of remembered food, how over the years a thrown-together lasagna can take on the properties of ambrosia, how the smell of Dole pineapple chunks can send you into the artistic rapture generated by Proust's madeleine. She summons up the lopsided chocolate cakes her mother used to make from a Duncan Hines mix; Lillian's Jell-O filled with fruit cocktail out of the can. You can feel that way about people too, she thinks. You can long for them knowing they're not good for you.

Henry finishes his yellowtail. Both their favorites, Henry saves it for last; Daisy eats it first. "There could be a fire, and we'd have to evacuate" is her reason. "You need a goal, something to work toward" is his. Perhaps these responses demon-strate why they were never meant to get along.

Sachiko clears the table. With silent efficiency she scoops everything onto a tray. When she's out of earshot, Henry whis-pers, "I should have married a Japanese. All that devotion to the male. All that fading into the woodwork. All that bowing. Plus I love the cuisine."

"It would be easier to hire a sushi chef," Daisy points out. "Imagine mastering Japanese characters with a middle-aged brain."

"I suppose you're right," Henry concedes. "Though there's a case to be made for middle age. The other day a neighbor said to Giselle—and he was just being nice—'You look so Mary Quant.' She hadn't a clue. And that's only the tip of the ice-berg. *You'd* know, Daisy. What I miss is a mutual frame of ref-erence."

Daisy thinks of her own mutual frame of reference with Tru-man, how much she's missing it. She has to force herself to keep Sammy in focus. She has to dwell on her doubts. She has to scroll through her fears. Otherwise her standoff with Tru-man seems like the Vietnam War: Who knows the reason for it, how they got into it, why they stayed? She turns her atten-tion to Henry. "Funny," she says, "I was sure you'd be marry-ing into saumon en croûte, bouillabaisse, coq au vin, washed down with a fine Merlot."

"More like Lean Cuisine with a diet Coke."

Sachiko brings the check on a red rectangular plate. This she slides toward Henry's wrist. Daisy reaches across the table. "My treat," she demands.

Henry curves his arm around the check like he's setting up a battlement. "No way. You're my guest."

"Then let's split it. *Divisez en deux.* In Japanese."

Henry looks stricken. "I can't believe how pompous I used

to be." He sighs. "Not on your life," he orders. He has already whipped out his American Express, which Daisy notices has graduated since Holden Green from appropriately green to platinum. Some things have improved for him. "Though if you insist," he declares, "next time you can take care of it."

"Next time?"

"Do you object?"

"I don't know." She pauses. "I thought we were having dinner to discuss our child, to figure out how to deal with his unhappiness."

"So we did. He's unhappy. There's not a damn thing we can do besides love and support. It's like a computer virus. You leave yourself open and—voilà!—you don't know what hit you. Part of it's his age. Young people come together and split up all over the place. I'm sure Andrea will have his heart broken. Phoebe as well."

"When it's your kid, though, it's hard to be philosophical."

"The whole love bit is hard for everyone. You and I have had our own malfunctions with togetherness. *La condition humaine,*" Henry pronounces with a slightly apologetic shrug. "Whatever the configuration, though, we're a family. And our students, no matter how flawed or annoying, are part of us."

He's on a roll now, fueled by sake, by what he'd no doubt call *le temps perdu*. Is he making any sense, defending that which only minutes before he'd dismissed? Daisy nods.

He gathers steam. "We can't assign blame. We have to forgive."

Daisy's pretty sure that in stating the general, he means the specific. But what the hell: Time has passed; he's miserable; she can forgive him. "I guess you're right," she acknowledges.

"Of course I am," he gloats. "There's no reason why we can't meet occasionally. I miss you, Daze. I miss our life together. I miss everything we had."

What is the subtext here? Is Henry trying to be more French than French by mining a past wife as a future mistress? Does he see himself, like Mitterrand, with a shadow family? Tinged by an American consumer preference for pretested goods? What would it mean if Daisy let him back into her life? Is her life so empty it's a vacuum waiting to be filled by the first offer to cross a platter of sushi? Henry misses her, but she doesn't miss him. She's forgiven Henry, but it's Truman she misses. Here's what she wonders: Is there anything about Truman she even needs to forgive?

"Daisy?" Henry asks. "Can we have dinner again?"

"We'll see" is how she answers him.

At home she calls Sammy. Nobody picks up. She dials again, deciding she's made a mistake. She's waiting for the machine with its ever changing oh-too-clever message full of esoteric references whose meaning even a Harvard graduate like herself could find obscure. Not to mention the background music with a thumping, migraine-making bass.

Speaking of which, she's got a headache herself. If it had been Chinese food rather than Japanese, she'd be blaming MSG. Now she's convinced it's Henry's fault. Her life feels like a revolving door: Henry's in; Truman's out. She's the unsuspecting host. And the door's spinning too fast to allow her own fingers to push against the glass.

Where is Sammy? she wonders now. Absenting himself from society? Turning into a wraith? Who is going to notice if he's not in class, not in the dining hall? Why has he unplugged his answering machine? She calls again. The phone rings seven times. She'll go to ten. At nine, somebody picks up. "Insane asylum," announces one of the wags who now shares Sammy's suite. From the background blares what could be an asylum's *cri de coeur*.

"Hi, Jonathan," Daisy says. "It's Sammy's mom. I'm hoping to get in touch with him." For a minute she's tempted to try the third degree. On a scale of one to ten, what is the level of Sammy's pain? she wants to ask. What shade of ash is his brow, what degree of red his eyes? What about drink? Drugs? Any of danger's ten warning signs? But it seems immoral, like spying on her son.

"Just a minute, Mrs. Lewis. Let me turn down this CD." The music sounds not a decibel lower when Jonathan returns. "Sam's out," he states.

Sam? "Out?" she repeats.

"Yeah. He went out. To a club with a bunch of friends."

"What friends?" asks Daisy. She can't stop herself.

"Oh, Phoebe, Andrea, some other kids."

"Phoebe? Andrea?"

"They're all buds."

"And everything's okay?"

Jonathan sounds surprised. "A-one, Mrs. Lewis. Nothing to worry about."

Daisy fishes in her pocket for some aspirin, which she chews without water. She thinks about Henry's talk of forgiveness, of not assigning blame, of the shifting configuration of relationships, how you might not know what hit you, how the ties between people may loosen but not break. She pulls out Andrea's letter. She tears a sheet from the memo pad on the kitchen counter. *Dear Andrea,* she writes, *Being a host family means just that. We will of course continue to be your host family. These things happen, as you yourself pointed out. Truman and I hope to see you soon.* She signs her name, looks at the *Truman.* Even reinstated, Andrea has no reason to be privy to her romantic ins and outs.

She climbs the stairs to her bedroom. The Mount Vesuvius etching she gave Truman hangs at a crooked angle over the headboard. Vesuvius is about to erupt. Daisy's already erupting. Shall she try to call him again? Shall she not? Is it too late? She circles the pros and cons in a continual loop. Should she? Would he? Will he? Will she? Never has her name felt more appropriate. Maybe if she had an actual daisy in her hand, she could abide by the dictates of its last plucked petal. Her head throbs. Her throat constricts.

She goes to bed in her jeans, hugging Truman's *Clinical Parasitology*.

FRANCE NATIONALE
CHARLES DE GAULLE 2
16
A 421 FRANCE

Daisy wakes up. It's still dark. Four A.M., she reads on the clock. Something's grinding into her ribs. She rolls over. She's been sleeping on Truman's *Clinical Parasitology*. The book is open, the spine bent, the pages damp and creased from her body like sheets after a night of love. She feels heat rise to her cheeks; she pulls the covers over her face despite the absence of a single soul to witness her shame. She remembers going to bed with her arm around the book, remembers a vision before sleep of Truman and the young woman through the windshield of her car, remembers thoughts of forgiveness, questions of blame. How she must have thrashed about wrestling with her problems to wake up with the book in such a condition of being wrestled with.

Daisy props herself against the headboard. She switches on the light. She's so mad at Truman she's taking it out on his book. She smoothes the pages of *Clinical Parasitology*. For all she knows, it's a first edition, out of print, the only other copy locked up in the vault at Widener or archived at Houghton, where they pamper rare manuscripts. She remembers when she and Henry were trying to decide what to call their baby, how they'd open books at random. Mordechai, Uriah, Gabriel had been the boys' names culled from this first dip into literature. For a while they liked Gabriel, but, as Henry pointed out, who would know they'd picked *Hardy's* Gabriel instead of Joyce's Gabriel from the story ominously called "The Dead"? Samuel had surfaced at the third tackle of the Old Testament.

Now Daisy turns the page open in front of her. "Relapsing Fever" heralds the chapter head. She stops. The hairs on her arm stand up. The burning in her cheeks feels like the start of a rash. She studies a drawing of *Spirochaeta duttoni*. It has pointed ends and large threadlike coils. So delicate, it could be a squiggle by Miró.

She reads on: Relapsing fever is borne by lice and is endemic to Europe, Asia, and Africa. The louse feeds on a host, then infects man when spirochetes released from a crushed louse enter abraded skin or are transmitted to the conjunctiva by contaminated hands. The symptoms are sudden chills followed by high fever, severe headache, vomiting, and often delirium. A rash may appear. Skin turns jaundiced. The illness clears but keeps coming back at one-to-two-week intervals.

Daisy takes the pulse of her own relapsing fever. Her flesh is goose-bumped. She has the same headache she went to bed with last night. Maybe her delirium comes not from love but from lice. Except she was spared the infestation; she was passed over like the firstborn son.

She thinks of the fragile scalps of her loved ones. However softened and moisturized with olive oil, they could still show patches of abraded skin. The conjunctiva could be reddened by bacteria, not sorrow. In the U.S.A., the disease is generally confined to the western states, she reads further. The paroxysms become progressively less severe, and recovery eventually occurs as the patient develops immunity. She expels a sigh of relief.

Which doesn't last long since the word *relapsing* has sent her thoughts spiraling out like this drawing of a spirochete. If you can relapse from parasitic disease, from twelve-step programs, from crash diets, from a blind faith in all things French, can you have a relapse of love? Or a relapse from the denial of love? She pictures her own heart veined with the residue of old suitors like the trace elements you find in minerals. Once she adored the Henrys, the Richies, the Olivers with a passion she was convinced would never die. Now she feels immune to all but the owner of *Clinical Parasitology*. Not for the first time this is what she wonders: Can you relapse into love as well as out of it?

She needs to act. To take a risk. She will call Truman as soon as the clock hits quarter to eight. The second she makes this decision, she starts a campaign against it. What if he's not there? What if he's waking up in a bed not his own? What if somebody else is waking up next to him in the cot at his lab? Maybe he's relapsed from Daisy and into somebody new. Certainly he's relapsed from Daisy into his whirling-disease worm. Married to one scientist, having lived with another, she still believes in magic. She's been known to turn over a tarot card, to toss the I Ching, to crack open a dozen fortune cookies until she found one acceptable. As a child she'd had a Magic 8 ball. Will I get an A in social studies? she'd ask it. Inside the ball, colored water would slosh until up floated a small white plastic disk on which she could just piece together: *The answer is yes*. It's hard not to feel that any fortune is a self-fulfilling prophecy.

Or any bad omen too. Why on earth did she go to sleep with that book? And what propelled her to check out the page on relapsing fever it lay open to? In penance she'll pack up

Truman's texts and store them in the basement. She should admit defeat. She needs to start exterminating the evidence of Truman's existence in her life, of his hold on her heart.

At the bottom of her closet sits an empty carton that once held a case of virus-protection software. In it she puts *Clinical Parasitology*. She picks up the *Physician's Guide to Arthropods of Medical Importance* from the night table next to Truman's former side of the bed. Is she important in one particular physician's view? She needs a guide.

This *Guide*'s cover is stained with olive oil. She sniffs it. She pictures Truman hunched over an article, dripping sweetly onto the footnoted bottom of the page. Near the back is tucked a folded-up bumper sticker. She smoothes it out. CELEBRATING 600 YEARS OF BUBONIC PLAGUE, it reads. FOR INFORMATION CALL 1-800-BUBONIC. Shall she call Truman? Shall she not? Will she? Won't she? She weighs the pros; she examines the cons. Resolved: Daisy Lewis will call Truman Wolff at quarter of eight.

At quarter of eight, Daisy Lewis calls Sammy Lewis.

"Mom, it's practically dawn." Sammy's voice is muffled, groggy with sleep.

"It's Wednesday. Don't you have a class?"

"I'll have to bag it. I'm wasted from last night. Don't worry. I'm two weeks ahead in the syllabus."

Normally this indication of academic preparedness would be enough to allay her Cambridge-mother-of-a-Harvard-student fears. Even her lovelorn-mother-of-a-lovelorn-son anxiety. After all, how debilitating is a depression if you can read and take notes and outline an essay on five obscure philosophers? No, it's the "wasted" and "last night" and the subtext of *with whom* she's worrying about.

"So where were you?"

"At Toad."

"When you have school the next morning?"

"I'm in college, Mom. Not in Kansas anymore."

"Very funny. Why were you at Toad? Who did you go with?"

"The Caterpillars were playing. What is this? The what, where, why, who of journalism?"

"I suppose it sounds like that," Daisy concedes. "I called last night. Jonathan said you were out with Phoebe and Andrea. I was a little concerned."

"Then why did you ask, if Jonathan already told you who?"

"He could have been wrong. I might have misheard. For instance, Jonathan might have said"—she pauses, thinks fast—"Fuji and Sandra."

"Yeah. Right. That's the name of a mountain."

"In the sixties I knew someone called Everest. Your father had a friend named Katahdin Schwartz."

"Oh, Mom." Sammy groans. "Everything's cool between Phoebe and me. She and Andrea are great together. He's an okay guy."

Daisy's sure she must be hallucinating. Delirium has come to stay. And her hearing has started to go. "What's that again?"

"Andrea. He's an okay guy."

"I thought that's what you said."

"Besides, Phoebe and I talked it over. We're better as friends than as—well, you know—a couple. What with you and Truman, it was much too incestuous."

"You didn't make that decision because of Truman and me?"

"Of course not. I'm no martyr."

"Because you know Truman has moved out, so if you and Phoebe—"

"Not a chance."

"I'd hate to think—"

"Mom! I've already met somebody else." Daisy hears a rustle, a soft voice, books thudding to the floor. Is the somebody else right at this minute coiled around Sammy's extra-long sheets? Is everybody a couple except for her?

She hears a few giggles. "Over there," Sammy whispers, "by the desk. Mom," Sammy declares, "mind if I give you a piece of advice?"

"Yes, I do mind."

"Very funny." Sammy's voice turns pontifical, not exactly seemly in someone only recently qualified to vote. "From my vantage point," he intones, "you and Truman make a much better pair than you and Dad ever did."

"I'll take that under advisement, Sammy." She gulps.

They say good-bye. Sammy's going back to sleep. Daisy's pretty sure she'll never sleep again. She should have known. Here she is imagining him curled into a fetal ball or heading up to the Eliot House roof, or at the very least paralyzed with misery. Instead, he's out on the town tapping his foot to the Caterpillars, eating pizza washed down with whatever's on draft. Holding the hand of a new girl. And ahead in his syllabus.

But if he's ahead, she's behind, repeating lessons she can't seem to learn. She remembers how Sammy once called her and Henry from summer camp. He was sobbing; some kid was bullying him, a counselor was being mean. He was going to jump in the lake. He was going to hide under his bunk. "Shall we come get him?" she telephoned to the director of the camp at the number starred strictly for emergencies.

"Let's give it a week," said "Uncle Spike," this colluder in Sammy's unhappiness.

They'd spent a week of sleepless nights. Should they have

ignored "Uncle Spike" and set out on a rescue mission immediately? Had they failed Sammy in their parental duties of
compassion and support? They worried at meals, in bed, canceled movies and dinner parties, put customers and consumers
on hold to consult and agonize over their office telephones.

At last they'd called, clutching the receiver with trembling
hands. "Gotta run," Sammy grunted. "Campfire night. We're
roasting hot dogs."

"But what about . . . ?"

He was already gone. Like fleas, his troubles had jumped off
him and onto them. And they had tortured themselves for a
week over what he'd forgotten in minutes.

Through the years there have been so many examples of
that, a trouble taking instant flight from him and lingering
for days for her to fret about. Not only has she not learned, but
also she's been making life-affecting long-term decisions for
herself based on the ephemeral glitches in Sammy's growing
up.

Or perhaps—she shudders—she's using Sammy as an excuse for her own doubts. His unhappiness has been a crutch for
her own fears of banishing intrenched habits and leaving herself exposed and vulnerable to love. Which takes her to Truman. Now that it's too late.

Daisy packs up the rest of the bedroom selection of Truman's books. She'll save his clothes for another day. His cappuccino machine, his corkscrews, his omelet pan, his meat
thermometer, his Marcella Hazan, his *Romagnolis' Table*, will
be put off for a period when she needs to flagellate herself.
Emptying the shelves in the study, the library, even the wicker
bookcase next to the toilet seat will require a toughness she'll
have to practice for. You'd think she'd already had training in
this, that the removal of white-jacketed rows of Henry's Editions Gallimard would prepare her for the absence of Truman's

thick volumes of parasites, his thin Italian language tapes; that, like lifting weights, she'd be able to go on to the next level of challenge with even more strength. But it doesn't work that way. Did Sammy's four weeks at summer camp two hundred and fifty miles away in Maine prepare her for the pain of separation when she drove him the three blocks to his freshman dormitory hall? No, Daisy Lewis is not the kind of woman for whom repetitions build muscles, for whom repetitive troubles build immunity.

Daisy drags the cartons of Truman's books down the cellar stairs. They thump and thud. The stairs are rickety. Mold pockmarks the walls. Cobwebs hang from the ceiling and festoon dangling bulbs. Here and there are the patches of cement slapped onto the plywood squares the wildlife control officer nailed up to keep the squirrels out. Propped against a trunk is the host-family award Daisy rescued from the flea market in Harvard Square. The leatherette case is cracked. What was once shiny crimson now has the brownish color of dried blood. It looks so neglected Daisy feels assaulted by guilt. Its state is a metaphor for her neglected host-family duties, for the bad direction everything took. You might even argue that being a host introduced lice into their house and cast Truman out. If you string events together, you can see how Pilombaya led to Giselle who in turn led to Andrea—a continuum that includes Truman, whom Daisy wouldn't have met if Henry hadn't picked an unsanitary restaurant at which to dump her for Giselle. It's a long line ending in misery. Daisy picks up the award. She puts it on the top stair. She'll take it to the kitchen. She'll clean it up. Perhaps resurrecting it will be a first step toward resurrecting her life.

Now she studies the rusted bicycles, broken tennis rackets, camping equipment, a hair dryer with a molded plastic head, toys, discarded furniture, college papers, Henry's most improved camper award from Camp Pockwockamus, Sammy's playoff trophy from Little League, his cross-country plaque presented by BB&N upper school. Abutting one wall is the old sofa bed from Holden Green, which neither she nor Henry could bear to trash when the Salvation Army declared its condition too ruined to accept. Springs extrude; stuffing spills out. On this bed they hosted Pilombaya. On these sprung springs, Daisy and Henry spooned peanut butter from the jar, chose children's names; and at least one time, for the novelty, they made love.

Piled on the sofa are more cartons. Though what they contain Daisy isn't sure, since she never got around to labeling them. On top of these rests a larger box taped on all four sides and wound with pink satin ribbon now discolored and ripped. It's Daisy's wedding dress—vacuum packed, sealed, preserved like a relic in an Egyptian tomb. "For your daughters," the wedding-dress conservationist/dry cleaner had informed.

"But what if I have sons?"

"For your daughters-in-law, then."

In all honesty, Daisy has to admit she has had fleeting thoughts of Phoebe in that dress, her ponytail wreathed with baby's breath cascading along a row of satin-covered buttons in their satin-covered loops. Now Daisy realizes there will probably be a roster of candidates for that dress before the winner is declared. Who may want to be married barefoot in a field wearing cutoffs and a turtleneck.

Or may not want to be married at all. Who is she to expect from someone else what she herself was so quick to reject?

Daisy picks up the box. She holds it against her ear. What is she hoping for? The rush of waves you hear inside a shell? She shakes it. She can just make out, faintly, the soft crackle of imported silk.

She puts the wedding gown back. She looks around the cel-

lar, at the shards of her life. She sits on a splintered crate. She
weeps. She wails. She must be making so much noise she stirs
the dust. She starts to sneeze. Now I feel so much better, she
tells herself.

She doesn't feel better. Work is the cure. She lugs Truman's
books to the wall opposite the sofa. She hoists them onto other
boxes of books like building blocks. On makeshift boards
propped up with bricks stands the *Encyclopedia Britannica*. She
selects Volume 17, *P to Planti*. She won't risk opening it at
random. In her present state of suggestibility she'd turn to
"Pineapple" and feel compelled to go back to soliciting canned
fruits and vegetables. She looks up "Parasitology." There's a
whole page of photographs of parasites.

Daisy studies them. A roundworm nestles in a kidney like
a cobra coiled in a basket. The heart of a dog exhibits an in-
vasion of *Dirofilaria immitis*. A tapeworm cyst bulges through
the skull of a sheep. Another graceful spiral of the organism
causing relapsing fever is braceleted by circles as big as balloons. These pictures don't bother her. In fact, the section of a
sheep's liver showing flat worms resembles a slice of a geode.
The lung of a tiger with Asiatic fluke looks like the landscape
of the moon. The foreign body that stimulates the formation
of a pearl in an oyster, she reads, is a parasitic worm; thus, con-
cludes the writer in an unexpected burst of poetry, the most
beautiful pearl is the worm's sarcophagus. This delights her.
Although the study of parasitic diseases must have advanced
well beyond the 1944 copyright of her encyclopedia, she assumes the malaria rosette has not changed its shape in over
fifty years. Parasites turn up in malt vinegar and wallpaper
paste. Traces of parasites have been found in mummies. Parasites are tenacious and identifiable. Unlike love, Daisy thinks.

Upstairs in the kitchen, she sponges off the host-family
award. She oils its cover with Andrea's extra-virgin in its pre-

sentation crock. The color comes back; a few daubs of dish detergent transform the soy stains into the badges of age prized in old documents. If only relationships were so easy to rehabilitate.

By the time she's dried her hair, dressed, made coffee, eaten toast, it's nearly eleven. She loads the dishwasher. She's practically ready for dinner since she's been up since four. She'll treat herself to something good tonight. Shrimp from the fish counter; that nice Vernaccia di San Gimignano on special this week in the wine and spirits section; from Produce, out-of-season asparagus and a baked potato with real butter; from the freezer, a pint of Rocky Road. God knows she deserves it, she's been trodding for so long her own rocky road.

As she leaves, the mailman is hiking up the walk. "Got a minute, Mrs. L.?"

"Actually—"

"Heard a really good one."

"If it's *really* good."

"Another tapeworm."

"Well, then . . ."

"This tapeworm walks into a bar and orders a dry martini. The bartender sets him up, figures what does a tapeworm know and charges him twenty bucks. The tapeworm knocks it back. The bartender says, 'We don't get many tapeworms in here.' The tapeworm replies, 'Twenty bucks for a martini, you won't get many more.'"

"Not bad," Daisy admits.

The mailman slaps the side of his bag. "Here's something better. How do head lice bake a cake?"

"I haven't a clue."

"From scratch."

Daisy laughs. "This one I like. Even though lice is a sensitive topic around my house. Still, my favorite is your tapeworm cookie joke."

"It's been around the block too many times. My sources have seen it on the Internet. In show biz you got to keep pushing the envelope. I'm lined up for two gigs at Comedy Cave in Mattapoisett next week. You want I should give you your mail or stick it through the slot?"

"I'll take it," Daisy says. She holds out her hands.

When she looks down at the stack the mailman places in her arms, she sees at once, right on top, a photograph of Truman Wolff grinning up at her. His mouth is crooked; his eyes are crinkled at the corners; his hair falls over his forehead like a little boy's; he's wearing his ladybug bow tie, the one he wore when she first saw him in the lecture hall at Mount Auburn Hospital. When she can bear to move her eyes from this compelling reproduction of the even more compelling, and rarely viewed, original, she notices the headline strung along the upper margin. In large red sans serif capitals, she reads: NIT NOTES: NEWSLETTER OF THE CAMBRIDGE PEDICULOSIS SOCIETY.

"Are you, okay, Mrs. Lewis?" asks the mailman. "Having second thoughts about my joke?"

"Second thoughts?"

"How's about I run you water from the hose?"

"I'll get some inside."

"If you're sure you're all right."

Daisy goes back inside. She grabs a tumbler propped upside down on the draining board. She fills it and drinks it. Fills it again. She takes it to the kitchen table. She slumps into a chair. Second thoughts, she ruminates. Second thoughts.

She picks up *Nit Notes*. She reads the article under Truman's photograph. It's written by Barbara Abernathy, sixth-grade teacher at the Peabody School. Barbara Abernathy catalogs

Truman's impressive academic credentials, that he lives in Cambridge, that he has a daughter at Harvard who's had her own problems with pediculosis. She proceeds with a factual account of Truman's talk. Which lists the steps to take to avoid lice. The steps to take once you have it. It's an impartial bit of reportage. No muckraking. No tabloid sensationalism. No indication that Truman broke a rule and tried on a hat. The last paragraph is devoted to what the author calls "the issues of shame." Even the best people get lice, she explains. Movie stars and sports figures, people in mansions, people in subsidized housing. People who wash their hair every day. Spanish speakers. English speakers. Asians. Italians. French. Africans. Americans. The Dutch. The article ends with a call to arms. It is time to form support groups, let the secret out.

Daisy moves to a profile of Lucy DiStefano, former school nurse, who has started a service of going to subscribers' homes to pick their nits. *Lice Busters*, announces her business card, *Have Comb, Will Travel*. She has seven employees already, she boasts. They are trying to unionize.

Daisy flips the page. Her eyes fall on a sidebar interview with Dr. Wolff by Brittany Gomez, age ten.

BG: How did you first get interested in lice?

TW: I've always loved bugs, since I was a kid.

BG: What is the ickiest bug?

TW: It's hard to pick out one. If you look them up in the school-library encyclopedia, you'll see a whole host of really icky ones. Which of course to me are part of nature and thus beautiful.

BG: Have you ever had lice?

TW: In the interest of full disclosure, yes.

BG: How did you get rid of it?

TW: Olive oil. And the loving support, and nit-picking skills, of family and friends.

BG: Does liking bugs make it hard for you to get a girl-friend?

TW: I'd be interested in your opinion on this.

BG: It wouldn't bother me. Will you wait till I grow up?

TW: I'm very flattered, Brittany, but I'm afraid I've already got a girlfriend.

BG: What's her name?

TW: Her name is Daisy.

BG: Thank you, Dr. Wolff.

TW: Thank *you*, Brittany.

Daisy turns over the newsletter and sees it is addressed to Dr. Truman Wolff, c/o Lewis. Thank goodness Truman did not go to the post office for a change of address. Imagine missing what that Woodward-Bernstein in training, Brittany Gomez, so brilliantly elicited from him. *Her name is Daisy. Her name is Daisy*, she repeats to herself.

Daisy takes another sip of water. If it weren't still before noon, she might consider champagne. That Truman Wolff has a girlfriend named Daisy is something to celebrate. The second she thinks this, she reminds herself it's all a matter of tense. In the amount of time it takes for a louse to jump out of a hat and onto a scalp, for a tapeworm to twist out of a sushi and into a gut, an *is* can become a *was*.

She remembers Truman's telling her about certain parasites that choose only female crustaceans. You need to have shel-tered nooks for liberating the offspring was the reason he gave. Well, she's liberated her offspring. Maybe she's started liber-ating herself. She doesn't need protection. What she wants is love. It's time she goes after it.

She calls Truman at his lab.

"Who wants him now?" asks a suspicious female voice.

This daunts her. She's tempted to hang up, to say never

mind, when the woman, exasperated, almost yells, "Who should I say is on the line?"

"Daisy Lewis."

"Daisy Lewis," the woman screams.

"No need to scream, Evelyn," she hears. Then silence.

Which makes Daisy panic. What if Truman says Who? What if Truman says Never heard of her? What if Truman says Tell her there are other fish in my personal sea? Other worms in my can of them. "Tell her I'll take it in my office," he instructs.

During the progression from lab to office, Daisy starts to fall apart. He must be preparing notes on how best to break the news. To inform her that in the interval between her first and second thoughts he's been doing some thinking too. And not just thinking. Daisy knows she needs to steel herself.

"Daisy!"

She holds her breath.

"I'm so glad you called. I've wanted to get in touch with you."

Her spirits soar.

"To find out about your lasagna. To copy down the recipe."

Her spirits drop. "It's on the box."

"What?"

"The recipe. You buy the noodles dry. The box is red. I forget the brand."

"Never mind that. We made Marcella Hazan."

We, Daisy notes. Her spirits plummet to her toes.

"Have you come to your senses?" he asks.

"Who made Marcella Hazan?"

"Livia and I. We messed up her kitchen so much, her husband was furious."

Livia has a husband! "What was the lasagna for?"

"Our class dinner. All the language partners had to produce an Italian dish."

"I thought you'd dropped out."

"Tapered off is a better word for it. Do you think I'd skip the class dinner, me who's been eating almost exclusively in a hospital cafeteria? We did have fun shopping for all the ingredients. Though talking to Livia in any language is a tribulation and a trial. She and her husband have no books, only bound back issues of *Consumer Reports*. Their condo is so sterile even a mite would turn away at the door. Oh, Daisy. I've started a million letters to you. Begun and abandoned a million notes. My wastepaper baskets are so full of crumpled, scribbled pages you'd think I was an aspiring novelist." He pauses.

Daisy holds her breath. What does this mean? That he wants his stuff back? That he's trying to find the kindest Dear John words?

"God, I've missed you," Truman exclaims.

"Are you sure?" Daisy asks.

Truman lowers his voice. "Are you?"

She pushes on. "Do you know about Sammy and Phoebe? That they're friends? That Sammy has a new girl. That—"

"Yes."

"And you didn't tell me?"

"You had to decide for yourself. Independent of the love life of the kids. Independent of my bugging you." He hesitates. "Have you?"

"Have I what?"

"Decided."

"Oh, Truman. Don't you think it's time you came home?"

Daisy calls in sick.

"Funny, you don't sound sick," says Bernie. "You sound in

the best of health. It's a terrible time not to come in. You know those benches we put up? The phone's ringing off the hook with people complaining about pigeon droppings, cigarette butts, teenagers doing God knows what. That green paint is already starting to peel. A mothers' group is worried that there's lead in it. They're planning a boycott. It's a crisis, Daisy. We need someone who's going to be in charge of our community relationships."

Not this someone, who needs first to be in charge of her personal relationships. Daisy tries to sound as vocally impaired as an invalid with advanced and highly contagious strep. "Bernie, I have every faith," she croaks.

Daisy slams down the phone, then turns into the kind of domestic whirlwind Martha Stewart might want to emulate. She runs to the cellar and lugs up the box of Truman's books. Earlier they weighed a ton; now, empowered by love, she might just as well be hoisting the finest down from the finest geese. She replaces the books on the shelf. The *Physician's Guide to Arthropods of Medical Importance* she splays open on the night table in the exact position she took it from. This is not hard, since its outline has been marked in dust. No sterile unwelcome environment forms her habitat. She changes the sheets. Makes room in the medicine chest, makes room in the closet. She multiplies by two her solitary meal of shrimp, potato, and asparagus. She buys a pint of Ben & Jerry's Purple Passion Fruit Sorbet. She puts champagne on ice.

At six on the dot Truman rings the bell. His arms are filled with bunches of daisies, more than she's ever seen either in fields or at the florists whose pots and flats garland the bricks along Brattle Street. "You must have cornered the market."

"There's not another daisy to be had in all of Cambridge, Boston, and the surrounding suburbs. Not a daisy left within the radius of 128."

"I've planned a wonderful dinner."

Truman showers her with the daisies. Flowers fall into her hair, float against her shoulders, pour onto her feet until she is ankle deep in a sea of them. Truman lifts her up. "Later," he says.

On the morning of Thanksgiving, Daisy and Truman get up early. They're due at Jessica's at four. They've volunteered to supply Sammy's favorite sweet potatoes. To roast chestnuts. "Don't you want anything more?" Daisy has asked. "I could cook the turkey and bring it over. You are, after all, feeding my whole family. Not to mention significant other and insignificant ex."

"*My* family too. I've annexed them. *Sua famiglia e mia famiglia*. Especially since Karl and Kiki will be with their father, the louse." Jessica laughed. "I never knew before how appropriate that term was until I met one up close and personal."

"I feel as if I'm not doing enough."

"You're doing plenty. I'm forever in your debt since you were responsible for Lombie and my getting together in the first place."

"I can't take credit. You met him on assignment for *Boston Bean & Cod*, remember?"

"But if you hadn't hosted him so well in the first place, he'd never have come back to Cambridge a second time. Besides, Lombie and I are turning into quite the cooks. We've signed up for a food and wine course this summer in Tuscany."

Now Daisy and Truman divide the newspaper over coffee and toast. The newspapers are larded with ads for the day-after-Thanksgiving sales. Daisy studies a page of lingerie, bits of lace in *vert absinthe* or *vieux rose*, 100 percent silk, made in France, greatly reduced. Would a wisp of silk at half price be worth bucking the bargain-hunting crowds? Still, now that Truman's back in her bed, prissy flannel or Sammy's discarded T-shirts of dissolved rock groups don't exactly sow the seeds of desire in the Cole Porter/Ella Fitzgerald set. Daisy examines a shoulder strap thin as a wire.

"Those Indonesians," Truman groans. "I wouldn't be surprised at a civil war."

"Those Republicans," Daisy complains. "Whatever could be in their heads?"

Truman sips his coffee. Daisy spoons out Three Fruits marmalade.

"And they're boycotting Star," Truman adds.

Daisy is confused. "The Indonesians?" she asks.

"No, mothers. They're protesting lead paint on the benches. Only in Cambridge. Still, it says here revenues are down. Hardly surprising, given this is a city of activists who would never cross a picket line."

"Imagine," Daisy says, trying to avoid a tone of sheepishness. She knows it's not her fault. She did not choose the paint. She is not responsible for shoddy goods bought on the cheap. Choices dictated by budget rather than sense. Nevertheless, she's the official scapegoat. Blame the ombudsman. Bananas spoiled, tuna tins dented, rude cashiers, automatic doors that don't swing open automatically—RSVP your gripes to Daisy

Lewis; she's hosting them. Daisy's relieved she's off till Monday. By Monday, the old clamor will have died down and a new furor will rise to storm the barricades.

Daisy layers the sweet potatoes into a casserole. Truman begins to carve Xs on the chestnuts. He arranges them in orderly rows on Daisy's broiling pans and cookie sheets. Honest Bob and the Factory-to-Dealer Incentives sing of love and tapeworms from the CD player. "They warned me about the steak tartare/They said I could get a disease/But I don't mind being ill so much/If I can have symptoms like these. . . . It's a welcome guest in/My intestine/I don't mind the things it makes me do/Each proglottid/That I've got is/Feeding on the love I feel for you. . . ."

Through the kitchen window, Daisy watches a feathery fall of early snow. She and Truman have built a fire in the woodstove. The kitchen smells of fresh-ground coffee and buttered toast. The marshmallows are already starting to melt on their sweet-potato bed. It's not a recipe to stir the nouveau haute cuisine tastes of Jessica and Pilombaya, but it's a dish she could no more veer from for Thanksgiving than she could ever again veer from love. She studies Truman, the object of her love, its origin.

She snuggles into her chair. Her house is a cocoon. No mothers picketing at her door. No outsiders trying to wrench their way in. When she looks around the room she sees such a vision of domestic bliss she feels ballooned by blissfulness.

Punctured by the ring of the telephone.

"Daisy, I'm so sorry to call you on a holiday," Elizabeth Malcolm exclaims. "But there's been an emergency. We've got a student stranded. Her host family just up and deserted her."

"What do you mean?"

"Moved to the West Coast. Didn't even leave a note."

Daisy finds it hard to match the tone of indignation spinning from Elizabeth Malcolm's tongue.

"Just like those summer people who buy a pet on Memorial Day and abandon it by the side of the road as soon as Labor Day rolls around."

"Maybe there were extenuating circumstances," Daisy says. She can certainly imagine extenuating circumstances. Natural disasters. Family crises. New opportunities. Old commitments. Or perhaps just a desperate desire to put space between you and somebody else. She can understand how someone suffering from host-family syndrome might need a change of scenery. Maybe the only way to dislodge a pest is to wedge fifteen states between you and it. Otherwise, how do you ever liberate the host from its parasite?

"There are no excuses," Elizabeth Malcolm goes on. "Youhayneah is desolate."

"You-hayne-ee-ah?"

"The Spanish pronunciation for Eugenia. A lovely girl. From Madrid. Studying anthropology. I told her I'd hook her up with another host family immediately. And you, Daisy and Truman, were the first that jumped to mind. The first ones I picked."

"I'm certainly flattered, but—"

"But?"

"Not on your life!"

"Daisy! I'm shocked." Daisy hears Elizabeth's shock sputtering like fat sizzling on a grill. "And you who won the Harvard host-family award!"

"That was *Henry* and me. It precipitated our divorce."

"The award?" Elizabeth's voice soars to a pitch of incredulity.

"Never mind," Daisy says. "Why don't you ask Henry?"

"I did." Elizabeth barrels ahead with not even a moment's

hesitation to acknowledge the shame of having lied. "Henry said that it was fine with him. He was highly receptive, in fact."

"I'm not surprised."

"Even though Youhayneah isn't French. But that Giselle . . ."

"Giselle?"

"She said *over her dead body*. Can you imagine, she actually used those words? Pretty sad when you think of it, how completely she's adapted to all things American. And from someone who herself enjoyed all the benefits, took great advantage even, from our host-family offerings."

When Daisy hangs up the phone, Truman asks, "Who was that?" He has finished his scoring duties and has piled the pans one on top of each other so the chestnuts look like cars in a multitiered parking garage.

Daisy explains. "They want us to host Yoo-hayne-ee-ah, a student of anthropology from Madrid."

"You've got to be kidding."

"Cross my heart."

"Over my dead body" is Truman's take-no-prisoners response.

Now Daisy throws her arms around Truman and kisses the top of his head. There is something about this particular section of his anatomy that she feels is totally hers. She knows it the way a farmer must know every acre he has plowed. The way a carpenter knows the gnarls and knots he has sanded smooth. Strand by strand she has put in her time. She has reaped her reward.

She goes into the dining room, where on the sideboard she has assembled her hostess gifts. Two bottles of wine—Beaujolais nouveau and Chianti classico—a jar of macadamia nuts, a pair of paper frills to adorn the turkey legs. Holding pride of place is the box of chocolates she found yesterday in the Coop.

She had double-parked, hazard lights flashing, to dash up to the front counter for pen refills. They'd moved the pens. In their place a sign announced HARVARD CANDIES. Where once stood Parkers and Mont Blancs now towered box after box shaped like a crimson shield, tied with a crimson satin bow, and displaying inside chocolate Harvard seals, each stamped with a *Veritas*. Daisy thought of Pilombaya's *veritas* tie from twenty years ago and of his current Kennedy School affiliation twenty years after he'd first knotted it. Perfect symbols to bookend a Harvard career. "I'll take two," she told the clerk.

Outside, the meter maid was just folding back her ticket pad. "This is a No Pahking zone, ma'am. I figure anybody lives near Hahvahd oughtta know how to read."

"It was an emergency."

"The nature of which?"

"Chocolates. For Thanksgiving. A hostess gift."

"Well, then." The meter maid smiled and retracted her ballpoint into its blue plastic shell.

Now Daisy has another thought. Triggered by Elizabeth Malcolm's telephone call, she realizes she must give credit where credit is due. She digs up her restored host-family award. She searches through her wrapping paper drawer, where she is amazed to come upon a sheet printed with turkeys and pilgrims and sheaves of yellow corn. She tucks the award inside the paper. She tapes together the ends. She attaches a bow. This she adds to the pile on the sideboard. It makes a nice symmetry, nuts to start, wine for dinner, ruffled collars for a turkey drumstick, chocolates and an award for dessert.

By the time Truman and Daisy arrive at Jessica's (Truman lost his keys; Daisy snagged her pantyhose), everybody else is already there. From the entrance hall Daisy peers into the living room. Jessica's guests sit on facing sofas like two opposing sports teams psyching themselves for the tournament cup. Everyone's features seem marked with a grim determination to have fun. On one sofa Andrea and Phoebe hold hands. On another, Sammy's fingers lace through the fingers of a young woman whose voice Daisy supposes she heard over the phone. Both Giselle and Henry bounce a twin on each lap and look tired. Between them is a glass coffee table crosshatched with trays of hors d'oeuvres. Over by the bar, Pilombaya is tipping a silver cocktail shaker back and forth like a character on the set of a Noel Coward comedy.

"Daisy! Truman!" Jessica cries out. She kisses them twice on each cheek. She takes their coats. She's wearing wide black pants and a matching shirt, what Henry's mother would have called a "hostess outfit," though minus the ropes of beads and glittering shoes Lillian would have added to embellish it. Circling Jessica's waist is a perky apron of orange and yellow batik.

Daisy touches a corner of the apron's ruffled hem. "This is a new accessory," she notes.

"Lombie asked his mother to have it made especially. She was so worried it might not arrive in time." Jessica gives the ruffles a little fluff. They undulate around her like the tutu of a ballerina in mid-jeté. "Isn't it adorable? In fact we're thinking of starting a cottage industry with a group of economically deprived women in some of the more primitive villages. I've been on the phone to Filene's. The head of Neiman Marcus is getting back to me."

Pilombaya dances into the hall, cocktail shaker jiggling like a castanet. "Jessica is an amazing woman. In January we travel together to my country and visit the poor."

Daisy envisions rows of small dark men trailing Jessica through rice paddies and bamboo groves.

"Together we make a good team to do good. Too bad we didn't meet on my last trip to Cambridge." Pilombaya giggles.

The scene from the past sets off a flash in Daisy's head. Thanksgiving. Jessica steps over the threshold, sniffs Pilombaya's mothballed Sunday best, takes in Daisy and Henry's sorry-looking spread. "Oh dear." She grimaces. "Can't stay. The in-laws will throw a fit if I'm late."

"But you did!" Daisy exclaims now.

"Did what?" asks Jessica.

"Meet. At our apartment in Holden Green."

"Never!" insists Jessica. "I know you've told me this before, but I would have remembered Pilombaya."

"And I," adds Pilombaya, "could never have forgotten Jessica."

Pilombaya sails into the living room to hand a martini in a Y-shaped martini glass to Henry. Daisy's surprised he's not requesting Lillet or the paregoric-tasting Pernod he used to affect in imitation of the demimonde slumped in Montparnasse cafés in the paintings of the French Impressionists. Or even absinthe, which the *New York Times* has pronounced newly fashionable. Pilombaya passes another martini to Giselle, who gulps it down like a cowboy quenching his thirst at the O.K. Corral. Then he bounces back out into the hall to relieve Truman and Daisy of their pans of chestnuts, their sweet-potato casserole. "This is so much fun." He chuckles. "The last Thanksgiving I attend was with my host family twenty years ago."

Daisy pictures the lopsided turkey, its cavity still frozen and thus refrigerating a stuffing that wouldn't cook. She remembers the accompanying instructions on how best to defrost, the steps to take to avoid salmonella poisoning. She remembers the watery cranberry sauce poured from a can and a cheap pumpkin pie in a box. She remembers fearing a tripartite trip to Harvard's Stillman Infirmary, where the only room left would be a three-bedded one. But though the meal was gut-wrenching, the aftereffects came not from the food. She remembers Henry's anger. "Sometimes the third world is too much with us," he had yelled and pulled the doorknob off in his fist. She remembers how little Pilombaya was. What a large amount of space he took up.

"That Thanksgiving was terrible," Daisy confesses now.

"It was wonderful. I carry it around in my heart so long"—Pilombaya places his hand over his heart in a pledge of allegiance—"and it inspires me to come back to America and have my own Thanksgiving dinner."

When Truman and Daisy go into the living room, the guests rise and form two rows like receiving lines at weddings or the arch of crossed swords assembled by West Point cadets.

Sammy steps forward. "Mom, this is Grace."

Daisy takes her hand. Though Grace has clear amber eyes and an endearing lopsided smile, she seems to be doing everything possible to contradict her name. Her Minnie Mouse shoes appear to have the weight of bowling balls. She keeps pulling down her Band-Aid of a skirt and keeps pushing up the droopy sleeves of her shirt. A gold stud glints from her tongue. Her face is sweet, Daisy notices, and Sammy's sweetly smitten. Which is all that matters here.

She makes her way down the line. Andrea lifts her fingers to his mouth, an affectation, even if he does look like Marcello Mastroianni courting Sophia Loren. But maybe Andrea's feeling awkward among them, not sure what his position is. What is his position? Is he with Phoebe for the long haul? They certainly seem content. Their shoulders jam together; their hips conjoin. And what about Sammy and Grace? Perhaps you need to keep trying things out until, like Goldilocks's chair, you can find one solid enough to settle into comfortably.

"Oh, Daisy, I'm so glad you're back with my dad," Phoebe whispers in her ear.

"Me too," Daisy says. Who is she to bear a grudge if the one spurned doesn't? She gives Phoebe's shoulder a squeeze.

Henry busses her cheeks like Charles de Gaulle awarding the Croix de Guerre. Giselle follows suit. Daisy chucks Jean and Jeanne under their charmingly dimpled chins.

"What did Papa tell you?" the proud papa asks.

"*Enchanté,*" squeals Jean.

"*'Chanté aussi,*" sings Jeanne.

Daisy waits for the moments of awkwardness. They are, after all, an odd assemblage not entirely related by blood. They've been thrown together by shifting allegiances, by geography, history, academia, by love and by lust. Connected and isolated by language and the foreign relations of their governments. And yet here they all are, all together, all giving thanks.

Truman loops his arm around Daisy's shoulder. Sammy leans into Grace. Andrea strokes Phoebe's wrist. Pilombaya plays with Jessica's batik apron string. Jean and Jeanne chase each other around the room. Although they don't touch each other, Henry and Giselle both beam at them. In a way, everyone here makes up a family. If not the conventional one.

They start talking all at once, the way families do. There's a new computer virus called Turkey in the Straw, Henry informs. Which reminds Truman of parasites found in poultry and their astonishingly interesting properties.

"Are you saying . . ." Jessica sits up.

"Nothing to worry about here," Truman reassures her. "There are stringent government precautions in effect."

"That's all we'd need," sighs Jessica. "We followed the instructions to the letter. Rinsed the bird. Boiled the cutting board. We're cooking the stuffing separately."

"Then there's not a thing to be concerned about."

"Speaking of parasites," Andrea says, "in my reading of how history is affected by epidemiology, I came across the term 'definitive host.'"

"The definitive host harbors the adult parasite. The intermediate host nourishes it only in its larval stage," instructs Truman.

Pilombaya and Andrea compare ice cream. "*Noccia gelati* from the Piazza Navona is the best," Andrea insists.

"Except for Jerry and Ben's Jerry Garcia," says Pilombaya.

"It's Ben and Jerry, Lombie," Jessica interjects. "*Cherry* Garcia. But for me, nothing beats plain old chocolate."

At the mention of chocolate, Daisy goes to get the shopping bag Pilombaya whisked away with her coat. She presents the chocolates to Pilombaya.

He rips off the wrapping. He laughs. He claps his hands. He holds up the box. Which elicits a chorus of oohs and aahs. "We eat after turkey," he says. "I used to have a necktie with *Veritas* all over it. I wonder where it is? What I did with it?"

"No matter," Jessica says, "we can get you another. The Coop is full of them."

Now Daisy passes him the host-family award. He praises the wrapping paper of pilgrims and turkey. He especially likes the sheaves of corn, which he calls may-eeze. Carefully, he undoes the triangled ends.

Pilombaya admires the leatherette case, rubs his fingers over its richly oiled surfaces. Says nothing about its Mediterranean smell masking an older odor of soy sauce and tamari marinade. He opens it. Reads it carefully. "Oh Daisy! Oh Henry!" he exclaims. "You're giving me your host-family award!"

Henry leans forward. "We're giving him our host-family award?"

"This is such an honor," Pilombaya crows. "I will cherish it."

"*Our* host-family award?" Henry repeats.

"Because you were our first student. And because we're back together after all these years," Daisy explains.

"In a manner of speaking," Henry says.

"This is the nicest award I ever receive," Pilombaya states.

"And you've had many of them," Jessica adds. "Whole drawersful," she boasts.

"Thank you, Daisy. Thank you, Henry," Pilombaya executes a graceful bow.

"It's all Daisy's doing," Henry points out. "She never consulted me."

Pilombaya passes the award around.

"I'm surprised it's only a couple of years old," Sammy says. "It looks yellowed with age."

"Foxed," adds Truman, "like antique documents."

"Cool," says Grace. "This is really, like, sort of nice." She lisps slightly, caused, Daisy supposes, by the small gold ball pierced through her tongue.

"I must be really hungry or something," Phoebe says, "but I could swear this smells like one of Andrea's pasta specialties."

"I was there the night you got this award," Giselle says. "Henry wore a beret."

"I never—" Henry protests.

"Moi. Moi!" shout Jean and Jeanne, who each grab for it. Jeanne sticks a corner between her teeth.

"Take that out of her mouth, Giselle. The thing is filthy," Henry orders.

"These Americans," Giselle says, "and their mania for cleanliness."

"Which is hardly a despicable quality," adds Henry. "Ask Truman. He knows where the germs congregate."

"Not here. Daisy did a fine job of cleaning it up," defends Truman.

"I'm not surprised you and Daisy won this award," Andrea

says. "From personal experience, I'm sure there couldn't be better hosts in all of Cambridge."

"Actually, it was Daisy and *me* who won that award," Henry says. "In another life." He sighs.

"Daisy and *I*," Giselle corrects. "I'm sure *Daisy* earned it."

"Thanks for the vote of confidence," says Henry.

"You are a sensitive plant, Henry." Giselle laughs. "A new phrase I just learned in my woman's group."

The award makes its way around the circle and comes back to Pilombaya, who holds it against his chest, a chest Daisy can visualize ornamented with the drawersful of medals any ceremonial occasion in his native land would have made compulsory.

"Dinner is served," announces Jessica.

As the others go into the dining room, Henry hangs back. He pulls Daisy aside. "You gave him our award," he complains.

"Do you care?"

"Well, it is *ours*."

"Which meant so much to you at the time you abandoned it at the Sea of Japan. And never went back for it."

"And you went back for it?"

"Absolutely not."

"But where did you find it, then?"

"At a flea market in Harvard Square."

"You're kidding."

She shakes her head.

Henry actually smiles. "It's kind of nice, though," he concedes. "The things you can't get rid of."

"I know," Daisy says.

"After we had our talk at Roka, I've done a lot of thinking. I've pretty much resigned myself to the fact that Giselle and I will make a life together. I've learned my lesson. But no matter what happens, what has happened, there's always a connec-

tion between the two of us. Through Sammy. Through everything we've shared."

"And that's somehow rather comforting," acknowledges
Daisy. "Sorry about the award. I didn't realize you might have
wanted it."

"It's in the best hands," Henry says. "Under the circumstances."

Jessica and Pilombaya's cooking classes, or the anticipation of
them, must have paid off, because dinner is wonderful. The
turkey is moist, its skin crispy gold, the stuffing inspired. Pilombaya carves it expertly with a Balinese sword. Daisy's
sweet-potato casserole gives rise to a clamor for seconds and
thirds. "I've forgotten how great this is," Henry cheers.

"What a perfect garnish is the marshmallow," says Giselle.

By dessert—pumpkin, mince, and apple pies made from
scratch, with crème fraîche brought by Giselle—the twins,
curled on the floor at opposite ends of the table, are asleep and
six bottles of wine have been consumed. Truman opens a seventh. He pours all around. He raises his glass. "To our hosts,"
he says.

"Hear! Hear!"

"*Bonne santé!*"

"*Prosit!*"

"*Skoal!*"

"*Salute!*"

"Cheers!"

"Especially the hostess with the mostest. A phrase we are
going to have sewn on our aprons for the English-speaking
market." Pilombaya lifts his glass to Jessica.

Jessica hoists her own goblet aloft. "To our guests."

*　　*　　*

It is still snowing when Daisy and Truman walk through the courtyard to their car. Grass and bricks, branches and benches are feathered with a cotton-batting white. Christmas lights, already strung on the trees, twinkle on and off like stars. They pass one of those metal newspaper stands with a glass door. On its front a sign reads FREE. HELP YOURSELF. These are usually filled with copies of *Boston After Dark* or *The Cambridge Tab*. Or fliers promoting computer courses, aromatherapy, and herbal massage. Daisy takes a closer look. From under the snow-speckled glass Truman Wolff's face peers out.

"Truman." Daisy points.

Truman groans. "Will I ever live down *Nit Notes?*"

From somebody's apartment drifts the voice of Ella Fitzgerald singing "I've Got You Under My Skin." A few blocks away the Andean Drummers pound and chant, huddled in the entrance to the Coop. Daisy laces her arm through Truman's. "That was fun," she says.

"*This* is fun," he says, squeezing her hand. He starts humming "A Bicycle Built for Two."

"Isn't it amazing," she says, "that Jessica and Pilombaya are a couple, that they're going off to Indonesia to set up a cottage industry for the poor?"

Truman chuckles. "I don't know what I find more amazing, their twosomeness or their mission of mercy." He pauses. "There was a cholera epidemic in Indonesia about eighteen twenty, carried from India and Ceylon by British soldiers. Of course parasites grow more rapidly in the well-fed middle class than in the bodies of the poor."

"Don't tell that to Jessica."

"My lips are sealed."

"Though I must say she was pretty good with Pilombaya's lice."

"The power of love, dear Daisy, to transform a caterpillar

into a butterfly." He pauses. "As recently as the eighties, Indonesia had a massive outbreak of the chikungunya virus, mosquito-borne."

"Chikungunya," Daisy enunciates. "It sounds like a food. Chicken satay. Or an Indonesian name like Pilombaya."

"Actually African. It means that which bends up."

Daisy turns to him.

"Not *that*." He laughs. "It refers to muscle aches so awful people are doubled over in excruciating pain."

The window of the Rialto bar blazes with light. She and Truman stop in front of it. There are people scattered at tables, though the dining room isn't full. More people crowd the bar. Guests, Daisy supposes, staying at the Charles. She's sorry for them, forced into the impersonality of a hotel, the anonymity of a restaurant, on this most sacred over-the-river-and-through-the-woods family-gathered days.

She's feeling superior, surrounded by loved ones. It astonishes her how, like broken bones or the split branches of trees, severed connections between people mend so cleanly you can barely see the scars.

She clears a circle of snow off the window and peers inside. Two women are seated at the bar. Between them, twirling on a stool first one way then the other, is a small man in a navy sweater. He turns his head. It's Barry Sweiker! He's unmistakable. Barry Sweiker: Caterpillar jeans salesman, man about town, man on the make, supplier of cutoffs and lace-ups. The first man she met after Henry asked for a divorce.

Who is now here alone on Thanksgiving Day, cooling his heels at a bar. No home-cooked meal. No welcoming hearth. Daisy feels a familiar pang, one she's finally come to recognize—it's her host-family instinct: the desire to take everyone in, to be the ombudsman for lost souls. Even if the jeans were awful, she reminds herself, the thought behind them was nice.

Barry Sweiker made her feel desirable at a time when she was convinced she'd never deserve the adjective. Perhaps she and Truman should invite him home for a drink.

Barry Sweiker jumps off the stool. From his pocket he pulls out a measuring tape. The woman steps down from her perch. Hands on hips, she struts in front of him. With a flick of his wrist, Barry Sweiker winds the tape around her waist. Daisy gasps.

"What's the matter, Daisy?" Truman asks. "You look like you've seen a ghost."

"I have."

"And?"

"And"—she steps away from the window—"I've vanquished it."

She loops her arm tighter through his. She pulls Truman's elbow into her ribs. How does she tell him that he's rescued her from small talk with jeans salesmen in bars, from blind dates with the discards in Jessica's retinue, from a level of desperation that might cast even Bernie and Billy and Jimmy in a potential escort light, from another possible impossible misalliance with Henry?

A passerby stops in front of the newsstand and takes his copy of *Nit Notes*. In seconds it's obvious he hasn't shut the door properly because, one after the other, pages of *Nit Notes* blow out into the night air and swirl around them. Truman lunges after the fluttering cascade of paper, then gives up. From all over the courtyard, Truman's face is raining down on them. Daisy plucks a newsletter from the sky. "Let's get married," she says.

Truman halts. He puts his hands on her shoulders. He searches her face with such scientific scrutiny he could be examining each pore for its microscopic mites, each eye for the loa loa worm's migration across its love-struck surfaces. "Are you sure?" he asks.

She takes another look at Barry Sweiker. Who now has the tape strung from the woman's ankle to the top of her thigh. Barry Sweiker scuttles around her. The tape flutters out like the streamer on a maypole. She thinks of intermediate hosts. Of Barry Sweiker. Of Henry. Of working through her larval stage. She thinks of change. Of growth. I've been wrong, Daisy tells herself. So terribly wrong. She knows now that love is every bit as identifiable and tenacious as one of Truman's parasites. That her love for Truman has found its permanent definitive host in the walls and chambers of her heart. She folds Truman's photograph. "Yes," Daisy says. "Yes."

ACKNOWLEDGMENTS

I am grateful to Mary E. Wilson, M.D., for answering my questions with patience and humor and letting me pore through her tropical disease journals and atlases of parasites. And to the writer Jennifer Ackerman, whose article on parasites for *National Geographic* I had clipped even before I had the privilege of claiming her as a friend. Martin Solomon, M.D., looked up sushi worms for me; Sami Gottlieb, M.D., waxed eloquent on the loa loa bug; Roger Swain dissected the botfly; Steven Lipsitt gave me musical terms; Evelyne Otten, French ones; Dennis Purcell, computer viruses; Barry Solar, car talk; and Massimo Morelli provided counsel on all things Italian.

It's no surprise the folks at Warner Books rated first in the Authors' Guild survey of writers' satisfaction. My beloved editor, Jamie Raab, has no equal. Her associate, John Aherne, is wise beyond his very young years and a wit, besides; between the two of them, one author couldn't be in four better hands. Tina Andreadis, who is called Bubbles of Love for good reason, sparkles both as publicist and pal. Ace sales rep Conan Gorenstein not only puts my books on the shelf but also bakes delicious cookies.

I'm Velcroing myself to my agent, Lisa Bankoff, the best, most delightful guide through the geography of publishing. In addition, much appreciation to George Tobia for his sharp legal eye.

Special thanks to my family and friends: a few—Ellie, Marjory, and Susan—looked at the manuscript; all offered support. Gold stars to my dear children, Daniel and Jonathan, for their nit-picking copyediting skills. And the heartiest welcome to Sharissa.

Most important is my debt to Howard, my first reader and sweet, steadfast husband. Once again, kid, and with my love.

ALSO AVAILABLE FROM WARNER BOOKS

MAIL
by Mameve Medwed

Mameve Medwed's debut novel introduces Katinka O'Toole. High school valedictorian. Radcliffe graduate. Published author. Ex-wife of a noted Joycean scholar. Writing instructor at Harvard. And in love with her mailman. Sharp, poignant, and uproariously funny, *Mail* showcases a talented writer totally in sync with out-of-sync relationships.

"Wacky . . . funny . . . an off-the-wall sendup of the take-charge-of-your-life novel." *—New York Times Book Review*

THE HONK AND HOLLER OPENING SOON
by Billie Letts, author of the
New York Times bestseller *Where the Heart Is*

A fateful misunderstanding with a sign maker gave Caney Paxton and his café, The Honk and Holler Opening Soon, the flashiest joke in the entire state. Twelve years later, the once-busy highway outside his establishment is dead, and the joke is as old and worn as Caney. Then one day, a Crow woman comes to town and shakes up business, the locals, and Caney's heart. Billie Letts's refreshing, original voice sparkles in a funny, quirky, and moving story.

"Filled with humor and fascinating twists and turns. . . . You'll be thinking about these people long after you've finished the last page." *—Chicago Tribune*

AMANDA'S WEDDING
by Jenny Colgan

Sharp-witted Melanie Pepper is broke, decidedly unglamorous, stuck in a boring job, and wants revenge. When her old nemesis plans to marry Melanie's former crush, this fed-up-to-here woman must stop "the wedding of the next century." With irresistibly wicked wit, here is a novel about love, friendship, the usual mayhem in between—and living life by your own rules of engagement.

"Compulsively comical." *—Cosmopolitan* (British)